A Promise *for* Ellie

Books by Lauraine Snelling

RED RIVER OF THE NORTH

RETURN TO RED RIVER

DAUGHTERS OF BLESSING

DAKOTAH TREASURES

A SECRET REFUGE

HIGH HURDLES

LAURAINE SNELLING

A Promise *for* Ellie

BETHANYHOUSE
PUBLISHERS
MINNEAPOLIS, MINNESOTA

A Promise for Ellie
Copyright © 2006
Lauraine Snelling

Cover design by Dan Thornberg
Cover image by William Albert Allard/National Geographic Image Collection

Unless otherwise identified, Scripture quotations are from the King James Version of the Bible.

Published by Bethany House Publishers
11400 Hampshire Avenue South
Bloomington, Minnesota 55438

Bethany House Publishers is a division of
Baker Publishing Group, Grand Rapids, Michigan.

Printed in the United States of America

Paperback: ISBN-13: 978-0-7642-2809-4   ISBN-10: 0-7642-2809-9
Large Print: ISBN-13: 978-0-7642-0259-9   ISBN-13: 0-7642-0259-6

Library of Congress Cataloging-in-Publication Data

Snelling, Lauraine.
    A promise for Ellie / Lauraine Snelling.
        p.   cm. — (Daughters of Blessing ; 1)
    ISBN 0-7642-2809-9 (pbk.)—ISBN 0-7642-0259-6 (lg. print : pbk.)
    1. North Dakota—Fiction. I. Title. II. Series: Snelling, Lauraine. Daughters of Blessing ; 1.

PS3569.N39P76   2006
813'.54—dc22   2006013799

DEDICATION

To all my readers who have been pleading for more about the Bjorklunds and Blessing, thank you for your love of Ingeborg and her family. *A Promise for Ellie,* book one in the DAUGHTERS OF BLESSING series, is dedicated to all of you.

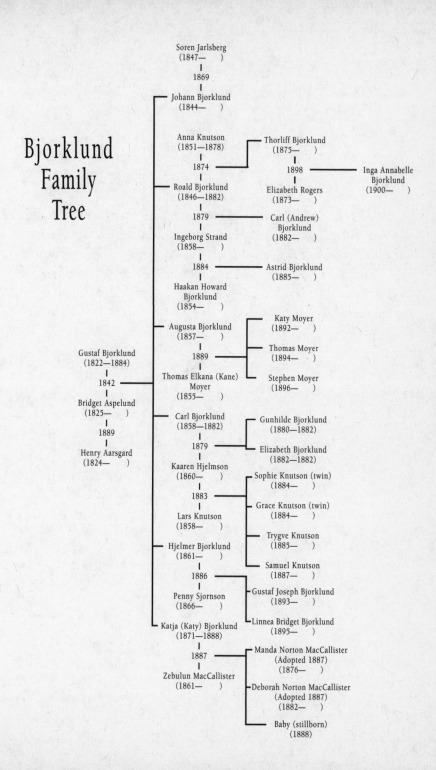

Bjorklund Family Tree

Soren Jarlsberg
(1847—)

1869

Johann Bjorklund
(1844—)

Anna Knutson
(1851—1878)

1874

Roald Bjorklund
(1846—1882)

1879

Ingeborg Strand
(1858—)

1884

Haakan Howard
Bjorklund
(1854—)

Thorliff Bjorklund
(1875—)

1898

Elizabeth Rogers
(1873—)

Inga Annabelle
Bjorklund
(1900—)

Carl (Andrew)
Bjorklund
(1882—)

Astrid Bjorklund
(1885—)

Gustaf Bjorklund
(1822—1884)

1842

Bridget Aspelund
(1825—)

1889

Henry Aarsgard
(1824—)

Augusta Bjorklund
(1857—)

1889

Thomas Elkana (Kane)
Moyer
(1855—)

Katy Moyer
(1892—)

Thomas Moyer
(1894—)

Stephen Moyer
(1896—)

Carl Bjorklund
(1858—1882)

1879

Kaaren Hjelmson
(1860—)

1883

Lars Knutson
(1858—)

Gunhilde Bjorklund
(1880—1882)

Elizabeth Bjorklund
(1882—1882)

Sophie Knutson (twin)
(1884—)

Grace Knutson (twin)
(1884—)

Trygve Knutson
(1885—)

Samuel Knutson
(1887—)

Hjelmer Bjorklund
(1861—)

1886

Penny Sjornson
(1866—)

Gustaf Joseph Bjorklund
(1893—)

Linnea Bridget Bjorklund
(1895—)

Katja (Katy) Bjorklund
(1871—1888)

1887

Zebulun MacCallister
(1861—)

Manda Norton MacCallister
(Adopted 1887)
(1876—)

Deborah Norton MacCallister
(Adopted 1887)
(1882—)

Baby (stillborn)
(1888)

PROLOGUE

Blessing, North Dakota
May 1900

THE CLANGING CHURCH BELL woke them all.

Andrew Bjorklund and his father, Haakan, met at the bottom of the stairs, pulling up their suspenders as they shoved their feet into their boots by the back door. Clanging bells in the night always meant fire.

Astrid pounded down the stairs, tying her hair back as she came. "Where is it?"

"No idea yet." Haakan stepped out onto the front porch of their two-story white house and scanned the area for the red of flames and billowing smoke. "Looks like the Olsons' place. Andrew, you get the horses. Astrid, help me get buckets and shovels in the wagon. Andrew can ride on ahead." He raised his voice. "You bring the rugs, Ingeborg."

"Ja, I will," she called from the bedroom. "I'm almost dressed."

"Was there heat lightning?" Andrew asked a few minutes later as they threw harnesses over the horses' backs.

"Coulda been. I was sleeping too sound to hear any thunder. Besides, it's clear now." Haakan finished snapping the traces onto the doubletree. "You take Jack and get on over there."

Within minutes Astrid and Ingeborg were in the wagon and they started down the lane, Haakan driving the team all out.

"Lord God, please protect our friends. Keep everyone safe," Ingeborg prayed, her eyes open, hanging on for dear life as they took a sharp corner at only a slightly reduced speed. She kept praying the entire way.

Haakan pulled the team to a skidding stop, the second wagon to have arrived. Already a bucket brigade had formed, but they were dumping water on the barn roof and soaking the other buildings. The fire roared as it devoured the machine shed, which was too far gone to try to drown the flames.

"What happened?" Haakan hollered as he climbed a ladder to throw water on the house roof.

"Don't know. Woke to the dog barking." Ole Olson handed up a bucket of water and reached for another from below as the lines grew with more wagons and horses arriving by the minute. "Just got to keep it from spreading."

As the flames died down, the firefighters gathered together. "Thank God there was no wind." Ingeborg wiped the sweat off her face with her apron and glugged the cup of water someone handed her. She turned to the woman behind her. "Any idea what started it?"

"None." Mrs. Olson wrung her hands. "But if it weren't for all of you, the entire place might've gone up. Thank the good Lord for friends."

Reverend Solberg nodded and drank deeply. "That church bell saved us again. And to think we almost didn't put one up."

"We've talked about a fire wagon. I think it's time to stop talking about it and start doing something about it." Haakan clapped Andrew on the shoulder. "You young men did a fine job with the barn roof. That would have gone up next. And if the ground had been drier, a prairie fire may have started."

"Lots of maybes and might haves. Let's pray and thank our God for what is." Reverend Solberg waited for silence. "Father in heaven, we offer our heartfelt thanks for your providence, for keeping the fire within bounds, for all the willing hands who came so swiftly, and for keeping us all safe. To you, O Lord, we commend our work, our dreams, our lives. In Jesus precious name we pray." Everyone joined him on the amen.

"Uff da, what a stench a fire can make."

"Pa, you better come look. I think there's a body in that shed." Andrew's face appeared green behind the smoke stains.

1

May 1900

BLESSING. *I'm going home to Blessing. Home to Andrew.*

"Ellie, you daydreaming again? I asked you to take this over to your pa." Her mother, Goodie Wold, peeked around the doorframe, a handled water jug in her hand. "Uff da, look at you. One would think you're pie-eyed or some such."

"Pie-eyed?" Ellie turned from holding her graduation dress in front of her to see in the mirror. A lock of wavy golden hair lay over one shoulder. Concern wrinkled her wide forehead until she saw the teasing glint in her mother's eyes. "Pie-eyed?"

"You know, mooning over that young man of yours. Here we've been gone from Blessing for two years, and you ignored every suitor who has come to call. Now take that handsome Mr.—"

"No, you take him and send him elsewhere. Andrew Bjorklund is the only man for me, and he always has been." She swung back and drew the waistline of the baby blue lawn dress against her slim middle and, with the other hand, held the bodice to her chest. "This turned out well, don't you think?"

"Of course it did, you silly child. Everything you sew turns out beautiful." Goodie sat down on the edge of the four-poster, the lovingly turned posts a tribute to Ellie's adoptive father, Olaf Wold, who made the most beautiful furniture west of the Mississippi. Right now he was working on a table and six chairs for Ellie and Andrew's wedding present.

"Perhaps I should have made this in white and used the same dress for both graduation and my wedding. That would have been more practical."

"Ah, Ellie, dear heart, you are always so practical. This is a good time for you to be at least a little bit impractical. Besides, I think we can afford a few extra yards of dress goods."

Ellie finished studying the dress and glanced at the smiling face above it. Dreamy might be a good word to apply to her. Her father said she looked like an angel, but she knew too well the streak of stubbornness that ran like double-strength whalebone up her spine. While some might say she was persistent, she knew it went beyond that. Bullheaded, more likely, although she managed to cover it with sweet smiles and soft words. Andrew likened her hair to golden wheat flowing down her back, so for him she kept it long; although she'd been tempted to follow the new trends and cut it shorter when some of her friends did. Short hair on her forehead might cover the marks that remained from her bout of chicken pox as a small child.

One thing bothered her—her eyes. They were gray and slightly tipped up at the outer edges and always reflected the color she wore. Toby Valders had once called her Cat Eyes when she was wearing a green dress. She shuddered at the memory. Andrew had nearly beaten him into the ground for that and had later promised her he would never fight again.

Andrew, whom she hadn't seen since Christmas, when the entire family took the train back to Blessing. Andrew, who'd been her protector since the day she was carried into the Bjorklund home, ill and half starved. Her whole family would have died had it not been for Hjelmer Bjorklund, who had stopped by their soddy on his way home all those years ago. Andrew, whom she'd had to leave behind when Olaf decided to move his family out of the flood plain of the Red River Valley and settle in Grafton. Not that far away from Blessing yet more than half a day's journey by buggy or horse.

She'd be forever grateful that Reverend Solberg said she could come home to graduate with her class—the friends she'd grown up with.

"Tante Goodie?" her young cousin Rachel Anderson said from the doorway. "Onkel Olaf says he needs you." Rachel had come to stay with them the year before, when her mother died. The little girl was the only member of the family to survive cholera.

"Tell him I'll be right there." Goodie stood with a bit of a groan.

"I will." Rachel dashed off, never walking when she could run.

"Your knee still bothering you?" Ellie asked as she hung her dress on a padded hanger and then on the bar in the clothespress.

"Some, but mostly when I get up. Falling like I did . . ." Goodie shook her head. "Enough about me. When Rachel gets back, you two go get the mail, would you please?" She smiled at the delight bursting on Ellie's face. "I know. Most likely there's another letter from Andrew, but the rest of us get mail now and then too. Poor Rachel, she is already feeling sad that you'll be leaving us."

"Mor, I won't be gone, just a ways away. Besides, the wedding isn't until the end of June. We have to get our house built first."

Soon after Rachel returned they headed out to pick up the mail. Ellie swung her cousin's hand as they strolled the four blocks to the post office.

"I don't want you to go away." Rachel stared at Ellie from under the wide brim of her straw hat—the same hat Ellie had worn the year before.

Today Ellie wore a new straw hat, this one with a narrower brim and a more rigid crown. A pink rose centered the white ribbon with strings down the back.

"Who will listen to me in the middle of the night when I have a bad dream?"

Ellie smiled at her young cousin. At ten, Rachel looked more like a bundle of sticks walking than the lovely young woman she promised to become. She would rather fish and chase with the neighbor boys than worry about keeping her nose from freckling. But her silky eye-lashes and curly hair were the envy of all the budding girls at their church. Rachel just didn't recognize such things yet. "You haven't had a bad dream in a long time. I think you are over them."

"But who will braid my hair so it doesn't fly all over the place?" Her pleading glance near to broke Ellie's heart.

"Tante don't braid—"

"Doesn't."

"You know what I mean."

"I know, but you have to speak properly, otherwise you sound slow and stupid."

"I'll never be like you."

"Ah, Rachel, you don't want to be like me. You want to be the best you that you can be. God made you special in His eyes, and He has a plan for you that only you can fill."

"How come He don't . . . er . . . doesn't tell me?"

"He often doesn't, just gives glimpses and peeks sometimes. But look at your feet." They both stopped and looked down. "Now step with your right foot." They both did. *Oh, Lord, how to explain this?* "See, until you took one step and then one with the other foot, you couldn't take the second with the first. Some things you just can't know ahead." They looked at each other, and Rachel shook her head.

"Hmm. I see what you mean." She stepped one foot at a time again. "So if I just keep walking, God will guide my footsteps?"

"He said so. But you have to read your Bible to hear His in-structions."

Rachel groaned.

"I know you think it doesn't make sense sometimes, but some things are very clear. Every story in the Bible is there to teach us something."

"Like David and Goliath? I like that one." Rachel made a whirling motion with her hand. "Three little pebbles from his sling, and bam, the giant fell."

"So, what's the lesson in that story?" They were nearly at the post office.

"Learn to use a sling real good. I've been practicing but don't get it yet."

"*Well*, not good. Food tastes good. We do things well."

"See, you go away, and who's going to teach me to speak proper?"

"You might listen in school instead of writing notes to Elspeth." She opened the door of the post office, and they both stepped inside.

"Wold mail, please," Ellie said to the man behind the counter. He turned to the rows of boxes and pulled out a packet, then handed it to her.

As soon as she saw Andrew's handwriting on an envelope, Ellie wanted to find a quiet spot and read it, hugging all his words to herself, letting them soak in and join all the others she had stored away in her heart.

Rachel groaned and rolled her eyes. "Andrew is a buttinsky."

"What a thing to say." Ellie tucked Andrew's letter into her pocket and sorted through the remainder of the mail to make sure nothing that didn't belong to them had made its way into their box. The day before she'd had to bring back something belonging in the post office box next to theirs. The young woman putting out the mail was in love, and even if the whole town collapsed, she'd never notice. Pie-eyed, for certain.

Good thing I'm not that way, she said to herself. *But does that mean I'm not really in love with Andrew?* The thought stopped her short. What if she'd loved him for so long that she was not in *love* love but in brotherly love? Like the way Astrid loved her brother. *Lord, do I know the difference?*

"Come on, let's hurry. I'm going over to play with Elspeth after we get home."

"You go on ahead. I'll be along shortly."

"Give me the rest of the mail, then, so you can go mooning over Saint Andrew's letter."

Ellie gave her the mail and a swat on the bottom. "Someday you'll be in love, and then I'll get even." She arched her eyebrows. "Why, Mr. Whatchamacallit, did you know that Rachel used to chew her fingernails and her braids too? Why, I remember when . . ."

Rachel hooted and took off up the street. "Ellie and Andrew sitting in a tree, K-i-S-s-I-n-G."

Ellie shook her head. Why not let the whole world know their private business? She took the envelope from her pocket and stared at the handwriting. Andrew, so big and strong yet gentle and kind. A warmth started in her middle and curled lazily up to set her heart to thudding. She'd not been running, but she felt like she might have been. Surely one didn't feel this way about a brother. Surely this was love so true as to be ready for marriage. The length of their love only strengthened it.

She sat down on one of the benches by the town park and carefully slit the drop of wax free from the paper. Andrew had drawn a small heart in the wax. She caught it in her skirt, picked it up, and slid it into the envelope. One more thing that Andrew had done especially for her. She unfolded the paper.

"Ellie, Ellie?"

Only Maydell would call like that from half a block away. Ellie sighed and tucked her letter into her reticule. She watched her best friend in Grafton come dancing across the grass, holding her hat with one hand and, of all things, a fan in the other. Now what scheme was she concocting to attract poor Mr. Farnsworth, the new choir director at their church? In a pink dress matching her cheeks made more pink by the run, Maydell was as short and round as Ellie was tall and slender. They were matched in determination.

"I was afraid I wouldn't see you before you left." Maydell sank down on the bench beside Ellie and unfurled her fan to cool her face.

"When did you start carrying a fan?"

"Well, I've been reading about how to attract a man by use of a fan." She fluttered it close to her face, her dark eyes dancing above the beribboned fan edge. "Doesn't this make me look more mysterious? Men like mystery in a woman, you know."

Ellie shook her head. "No, I wouldn't know."

"But you should learn, perhaps teach Andrew a thing or two. Make him wild for you."

"Maydell, what have you been reading?" The thought of some of the things Andrew had said in his letters unfurled the warmth in her middle again.

"About romance, silly. Ah, remember reading Romeo and Juliet? How Romeo called beneath her window? Now that is romance."

"But they both died. Remember?"

"And Juliet is the sun. . . ." Maydell fluttered her fan and gave a good imitation of pie-eyed. "Here." She snapped the fan shut and pulled the string from her wrist, then thrust it at Ellie. "Now you try it, so I can see what it looks like. Although I have to admit I've spent time in front of the mirror practicing."

"Oh . . ." Ellie took the fan and, when trying to open it, dropped it in her skirt. She looked at her friend, and they both chuckled. Maydell repositioned Ellie's fingers and showed her how to spread the fan wide, then hold it open using her thumb against her fingers. She fluttered it close to her face and stared deep into Maydell's eyes. This way she could hide the twitch of her lips behind the fan. Her voice deepened and grew husky. "Ah, my dear, you are so ravishing."

Maydell clutched her clasped hands to her throat. "Ah yes."

Ellie snapped the fan closed. "Yes? What kind of answer is that? Someone says you are ravishing, and you say 'yes'? What happened to thank you or tell me more?" She shook her head again. "I don't need a fan when I go see Andrew. I need extra aprons because we're going to be building our house and barn." *That is, if the house arrives anytime soon.*

"Well, if you are sure." Maydell stood and raised her attention to the rustling leaves of the elm tree above them, trying for a dramatic pose.

"I'm sure." *At least I think I'm sure.* This was love she felt, the kind of love she saw between her ma and pa. "I hope graduation exercises go well for you."

"Mr. Farnsworth will be playing the organ."

"Try to pay attention to the ceremony. I wouldn't want you faint-ing or something, but then, you'll have your fan, right?"

Maydell leaned over and gave her a hug. "I'll see you again before the wedding?"

"Yes. I'll be back to get my things."

"You could take extra hankies to drop."

"Go practice your fan." Ellie shooed her away, laughing at the pout Maydell half hid behind the fan. "Very good. That one should get him." As soon as her friend was on her way home, Ellie took out the letter again, unfolded the page, and began to read.

May 13, 1900
Dearest Ellie,

Her heart skipped a beat as she heard his voice in the reading.

I am counting the days, nay the hours, until I see you again. I am supposed to be writing my final essay, but I couldn't quit thinking of you, so I am writing this instead. I will be like Thorliff used to be, burning the midnight oil to finish my lessons. Only he went on to college, and in spite of Mor's encouragement, I do not plan to do that, as you know. She would like me to go to Grand Forks to the agricultural school, but I will learn all I need to learn about new farming ideas from the magazines, newspapers, and books that Thor-liff makes sure find their way into our house. Besides, we couldn't get married if I went off to college.

The whole family is excited about Thorliff and Elizabeth's baby coming soon. The women think men shouldn't discuss such happenings, but you know me. I think that is downright stupid. Having babies is as ordinary as cows having calves. Except that calves are cuter. Now don't go getting riled up. You know I am only teasing you.

She stared up at the branches over her head. Andrew did love to tease, but he was never malicious about it like Toby Valders had been when they were in school together. Toby most likely would be at the graduation, but surely she was beyond letting him bother her any longer. Maybe he had changed.

Leave it to Andrew to talk so easily about having babies. But then he'd not been there when her mother nearly died in childbirth and the baby was born blue and waxlike. No matter that she'd been so young. She still remembered that day. The thought of suffering like her mother had for hours and hours had dug a hole down inside her and filled it brimful with fear—a ripping, tearing fear that infected her joy when she allowed herself to think on it. Something that was happening more often as the wedding date drew near.

She returned to her letter, the sun having dimmed slightly even though no cloud crossed the sky.

> Pastor Solberg said to send you his greetings and to say that he is happy you are coming back to graduate with the rest of us. I asked him if he would conduct our wedding, and he said he thought I'd never ask. And if someone else came to do that, he'd have to do battle with him. Isn't that typical of our Pastor Solberg?
>
> Astrid has written a letter, and I will include it with mine. Don't believe everything she says about the way I've been acting.
>
> Your loving Andrew

Ellie read the letter again and put it back into the envelope. Maybe seeing Andrew would allay her fears. But what if it didn't?

"EASY, OLD GIRL. Just finish pushing that calf out so I can go back to bed." Andrew stood from his kneeling position beside the birthing cow.

"Thought I'd find you out here." Haakan leaned on the half wall of the calving stall, watching his younger son in action.

"She needed some help, is all. She'd been laboring too long." Andrew washed his hands and arm in the bucket of water now gone cool. "I went in and straightened that front leg, and now they're all right." They watched as the calf slid out onto the straw, still encased in the birth sac but for the two front hooves now parallel to each other. Andrew picked up some straw and began scrubbing the sac away, clearing the calf's muzzle. It shook its head at the intrusion and bleated, coughing out phlegm. While it lay still for a moment, gaining strength, the afterbirth followed, and the cow surged to her feet, then turned to begin licking her baby. She glared at Andrew and shook her head, warning him to stay back. She was now in charge.

"This one's yours, you know." Haakan rested on his crossed arms.

"You don't need to do that. You already deeded me the land for my house and barn."

"I know, but your mor and I decided that the calf crop this year would belong half to you. What do you have there—a bull or heifer?"

"Bull."

"That won't help much with your milking herd, but he'll taste mighty good when he grows enough." They usually castrated the bull calves and fed them out for beef, unless one was of particularly good breeding and build. Then they sold it for a breeding bull. Some of the farmers to the west would often write and ask if they had dairy bulls for sale. The Blessing Cheese Company Ingeborg had started was known coast-to-coast for its delicious cheese, while the Bjorklund name stood for farming success due to hard work and good management. Twenty years earlier two brothers with their families homesteaded on the banks of the Red River of Dakota Territory. The town of Blessing, located north of Grand Forks and northeast of Grafton, grew after the arrival of the train lines that crisscrossed the fertile Red River Valley, hauling wheat east to the flour mills of Minnesota and supplies west to the prairie farmers.

Andrew shut the stall door behind him, satisfied now that the calf was nursing and the cow clearly wanting him to leave. Like his mother, Andrew had inherited the gift of healing, but most of his talents went to helping animals, not humans. People were Ingeborg's province, or they had been until her older son, Thorliff, came home from college bringing with him a budding newspaper career and a wife, Dr. Elizabeth Bjorklund.

Father and son strolled back to the house, the star canopy arched above them. A thin sliver of moon hung in the west with a bright star dangling off the lower point, as if caught like a fish. The breeze carried the fragrance of spring—burgeoning earth, newly turned and seeded, and grass growing so fast as to be measured daily on a yardstick.

A few minutes later, when he slid back between the cool sheets, Andrew thought again of the letter he'd received from Ellie. Locking his arms behind his head, he let his mind play both backward and forward. Back to the last time he saw her at Christmas and ahead to their wedding and a lifetime together. Ellie, his Ellie, ever since the sick little girl was carried into his mother's house in the dead of winter. Mr. Peterson had died, leaving his wife and two children to manage on their own. Andrew had never forgotten the look of her, all gray eyes in a face so thin and tiny that it seemed you could see right through her. As she grew stronger, he'd appointed himself her guardian and had never stopped. The family teased him when he'd stated that when they were big, he was going to marry up with Ellie.

He'd never changed his mind, not even after Onkel Olaf decided to move his family to Grafton, farther away from the banks of the Red River and the horrible floodwaters of 1897. He had all of her letters of these past two years tied with a leather thong and in a box under his bed. When he needed a shot of Ellie's good common sense, he took them out and read them by kerosene lamplight.

Three more days until graduation, and then little more than a month until their wedding. If all went well, the planting would be done and the grass not ready to hay. The week after graduation, they were having a house raising on his own land. He'd ordered the house package from Sears and Roebuck, and it should be arriving on the train any day now. He'd used his savings and borrowed from the farm to buy the house. He'd use the one hundred dollars each graduate received for future schooling to pay back Mor and Far.

"Soon, Ellie, my heart, soon." His whisper floated on the breeze coming through the window, playing with the white lace curtains all newly washed and starched after his mother's annual spring cleaning. No dirt dared to reside in the Bjorklund home after the women scrubbed it inside and out. At least this year there had been no flood to leave all the dirt behind.

~

At school the next day Andrew took his final exams. While he struggled with some of the arithmetic equations and didn't have the writing skills of his brother, Thorliff, he knew he'd passed with reasonable grades. Perfection in the field, with straight rows and weeds afraid to even peep out of the soil, was necessary, nay obligatory, but the same rules did not apply in the classroom. At least not according to Andrew.

For his young sister, Astrid, that was a different matter. She upheld the tradition that Thorliff started of all straight A's and threw extra in for good measure.

Andrew handed in his final exam.

"Thank you. You may be excused." Reverend Solberg laid the papers on a growing pile.

"You mean I'm done for the day?" Andrew kept his voice to a whisper so he wouldn't disturb those still writing.

"That's what I mean, but I expect you back tomorrow morning to help with cleaning the building. Must have a clean school for graduation."

"Everyone will be cleaning?"

"Some will be finishing their tests. I thought you seniors could start on the outside, cutting the grass around both the school and the church, washing the windows—those kinds of things. Bring cleaning supplies." Reverend Solberg smoothed his thinning hair back with one hand. He sometimes said he was not only turning gray but was losing hair over the antics of some of his students.

Andrew clapped his hat on his head as soon as he exited the school and leaped the two steps to the ground. He felt like yelling "I'm done" loud enough to scare the birds and reach the heavens, but that was surely the antics of a child. And he no longer considered himself a child—hadn't, in fact, for several years. Ever since Thorliff left home to go to St. Olaf College in Northfield, Minnesota, Andrew had been the oldest of the children at home. And he had long done the work of a man—milking cows, doing fieldwork, helping in the cheese house, whatever needed to be done. He'd rather work outside than study any day of the week.

He stuffed his hands into his pockets and set off for the general store owned by his tante Penny, whistling as he went. Perhaps his house had come in on the train, although you'd have thought they'd come ask him to help unload it. Buying the Sears and Roebuck house package so that his and Ellie's house would go up more quickly had seemed a stroke of genius on his part. No longer were there enough trees available to cut their own logs for a sawmill that Haakan used to run. He needed to buy the lumber for his barn too. Had he been wise in starting with the house? They could have raised a soddy, but the thought of taking his new wife into a soddy made him shake his head. He'd thought long and hard on it. Ellie needed sunlight like a sunflower did, not the dank darkness of a soddy.

At least the ground had dried enough that the gumbo no longer weighted down his boots. He kicked off any dirt on the store steps and scraped his soles over a scraper by the door. Tapping on the window, he caught Tante Penny's attention as she rearranged the window display.

"How come you're not in school?" she called back.

"Finished." He pushed open the door, setting the bell above to jangling. "That looks right nice." His compliment made her smile widen.

"Andrew, you always say the nicest things." Penny climbed over the small picket fence made to protect her window display and gave him a hug. "I can't believe you are really graduating—so soon. I close my eyes and you're still a little guy dragging after Thorliff or down playing with whatever animal babies there were." She stared up into his eyes. Bjorklund blue eyes, they were called. "You and Paws." She sniffed and locked her arm through his. "Here I go getting all weepy. It's not like you are moving away or anything."

"Just from one house to another." He squeezed her hand against his side. "You have any mail for me to take on home, and did my house come?"

"Sorry, no house, but do you think that dear Ellie would let more than a couple of days go by before writing to you?" She went behind the counter to the wall of cubbyholes and pulled out a newspaper and several pieces of mail. "I'll bet half of these are cheese orders." She held one envelope back. "Except for this. What am I offered?"

Andrew shook his head. "Have to pay for my own mail?" He scrunched up his eyes. "What would it take?" He opened his eyes and shook his head. "Please don't say you need wood chopped."

"Now that you volunteered . . ." She laughed and handed him the letter. "I'd be truly grateful if you'd fill the woodbox for me. I'm baking something special for Hjelmer so that he remembers how good things are at home."

His onkel Hjelmer, youngest of the Norwegian-born Bjorklund brothers, had been elected to the state assembly and now spent more time on the road than he did at his blacksmith and machinery sales businesses. Old Sam took care of the one and Mr. Valders the other, as well as being the bank manager when needed.

"I will." He folded the letter carefully and put it in his breast pocket, right over his heart, where he usually carried Ellie's latest letter. Never would he have dreamed that he could be such a faithful correspondent.

"So when are the Wolds coming?" Penny asked.

"Tomorrow."

"They going to stay at the boardinghouse?" His grandma Bridget ran the boardinghouse just up the street.

"I doubt it. Mor offered them a room upstairs." He headed back to bring in wood. Instead of being stacked neatly against the woodshed, it was tossed in a pile, and there was not much of it. Should he split some now or come back later? Like his mor had said more than once, it was great having Onkel Hjelmer helping run North Dakota, but when his family needed him, he wasn't often around. Like now to chop wood. Andrew took off his shirt and hung it on the clothesline so he could be free to chop. He set a butt up on the block and brought the ax down right in the middle. When it took a second swing, he shook his head. The ax needed sharpening. His pa had been a lumberjack before coming west to help his relatives and had drilled into his sons the necessity for a sharp ax.

Keeping one's ax sharp was a good metaphor for life, one that

Andrew understood clear to his heart. He took the ax over to the blacksmith shop and sat down at the stone wheel to grind an edge on it again. Haakan always set a good example, taking care of his tools and machinery, fixing anything that came loose or cracked or showed wear. Sparks peppered Andrew's bare chest as he peddled the wheel and held the ax bit against it until the edge was sharp enough to shave with. Or at least that was the joke. Since he'd only had to shave a couple of times in his whole life, he didn't want to try doing so with the ax bit.

Back at the woodpile he split enough to last a couple of days and loaded his sweaty arm high. It took him four trips to fill the woodbox.

"Leave it to you, Andrew, to go far beyond what I asked for." Penny handed him a napkin filled with cookies. "So you don't starve on the way home." She reached up and kissed his cheek. "I don't know what I would do without you."

"I don't think you have to worry about me going anywhere." He shrugged into his shirt. "Me'n Ellie—we'll be right here. See you later."

He waved and headed for the door, only to have it pushed open before he reached for the handle. Stepping back, he groaned inside.

"Well, well, if it ain't Prince Andrew." Toby Valders took a step back and gave a half bow.

"That's enough, Valders." Andrew kept a smile on his face with sheer effort. Why did Toby always have to say something that set Andrew's teeth on edge?

"Ah, a bit surly today. Has not the fair Ellie arrived yet?" Toby's dark eyes narrowed slightly. While Toby had never gained the height of the Bjorklund boys, he had filled out in the chest and shoulders since he left school. Hard work had a tendency to do that. The dark hair and swarthy looks of both Gerald and Toby stood out in this land of blond Norwegians.

Andrew ignored the barb. "How's Gerald?" Toby's older brother had returned from the Spanish-American War in ill health, although he'd not been wounded.

Toby shrugged. "Malaria comes and goes. He's helping Pa out, getting the bank and post office building ready." The new building was across the street from Bridget's boardinghouse. "I heard the sheriff came to see about that body burned in the fire."

Andrew shook his head. "I was in school."

"Yeah, that's right, still one of the kids." Toby pushed on by to go into the store, his mocking laugh floating back behind.

Andrew gritted his teeth, but if this was the worst Toby had to dish out, he'd not have a problem keeping his promise to Ellie.

Once again he waved to Penny and headed back to the school-house to harness up the wagon. His cousin Trygve would have to be in charge of the wagon next year. Hard to believe Trygve would be the oldest Bjorklund boy in the school next year. Not that Astrid, Sophie, or Grace couldn't harness the horse and drive the wagon, but the task had always fallen to the boys.

Astrid leaped off the steps, as did most of the other students, and within minutes Andrew had a wagonful of laughing and shouting children.

Reverend Solberg waved them away. "Remember, tomorrow we clean, so bring soap, buckets, and rags."

"No more homework, no more books, no more teacher's dirty looks." Sophie led the chant and had them all laughing.

Tomorrow he'd see Ellie again. Andrew clapped his hand over his pocket. He'd forgotten to read her letter.

3

Dear Ingeborg,

Thank you for the invitation to come to Andrew's graduation. I do wish we could attend, but spring came late here, and Kane is just now seeding the wheat. He feels he cannot take any days off, and while he said we should go ahead without him, I would rather wait and come after harvest. I know I will miss the celebration, but I hate to leave him. It seems I always do that. How I would love to see Mor more often. I wrote to her also, and I know she will be as disappointed in not seeing her three grandchildren. They are disappointed too. They were so looking forward to playing with their cousins.

Forgive me for not being a better correspondent, and I will try to write more often. Give my love to all my family in Blessing. I wish you could all come down here. We have plenty of room on the ranch and Kane says he'll even round up some horses for the boys to ride, after they break them, of course.

Better close and get to making supper.

Yours affectionately,
Augusta Bjorklund Moyer

Ingeborg sighed and refolded the letter. *Having the entire family here would have been nice for a change. Doesn't Augusta understand her mother is getting up in years?* After the last spell that Bridget had, Ingeborg had come to the realization that her mother-in-law might not live forever, in spite of her protestations to the otherwise. Bridget did not appreciate any advice suggesting she slow down. When guests came to her boardinghouse, they expected good food, a clean bed, and a cheerful time. She was known far beyond the outskirts of Blessing since Henry Aarsgard, her husband of nearly ten years, had been a railroad man. He always said it was her cooking that caught his attention and her smile that caught his heart.

Ingeborg's knees creaked when she stood up. She shook her head. Her coronet of braids was not as bright as when she was younger but was still thick and her husband's delight, especially when, sitting on the edge of their bed, she let the braids down and brushed her requisite one hundred strokes a night.

Something nagged at her.

"Uff da, I'm getting to be an old woman, forgetting things, creaking when I walk. What was it I said I'd do?" Lines deepened on her forehead and between her eyebrows. She pulled the coffeepot to the hotter part of the stove. Perhaps a cup of coffee would revive her memory.

She checked the bread baking in the oven, not quite brown enough, and glanced over at the pies waiting to be put in the oven. She'd used the last of the dried apples, and the two pie shells would be used for chocolate cream, Andrew's favorite. While everyone in Blessing would share the dinner after the graduation ceremony, she wanted some left here for their personal celebration.

Barney barked a welcome, the tone saying it was someone he knew.

Ingeborg changed her apron and went to the door. "Elizabeth, what a wonderful surprise." Her daughter-in-law smiled and waved, then stepped carefully down from the buggy. While she'd said the baby wasn't due for another month, her girth said otherwise. But in the family way or not, Dr. Elizabeth Bjorklund had not slacked on her medical practice one bit.

"I was hoping you had the coffee on. I'm in dire need of your outhouse and then sustenance." She tied her horse's lead rope to the hitching rail in front of the white picket fence that surrounded the white two-story farmhouse. "The Swenson baby came with no trouble, a boy big enough to start crawling next week. That woman's pelvis must be made of elastic, the way she has such big babies so easily."

"I'll pour your coffee. Will a sandwich be enough, or should I warm some soup too?"

"Yes to all the above. Uff da." Elizabeth smiled at adopting one of Ingeborg's Norwegian expressions. She massaged her lower back as she made her way around the house and followed the well-worn path to the privy.

She'll not go another month, Ingeborg thought as she turned back into the house. *Doctor or not, she will have that baby when it is ready to come.* She smiled to herself. While she was still called to assist some births, Dr. Elizabeth did most of them nowadays. The people of Blessing and the surrounding area felt great relief at having a board-certified doctor in their midst, taking much of the pressure off Ingeborg, who'd used her gifts of healing for anyone who called her. Her doctoring began when she and her first husband, Roald Bjorklund, staked out their homestead near the confluence of the Red and Little Salt rivers in the spring of 1880.

Ingeborg went out to the well house, where they kept things cool, and brought in the kettle of soup she'd made the day before. Since it was time to begin dinner anyway, she'd have a bit of a jump on the preparations. Soup along with bread right out of the oven—dinner fit for a king, or queen, as in this case.

She shaded her eyes to see Haakan and his team out plowing the acreage he'd been seeding in oats for cattle feed. He and Lars worked in tandem, one team plowing just behind the other, both with double-bottom plows and four up. When the sun stood straight up, they'd head for the house, both eating here because Kaaren's school for the deaf was still in session. Both schools would be out tomorrow afternoon. Most of the deaf students would be picked up or put on the train to go home on Saturday morning.

Ingeborg added more wood to the firebox and gave the soup kettle a good stir so the vegetables wouldn't burn on the bottom. Taking two eggs from the basket on the table, she whisked them to a froth and, after measuring it in the palm of her hand, dumped salt into the eggs and beat in flour until she had a dry dough that she could drizzle into the soup to make spaetzle, tiny dumplings that looked like fat strings.

Elizabeth washed her hands at the bench outside and entered the kitchen. "Much better. Oh, it smells so good in here. Ingeborg, you bake the best bread. No matter how hard I try, mine just doesn't measure up."

"Thank you. I'll have those loaves out in a minute or two, and you can take one home with you." She gave the soup another stir. "Sit down. Rest yourself in that rocking chair." She glanced down at Elizabeth's feet. "Those boots look a mite tight. Better get your feet up too."

"I know. My feet started to swell last week when the warm weather hit. I can't take long here. I'm sure I have folks lined up at the office."

"Just for starters." Ingeborg handed Elizabeth a cup of coffee with a cookie on the saucer. "How's Thelma working out there?" She smiled as she remembered the woman who had arrived on the train one day looking for a job.

"She's a godsend." Elizabeth laid her head against the chair back. "What with Thorliff gone again, I don't know what I'd do without her."

"He'll be back for the graduation." He was going to be the speaker at the service, so she knew he would be.

"Of course. He said he'd be back on the train tomorrow." Elizabeth closed her eyes with a gentle sigh. "Guess I never realized how carrying a baby would make me feel so tired."

"You might want to cut back on taking care of other folks and look to taking care of you." Ingeborg opened the oven door, and the fragrance of baking bread filled the room. She inhaled deeply and heard Elizabeth do the same. *Don't you go giving advice where it may not be wanted,* she reminded herself. *She's the doctor, not you. Ah, but she is carrying my first grandchild, and surely that gives me some kind of reason for my concern.*

"Now you sound just like my mother." Elizabeth opened her eyes and smiled. "And yes, I know I should. Especially after we lost the first one. But that was so early in the pregnancy that the baby hardly seemed real." She rocked gently. "But I've so often wondered, was it a boy or girl? And did I do something to make it happen?"

"I still think about the baby I lost so many years ago." Ingeborg paused in turning the loaves out of the pans and onto a wooden rack so they could air. "And when I had no more after Astrid, for a while I wondered if God was punishing me for my willfulness."

"And what did you decide?"

"What I read in the Old Testament was about a vengeful God, but in the New Testament Jesus said His Father is love and that who-ever has seen Him has seen the Father. I reread all the Gospels, and the only people Jesus spoke harshly to were the Pharisees for their hard hearts. Everyone else He loved and healed. I reminded myself of those verses over and over. 'Come onto me, all ye that labour and are heavy laden, and I will give you rest. Love one another, as I have loved you. . . .' That's running them together, but I chose to believe them all. And I did what the Psalms and Paul said. I ate those words. I meditated on them day and night. I had no choice, and it seemed that thinking on the Word in the hours at night when I could not sleep was better than pacing and fretting. Another good verse, a simple one—'Fret not.'"

"You are such a good example for me. It is easy to think all my training heals people, but I know that I just do what I can, and God does the healing." Elizabeth smiled her thanks for the buttered heel of a warm loaf of bread. "You spoil me."

"My privilege. Just think, I now have two daughters and will soon have a third." She stirred the soup again. The spaetzle were cooked enough, so she pushed the kettle to the cooler part of the stove to let it simmer. She patted Elizabeth's shoulder and stepped outside to beat the iron bar around the insides of the iron triangle hanging by the back door. By the time the men arrived from the field, she would have the table set and the bread sliced.

Dishing up a bowl of soup for Elizabeth, she set it on a plate and put the plate in her daughter's lap. "There now, take your time."

"Do you think you can spare Astrid to help me part of the time? Even with Thelma helping, there is plenty to do, and Astrid has such an aptitude for caring for the sick. I'm hoping she will choose to go for a nursing degree or even study to be a doctor."

"Of course, although she usually helps Penny with her little ones and at the store in the summer."

"That Penny, now there is a wonder woman. How she manages the store, Hjelmer's businesses, her family, and all her church things I'll never know." Elizabeth wiped her mouth on a napkin. "This soup is really good. Our cook at home made spaetzle like this."

"It's easy. We like dumplings of all kinds." The dog's barking announced that the men were nearing the barn.

"I better be on my way." Elizabeth stood and set her dishes in the enameled dishpan sitting near the reservoir. "*Mange takk* for the refreshment."

Ingeborg wrapped a loaf of bread in a clean towel. "Here." She added a wedge of cheese cut from a larger wedge sitting under a glass dome. "Try this sharp cheddar and tell me what you think. Now with the cows on grass again, we'll be making plenty more cheese."

They tried to sell out their supply of cheese each year before the possibility of spring flooding so that none would go to waste. Orders came for Bjorklund cheese from as far away as St. Louis and Seattle. They'd even had orders from New York after she sent their benefactor, David Jonathan Gould, a small well-waxed wheel one Christmas.

Since Onkel Olaf now made cheese presses of various sizes, they produced more variety. She'd thought of adding Swiss cheese this year and ordered the culture to begin experimenting with. Her gammelost was a permanent success with all the Norwegians, including the new wave of immigrants.

She hugged Elizabeth and walked with her out to the buggy, where her horse dozed in the sun. "I'll see you for supper on Saturday, then, if not before."

"Yes." Elizabeth gave a discreet *oof* as she settled onto the seat. "If Mrs. Geddick has that baby anytime soon, shall I send them over here?"

"Gladly." She smiled up at the doctor. "You need to sleep through the night, and babies seem to want to come in the early morning hours. I think it's so their entrance can cause a stir."

"That they do." Elizabeth rolled her eyes. "Will you please untie that lead rope for me? How I manage to forget that little chore so often is beyond me."

"We were talking. That's why."

"Hey, Doc, what's your hurry?" Haakan called from where they were unharnessing the horses in front of the barn.

"Got people waiting for me." She waved and turned the rig around to jog down the lane.

Ingeborg watched her go. If she knew anything about babies, this one for sure wasn't going to wait a whole month, no matter what the good doctor thought. Perhaps she'd be delivering more than the Geddick baby.

The men had just finished eating when Barney announced a stranger arriving. Haakan set down his cup. "I wonder who that can be?"

Wiping her hands on her apron, Ingeborg went to the screen door. "Can I help you?"

The man dismounted from his horse, flipped the reins over the hitching rail, and pushed open the gate of the picket fence. "Mrs. Bjorklund?"

"Yes."

"I'm Sheriff Becker from Grafton. I'm here to see your husband if possible."

"Of course. Come on in. Have you had dinner yet? We're just finishing." She held the door open for him.

He removed his fedora as he came through the doorway. "I think we've met before at some of the county meetings." He nodded to the men at the table. "Haakan, Lars, I was hoping to find you where we could talk a bit."

"Sit down. Astrid, bring the man a plate."

"I hate to put you out this way."

"Have you eaten?"

"No."

"Then take that chair."

While the men spoke, Ingeborg dished up some soup from the kettle on the stove, and Astrid filled a coffee cup and set it and the silverware in place.

"So, Charles, what brings you clear over here?"

"That body you found after the Olsons' shed burned. You know anything more about that?"

"No. Since we've not heard of anyone missing, I think it was some bum off the train who holed up in there, and maybe it was him smoking that started the fire. We buried him over to the church plot. Didn't know what else to do."

"Was there any kind of identification on him?" Charles took a spoonful of the soup. "This is mighty good, Mrs. Bjorklund. Thank you."

"Nothing remained from the fire. He was burnt near to a cinder." Lars dunked his cookie in his coffee.

"No one had seen a stranger around these parts?"

"Nobody said they had. You know, the people here would come right out and say so if they knew something. We all just responded to the church bell tolling. Olson's place is right near the church."

"So you don't think there was any foul play?"

"In Blessing?"

"Well, ya never know, and it's my job to look into things like that." He sopped the soup up with the last of his bread.

"I have plenty more," Ingeborg offered.

"Thanks, but that was enough. I'm going on over to the Olsons' next. Anyone hears anything, you'll let me know?" The sheriff nodded to Ingeborg. "Mighty fine, ma'am. Thank you." He shoved his chair back.

"Thorliff was planning to put something about it in the paper. Perhaps that might bring out some information." Haakan stood up. "Come again some time when you can stay longer."

Ingeborg watched the men file out the door. Someone, some-where was missing a family member. How tragic.

By the time they blew out the kitchen lamp, the sheriff's visit had been discussed soundly. Later, when Ingeborg and Haakan retired to their room, he lay against propped-up pillows, his hands locked behind his head, watching his wife brush her hair.

"I've been thinking."

She turned to look at him. Even after all these years of marriage, the sight of his muscled chest and shoulders made her heart trip over its own beat. The silver in his hair caught the lamplight, silver that was getting more pronounced, as were the lines in his face. More scalp showed, giving his already broad forehead more skin, and a distinct line divided his tan face and the white of his hat-hidden head.

"Thinking what?"

"You know Andrew's house is not coming on time?"

"Ja." She kept up her strokes, no longer needing to count but doing so anyway, content with the rhythm.

"Perhaps they should put off the wedding. Wait until we get the house and barn both up and the harvest in."

"They are so young, but I sure don't want to be the one to suggest this to Andrew." Ingeborg shook her head slowly. "Guess we should pray about it first. If you believe this is what's best, we need God to give you the right words and Andrew to have willing ears to hear it. He thinks he's a man now, you know."

"It isn't like we are saying to wait forever—only two, three months or so. They have their whole lives ahead of them."

Ingeborg set her brush on the washstand and brought her hair over one shoulder to braid it loosely for the night.

"Leave it down."

His request tickled the hairs on the back of her neck. She knew what he was asking, and yet the thought made her sigh. She should be glad he still cared for her in that way. When had she first yearned to put off her husband's advances? Most likely at the same time she stepped into being contrary. She wished she'd trapped that loud sigh before she blew out the lamp and crawled into bed. Sometimes loving him more than herself took extra effort.

Later, when he'd turned over and his breathing deepened into sleep, she lay there watching the moonlight paint designs on the floor. *You should be grateful,* a small voice nagged.

Should be grateful and *were* grateful were two different things and never more obvious than right now. What would Andrew say when his far asked him to put off the wedding? "Uff da," she muttered to herself. She had meant to bring up the subject of leaving more fields for pasture and hay, but she'd forgotten. Or did she just not want to get into another argument? It seemed they'd been gnawing at this bone of contention for years instead of only months.

"YOU WANT ME TO WHAT?" Andrew stood with his mouth agape.

Haakan raised a hand. "Now take it easy. Let's talk about this."

"Whatever gave you any idea I'd even consider such a thing?" Andrew fought to keep his voice at a low pitch. Long ago he'd learned that shouting never did anyone much good. So having to work to lower his voice caught him by surprise—nearly as much as his father's words had. He looked deep into Haakan's eyes, searching for he knew not what. "Pa, you know I've been planning to marry Ellie as soon as we were out of school ever since I was in short pants. Seems I've waited long enough."

"I know, Andrew, I know. But perhaps your house not coming on schedule is God's way of telling you to wait."

"But why?"

"I don't know why, and I've never doubted a day in my life that you and Ellie were meant for each other. But . . ." Haakan, his Bjorklund eyes clouded like the sky above, stared into the distance, as if he too were seeking answers.

"Pa, I've done what you said all my life. I've tried to be a son you can be proud of."

"And I am, Andrew. I am so proud of you I sing your praises to the sky. I thank our God for giving me sons like you and Thorliff. Especially you, Andrew. You love this farm and this land the same way I do—I couldn't ask for anyone better."

Andrew stared out over the land as he scuffed a chunk of black soil with the toe of his boot. Haakan was never one to throw words away. If he said something was so, it was so. But everything within Andrew screamed at the injustice of this request. For he understood it was a request or a suggestion, not an order. "I have waited so long."

"Look at it this way. We'll have the summer to get your house up, and then between haying and harvest, we can have a barn raising. A month or two, three at the most. Ellie could stay here in Blessing, work for Penny at the store. Astrid wants to help Elizabeth, so she won't have time to help Penny. Andrew, your mor and I, we just ask you to think about this, to pray about it."

"And if I say no?" A quick kick shattered the clod.

"I'd hope you'd talk this over with Ellie first. Make this decision together."

"And if we decide to go ahead?"

"Then we'll have the wedding near the end of June just like you planned."

"You won't be mad?"

"Sad, perhaps, and maybe disappointed. But mad? No, son, I won't be mad."

"And Mor?" Andrew glanced out of the side of his eye.

"You'll have to ask her. This was a surprise to her too. Like it was for me."

Andrew clamped his teeth together. His jaw ached from the fight against saying more. "I better get the cows up." He whistled for the dog and headed for the barn. While some of the twenty-five head of milk cows would be lined up at the door, there were still those stubborn ones that had to be rounded up. That's what a good cow dog was for. It saved a man a lot of tramping through the grass.

Although right now, stomping through the grass might have done him some good. How could they ask this of him? It wasn't as if this wedding was a recent thought. All the chaste kisses when his body screamed to hold her close, when he hated to say good-night, when he thought if he had to write one more letter rather than getting on the train and going to fetch her home . . . His heart had nearly shattered when Onkel Olaf, Ellie's adoptive father, decided to move his woodworking shop farther away from the flooding river. Soaking in dirty river water was pretty detrimental to the hardwoods he used for building good furniture. Not that the floods weren't hard on everyone, but Onkel wasn't locked onto the land like the rest of them and so could wisely move.

Mor had reminded him to be grateful that Ellie wasn't days away, like on the East Coast or the Pacific, where his cousin Hamre now lived. The train made the distance to Grafton in little more than an hour, but it felt like more. Through her tears, Ellie had said that they would get to know each other on a deeper level through letters, because when she was with him, her mind seemed to go off and flit with the clouds or some such. Then they'd laughed together.

Ah, it was so easy to laugh with his Ellie.

One by one he dropped the short boards in the stanchions to close the board against the cow's neck, keeping her from backing up and leaving the barn before she was milked. When the final three came in, thanks to the dog, he poured a scoop of feed in front of each cow, talking to them as he moved down the line.

"Hey, Andrew," Trygve, Kaaren's oldest son, called as he strolled into the barn swinging a metal milking pail in each hand. "You want me to bring over the milk cans?"

"Please, and don't forget the buckets of soapy water."

"I won't." He left, whistling as usual. One always knew when Trygve was coming. Mor said he could outwhistle the birds, and often one would think a bird was singing when, in reality, it was Trygve.

Right now Andrew knew he would give anything to be as carefree as Trygve, sure he would work along with the men, no longer left to weed the garden or help however his mor required. Trygve's younger brother, Sam, had taken on those chores. The whole family called him

Little Sam, as if the two words were hitched together. Old Sam Lincoln ran the blacksmith shop for Hjelmer.

Just the thought of bringing this idea of postponing the wedding up to Ellie made his stomach do flip-flops. How could they ask this of him? *But they never ask anything of you*, a little voice in his heart said. *At least nothing like this. There has to be a good reason.*

But even Haakan didn't know the reason, just said it was a feeling he had. And Mor even agreed.

As soon as Trygve returned with the buckets of soapy water, Andrew washed down the udder of the cow he was about to milk and set his stool in place. With his forehead planted in the cow's warm flank and the milk pinging into the bucket, he could let his mind roam. Cow milking time was always good thinking time. He'd daydreamed many a milking hour about the life he and Ellie would have once they were married.

But it's only three months or so. Surely ninety days isn't going to make a difference in all the years we will have together. He recognized his reasonable side. But when he realized his jaws were clamped, he knew this went beyond reasonable. *I will not get angry over this,* he promised himself. *Look at all the wood I've split because I got angry. It's just not worth it. Besides, chopping wood for my own house will be a time of pleasure.* His mind took off on another daydream—Ellie's smiling face as she served him a cup of coffee at their own table. Of planting roses by their front porch, apple trees, and their own garden. Of reading by the lamplight on a winter evening. Ellie had such a sweet voice and loved to read aloud. He would lie on the sofa with his head in her lap, and— He cut off that picture when he could feel his neck heating up.

❧

Andrew stood at the train station waiting for Ellie and her family to arrive that afternoon. He wore clean shirt and pants, his boots were polished, and he'd brushed his straw hat the night before after the haircut. Mor always gave him a good haircut. While many of the men went to the new barber in town, he could see no sense in wasting his money on that when his mor cut hair for free. Did Ellie know how to cut a man's hair? Of course she did. Ellie could do anything.

The train whistled in the distance, as if announcing it was bringing him a gift. Nothing sounded more lonesome than that train whistle across the prairie on a cold winter morning, but not today. Each clack of the wheels brought her closer.

His feet refused to stand still, so he paced and willed the train to come faster.

"Hey, Andrew, could you come help me a minute?" Penny called from the front of her store.

Andrew stared from the train to the store and back to the train. "I . . . ah . . . of course." He started toward the store, dogtrotting so he could get back quickly.

But Penny laughed and hollered back, "No, Andrew, I was teasing you. I know you're waiting for Ellie." She waved again and returned inside.

Andrew grinned and shook his head. *Leave it to Penny to tease me like that.*

The train slowed, the brakes screaming and the steam billowing. The engineer pulled the whistle again, announcing to all the world that the eastbound Northern Pacific had arrived.

The engine passed, the tender loaded with coal, the mail car with a man waving from the open door, and finally the passenger cars. Shrieking and squealing, the brakes stopped the train with the door right in the center of the platform. The conductor stepped down, reached back in to fetch his stool, and set it in place.

Onkel Olaf came first, carrying Arne. Then he turned and handed Mrs. Wold down. Rachel, the young cousin, followed Goodie and took Arne's hand as soon as his pa set him on the platform.

Andrew greeted them all, but his boot soles nearly wore a hole in the wooden planks. Finally, there she stood on the bottom step, her smile dimming the sun, even when shaded by a broad-brimmed leg-horn hat, decorated by a wide blue ribbon with streamers down her back. He noticed everything about her, cataloging them instantly, paying attention especially to her smile and the love shining from her wide gray eyes. Her cheeks turned pink, and she waved a white-gloved hand.

As soon as her black-slippered feet touched the platform, she flew into his arms, then grabbed her hat as he whirled her around.

"Andrew, that is not seemly." But her smile said she loved every minute of their embrace.

He sighed as he set her down, staring deep into her eyes, his slow smile making both their hearts speed up. "I was beginning to think you'd never get here."

"Why, you knew what time the train would arrive." She stepped back and locked her arm through his.

Ever practical, his Ellie. He covered her hand with his own. "I better help them get the bags."

"No. Pa will take care of that. He has help. Come, Ma, Andrew has the wagon waiting over there."

Rachel took her cousin's other hand and grinned up at Andrew. "Ellie changed her dress three times before she could make up her mind what to wear."

"Hush." Ellie ducked her head. "You shouldn't tell family secrets like that."

"Oh, really? She sure looks pretty, don't you think?" Andrew grinned at Rachel.

"Ellie always looks pretty. Even when she has her hair tied up in a towel after she washes it. Like yesterday."

"Rachel, that's enough." As if trying to hide the blush that bloomed on her face, Ellie put her hands to her cheeks.

"Well, you said—"

This time Ellie clamped a gloved hand over her cousin's mouth. "I don't care what I said."

Andrew's laugh drowned out the conductor's "All aboard." The train whistle blew as Andrew handed Ellie up into the wagon and climbed up to sit beside her, Onkel Olaf taking the outside seat.

"Ma, would it be better if you sat up here?" Ellie turned to look at her mother, who was sitting with Arne in the back of the wagon. In the turning, her broad hat brim bumped Andrew's hat forward onto his face. With a quick grab he kept his straw hat from blowing off and tumbling into the dirt.

"Sorry."

"That thing is a menace." He chuckled to see her cheeks flaming again and not from the sun either. "But you look so pretty in it that I'll forgive you." He whispered the words for her ears alone but knew by the snicker from the rear that others besides hers had heard.

And Far is asking me to wait when I can never have a moment alone with her as it is. The thought clamped his jaw, and he backed the team instead of letting his mind dwell on the request. When would he even have a chance to ask her?

In spite of his good intentions, Ellie knew something was wrong. He could tell by the way she watched him and had managed to brush her shoulder against his when she'd turned to admonish Rachel.

"Has our house arrived?" She looked up at him.

He shook his head. "No, we got a letter saying there was a delay. It should come in the next two weeks." He flicked the reins for the horses to pick up their trot. *Don't ask me any more.* He stared straight ahead. Things were not going the way he'd planned, that was for sure. Mor had reminded him that God's plans weren't always the same as our plans. Who wanted to hear such a thing as that right now?

"It'll be all right," Ellie said as she patted his arm.

"Ja." He nodded. If only he could skip all this and enjoy graduation and getting ready for their wedding.

He stopped the team by the gate in the picket fence that now surrounded the front yard and kept any stray cattle out of his mother's flower gardens. She'd already rooted starts of the rosebushes for them to plant by their new house. Everything was ready but the house.

"Goodie, Olaf, how good to see you." Ingeborg flew down the

steps and across the yard. "Come in, come in. Supper is nearly ready. You've just enough time to wash up. Andrew, help carry their things inside." She and Goodie hugged each other like long-lost sisters, which they'd nearly become in the years they'd worked so closely together, both on the farm and at the cheese house. When the Wolds moved to Grafton, the split had been hard for everyone.

Ingeborg locked her arm through Goodie's, and together they walked into the house. Olaf handed the boxes out to his soon-to-be son-in-law. Andrew led the way to the bedroom he and Thorliff had once shared. While Ellie's parents and Arne would take over Andrew's room, Ellie and Rachel would room with Astrid. Having company had been easier before the flood took out the soddy. Any time they referred to *the flood*, they meant the horrendous one of 1897. People referred to that one as the hundred-year flood, and they all hoped and prayed another would wait that long but preferably never happen again.

All the soddies in the area had been destroyed, the dirt walls melting away with the force of the water. But while loss of livestock and buildings had been high, no one had died during the flood, which was a miracle in itself.

As soon as Andrew unloaded the wagon, he drove the team to the barn and removed the harnesses. Off to the west he could see Haakan coming in from the fields, walking behind the team he'd unhitched from the seeder.

To the north he saw Astrid come running across the small pasture, as they called the fenced-in plot between their house and Tante Kaaren and Lars's house. Three years younger than he, Astrid seemed not nearly as grown up as his Ellie, although he had noticed that some of the young men around Blessing had come to visit more often than before. While they said they came to see him, he knew Astrid and Tante Kaaren's twins were the reason they came. Astrid would say they came because Sophie was such a flirt.

Andrew hung up the harnesses and let the horses loose in the corral to cool off before he released them into the pasture, where the water trough waited.

"Gettin' warm," Haakan said, stopping the team in the shade of the barn. "Want to help me here?" He lifted his hat to wipe his sweaty forehead with the back of his arm.

Andrew set about removing harnesses again, not purposely ignoring his father but not having much to say either. He draped the harness across the pegs on the outside of the barn wall, hung up the collar, and took off the bridle. When Haakan finished doing the same, Andrew led the two horses over to the corral and released them. Sliding the bars back in place, he sighed before heading for the house. This surely was the hardest thing anyone had asked of him. When could he talk it over with Ellie?

5

"ELLIE, WE HAVE TO TALK." Andrew got up from the swing on the porch and began pacing.

Ellie watched his face. From the moment she'd gotten off the train, she'd known something was wrong. But Andrew would tell her in good time if it was something to do with the two of them. He'd always been that way. If the tales she'd heard of his uncle were true, Hjelmer had been a master poker player. Andrew had not inherited those skills, especially not a poker face. Perhaps she just knew him better than anyone else. She'd given everything about Andrew Bjorklund plenty of thought. He'd been her best friend from the day she woke up after being terribly sick to find him sitting in the chair by the bed, watching her. He got her anything she wanted and told her stories about the animals on the farm to entertain her. By the time she was well again, they were inseparable. And had been ever since.

She promised herself then that she would never be parted from Andrew again, but she'd had no control over the move to Grafton. And now something was seriously wrong. Fear gnawed like a rat in the grain bin.

She watched him pace the length of the porch and back again. "Just tell me what it is before you wear out the floorboards." She kept her voice calm while her insides screamed and her fingers creased the folds of her skirt.

He dropped into the swing and took her hands in his. "I-I don't know where to start."

"I've always thought the beginning was the best place." *Andrew, what is wrong?*

His face tightened, more so than it had been. "You know how much I love you?" His grip strangled her fingers.

"I believe I do, but I don't think that is the beginning." Ellie kept her voice even, in spite of the arrow of fear that nicked her heart.

Andrew sucked in a deep breath. "Sorry." He relaxed his grip on her fingers, then stroked them gently in apology. "Far asked us, or rather Mor and Far have asked us, to postpone our wedding."

Ellie breathed a sigh of relief. While she'd not put words to her fear, this wasn't it. "For how long?"

"Until after harvest."

Ellie collapsed against the back of the swing with an unladylike snort. "Ho, what a relief."

"Relief! Did you hear what I said?"

Now it was her turn to stroke his hand. "In my mind you were dying of some terrible malady or you'd decided you didn't love me anymore." She patted her chest. "Be still, heart—this is going to be all right."

Andrew shook his head, his eyebrows slashing into a straight line. "Don't you care?"

"Of course I care." She sat up straight and planted her feet firmly together on the floor. "All right, let's start over before we get carried away. Tell me the whole thing. I know they must have a good reason to ask this of us."

"How can you be so calm?" Andrew clamped his arms across his chest. "Far said it was something that came to him, and he and Mor talked it over, and since our house hasn't come yet and we've only started building the barn, he said we would have the summer to get the building done. He just felt this was the best way to do things.

When I asked him more about it, that's all he could, or would, say."

"Haakan is a wise man."

"I know. Most of the time."

Ellie leaned against his shoulder until he relaxed and put his arm around her. "Why does this upset you so much?"

He jerked away and turned to stare into her face. "I've waited for years to marry you."

"Then a couple more months shouldn't make a great deal of difference."

"Ellie Wold, I thought you'd feel the same as me. We don't have to do this, you know."

"Oh, Andrew, don't be silly." *Oh-oh. Wrong thing to say. Be careful, Ellie.*

"So now I'm silly for getting angry when I'm asked to change all my plans? Plans I've been dreaming of forever?"

Ellie rolled her eyes but refrained from saying more. She reached up and kissed his cheek, then took one of his hands in hers. "I don't want to go back to Grafton for the summer—that I don't want to do. Even if we aren't married, I want to be close by."

"Far said he was sure Penny would hire you to work in the store. Usually Astrid helps Penny out all summer, but this year she is going to help Dr. Elizabeth."

"Then I would have money to buy some of the things we will need for our house."

"That's my job."

"What?"

"Providing things for our house."

"Oh, Andrew." She kept from telling him not to be silly again. He did not like to be called silly. She thought for a bit, letting the evening song of the crickets and peeper frogs bathe her in peace.

"Are we fighting?" She could feel the weight of his cheek on her hair as she snuggled in the circle of his arm.

"No . . . yes." He heaved a sigh. "I thought you'd say we couldn't—"

"Couldn't?" She interrupted him.

"Wouldn't want to wait." He corrected himself.

"I don't want to wait. If I had my way, we'd get married the day after graduation. But there has to be a reason for this." She tilted her head back to look up at him. "Have you prayed about this?"

"Yes."

"Yes, meaning sort of, or yes, meaning a lot?"

"Well, Far just told me this the other day."

She could feel him drawing back even though he hadn't really moved at all. She sensed sometimes that while Andrew believed all the things they'd said at confirmation, he was not really comfortable talking about prayer, especially when it related to his praying. She tried to think back. Had she ever heard him pray out loud, other than grace? "I think we need to pray about this."

"Ja."

"Together."

Silence but for the sound of his heart thudding. She could hear it clearly through his chest wall. In all their years together, they'd only sat close like this a few times. She fully expected one of their mothers to come and check on them or send one of the children out. The warm, solid feel of his muscles made her want to snuggle closer. But she didn't, hearing her mother's comments on what was proper and how Jeanne Smith, a neighbor in Grafton, had overstepped the bounds of propriety and look what happened to her. Ellie wondered what indeed had happened to her friend. She'd gone to visit her aunt in Minneapolis, promising to write, but Ellie had never heard from her. *I should have asked more questions.* She and Maydell had talked the situation to death but decided it was one of those mysterious things they'd learn about when they were older.

Ellie was sure she could be content for the rest of her life if she could always sit like this with Andrew. But instead of allowing herself the pleasure, she pulled away and looked up at him. His handsome face with a strong chin and smiling mouth—not right now but usually—and those blue eyes that caught pieces of a summer sky and shared them with her. What would it be like to smooth the hank of hair that always fell over his forehead when he wasn't wearing a hat or cap? To run her fingers through his thick blond hair not yet bleached nearly white like it would be by the end of the summer in spite of the hats he wore?

"You didn't answer me," she whispered.

"I didn't know you wanted an answer."

"Andrew, this wait won't be the end of the world. As long as we can see each other and talk and laugh . . . Just being together is so much better than not seeing you for months, and while I love your letters, they weren't enough."

"I know."

"So please, don't be angry at your mor and far." She watched his eyes. "Or me, for that matter."

She could see his jaw tighten and reached out and laid her hand along his jawline. When he turned his head and placed a kiss in the palm of her hand, she sucked in a breath. Ooh, what was it that shot up her arm? Her skin burned where his lips had touched it.

"We better go in." He stood in one smooth motion and pulled her up with him. "I will go along with this, but I can tell you right now it won't be easy—and I'm not happy about it."

Ellie cupped her burning hand with the other. She stared at Andrew as if seeing a perfect stranger. Granted they'd not shared more than a few kisses, in fact she could remember every one of them, but never before had she felt like this. How could a kiss in her hand have burned all the way to her middle? Why it even affected her knees. She took in a deep breath, hoping and praying for it to bring calmness, but like an open door fanning flames, the breath seemed to increase her awareness of the man in front of her.

Andrew opened the screen door and turned to see what happened to her when she wasn't right behind him like he expected. "Are you all right? Ellie, is something wrong?"

"Ah . . . yes . . . um . . . I mean no."

"Ma says to come for dessert." Astrid paused at the door Andrew was still holding open. "Is something wrong?" She looked from Andrew to Ellie.

"Only if you call postponing our wedding something wrong."

Andrew's curt tone jerked Ellie from the stupor that had attacked her. She forced a smile to lips that quivered. Why did she feel like crying? *Lord above, what is wrong with me? And we didn't pray about this. Is Andrew afraid of praying with me? Isn't that important in a marriage? If I tell him how afraid I am of having a baby, will he pray with me or just turn away? Oh, Andrew, maybe I don't know you as well as I thought.*

6

"WHAT'S WRONG WITH ANDREW, Mor? He's ugly as a bear with a sore paw."

"Now, Astrid, how would you know what a bear feels like?"

"I heard that somewhere. It seemed to fit. I thought he'd be all excited today, what with graduation and all." Astrid wiped the last dish and set it in the cupboard, then draped her dish towel on the rack behind the stove. "I'll go change now, all right?"

"Fine." Ingeborg untied her apron. While she'd known Andrew would not be happy with Haakan's request, she'd not expected him to be surly. But come to think on it, he'd been glum but not out of sorts like this until he'd talked with Ellie the night before. That was the key. How would she get this son of hers to talk with her, especially since he blamed her too. *I'm sorry, Andrew, but I trust that Haakan would not have said something like this if he'd not had a strong feeling about it.* Knowing that God had used her husband this way in the past made her trust He would do so again. *Lord, please help our son to be patient, to look to you for help in dealing with this disappointment. I know you love him far more even than I do and you want the best for him. It's so hard for me to believe my sweet little Andrew is really old enough to graduate and to think of marrying. And Ellie has been like a daughter to me for so many years. This will be one more thing to draw us closer.*

Ingeborg checked on the two chickens she had baking in the oven for the community dinner at the school, since the graduation ceremony would be held in the church. Andrew and Ellie had taken the buggy over already. The rest of them would come in the wagons.

"Anything I can do to help?" Goodie asked after coming down the stairs.

"You don't want to muss your good clothes."

"Ingeborg Bjorklund, this is me you're talking to. Can I use that apron?" Goodie pointed to one of the aprons hanging on a peg on the wall behind the stove. "Things ready to be loaded?"

"You can pack those baskets if you like." Ingeborg pointed to the table laden with baked pies, rolls, and three loaves of bread. Baskets waited on chairs.

"Slice the bread first?"

"Please."

Rachel followed Astrid back down the stairs, both of them with their hair gathered up from the sides and front and tied with a bow to flow down their backs.

"I thought you were going to ask Astrid to braid your hair."

"I want it like hers and Ellie's."

"But it will get all tangled when you are playing."

"No, I'll be good."

Ingeborg and Goodie swapped mother looks that included smiles ripe with memories—of Ellie and Astrid wanting to wear their hair up, of them coming in muddy or covered with hay or straw dust, their knees dirty from kneeling as they weeded in the gardens. How they'd loved playing with the calves, even the chickens, which had always been Astrid's specialty, some of the hens her pets. They especially loved the fluffy chicks, cuddling them gently under their chins.

Rachel leaned against her aunt. "I don't want Ellie to go away."

"I know. Me neither, but she's grown up now, and she loves Andrew."

"He don't love her much as I do."

Again the mothers exchanged looks as Goodie hugged her niece and kissed the top of her head.

"Andrew could come live at our house. He could have Hans's room."

Ingeborg glanced up at the carved walnut clock on the shelf, both shelf and clock gifts from Onkel Olaf. "We better hurry. Astrid, you and Rachel go bring the team and wagon up. Haakan has them harnessed."

Astrid grabbed Rachel's hand and out the door they went, laughing at something only they knew.

"Let Astrid comb out the snarls. She's enjoying being 'big sister' to her."

Goodie chuckled but used the hem of the apron to wipe away the moisture in her eyes. "I don't know how I'm going to bear it with Ellie gone."

Ingeborg wrapped her arms around her friend. "And here I've been so selfishly looking forward to having my other daughter back. Oh, Goodie, I have missed you all so much. Much as I enjoy your letters, there's been a hole here without all of you."

"Grafton just isn't the same as Blessing. The people are nice enough, and we have a good church. The children have done well in school there, but our family is here." Goodie leaned into Ingeborg's arms. "Ellie told me what Andrew said. He seems some upset."

"He is—more so I think since he talked with Ellie. I thought that would help, but . . ." She shook her head. "Can't say as I blame him. He's talked about marrying up with Ellie ever since he was in short pants."

"I know. Andrew is always so sunny, I hardly recognize his face behind the frown."

"Mor, we're ready," Astrid called from outside.

"Oh my, and here we stand gabbing instead of packing." Goodie brushed the backs of her hands across her eyes. "It will all come out all right?"

Ingeborg knew her friend didn't really mean that as a question. "I have to keep reminding myself that God is in control. He has a plan, and He holds all of us in the palm of His hand. I believe Haakan is acting on divine guidance, so there is some reason for this."

"Yes, I believe so too."

While Goodie finished packing the baskets, Ingeborg took the chickens in the roaster from the oven and tied a dish towel across the lid to keep it in place. "There, I think that is everything."

"There will be plenty of food. Always is. I feel bad not bringing anything."

"Coming on the train like that? I think not. You get to be the guests this time."

Astrid and Rachel charged in the door. "We'll start carrying things out."

"Be careful you don't spill on your dress."

Astrid glanced down, and a smile made her eyes twinkle. "Not when we sat hemming it half the night." The blue-and-white dotted Swiss draped from gathers at her waist, a deep ruffle around the bottom skimming her ankles in the newer, shorter style. The ruffle had made for a lot of hemming. A matching bow at the waist and the one in her hair proclaimed her still a girl, but one right on the verge of womanhood. At fifteen, Astrid was unaware of her charm, but Haakan had noted how she caught the gazes of males of all ages. Young Abner had blushed when he'd seen her at the train station one day.

Haakan rushed in now as they put the last basket in place. "Sorry I'm late. I'll be ready in a moment."

Ingeborg followed him to the bedroom. "What happened?"

"The sow is farrowing. I'm so used to Andrew taking care of the sows, I almost forgot to check on her. I put the babies under the bar in the corner. She'd already lain on one." Haakan changed clothes as he talked. "Don't tell Andrew, or he might just come home to take care of her."

"How many does she have?"

"Six live. I think she'll have more. But I can't miss Andrew's graduation."

Ingeborg handed him his tie and, taking his coat off the hanger, brushed the shoulders and gave it a shake before holding it for him to put his arms in. "Astrid can drive the team while you tie your shoes and put on your tie."

He grabbed his fedora from the peg as they went out the door.

Haakan let Astrid drive the team all the way, nodding to her smiles at him. "You're doing just fine. I'll sit here and enjoy the ride."

"Your shirt isn't buttoned right."

He glanced down. "You're right. Thanks for telling me. We wouldn't want your mor embarrassed that her husband wasn't dressed right."

"I heard that," Ingeborg called from the back.

Astrid giggled and smiled again at her pa. They were often co-conspirators in teasing Ingeborg.

It was a good thing that pews had been saved for the families of the graduates, or they would have all been standing against the walls like some of the others. As they came down the aisle, Lars pointed out their pew across the aisle from where Kaaren and the rest of his family sat. Two of the students from the deaf school were graduating, and since their families couldn't, or didn't, come, Kaaren stood in for them, as she had for many others.

Ingeborg patted her sister-in-law's shoulder when she passed by her. After all they'd been through together, from the beginning of the trip from Norway until now, the two were closer than sisters, especially after both their husbands died in the same terrible winter.

As soon as everyone settled, Pastor Solberg took his place in the front of the congregation and, with a broad smile, announced, "Welcome to the graduation for our fine young men and women in this year of our Lord, a new century, nineteen hundred." He nodded, and the pianist crashed into the opening chords of "Pomp and Circumstance."

Everyone turned to see the first two, Ellie and Andrew, step through the doors, each carrying the Bible they'd been given at confirmation. Deborah MacCallister and Abner Thorensen brought up the rear. Eight students this year, the largest graduating class of Blessing School. As they marched to the front row, the first two went to the left, the next to the right, and at the final chord they sat as one.

Ingeborg sniffed. Her second son was graduating. Thorliff, sitting in the row behind them, laid a hand on her shoulder. He leaned forward to whisper, "You did well, Mor. He is a young man to be proud of."

Ingeborg patted his hand and let out a breath she didn't realize she'd been holding. Andrew looked nervous, but the frown had been left at home.

"We are gathered here today to bestow graduation honors on eight fine young men and women. They have all studied hard, learned things they were not sure were necessary . . ."

A titter danced along the rows of those in attendance, from the graduates and from those who'd encouraged them.

How many times did I hear that, I wonder? Ingeborg wanted to pat Andrew's shoulder, but she refrained. She glanced at Astrid, who had no compunction about poking her brother in the back. Andrew sat straighter.

". . . and discovered new worlds through their reading and discussions. The Bible says to train up our children in the way they should go, and they will not depart from it. I say to you that even if they depart for a time, although we pray they won't, God will not let them go. He has promised that His own will not be lost."

A shiver ran up Ingeborg's back. She tucked her hand under Haakan's arm, needing the feel of his strength beside her. He laid his other hand over her fingers and squeezed. *Thank you, Lord, for this man you have given me and for all those gathered here.*

"Let us pray." Pastor Solberg waited for silence and continued, "Heavenly Father, we come to honor these young people, your children, and to ask your blessings on all of us as we grow in grace and learn to walk in your ways and remain in your will. Be with us now as we are gathered in your name. Amen."

He looked up and smiled across the room. "I have asked each of our young people to share with us a Scripture that they feel God has given them for this moment in their lives. Andrew, we'll begin with you. . . ."

After all eight of the graduates had shared their verses, Pastor Solberg returned to the podium. "I have invited a former graduate to bring us a message today. Thorliff Bjorklund will share some words of wisdom he has learned in his years at college and while working in the newspaper world. Thorliff?"

Ingeborg thought she might burst with joy. While she knew pride was a sin, she couldn't help the tears and didn't try to stanch them.

Thorliff smiled at each of those in the front row. He'd filled out in the years since he left home to attend St. Olaf College in Minnesota. His blond hair had darkened because he no longer worked out in the fields. Instead, he published a biweekly newspaper, the *Blessing Gazette*, and wrote as a stringer for several others, including the *Northfield News*, where he'd learned his trade.

"Graduates, families, friends, and neighbors, I thank you for this honor and privilege. If someone had told me when I was sitting where you are"—he smiled at those in the front row—"that these years would fly by so swiftly, I would have perhaps laughed. After all, I knew what I wanted to do. I wanted to go on to college, I wanted to write, and I dreamed of marriage to a fine young woman."

Ingeborg knew he meant Anji Baard, now Moen, who had been his sweetheart for his last year before college and a good friend since they were young. But that had not been in God's plan, it seemed. *Perhaps that is why Andrew wants to marry now, in case something happens as it did with his brother.* That thought made her want to say something to Haakan, but she kept still. He was right. Both Andrew and Ellie were young and would have many years together. The wait was not for long. She brought herself back to listen to Thorliff, knowing she'd missed something. Sometimes her mind just took off without her permission, and she'd know she missed something or forgot something, and the thought would drive her crazy.

"I believe it is important that we have dreams and plans, and if we are reading God's Word and searching for His will, He gives us dreams to follow. Our dreams become plans, and when we work hard at them, our plans can come to pass. But perhaps not all of them. When we pray 'Thy will be done,' we are stating that we believe God's will should supersede our own. We must trust that His will is perfect. He has a plan for you, a plan 'for good and not for evil.' As children we sang the song 'Trust and Obey.' Trusting and obeying are not always easy. In fact, there will be times in your lives when those two will be the hardest things you will ever do. Trust and obey." He looked each graduate in the eyes. "Trust and obey God, and I promise you that He will fulfill His part. I know He did and is still doing so for me, for my family, and for each of us. His grace is sufficient. It is new every morning. May God bless your dreams and plans and keep you until the day He comes again."

He sat down to the applause and more than a few tears from the congregation.

Ingeborg clung to Haakan's hand. Plans, so many plans they'd had, and God had blessed them in ways beyond measure. Not all exactly when they wanted, but . . . Another thought popped into her head. Some He ignored or changed, like her desire for more children. She and Haakan had had no more children after Astrid. She'd wanted lots of children, but that dream had been denied. While she'd quit asking why and most of the time was content, the loss was there. But now she would be having children in a new way. Grandchildren. And the first would be coming at any time. Elizabeth and Thorliff would have a baby, and she would be there to assist that baby into this world. *Thank you, Father.*

She brought herself back to the moment and saw that Pastor Solberg was again at the podium.

"And now, as I call your name, please come forward for your diploma. Andrew Bjorklund."

Andrew stood and walked up to Pastor Solberg. Taller than his father and Thorliff, with squared shoulders and an easy confidence, Andrew wore the suit his mother had made for him for this day. He took his ribbon-tied diploma, along with the envelope containing Mr. Gould's gift of a hundred dollars, and shook the pastor's hand.

"Thank you, sir."

"Go with God, Mr. Bjorklund."

"I will." As he returned to his seat, the next name was called and the next until Pastor Solberg said, "Ellie Wold."

Ingeborg heard Goodie sniff when her daughter stood and walked to the podium. Ellie glowed like the sun shone just on her. Her smile brought an answering one from Pastor Solberg. "Thank you for letting me be part of this celebration."

"You are so welcome. Go with God."

"I will." Her sweet voice carried to the corners of the room. Her eyes sparkled with tears as she made her way back to her seat.

The ceremony closed with the singing of "Blest Be the Tie That Binds" and Pastor Solberg's benediction. The graduates lined up at the door so they could accept the congratulations from all those congregated.

"I'm so proud of you," Ingeborg whispered, hugging her son.

"Thank you, Mor. You didn't cry too much, huh?"

"No. I did well." She hugged Ellie. "You looked so beautiful up there. Your ma nearly melted into a puddle."

"I did not," Goodie protested and dabbed at her eyes again.

Inside the schoolhouse the food was set up on tables, and outside, tables draped with cloth waited for the people to sit and enjoy themselves. Small children played tag among the groups of adults, and the older boys gathered in one group, eyeing the girls gathered in another.

At Pastor's instructions they sang the grace, and lines formed for folks to help themselves to the bounty spread in celebration of the graduates.

"Hey, Prince Andrew, thought you was goin' to announce the big wedding." Toby Valders looked up at Andrew. While the smile said this was friendly, the eyes held no warmth.

"That's none of your business." Andrew smiled too, but the curt tone didn't.

"Now, ain't that a shame." Toby shrugged and narrowed his eyes. "Maybe everything in life ain't going your way all the time."

Andrew clenched his fists but stepped back when Ellie laid a hand on his arm.

"Thank you, Toby. I know you wish us the best." Ellie smiled from one man to the other.

"'Course I do."

"Toby?" Grace stopped beside him. "I was hoping you would sit with Sophie and me."

"Ah . . . well, thank you, but I—"

"Oh, come on." Grace had learned to talk in spite of her deafness, but her fingers formed the signs as she spoke.

"All right."

Ingeborg caught her breath. Toby was blushing. Was something going on here? No, of course not. Grace was just being Grace, the peacemaker of the family. But still . . .

7

"ANDREW, DON'T LET TOBY get under your skin like that."

"I try not to, Ellie. I really do." He shook his head slowly from side to side, as if his head were too heavy to hold up. Or something were too heavy to hold up.

"I know."

"No, you were gone the last year he was in school. We chopped enough wood to power the Great Northern from coast to coast. But he wouldn't leave off pestering the weaker ones, and it made me so mad."

"And you'd hit him, and he'd yell and bleed, and you'd both be out chopping wood. There must be another way."

"Well, if you can figure it out, you let me know. I'll tell you one thing—if he ever gets any idea about Gracie, I'll beat him into the ground." Andrew glared over at his cousin still talking to Toby. "Why is she so good to him? He used to tease her too."

"You and Grace do the same thing, only in a different way."

"What's that?"

"Stick up for the underdog."

"If we don't get in line for ice cream, it'll be all gone."

Ellie smiled up at him. *Ah, Andrew, I wish I could help you.* But she let him change the conversation and take her over to the ice cream line, where the ladies were ladling ice cream out of one freezer while the Knutson boys were out cranking two more.

"So you finally came over here." Kaaren Knutson, Andrew's tante, was pouring more of the egg, cream, and sugar mixture into another mixer while her husband, Lars, using the flat side of a heavy axhead, bashed a gunnysack that had once held a block of ice. He'd made sure it was now in small enough pieces to feed around the cylinder holding the future ice cream.

"Doesn't look like there is any chance of running out." Ellie grinned up at Andrew.

"We shouldn't. I have another one done, waiting in the ice pack," Kaaren said.

"Do you know that in cities they have machines that make ice?" Thorliff stopped beside Andrew. "They have refrigerated cars for the railroad and rooms cold enough to freeze meat, and I heard that some inventor is dreaming of ways to bring a machine like that into homes. No more iceman in the cities, no more icehouses like we have here."

"I s'pose that goes along with the electricity that is replacing gas-lights, not that we have even that here."

"I'll never forget seeing all the light bulbs at the Chicago fair. Near as bright as day." Thorliff stuck his hands in his pants pockets. "Wish you could have come."

Andrew shook his head. "Nah. I just don't care for cities like you do. Not even to go to the World's Fair."

"I wanted to go. I read as much as I could find in the papers. The Ferris wheel—wouldn't that have been something to ride on?" Ellie smiled at Thorliff. "I'd love to see Chicago."

"I'd rather ride a horse any day." The grump had returned to Andrew's voice.

"How do you know? You never rode something like that or ever went into a building that tall," Thorliff insisted. "There's a lot of world out there beyond the farm."

"I've been up in the grain elevator. That's tall enough for me."

"Thank you." Ellie took her dish of ice cream and spoon and, after savoring her first spoonful, smiled in bliss. "I don't think anything tastes better than ice cream."

"Mor's apple pie is better."

"Andrew Bjorklund, if I said the sun was shining, you'd say the moon was. What is the matter with you?"

"Why would I say that?"

"I think I'll take a dish of ice cream back to my wife." Thorliff winked at Ellie. *Good luck,* he mouthed before he turned and left.

Ellie looked up to see Andrew staring at something. She followed his gaze and saw why his jaw was tight.

Grace was still with Toby, and they were laughing about something.

"Hey, Andrew!" Pastor Solberg called. "Bring Ellie and all the others. The man is here to take the graduation pictures."

Andrew waved in acknowledgment. "We will." He glanced around to find the others. "Come on. You find Deborah."

"Of course." Ellie finished her ice cream as she crossed the grass. While some of the people had already left, most were still visiting in groups in the shade of the schoolhouse and church. Some of the younger mothers sat with the babies and very small children, many asleep on blankets under the growing cottonwood trees. So much had changed in the years they'd been gone. She and Deborah had been good friends all through school, ever since Deborah and her sister, Manda, arrived in Blessing with Zeb MacCallister. He'd found them in a dugout, alone since their mother died and their father disappeared. Deborah had been living with the Solbergs, who took over the MacCallister ranch when Zeb moved west.

After Toby fell in step beside her, Ellie asked, "Did you go on to college with your gift from Mr. Gould, Toby?"

"Nope. I never cared much for school. Never graduated."

"What are you going to do?"

"My pa said I should go to work for the railroad, laying track, but I don't know. If there was a war still going on, I'd go fight."

"Oh, how awful. Look what happened to your brother."

"You better quit talking to me. Here comes almighty Prince Andrew."

Ellie made a face. "Toby!"

He arched his eyebrows at her and, hands in his back pockets, strolled off.

"All right, let's get started here." The photographer pointed his camera, already set up on a tripod. "Line up there on the steps. You boys in the back, young ladies in front."

Andrew stood behind Ellie. She could feel the brush of his jacket through her dress and knew if she leaned her head back, she could touch him. Why all of a sudden did she have this need to touch him? Ever since that kiss on the palm of her hand, she'd wanted to be as near him as possible. Thoughts of the way he was acting flew off like a bird winging away, leaving only sensations. The touch of his hand on her shoulder, the sound of his voice, his smile, the love light in his eyes.

"All right now, everyone look right here, and when I say 'hold it,' don't breathe, don't move." The man ducked back under his black drape and raised a hand. "Look here. Now hold it."

Ellie had the most necessary urge to rub the itch on her nose, but she held her pose.

"Okay, you can breathe now."

They all sucked in breaths along with nervous giggles. Ellie looked beyond the photographer to see Rachel making faces at her.

She shook her head and shot her cousin a warning look. Laughing, Rachel ran off with two other little girls, and those on the steps settled in for another picture. Andrew tapped her shoulder when the man ordered them to not move again. She felt a giggle rising and ordered her lips to remain at the half smile. *Ellie Peterson Wold, you will do as you are told. You will not giggle or move or breathe.*

"Good. You can breathe now." The man popped out from behind the camera. "I'll move this inside now, and we'll take the individual shots. One of you big strong men want to give me a hand here?"

"Leave it to the prince," Toby, standing off to the side, muttered just loud enough for Ellie to hear as Andrew stepped forward.

She snapped her head around and gave him a glare, icy enough to freeze a flowing river.

He raised one dark eyebrow.

Ellie could hear Pastor Solberg's voice as if he were standing right behind her. *"If you ignore his teasing, he'll quit, because it's no fun to tease someone who doesn't respond."* Ellie pasted a smile on her face, sweeter than caramel candy, and cocked an eyebrow back at him before following the others inside the church.

"Miss, would you like to be first?"

"Me?" Ellie pointed to herself.

"Yes. Just sit right here." The photographer pulled the chair closer to a drape he had hanging on the wall.

Ellie sat down and allowed him to arrange her skirts, place her hand in her lap, and cock her head just so. While nerves made her want to squirm, she held still. Feeling the heat of Andrew's gaze, she resolutely watched the photographer, ignoring the heat blossoming up her neck and onto her face. *Andrew Bjorklund, don't look at me like that.*

"Now, miss, look right here, and let's have a bit of a smile. Think about your nice young man. Keep your back straight . . . there you go." The photographer swapped out plates. "Hold it again, please. Look over here . . . that's excellent. Good. Now breathe." He ducked out from under the drape and smiled at her. "If all my subjects were as easy as you, this business would be a delight."

"Thank you." Ellie stood and moved off to the side as another of the girls took her place on the stool.

"I want one of those pictures." Andrew stopped beside her.

"Why? You'll see me every day."

"Because someday when we are old and gray, we will look back and see how lovely you were back when we were young."

"What about you? I want one of you for me."

He shrugged. "If you want."

"And in the fall we will have a picture of us after we get married. My dress will be similar to the one I have on, only in different material and white."

"I want us married in one month, not three or four." The frown carved a line between his eyebrows.

"I know you do. So do I. But this will turn out for the best, I'm sure. You wait and see." When Andrew didn't answer her, she peered up to his face. She wished he'd not brought up the subject when it did nothing but make him unhappy. "Smile," she whispered, "so you look happy in the picture."

When his turn finally came and he stood posed for the picture, it was all she could do to not dance around singing, "That's my Andrew, and I'm going to marry up with him." The phrase that Andrew had used the first time all those years ago had stuck. Marry up. *Oh, Andrew, I cannot begin to tell you how much I love you.* A thought caught her. Had Andrew ever really asked her to marry him?

They gazed at each other across the space until the photographer ordered Andrew to look at him. Sensations coursed up and down her body—not shivers but tiny bursts of heat like slender flames licking the underside of a log. The urge to touch him poured through to her fingertips, setting them to tingling. She looked away and then back, catching his eyes watching her. The tip of her tongue sneaked out to water lips gone dry.

When he finished, he walked back to her, never taking his gaze from her face. He reached for her hand and led her out the open doorway.

"Would you like to go for a walk?"

Wherever you would like to go. Instead, she shook her head. "I'd really like more ice cream."

"If there's any left."

"Oh, they're still cranking there under the trees." They made their way over to the ice cream table, stopping to talk with friends and neighbors on the way.

"Chocolate sauce or caramel?" Dr. Elizabeth asked. Seated at the table, her bulging form was slightly hidden, although she had to reach to pour the syrup on the dishes of ice cream.

"Plain for me," Ellie said.

Elizabeth held the dish of scooped ice cream Thorliff handed to her.

"I'll take both. I make up for her." Andrew grinned.

"Andrew, I don't know where you put it all." Elizabeth poured a healthy dollop of each on his mound of ice cream. "So how does it feel to be graduated?"

Ellie sat down across the table. "When I think of never going back to school, it makes me a bit sad. I have always loved school."

"I didn't hate school," Andrew put in, "but there are so many things that need doing around the farm, and now I'll be able to catch up on some of them, along with getting our house and barn built."

"Did it come in?" Thorliff asked.

"Not yesterday, and surely Penny would have told me had it come today. They said it might be an extra two weeks or more."

"Lot of people must be building houses." Elizabeth picked up the fan lying in front of her on the table and waved it slowly in front of her face. She smiled at Ellie. "I'm looking forward to getting to know you. I'm sorry your wedding has to be postponed."

"She'll probably be working for Penny at the store, since Astrid will be helping you." Andrew swallowed a spoonful of ice cream.

I can answer for myself, Andrew. The thought caught Ellie by surprise. Had Andrew always answered for her? She'd have to think back.

"Really? That's wonderful. For an only child like me, this big family is such a pleasure." Elizabeth smiled.

"Ja, Ellie will be one more Bjorklund woman to make trouble for us men," Andrew said with a straight face.

"Oh, you." Ellie pushed at his arm. "You won't let anyone else tease us, but that doesn't seem to apply to you."

"Should it?" He paused midspoonful.

Ellie rolled her eyes and exchanged smiles with Elizabeth.

"I saw you and Toby pushing at each other." Thorliff dished up another bowl of ice cream and handed it to Lily Mae, old Sam's youngest. "There you go."

"You 'bout out?" Sam's dark face shone with sweat.

"No."

"Good. The ball players are on their way over."

"You want some help?" Ellie asked Elizabeth.

"Sure. You hand the bowls to Andrew. He can dish while Thorliff unpacks the next freezer."

Laughing, cuffing, and sweating, the young men and boys lined up for their ice cream. "How come the Bjorklunds didn't come play?" someone called.

"Then who would have made the ice cream?" Thorliff answered.

"The old men."

"Sure wish someone had told me that." Thorliff handed out another dish. "See the women for syrup."

Ellie glanced at Elizabeth with a giggle. "Women? Guess you are but not me, not yet."

"I might be big as a house with baby, but I don't think of myself as a woman either. I guess *doctor* took the place of *woman*. Now, I'll tell you, I like *wife*."

"Is that so?" Thorliff wiggled his eyebrows.

"Hey, Dr. Bjorklund, you sure did a good job sewing up my brother." A young boy stepped up to the ice cream table. "Ma said that one was beyond her needle and thread."

"Thank you. My mother said I never learned to sew. You might write and tell her I did all right."

"The doctor in Grafton was too far away to go, bleeding like he was."

"Glad I could help."

"It sounds like you saved the boy's life. What happened?" Ellie poured the last of the chocolate syrup.

"The boy ended up on the wrong end of an ax. Slipped and fell. Had his brother not put a tourniquet around his arm, he'd have bled to death. I'm so grateful he has the use of his arm. I prayed so hard for that one. It could have been useless. And thank God there was no infection."

Ellie thought back. "Maybe if you had been here, Agnes might have lived longer."

"Maybe. But Ingeborg and I talked about that. From the sound of it, Agnes had cancer, and while I might have been able to remove the tumor, the vicious stuff comes back."

"We all grieved for her. Agnes Baard was a wonderful woman. I'm so glad you are here now." She glanced over to see Thorliff and Andrew emptying out the ice and putting the freezers in a box, then looked back to Elizabeth. "Are you all right?"

Elizabeth nodded. "But I think we better head home." She raised her voice. "Andrew, will you take care of those things? Thorliff, you need to bring the wagon over now." She emphasized the last word and flinched afterward.

Ellie stared at her. "Are you . . ? I mean, is it time?"

"Unless this is a false labor, we have a baby on the way. Please go ask Ingeborg to come too."

Ellie glanced at Thorliff. He stood staring at his wife, not moving, as if he'd been cast in stone.

"Good thing Andrew knows what to do." Elizabeth nodded to the figure flying toward the teams tied along the hitching rails.

"Thorliff!" Ellie took his arm and led him over to his wife.

"I-I'm sorry. I-I'll get the team."

"Andrew is doing that. Please get my things out from under the table."

Ellie shook her head. How could Elizabeth be so calm? Here she was shaking like she was the one having the baby. Maybe not getting married yet was a good thing. *What if Elizabeth's baby dies like Mor's did?* The well-remembered picture made her shudder. *How can I get married and not have babies? I know Andrew wants children, and so do I. But I'm afraid to have a baby. Dear Lord, what am I going to do?*

8

"THORLIFF, COME HELP YOUR WIFE," Ingeborg ordered some hours later.

He leaped to his feet and followed his mother into the bedroom, where Elizabeth reached for his arm.

"Help me walk. It helps when I have someone to lean upon."

"Shouldn't you be lying down?" he stuttered as he put an arm around her.

"No, silly. The more I walk, the easier the labor will be. So far everything is perfectly normal."

Ingeborg smiled at her daughter-in-law and shook her head. Thorliff, always so sure of himself—at least he gave others that feeling—was now a bundle of contradictions. He'd assured them he was fine, but his hands were shaking, no matter how hard he tried to keep them still, and fear lurked in his eyes.

"Thorliff, I'm not going to break. We walk, not shuffle." But when at that moment she grabbed his hand and nearly strangled it, he stared at his mother, his mouth working but no words coming out.

"Keep her walking, son. She has everything all ready." Ingeborg wiped her hands on her apron after placing the scissors, narrow strips of cloth, and a couple of towels into a pan of water on the stove to boil them to make them sterile.

"Oh." Elizabeth stopped and a puddle formed on the floor. "Good. Now we'll get this going." She patted her rounded belly. "The time has come, little one. No more dallying." Smiling up at her husband, she shook her head. "You men, you see a puddle of fluid and you freeze. I tried to tell you all the stages, and you didn't want to hear."

"I know." He took the rags from his mother and knelt at his wife's feet to mop the floor.

Ingeborg tapped him on the shoulder. "I can do that. You keep her walking."

"You walk with her. I'll catch up."

Ingeborg nodded and took Elizabeth's arm. "He'll be all right now," she whispered in her ear. "Our Thorliff's back."

"Good thing. I'm going to really need him pretty soon. I've always thought the husbands ought to help their wives. That old idea of banishing them from the birthing room is sheer idiocy." Elizabeth stopped and took several breaths, blowing them out. Looking out the window to the faint lavender tinge left on the western clouds, she said, "I missed the sunset. I didn't realize we'd been at this so long."

"Things are moving right along for a first baby."

"I know, but it's different when you're the one having it." The two women kept a steady pace, wandering all through the first floor of the house.

"I remember when Andrew was born. We lived in the soddy then, and there wasn't a whole lot of room to walk in. Kaaren was still recovering from losing her little ones. Ach, such an awful time we had."

"Kaaren told me that you saved her life, that she lost all desire to live, but you wouldn't let her give up." As she walked near him, Elizabeth took her husband's arm, and the three of them walked together.

"And then when I hit the pit of despair, she pulled *me* along. That black pit . . . it is a terrible thing. Blows out the light, and all you can think is dark."

"Mor wore men's pants, went hunting, and worked in the fields.

She nearly worked herself to death." Thorliff shuddered. "Those were terrible times."

"But I saved the land. Roald and Carl had worked so hard for this land to give to their sons that I couldn't let the homestead be lost."

They waited while Elizabeth huffed through another round of contractions. She looked up at Thorliff afterward. "Don't get so worried. I keep telling you this is the way it is supposed to be."

"And I'm supposed to think you've done me a favor by letting me help?"

Ingeborg chuckled. "This is why most men would rather wait out in the barn, preferably with a jug for company."

"They're coming closer." Elizabeth caught her breath after another one. "Walk!" She caught her breath again. "Tell me more about the early days, please."

"One time Andrew got lost in the tall grass, and Wolf found him and saved him," Thorliff said.

"Wolf?"

"I told you about Metiz, our old Indian friend?"

"Yes."

"She had saved a young wolf from a trap, and he remained her friend the rest of her life. He decided we were part of her family and watched out for us too. One winter he fought off a pack of wolves that were attacking our sheep."

"You remember that?" Ingeborg smiled at her tall son who'd been such a serious little boy. They entered the kitchen on their continuous circle through the house.

"No, but you told the story many times."

"We never saw Wolf much. He was more like a silver shadow, but we'd see his tracks, the one front foot deformed so you could recognize it."

"He came back when Metiz died, you know," Ingeborg said. "I heard him howling but didn't realize why till the next day, when I found her. Metiz was so old, but she refused to come stay with us. Wanted to stay in the small cabin we built for her by the river.

Between her and Agnes, I've had the best friends."

"And they're both gone now?"

"Ja, I still miss them so much at times it hurts." Ingeborg moved the boiling kettle to the cooler side of the stove.

"Mor, Thorliff, may I come in?" Astrid called from the back door.

"Of course. Come join the party." Elizabeth looked to Ingeborg. "That's all right, isn't it? I mean, is she too young?"

"Not at all. Some women are having children by her age," Ingeborg answered softly.

Astrid kept the screen door from banging as she entered the room. "You're having a party? I thought you were having a baby."

"Soon." Elizabeth clenched the hands that held her and puffed her way through another contraction.

Thorliff shook out his hand when she straightened again. "I never realized how strong my wife is."

"You want me to take your place?" Astrid volunteered, grinning at her brother.

Thorliff nodded and tried to retrieve his arm.

"Wait a minute." Elizabeth smiled while Ingeborg wiped the perspiration from her brow. "You know, I have a fan upstairs in the top right-hand drawer of the tall chest. Would you like to get it?" She shrugged at her husband. "Sorry, dear, I still need you."

"Sure. Thorliff most likely couldn't find it." Astrid headed for the stairs, laughter at the look on her brother's face floating over her shoulder.

When she returned, Astrid waved the fan in front of Elizabeth as they trudged back across the parlor.

"That feels so good. Thank you."

"At least this baby won't have to fight off the winter cold." Ingeborg shook her head. "Sometimes when they're born in the dead of winter the only way to keep them warm enough is in a box on the oven door."

"Or wrapped and carried in a sling cuddled against the mother's chest." Elizabeth stopped again. "About time to lie down, I think."

"Do you, I mean . . ."

"Don't worry, Thorliff. We'll tell you exactly what to do. After all, I'm the one who has to do all the work." Elizabeth sounded a bit testy, which made Ingeborg smile.

"You ready to push?"

"Soon, I think. Having had one of my own will make me a better doctor, I hope. Uh!" When she could walk again, they headed for the bedroom.

"All right, Thorliff, you sit with your back against the headboard there, and Elizabeth can use you to push against."

When they had Elizabeth settled, she groaned and her face twisted with the pain.

"A doctor once tried to tell me that . . . women didn't . . . feel pain with birthing . . . only pressure." She groaned and sucked in a breath again. "He was wrong!"

"I can see the crown." Ingeborg knelt on the end of the bed. "Easy now. All right, give a good push."

Elizabeth pushed and screamed at the same time, then lay back panting.

"Take a cloth and dip it in that basin. You can wipe her forehead."

Astrid did as her mother told her, then flinched as another contraction rolled through Elizabeth.

Ingeborg gave her son a reassuring smile. His face about matched the sheets. "She's doing fine. One more good one, Elizabeth, and we'll be done, I think."

Elizabeth nodded, clamped onto Thorliff's hands, and with another thin scream, pushed and grunted.

Ingeborg turned the baby's shoulders and, tears streaming down her cheeks, held her granddaughter in her hands. *Oh, dearest Jesus, mange takk. Oh, mange takk.* "You have a beautiful daughter, my dears." She laid the baby on her daughter-in-law's chest. "There. You three get to know one another while I clean things up a bit here." She used a clean corner of her apron to wipe her eyes.

"She's so tiny." Astrid clutched the cloth between her shaking hands. "Mor, can she see?"

"Oh yes. Human babies can see immediately, not like kittens and puppies."

"Oh, Lord, thank you, thank you, thank you." Thorliff could hardly talk around his tears.

Elizabeth and the baby stared at each other, then the mother reached out and stroked her daughter's cheek. The baby turned her head, lips puckering.

"See, she's a smart one. She's ready to nurse already." Ingeborg folded back the towel, picked up the strips of cloth, and now that the cord lay flaccid, she tied it off several inches from the baby's navel and then again a couple of inches farther toward the mother, cutting between the knots with the scissors. As soon as the afterbirth appeared, she folded up the pad of sheeting and went about cleaning up Elizabeth, all the while explaining everything she was doing to Astrid.

"Now we'll wash the little one, get her diapered and in a gown. Thorliff, you help Elizabeth into a clean nightdress. Then we'll change the bed, and these two can settle in for a much needed nap."

"What are you going to name her?" Astrid asked.

"Inga Annabelle, after both our mothers." Elizabeth yawned. "Astrid, dear, could you bring me a drink of water? I am so thirsty." She raised her arms for Thorliff to remove her gown and bring her a clean one. "Ah, this feels so nice." She yawned again and shifted around. "Massage my belly, please, Thorliff. That helps the uterus shrink more quickly."

"What's a uterus?" Astrid asked, handing Elizabeth a glass of water. She propped her elbows on the bed so she could watch.

"That's the part inside of a woman God created to grow and hold the baby. All the other mammals have them too." Elizabeth took her swaddled daughter in her arms. "Little Inga, you are so perfect. You want to hold her, Thorliff?"

"I suppose so." He sat down on the edge of the bed and took his daughter in his two hands. When she screwed up her face and a whimper turned into a cry, he handed her back. "You need your mother, baby girl. She's probably hungry."

"Oh, Thorliff, babies cry for all kinds of reasons. But speaking of hungry, while I feed her, perhaps you could warm up that soup I made yesterday."

"I will." Astrid got to her feet. "Mor, would you like some too?"

"Why don't you and Thorliff fix something for all of us?"

"All right. Come on, big brother. Mor said."

He stood and tugged on a lock of her hair. "You act mighty grown up, young lady. As soon as we take care of these things, I'll go send that telegram to let your folks know they are grandparents."

Elizabeth nodded her thanks.

"I just helped with my first birthing," Astrid said proudly. "Other than kittens and puppies, that is. I think seeing babies born is the most beautiful thing in the whole world. Someday I'm going to help women have babies, just like Mor and Elizabeth do."

Ingeborg and Elizabeth exchanged smiles as they heard her declaration.

"So we have another doctor on the way?" Ingeborg asked, helping nestle tiny Inga against her mother's breast.

"Or a nurse." They both watched the baby root around, questing for the nourishment she needed. Ingeborg assisted again, and the little mouth settled onto the nipple and began to nurse.

"Oh, ouch. Guess that's another thing you have to experience to know it can hurt." Elizabeth twisted a bit to get more comfortable. "She sure is a strong sucker."

"She's a healthy one, all right. My first grandchild. And to think you named her after me. What an honor."

"She has a lot to live up to."

"Oh, Elizabeth, you are so kind and thoughtful."

Elizabeth stared down at the infant in the crook of her arm, now soundly sleeping. "I'm going to join her. Thank you for taking such good care of us."

"My privilege." Ingeborg smoothed Elizabeth's hair back. "You did a mighty fine job." She met the other two at the doorway. "We'll let her sleep now. She can eat later."

Sometime later, after Astrid had gone home, Ingeborg entered the parlor to find Thorliff staring out the window. She stood beside him. "You're awfully quiet."

"I never knew having babies would be so hard." He cleared his throat. "I guess I just never thought about it."

"Most men don't. But Elizabeth had an easy time of it. Some take so long the mother is too tired to push anymore. This little one was in a hurry to get here."

"She didn't look too happy when she let out that first yell."

"True, no whimper there, but a good strong baby girl."

"So . . ." Thorliff jingled some change in his pocket.

Ingeborg waited, knowing her eldest son would take time to think through what was bothering him.

"So we are past the danger stage?"

"One of them. But Elizabeth is in good health. This is her first, and we took precautions to sterilize everything we could. We've done all we can, and now it lies in God's hands, where it really was all the time."

"I know all that, Mor, but this is my wife and baby we are talking about."

Ingeborg stared out the window at the shadows thrown by a half moon hanging above the cottonwood trees planted a couple years earlier in preparation for the turning of the century.

Blessing was changing, Thorliff's life had just changed, Andrew's would be soon, and thus all their lives were changing. *Please, God, let the changes all be for the better. Inga Annabelle Bjorklund, born May 20, 1900, you, dear baby, had the biggest change of all.*

9

ANDREW STOOD WAVING as the train left the station heading west. Even knowing that Ellie would be back in a week did not leave him feeling secure. Too many things that should have been decided by now were still up in the air.

All his plans, for all these years, were in disarray. At least that's the way it seemed to him. The house not coming on time was the catalyst.

He rammed his hands into his pockets and, turning, headed back to the wagon. Ellie and her family were on their way back to Grafton, and that's all there was to it. Time to get going. If he hurried, he could get the field he was to plant done before dark. Maybe he'd even have time to start scraping the sites for his house and barn, sites he'd measured and marked out long before. He'd plowed and disked the garden spot earlier, and yesterday he and Ellie had taken Astrid and the twins to help rake and plant so they would have provisions for the winter.

He backed the team and turned for home. If only Ellie would be in the kitchen when he came in for dinner. But then, as he'd often heard Mor say, *"If only' will defeat you every time."* If that were true, then why was it so easy to slip into thinking that way? Of course she'd often quoted one of her favorite Bible verses about the enemy being like a lion prowling around, searching to destroy. Right now he felt that lion would love to devour him. But fight back he would. He slowed the horses. No sense taking his hurry out on them.

"Sorry, boys. Although I'm sure you'd like a good gallop, not with the wagon banging behind you. Pa would really get after me then." Their ears flicking back and forth showed they'd been listening.

He could hear Mor's voice as though she were in the wagon with him. *"Pray about it, son. God longs to hear your prayers and to answer them for you."*

Why was it so hard to pray about his house, his barn, his not-so-soon-to-be wife? He thought on that. While Thorliff was the thinker in the family, Andrew knew he had a good head on his shoulders too. How to pray? Why did he feel his prayers went no higher than his head?

"I could always ask Pastor Solberg." Again the horses' ears flicked back and forth.

But who had he taken his questions to in the past? The answer exploded into his mind. Far. So why not this time? He knew the answer to that one. Because putting off the wedding was all Haakan's idea. Resentment burned at the back of his throat. And if he was right that God had sent the suggestion, then God was to blame.

Andrew trotted the team to the barn and stopped to unharness the horses. Since he shouldn't be mad at God, then surely this was all Haakan's fault.

"God, I sure wish Ellie was here to help me think through all this. She didn't even get the least upset."

"Andrew, are you all right?" Astrid stood on the other side of the team, unbuckling the harness without being asked.

"Ja, why?" He knew his tone was curt. Knew it and didn't change or ask her pardon.

"Are you mad that Ellie had to leave?"

"Some."

"She's coming right back."

"So she said." He pulled the harness off and carried it over to the pegs in the wall to drape it into place. The harness needed cleaning, and he could see a place where it needed repair before it broke.

"Are you mad at Ellie?" Astrid lifted the harness off the other horse, but Andrew took it from her to hang up. "Are you?"

"Astrid, this is really none of your business."

"All right, Andrew Bjorklund, be that way. I never thought I'd see my brother being mean, but you are, and you have been. If I were Ellie, I'd want to leave too."

Andrew watched her spin and head for the house, her bare feet spurting up dust as she slammed them against the earth.

Wonderful. Now even Astrid was angry at him. He let the light team loose in the corral and brought in the heavier horses, harnessed them, and started for the field.

Ingeborg stepped out on the back step and rang the triangle for dinner. When she finished, she waved and called to Andrew.

Although he really wanted to ignore her, he stopped and answered. "I'm not hungry, and I want to get that field done."

"You're not sick, are you?"

"No, Mor. I'm not sick, just in a hurry." He waited while she crossed the dirt yard to stand beside him.

"I can send Astrid out with a lunch."

"No. She'd probably spit on it."

"Andrew, what a thing to say."

"Well, she's mad at me, and . . ." He started to say "I deserve it" but didn't. One more sliver under the skin to fester along with the others.

Ingeborg studied him, then nodded. "I think you and I need to have a good long talk."

"Later." He clucked the team forward and strode after them. Surely he could work this mad off and come home feeling more himself.

Or maybe he needed to go chop wood.

Trygve came bounding across the field halfway through the afternoon, waving his straw hat to catch Andrew's attention.

Andrew whoaed the team and got off the seeder. He stretched, arching his back and wishing for a drink. He'd not even thought to bring a jug of water with him. "Nothing like a stubborn Norwegian," he muttered as he checked the seed drills.

"You want to go fishing?" Trygve asked as soon as he caught his breath.

"Sorry, I have to finish this field, then the seeding will be done."

"Nobody wants to go fishing."

"Astrid always wants to go fishing."

"She went over to help Elizabeth."

"What about Samuel?"

"He went over to Tante Penny's. I got my chores finished early so I could go."

"And neither of the twins wants to go?"

Trygve gave him a rolled-eye look. "They don't like fishing. You know that."

"Why don't you ask Tante Ingeborg? She loves to go fishing, and she hasn't gone for a long time."

"She's out in the cheese house. Sophie and Grace went to help her."

"Guess you'll have to go by yourself. Sorry."

"If I go home, Ma will make me help in the garden." He dug a cork and hook out of his pocket, then another. "See, I even brought you one."

Andrew stared across the field. He only had two more rounds to go, and he'd be done. Might be nice to make someone in his life happy. "You go dig some worms out by the manure pile while I finish this field, and then we'll go."

"Thank you. See you in a while." Trygve waved his hat and set off across the field, hands in his pockets, whistling as he went.

"Well, at least I made someone happy today. Maybe a mess of fish will mend a few fences."

After finishing the required rounds and letting the team loose, he headed for the house, cut some bread and cheese, drank two glasses of water, and found Trygve ramming the pitchfork back into the manure pile, the worms in a can with dirt.

"Let's go."

The one bad thing about fishing was it gave a person too much time to think. And today, all the fish seemed to prefer Trygve's hook. The one time Andrew's cork went down, the fish took the bait and vamoosed.

Andrew rebaited his hook. Perhaps a fresh worm would help.

"I have ten."

"Braggart. If this doesn't work, I'm going upriver a bit. There's always fish by that old log."

"There's plenty of fish here. They just don't like you."

The fish and everybody else.

"Pa said I could help you build your house."

"Good. It should go up fast." *If it ever gets here.*

"Your cork!"

Andrew jerked back on his pole, and a fish flew through the air, just missing his head, close enough he heard it whiz by.

"You finally got one."

"Right, and it's big enough to equal two of yours." He removed the hook, stuck a stick through the gills, and anchored it to another on the bank, leaving the fish in the water.

By the time they heard the bell cow leading the herd in for milking, they both had enough fish for the families and headed home. A spike deer bounded away when they reached the field.

"How come we didn't bring a rifle?" Andrew gave a snort of disgust. Fresh venison would have tasted mighty good. They'd had to hunt farther afield these last years. While game used to be abundant in the woods along the riverbank, now with the big old trees gone and so many more people hunting, the game trails had fallen into disuse.

"I got three rabbits in the snares this morning."

"Been a good day for you."

Trygve eyed Andrew's string of fish. "But not as good for you, huh?"

If you only knew. "Tomorrow will be better."

"You want some of my fish?"

Andrew reached over and knocked Trygve's broad-brimmed hat forward on his head. "No, but thanks. This is plenty for supper. If you have extra, take them in to Bestemor. She likes to serve fried fish."

Bridget still ran her boardinghouse, but Eulah, Sam's wife, did most of the cooking. His daughter, Lily Mae, waited on the folks in the dining room and did much of the cleaning.

"Maybe I'll go out tomorrow and get some for her. I'm going to run these over home, and then I'll be back for milking." He took off across the field, finally grabbing his hat so it wouldn't go sailing.

Andrew watched him go. That had been him not too many years ago. He sucked in a deep breath of cooling air and picked up his pace.

"Mor," he called from the stoop. "I brought fish for supper."

"Oh, good. I was about to start slicing that last ham." She met him at the door and took the string.

"Trygve caught twice as much as I did. I think I'm losing my touch."

"I'm glad you went fishing. You needed to."

"Guess I did."

"The milk pails are ready."

"Thanks."

"You are welcome." She patted his shoulder. "You look better."

Between fishing and milking, Andrew felt more like himself by the time he dumped the last bucket into the milk can. He set the lid in place, hauled the can to the end of the aisle, and went down the stanchions, letting each cow out. They'd pause, back up slowly, and turn toward the door, none in a hurry, following the line out the door and on the same path to the water tank, where each one would drink, and then head out to graze awhile before lying down to chew their cud. He dropped the bar across the door to keep them from coming in during the night and leaned against it. Several stars had joined the evening star, the sky above already a dark azure while the sunset lingered yellow on the horizon. A nighthawk called from the brush while a cricket tuned up for the evening chorus. A bullfrog harrumphed from the swamp, and soon the peepers would join him.

"You coming, son?" Haakan asked from the other door.

"Ja. You already slopped the hogs?"

"Done. And checked on the sows. All done but taking this last can to the well house. I ordered a load of lumber. Should be on tomorrow's train."

Andrew joined him, and they each took a handle of the milk can. "For what?"

"Your barn. Thought we could lay the footings. Call for a barn raising before haying."

"Barn might be up before the house." They walked side by side, the milk can holding them together. *You didn't have to do that. We were going to put it up in the fall.* "Mange takk."

Haakan nodded. "Since we got the spring work done so soon and the house isn't here yet, I couldn't see any sense in waiting."

"You going to buy more cows?"

"Not if I can help it." In spite of his parents' trying to keep their disagreements from the children, Andrew knew his mother wanted to invest in more cows for milk for the cheese making and plant some of the wheat fields to hay, especially since the flour mills of the Twin Cities had again cut the price they would pay for North Dakota wheat.

Haakan disagreed. Strongly. So the discussion had gone on, mostly in the privacy of their bedroom.

Haakan sniffed as they washed at the bench beside the house. "Smells like fried fish."

"Ja, Trygve and I went fishing this afternoon after I finished seeding that field. Fool things wouldn't hit my hook for the longest time."

"Metiz used to say that fish came only to those of a peaceful mind.

Not her words exactly, but the gist was the same."

"Well, I did catch enough for supper. Oh, and there was a spike coming up from the river."

"Really? Don't tell your mor, or she'll decide to go hunting tomorrow."

While Ingeborg had hung up her guns and britches years before, the family still teased her about it. The last time she'd taken a gun out, after a few practice shots she'd still outshot all of them. Thorliff dubbed her "Annie Oakley" after the famous western woman shooter.

"Astrid still over to Thorliff's?" Haakan asked as they sat down at the table.

"She'd live there if she could. How she loves that baby." Ingeborg set the platter of fried fish in the center of the table between the bowl of string beans and one of creamed canned potatoes. "I will sure be glad when the garden comes in."

"There's a big patch of dandelion greens out by that big oak in the pasture." Andrew thought a moment. "And I saw fiddleheads down on the riverbank. I'll go get some tomorrow."

Ingeborg set the bread plate down. "Or Astrid can. Perhaps she and the twins will get some for all of us." She glanced around the table at the empty chairs. "One missing sure leaves a hole." She took her seat and looked to Haakan.

He nodded. "Let's pray. I Jesu navn, går vi til bords. . . ." They all joined in the Norwegian grace, ending with the amen. Each started passing the serving plate closest to them, and other than "Please pass" or "Thank you," they ate silently.

Andrew could feel the tension between the man at the head of the table and the woman across from him. They must have been "discussing" again. Since all the land was planted, it didn't make much sense to buy more cows now. They didn't have enough pasture or hayfields for much more stock than they had.

"Did you pick up the paper when you were in town?" Haakan asked.

Andrew shook his head. "Wouldn't have been out yet. Soon as

we're done with supper, I'm going out to scrape the grass off the house site." He'd planned to start that tomorrow, but this way he'd get a head start. *Maybe I can start digging the cellar.*

"I'll help you in the morning. Trygve and Lars will come too."

"I'll make a picnic and bring it over," Ingeborg said. "What about little Sam? He'll help, I'm sure. Remember how you and the Baard boys split the shingles for our barn? It's a good thing Samuel and Trygve have started doing it for yours."

"Astrid was good at it too."

"Astrid is good at most anything she does." Haakan leaned his chair back, caught the glance from his wife, and set the two front legs back down gently. "Maybe we should put a salt lick out on the game trail again."

"Maybe I'll go out in the morning." Ingeborg got a faraway dreamy look in her eyes.

Andrew caught a frown on Haakan's face that came and went fast as a blink. He wasn't the only one unhappy with the man. Mor was too. He watched as Haakan rose, took his pipe from the stand on the shelf behind the stove, opened a lid on the stove, and using his knife, cleaned the bowl, the ashes and tailings dropping into the fire. He took the worn leather tobacco pouch from the same shelf and brought it all to the table.

"You'll get your skirt full of burrs."

"I could always put on my britches again." Ingeborg pushed her chair back, the legs scraping against the floor. She never scraped the legs, always lifted her chair so as to not mar the wax she so laboriously rubbed into the pine planks.

"Hmm . . . thought you burned your britches." Haakan tamped the tobacco down in the pipe bowl, then with pipe stem clamped between his front teeth, he raked the match tip with his thumbnail. It took two scrapes before the match flared, filling the room with the scent of sulfur. He sucked on the pipe stem while holding the match to the tobacco, then nodded, blew out the match, and set the charred remains on his saucer.

He used to hold that match for Andrew or Astrid to blow out.

Ingeborg's muttered uff da as she cleared the table said far more than words about her lack of appreciation for the pipe smoke.

It wasn't like his mor to hold a grudge. Andrew couldn't remember when there'd been tension like this at mealtimes. *Ellie and I will never carry on like this,* he thought. He pushed his chair back. "I'll go get the paper."

Not too many days now and Ellie would be living at Penny's, and then they could go for long walks in the evening. Why did a week seem like a month—or more?

10

May 23, 1990
Dear Andrew,
    How I hated to get on that train and leave you behind.
Actually, leaving you is getting harder and harder. I am count-
ing the days until I can come back to Blessing and to you.

Ellie tapped the pencil against her teeth. How she wanted to
share her newfound feelings with him, but somehow that didn't
seem quite proper. All the letters she'd read in books never mentioned the heat that rose from her middle at just the thought of
him. Perhaps something was wrong with her; perhaps she was a
wanton. She'd read that word in a story once, and it was not a very
nice term. Nice girls only allowed chaste kisses on the cheek, if even
that. Her mother had drilled the proper behavior of a young lady
into her daughter's head for years. She'd never mentioned feeling on
fire with melting knees. Ellie laid her hands on her hot cheeks. At
least everyone else in the house was long in bed, so she wasn't giving
herself away. She'd planned to write Hans a letter too but caught
herself daydreaming about Andrew until she should be blowing out
the lamp.

Mother has finished the quilt she was making for our bed.

The thought of the two of them and a bed made her eyes widen. She rolled her lips together and kept writing.

Rachel is embroidering us a set of dish towels. She says we cannot get married until she finishes them. Is everyone in cahoots at putting off our wedding?

In cahoots. She'd once read that in a western novel. There were some delightful terms coming from the West, although Thorliff had explained to her that to the publishers, most of whom lived in New York, the Dakotas were considered the West too.

Manda peppered her letters with western terms, the few that she took time to write anyway. Since she and Baptiste had gone to Montana with Zeb those years ago, her letters were shared around the community when they did come. She said Zeb was off putting up windmills these days, while she and Baptiste took care of the horses and the home ranch, which had been moved to Wyoming.

What would it be like to travel west and visit with them, just she and Andrew? *My goodness, but my mind is just flitting all over the place tonight. Finish your letter, Ellie, and get to bed. After all, you need your beauty sleep.* She giggled at the thought. While she knew Andrew thought her pretty—he'd told her so—she didn't. Except in the dress she'd made for her wedding. In that she did feel beautiful.

I told Penny I would be there a week from today, although if I had my way, I'd put what I have in my trunk and get back on that train tomorrow. I know you are angry with Haakan, but please let that go. The Bible says to not let the sun go down on your anger, and I know for certain there have been several sunsets on yours. The time will fly past. You just watch.

Love from your Ellie

She folded the paper and inserted it into the envelope with a pansy petal she had dried, then dropping wax from the candle she lit for just that purpose, she leaned the already addressed envelope against the base of the kerosene lamp. Black smudged the glass chimney. Time to wash the lamps and trim the wicks. Surely Rachel was old enough to learn how to do that. Perhaps she would give a lesson on lamp cleaning in the morning. Strange how her little cousin had grown as close as a sister, while she often felt more like a mother than a sister to Arne.

She blew out the lamp and made her way up the stairs by the moonlight that kissed the lightly dancing Priscilla curtains at all the open windows. Upstairs she undressed in the room she shared with Rachel, carefully hanging her dress on one of the pegs along the wall. With her nightdress in place, she knelt by the window and crossed her arms on the sill. The moonlight silvered the maple leaves that whispered secrets in the breeze. Off in the distance a dog barked. Would she and Andrew have a dog to watch their place and bring in the cows? While they had talked of so many aspects of their life together, each day or even each hour she thought of more. Her mother had promised her a few chickens from her flock—somehow having chickens of her own seemed like wealth in abundance. She could sell the extra eggs to Penny so she would have money to store in a tin like her mother did. The wages paid her by Penny would allow her to buy some things for the house. Already she'd had promises of starts from flower gardens and seeds to begin her own.

My goodness, she thought, *there is far more to making a home than I ever believed.* No wonder Olaf had crafted her a large trunk to put all her treasures in. Treasures she'd been making and collecting since she was eight, when she finished embroidering her first sampler on linen she'd woven herself from the thread she'd been given for a present. While she'd learned to card and spin wool that she would knit, spinning flax was not so simple. With her chin propped on her hands, she thought of all the sheets she'd hemmed on her mother's sewing machine and the pillowcases she'd sewn and then embroidered. Fine handwork was almost as much of a delight as sewing on the machine. She'd made most of the clothes for Arne and Rachel, since her mother would rather cook and bake than sew.

Her eyes grew heavy, but before she fell asleep, she looked up to the sky and found the star she and Andrew both wished on every night. "God, please take good care of my Andrew and help him see that good will come of this time we are preparing for our marriage. And teach me to be the woman you want me to be, a good example of all the fruits of the spirit—love, joy, peace, longsuffering, gentleness, goodness, faith, meekness, and temperance." They had been part of her memory work for the last week as she continued to commit the book of Galatians to memory. Pastor Solberg always stressed that memorizing the Bible made it your own so that you could dwell on it, as the heavenly Father ordered.

"Thank you, Father. I believe you love me and want the best for us all. Amen." She'd hardly lain down before she joined Rachel in peaceful slumber.

"As soon as we finish washing the lamps, we can go to the post office, and perhaps we will stop by Pa's shop and ask him if we can have an ice cream cone at the drugstore." *And I can mail my letter to Andrew, but more importantly, perhaps there is one from him.*

Rachel sighed. "The boys are going fishing over at the creek. I was gonna go too."

"Rather than eat ice cream?" Ellie kept a serious look on her face. She knew how much her cousin would rather play with the boys who lived in the house next to them than do chores of any kind.

Rachel sighed again. "No, I guess not."

"If you'd rather go fishing . . ."

"Wouldn't you rather go fishing than clean sooty lamps?"

"Well, when you put it that way . . ." Ellie grinned at her young cousin's hopeful look. "No, I've never been one to like fishing much, especially when you have to put the worm on the hook. Now grasshoppers, I'll skewer them any day, but not worms."

"You think Onkel Olaf will buy us ice cream for sure?"

Ellie smiled and nodded. He'd been the one to suggest they drop in at the building where he had his furniture shop. "Let's hurry and get the lamps done. I have a real hankering for ice cream."

Together the two picked up lamps as they made their way to the kitchen, where Goodie sat in the rocking chair, her Bible on her lap.

"The lamp brigade is here." Ellie set her two on the table.

"Out on the back porch would be a good place to do that. It's cooler than in here." Goodie closed the book, stroking the leather cover with a loving hand.

"Good idea. We'll use the washing bench." Ellie picked up the lamps again and backed her way out the screen door, holding it for Rachel. "I'll get the wash pan set up while you bring out more lamps."

Rachel nodded and ambled back inside, whistling as she went.

"Whistling girls and crowing hens always come to two bad ends," Goodie intoned.

"Yes, ma'am." The music stopped, but Ellie knew the admonition never did more than cause a pause in the whistle. Rachel would just wait until she was out of earshot.

"I don't know what I am going to do without you here to help," Goodie said when Ellie returned to the kitchen.

Ellie nodded. She'd heard the words so often one would think they would fail to wound by now, but that wasn't the case. Since the wedding wouldn't be until fall, perhaps she should stay home to help. Not that Grafton was home, but it was where her mother lived. The thought of not seeing Andrew for several months made her toes clinch.

"But I have agreed to work for Penny so that I can take care of my garden and help with building the house."

"I know that. Don't pay any attention to my wishing." Goodie rose and placed the Bible on the shelf away from Arne's busy fingers then returned to the rocker.

"I wish Onkel Olaf would move back to Blessing," Rachel said on her way to get more lamps.

While her mother said nothing, Ellie knew she wished the same thing. But Olaf had found a ready market for his furniture in Grafton. People were coming to him from Grand Forks, and he'd even had some orders from Fargo, many miles to the south. Thanks to the railroad system, he sent his beautiful furniture far away and was developing a solid reputation. He now had four men working for him and was looking for another. Ellie had seen him talking to George McBride, a young man from Kaaren's school for the deaf who had worked for him before in Blessing. Olaf had trained several young men from the school in the craft of woodworking.

Ellie knelt by her mother's rocker. "If I didn't love Andrew so much, I would stay with you. You know that."

"I do." Goodie cupped her daughter's cheek with her hand. "First Hans left us for college and now you are leaving. I know that's the way of life but a mother always hopes her children will live close by. You will make a fine wife for that young man and he will make you a fine husband. A mother can hope for no more." She patted Ellie's shoulder as Rachel returned with another lamp. "Forgive me. I am feeling sorry for myself today. Uff da. What would Ingeborg say if she heard me carrying on like this?"

"She'd say let's sit down and have a cup of coffee and a good visit."

Goodie smiled and nodded. "That she would, and then she'd bring out the cheese to have with bread. Ah, I am so thankful for the many times she and I sat to visit."

"Or more likely visited while you both kept on working. I don't remember seeing the two of you sitting very often." Ellie pushed herself to her feet. "If I don't get moving, I might lose my helper. The boys wanted her to go fishing, but I bribed her with the promise of ice cream."

Goodie flinched as she rose to check on the cake baking in the oven.

"Ma, are you all right?"

"I'll be fine, dear. I best buy some liniment. I do wish I'd mentioned it to Ingeborg when I was there."

Ellie nodded and dipped water out of the reservoir into a pan where she shredded soap to make suds. Taking the pan, dishcloth, and clean towels outside, she set up for the washing. Adding a pan of clean water with vinegar for rinsing, she set the kerosene can on the bench too.

"Bring the scissors," she said to Rachel when she placed the last of the lamps on the bench.

"Where are they?"

"Hanging on a string behind the stove, where they always are, I imagine."

"No they're not. I looked."

"Oh, bother. I wonder who used them last." The rule was "Always return the scissors to the hook" along with "Put back in its proper place anything you took out." Goodie trained her family well in keeping things in good order.

"I'll ask Tante Goodie." Rachel darted through the door, leaving Ellie to set the lamp chimneys in the pan to soak.

With the chimneys removed, Ellie unscrewed the metal cap that held the wick, pulling the wick out at the same time. Once they were all disassembled, she poured kerosene into each lamp base, filling each to the base of the metal wick holder.

The door slammed open. "I found the scissors."

"Where?"

"With your writing things on your chest of drawers."

"Oops. Sorry." She'd been cutting out an article from the newspaper to put in her letter to Andrew.

"Always put the scissors—"

"Back on their hook. I know."

The air of superciliousness that surrounded her cousin made both of them smile.

"You want to trim the wicks?"

"Sure." Rachel picked up one of the metal pieces, inserted the wick into the neck of the lamp, and screwed the metal in place. Then, turning the metal screw, she cranked the wick high enough to trim. Cutting off all the black, she glanced to Ellie for approval, then adjusted the wick so about an eighth of an inch showed above the slot.

"Very good. You want to wash or dry?"

"Neither. I'll trim."

"I'll wash and rinse. You polish."

Chatting about a book they'd been reading, the two worked as a team until all the lamps were gleaming and returned to their places.

"Now, doesn't that feel like we accomplished something necessary? A good feeling?"

Rachel shook her head and rolled her eyes. "They'll just get smoky again."

"And use up the kerosene, I know. But still, for right now they look very nice."

"Let's go get ice cream, like you promised, before Mor—er, Tante Goodie says it is too close to dinner."

"It's okay. You can call her Mor," Ellie whispered.

Rachel nodded and wrapped her arms around Ellie's waist.

Ellie kissed the top of her head. "All right. Let's get the mail." Within moments they were out the front gate and on their way uptown, all without Arne, who'd been digging in the backyard, none the wiser. While Arne loved ice cream, they almost always had to give him a bath afterward. Neatness did not count, as far as he was concerned.

Ellie kept her letter to Andrew in her apron pocket, where her fingers could sneak in to caress the stiff paper. Such a flimsy tie to the other half of her heart.

In a week she would be leaving. This might be the last time she and Rachel would walk uptown like this. When she came back again, she would be a visitor. The thought stopped her like she'd hit a wall.

"What's the matter?" Rachel asked.

"Nothing. I just had a strange thought." She half trapped a sigh and smiled back at her cousin's questioning look. *So enjoy every moment before you leave.* While that was good advice, it wasn't easy to do. Regret lent everything a shadow.

Admiring the furniture her pa had made for her at his shop and answering greetings from others at the post office took longer than they had expected, so by the time the girls got their ice cream, they needed to hurry home to help with dinner.

Eating an ice cream cone and walking at the same time was not difficult, unless one let her mind wander off to the last time she'd had ice cream with Andrew. Ellie stumbled over a root in the path and, but for a convenient tree trunk, might have taken a header.

Rachel licked around her cone. "You should pay attention."

"Thanks for the advice." The two grinned at each other and kept on walking.

The letter from Andrew burned a hole in her pocket.

"Onkel said he'd be a few minutes late," Rachel announced when they walked in the door.

"Thank you. Please set the table, and Ellie, could you slice the bread?"

❧

Ellie couldn't get away until later in the afternoon when she stole out to the swing attached to a huge limb of an oak tree in the back-yard. Olaf had put up the swing with a wooden board for a seat not long after they moved to the house in Grafton, not long after Rachel came to live with them.

Ellie sat down and, using her fingernail, opened the envelope and withdrew the single sheet. While Andrew was a faithful letter writer, he never used more than one page.

Dearest Ellie,

She paused and reread the greeting. *Dearest Ellie.* What a beautiful thing to say. She sighed, a slight smile teasing the side of her mouth. *Dearest Andrew.* Soon she could say that to him in person. She continued reading.

This has to be fast, but even though I said good-bye to you yesterday, I wanted you to get a letter. Our house will be shipped in two weeks, so once the barn is up, we should be able to begin setting up the house. I'm not sure how many wagon trips it will take to move all the pieces to our land.

Our land, our land. Hers and Andrew's but not really. Not hers until after the wedding, but still, it made her feel closer to him.

We started laying the stones for the foundation for the barn. Even Thorliff came over yesterday to help. Astrid has been helping at their house and some at the store too. Far finally agreed to buy a few more cows, but now Mor must find some to buy. He has no time for buying cows right now. I think Far is right in waiting until more of our own heifers come in, but perhaps there are none to buy. No one in Blessing has any for sale, and everyone sells all their extra cream and milk to the cheese house anyway.

Trygve is keeping us all in rabbit meat with his snares. I remember when that was my job. Soon he'll pass that on to Samuel.

Elizabeth is back to work in her surgery, but Mor is still taking care of anyone who can't come to the office. She went out to birth a baby again last night.

We sold a few of the bigger shoats, but with the two younger litters we will have plenty to butcher come fall. Next year we'll have our own smokehouse, along with a cellar.

Sometimes I stand in a spot between where our house and barn will be and close my eyes so I can see it all. I'm thinking I want the barn red, but I know you said white with green trim would be good. We'll have to talk about that. Oh, I forgot to tell you. We will have the barn raising this Saturday and Sunday. We won't get it finished, but we'll have a good head start. I wish you could be here for that.

Ellie laid the sheet of paper in her lap. Why was she struggling so much with leaving her family? Did all young women have this struggle, or was she unique? *Heavenly Father, what am I to do? I want to be with Andrew, but I feel I am needed here.*

11

FIFTEEN MEN, INCLUDING A FEW BOYS, showed up.

"Andrew, if you don't mind, I'll lay out the jobs and such." Haakan kept his voice low, for his son's ears alone.

"I was hoping you would. You're the best builder around." Andrew knew Haakan's reputation and counted on his expertise to make sure the buildings were tight and sound. And up as fast as possible.

Onkel Hjelmer, who had just returned from Bismarck, clapped him on the back. "It is still a surprise to me that you are already old enough to be building a house and barn, let alone thinking of getting married."

"He's been thinking of that since the day he first laid eyes on Ellie." Thorliff picked up a hammer and slid the handle between belt and pants. "Got any extra leather gloves? I have a bad case of summer hands. Writing and even running that old press don't bring up the kind of callouses you all have. You better give some to Hjelmer too."

"See there, young man, are you making disparaging remarks regarding what I do?" Hjelmer's Bjorklund blue eyes twinkled, and a grin wiggled his mustache.

"No, just trying to protect you from painful blisters. Unlike the way you trained Andrew and me at the smithy those years ago."

While Hjelmer rarely ran his own blacksmith shop any longer, he had taught many of the boys, both local and from the deaf school, a few rudimentary smithing skills. Setting the rim of a wheel took more wood chopping than anything else in order to get a blaze going around the entire wheel. All of them had learned to make links for a chain. Andrew still had the six-foot chain he'd made, but now Sam and his son, Lemuel, set most of the wheels, and it was easy to buy any length of chain from the Sears and Roebuck catalog.

"All right, let's get started." Haakan pointed to Lars. "You take your crew and start on the south wall, and we'll do the north."

"Surely we have a bit of a wager as to who finishes first," Knute Baard, of Lars's group, said, one eyebrow raised, nodding to his team.

Haakan and Lars grinned at each other.

"Winners eat first."

The two leaders shook hands, and everyone fell to work, each taking the job he did best, be it measuring, cutting, drilling holes for the pegs on the beams, or nailing.

"You think we carved enough pegs?" Andrew asked.

"We'll soon find out." Haakan slapped his son on the shoulder. "Gus Baard brought a sackful with him. We'll just peg the beams and joists. The walls will be nailed. Go see how the boys are doing with the shingles."

Andrew nodded and headed over to the pile of butts, where four younger boys, Samuel at almost thirteen being the oldest, each sat with a froe and mallet, splitting the shingles off the butt. Each also had a frame to lay the shingles on so the bundles could be tied to be hoisted to the barn roof.

"I'll pay a quarter to the one who has the most bundles at the end of the day."

"No fair. Samuel is bigger," one of the boys complained.

"Bigger has nothing to do with speed. I used to out split Thorliff all the time."

"How come?"

"I didn't take time for daydreaming." Andrew grinned at the boys' laughter and headed back to help with his wall. At 11:30 their shout of victory brought a groan from the other team. With all of the men working together, some lifting, some pulling, others setting braces, the wall rose upright and was nailed into place. Fifteen minutes later the second wall went up.

"Dinner's ready." Ingeborg rang the triangle she'd brought from the house, and as soon as the men washed, they took their places on the benches lining the tables the women had set up, covered with tablecloths and food of all kinds: fried chicken, fried pork chops, baked ham, a venison haunch, canned vegetables, pickles, fresh bread, and cheese. As soon as Pastor Solberg said grace, they took their seats and fell to the feast.

"It's your own fault if you go away hungry," Ingeborg said as she carried the coffeepot around, filling cups and laughing with her neighbors.

"You got any cream?" Hjelmer asked.

"Cream in your coffee? Those fancy politicians turning you into a dandy?"

"Try it. You might like it," Hjelmer called back. "Besides, I always took cream in my coffee. Used to drive Mor crazy."

Andrew glanced up at his mother. Her smile and hand on his shoulder had always been a sure part of his life.

"Congratulations."

"For what?"

"Your wall went up first."

"Thanks to Far. He drives a nail faster than anyone I know. Three strikes at the most." He thought to how many he'd bent and had to straighten before pounding in again. Wasting a nail or leaving it bent over was not even a consideration.

"You're getting your stride." Haakan held his cup for his wife to fill. "How come you're pouring? I thought that was the job for the girls, so they could flirt with the young fellas."

"If you haven't noticed, there aren't many young fellas around these parts. Young fellas not spoken for, that is."

She's right, Andrew thought. Most of the young men in town were married, like he should be soon. *Ah, if only Ellie were here.* But her last letter said she would be delayed almost a week beyond her intended arrival because the ladies at her church wanted to throw her a party. She put off returning to him for a party! He'd wanted to get on the train and go fetch her but he knew it was useless. She also felt she needed to stay a few more days to help her mother. All the while he ate, he paid more attention to what was going on in his head than to the discussions ranging around him. Her mother and a party were more important than being with him—one more thing on the growing list of irritants.

Someone had asked Hjelmer when the government was going to do something about the graft going on at the grain elevators, and he was trying to come up with some acceptable answers. Hjelmer always had been a smooth talker. "I'll be going to Minneapolis myself to see if we can convince the mill owners to pay our farmers more for their wheat."

"Remind them, no wheat no flour. We could ship to Valley City if we choose."

"You know, maybe we should start a mill of our own."

"With what? They got the waterfalls for power in Minneapolis. Our river here don't move fast enough to turn nothing." Gus Baard surprised them all with his comment.

"Steam engines could do it. We could use that coal from down south to power it."

"Hey, Pastor, you ever heard anything about who that was got burned up in the fire at Olsons'?"

Solberg shook his head. "I sent letters to most of the large newspapers, but we've heard nothing. But it's been less than a month."

"Coulda been an Indian off the reservation. Coulda got drunk and crawled into that shed to sleep it off before going back home."

"Question is, how'd the fire get started?"

"You got any good ideas, don't go keeping them to yourself."

"Could be he was smoking and set himself afire."

"Went up mighty fast."

Andrew finished eating and swung his leg over the bench.

"Where you going?" Haakan asked.

"Over to check on that sow. She looked mighty close this morning."

"Don't you want dessert?" his mother asked.

"Later." He untied one of the horses from the wagon and swung aboard. This would be the first litter for his own gilt, and he wanted to be there to make sure she was all right.

When he got to the barn, he slid off and tied the horse before stepping into the dim interior. One of the barn cats twined around his boots, meowing her suggestion that even though it wasn't milking time, if he wanted to feed her, she wouldn't be averse.

He pushed her out of the way and headed for the farrowing stall. Glancing over the half stall door, he paused and crossed his arms on the doorframe. *Well, I'll be . . .* "How is she?"

Astrid looked up from putting a baby pig under the crossbar in the corner.

"Eight so far, all nursed. You think she'll have more?"

"Hope so. Thank you."

He watched as the sow lay flat out on her side, flapping her ear to chase a fly. Another baby slipped out onto the straw, wiggling immediately to free itself from the membrane, followed by another.

"Two more." Astrid smiled up at him. "She has teats for twelve."

"Just like her mother."

"You can go back and work on your barn. I'll stay here. I don't mind." She guided one of the babies around the sow's back feet and up to a teat. The baby nosed around until it got a hold and settled in to nurse.

"They sure are smart, aren't they?" She smiled up at her brother again. "Almost as smart as little Inga. She knows who I am already."

Andrew almost said *I doubt it* but caught the words before they came out. Why be nasty to Astrid when she was being so good to him? He leaned over and tugged gently on her braid. "Mange takk, little sister. I'm heading back."

"If she has thirteen, can I keep the runt?"

"Why not, but see if you can get it a good nursing first. It'll have a better chance that way." He stopped at the cattle trough and cupped his hand under the spigot from the pump to get a drink before mounting the horse and loping back across the fields to where they had the back wall nearly ready to raise.

"How many?" Haakan called.

"Ten. Astrid is with her."

"Good."

Andrew turned at a familiar laugh, one that always set his teeth on edge. Sure enough, the two Valders brothers had arrived while he was gone. Gerald was fine, but Toby could well have stayed home. Andrew looked up to see his pa watching him. He shrugged and grabbed the hammer he'd left in his toolbox.

"Where do you want me?" Toby asked.

"We'll start on the front wall. There's enough help on the back one to get that raised."

I don't want him working on my barn. Don't be stupid. Toby's as good with hammer and saw as anyone. Why would he come? At least he wasn't here for dinner. Andrew Bjorklund, don't be a fool. His thoughts raged, even as he tried to drive them out with every blow of the hammer.

By the time everyone headed home to do their own chores, the four walls were in place and braced, and half of the rafters were ready to raise. Andrew had hewn his own beam from a cottonwood tree that had been curing for several years. Andrew made it a point to shake the hand of every man who had helped him.

"*Tusin takk. Mange takk.*" He could not say the words often enough. When he reached to shake Toby's hand, the man hesitated slightly, then gripped his hand and nodded, never looking him in the eye. He turned and left, striding ahead of his brother, who shook Andrew's hand next, looked after Toby, and shook his head.

"I didn't think he'd come with me. Sorry we couldn't get here earlier."

"That's all right. I appreciate your help." Andrew smiled at Gerald, who never had regained his strength since his time with Teddy Roosevelt's Roughriders in the Spanish American War. He looked closer to middle age than the young man he was. A gray tinge around his eyes made him look as if he'd forgotten how to sleep.

"You'll have a fine barn. Shame your house hasn't come yet."

"They said soon." *I should have gone ahead and just framed it myself. Sometimes trying to save time only brings more frustration.*

"See you tomorrow, then."

"After church."

Gerald nodded and headed out.

The last to leave, Andrew stopped a moment and studied his barn. *My own barn. My land. Ah, if only Ellie were here, all would be perfect.*

On the way back to the house from milking, he leaned against the wind that had come up. Was the barn frame braced securely enough to withstand a storm? Dark roiling clouds hid the last color in the west and piled high into the heavens, as if seeking to obliterate the moon.

"There's nothing more we can do. We braced it as strong as possible." Haakan pointed to the table. "Sit down, let's eat. It's all in God's hands."

While Andrew had never wanted to be called a whiner, right now he felt like screaming. Would nothing go right? No house, no wife. What had he done to deserve all this?

Haakan bowed his head. "Let us pray." But instead of the normal Norwegian prayer, he said, "Father in heaven, tonight we pray for the protection of Andrew's barn. Keep it strong and upright against the storm just as you stand in front of us during life's storms. You are our shield and protector, and we thank you for that. Help us always to trust in you. Now we thank you for the food we have, the roof over our heads, and all the blessings you have heaped upon us. In Jesus' precious name we pray. Amen."

Lord, I want to believe. I really do. Andrew reached for the platter of corn bread in front of him. What if the barn fell down? What if Ellie never came back? So many what ifs.

12

"Perhaps you better stay home from church." Haakan stared at his wife, who looked as white as the sheet on which she lay.

"No. I will be fine." She knew she sounded less than gracious, but how long could one bleed like this? She'd been so long without a monthly that she thought she was finished with all that mess, and now here she lay. Was the flow any less when she was lying down? She thought not. But then, when had she ever been like this?

The flow had started when she got back to the house after serving dinner at the barn raising. And had not stopped. "Uff da." She glared up at her husband. "Just go on about your chores. I will be fine."

"Astrid can make the breakfast. I've already called her."

"Haakan, I tell you, it is nothing. Now go about your chores, and I will go about mine." Ignoring the gush she felt, she swung her feet to the floor and waited until he left the room. The rigid set of his shoulders told her she'd irritated him. After all, he was only trying to make things easier for her. One more strike against her. Guilt clamped frigid fingers around her heart. If she'd said what she really thought . . . A good thing she'd been able to keep some control of her tongue. Lately words just came out, something like the issue that was causing the problem. She checked. There was less flow than it felt like. Surely it was letting up. Right now she really understood the feeling of the woman in the Scriptures who'd been bleeding for twelve years. How did she ever manage? After changing the folded cloths, she set them to soak in cool water and made her way into the kitchen, braiding her hair as she went. At least, unlike the woman in the Bible, she was not an outcast.

"What are you doing up? Pa said you are sick." Astrid turned from beating the eggs for pancakes.

"I'm not sick. It's just a bad case of the monthlies."

"Oh." Astrid studied her mother. "Are you sure? You don't look good."

"Astrid, for heaven's sake, surely I know what the matter is." Ingeborg glared at her daughter, at the same time throwing her hands in the air.

Astrid narrowed her eyes and straightened her shoulders. "Maybe I should go get Tante Elizabeth."

"Maybe you should just do as you are told." At the sight of her daughter's eyes filling with tears, Ingeborg flew across the room and threw her arms around Astrid. "Forgive me, please. I am not myself. I promise that if I need to, I will go see Elizabeth." *Not that there is anything she can do. How I wish Metiz were still here. Surely there must be herbs to help with this.* She thought through her store of simples. Nothing came to mind, but then she was low on many things and needed the summer and fall to refill her stores. While Elizabeth had a lot of modern medical knowledge, she'd been quizzing Ingeborg and learning about herbs and the natural pharmacopoeia she harvested from the land. If Eve had had any idea what her desire to eat of the tree of life was going to cost her daughters through the ages, surely she would have resisted. "Uff da."

She shook her head but carefully, since that seemed to aggravate a headache that hovered at the edges of her eyes. "Please, Astrid, don't fret. I'll be all right. Older women just have to go through this time."

"Tante Penny calls it 'The Curse.'"

"Not a bad description." Ingeborg picked up the knife to cut slices off the venison haunch to fry for breakfast. How she missed the hams and bacon from last fall's smoking. Haakan had a venison quarter hanging in the smokehouse now. The spike that Andrew had seen was nicely supplementing their larder. As always, they had shared the meat with Kaaren and Lars. Haakan had come in bragging about one shot bringing it down.

I always used only one shot. Maybe that's what I need to do—don my britches and go hunting. Killing something sounds real fine right about now.

"Ma, are you truly all right?"

Ingeborg looked up to find Astrid staring at her. She'd sliced off far more meat than was needed for breakfast. Even now her hand was clenched around the handle of the knife so tightly that it whitened her knuckles. She laid the knife down, only then realizing she felt quivers race up and down her arm.

"I will be, Astrid. I will be." *If I could only touch the hem of his garment. . . .* Tears burned at the back of her eyes and made her nose run. Blinking quickly like a young girl batting her eyes at a suitor, she sniffed and reached for one of the cast-iron frying pans hanging on hooks behind the stove. "We'd best hurry or we won't be ready when they come in." Useless words to cover up the gnawing tiger she felt inside. She'd thought of asking Bridget about this time of life, but nothing ever seemed to faze her mother-in-law. If only she could ask her own mother, but a letter more than a year ago informed her that her mor had died one night in her sleep at the ripe old age of seventy-nine. Women in the Strand family lived a good long time. Her far had died years earlier.

If only she could have come to this country too and seen how good we have it here. That thought only made her want to sniff again. For Astrid's sake she had to quit acting strange.

She was forced to go change again once before the men came in and again before she climbed up into the buggy for the drive to church.

Perhaps I should knit myself some wool soakers like we use for the babies. The thought made her smile. Haakan reached over and patted her hand. Was he watching her all the time?

Henry and Bridget came walking up to the church at the same time they tied up the horses at the hitching rail.

"God dag." Bridget's smile revealed two missing teeth, but she didn't let that keep her from a cheerful greeting. Henry nodded and, like all the men, removed his hat when he entered the church.

"Why is it, Mor, that the men take off their hats for church and women make sure they wear one?" Astrid had always asked questions with difficult or no answers. She was wearing a straw hat that she would change the ribbons on to match whatever she was wearing. Today the deep rose of the ribbons matched the trim on her dimity dress and the ribbon that circled her trim waist.

Haakan would be frowning at more than one young man today, for more and more of them were noticing his daughter, especially the sons of the German family that had moved into the old Peterson place south of town. Their eyes nearly popped out of their heads when the twins joined Astrid and the three sat together, rather than with their families.

When Heinrich, the eldest of the brothers, caught Ingeborg's watchful eye, he blushed, red as the radishes that grew in her garden. As soon as Ingeborg sat down next to Kaaren, the two women glanced at each other and shared a mother smile. She'd noticed too.

The Valderses came in with only Gerald accompanying them. Mary Martha Solberg shushed her brood into the row in front of them. Anji, now Mrs. Moen, handed her nearly two-year-old son to one of his older stepsisters and smiled across the aisle at Ingeborg. From the looks of her dress, Anji would soon be a candidate for Dr. Elizabeth's ministrations. Thorliff and Elizabeth took their places, their tiny daughter soundly sleeping in her mother's arms.

Ah, Lord, please oversee all these your children, the young growing up so fast, the old feeling their years. And I pray for me that I manage to make it home without embarrassing myself or anyone else.

"Good morning this blessed Lord's day." Reverend Solberg,

wearing the new stole Ingeborg, Astrid, and several others had stitched in honor of the graduating class, smiled across his congregation. "Let us open with hymn number forty-three—'Holy, Holy, Holy.'" He nodded to the young woman who had taken Elizabeth's place at the piano since the coming of the baby.

The congregation stood and raised their voices in four-part harmony, the sound of which always gave Ingeborg the shivers. Surely that was a foretaste of the heavenly choir.

After the sermon Pastor Solberg announced that the Bjorklund baby would be baptized next Sunday. Ingeborg smiled to herself. She'd almost finished sewing the baby's dress, fussing over the lace on the tiny cap and the hem of the long garment.

"Thanks to all of you who helped out at the barn raising yesterday, and to those who can, we'll be putting up the rafters today." He glanced around the room. "Now if there are no more announcements, we'll close with 'Blest Be the Tie That Binds,' number three hundred twenty-three. Let us stand."

At the opening chords Ingeborg stood with the rest of those gathered, felt a gush, blinked, and tried to catch her breath. The room swirled, and before she could grab Haakan's arm, she crumpled to the floor. She barely felt the slam of her chin on the back of the pew in front of her before her world went totally black.

She came to with her head in Astrid's lap, Haakan patting her hand, and Elizabeth unbuttoning the top buttons of her waist.

"Welcome back." Elizabeth smiled.

"What happened?"

"You fainted. I believe you and I should have a talk."

"We tried to get her to go see you." Astrid smoothed a wisp of hair from her mother's cheek.

"Let's get you to my surgery, and—"

"No, I . . ." Ingeborg cleared her throat and closed her eyes when the faces above her faded in and out. She started again, in a whisper this time. "I want to go home."

Haakan scooped her up in his arms. "I'm sorry, but this time the decision is out of your stubborn hands. We are going to the surgery." By the time he set her in the buggy, leaning her against Astrid, he had to stop to catch his breath.

Foolish man. You're not the stalwart young buck who used to carry me around like I weighed a hundred pounds. But Ingeborg kept the thought to herself, enjoying a rush of good feelings that made her even dizzier.

Haakan turned to Andrew. "You go on over to the barn with the others. I'll be there as soon as I can."

Kaaren patted Ingeborg's hand. "Don't worry about feeding the builders. We'll all take care of that."

Ingeborg nodded and let her eyes close again, which they seemed to demand. The buggy shifted as Haakan climbed in and backed the team.

"You tell me if you need to stop."

"You're not carrying me into the surgery, so don't even consider it." She tried to put some steel in her voice but knew her words came out like a mewling kitten.

Once he'd stopped the team at the side door of the house that led to the surgery, Haakan and Thorliff locked hands and carried Ingeborg in together. They laid her on a bed, and when they stepped back, Ingeborg could have melted through the mattress in mortification. Both their hands and shirt cuffs were stained with her blood.

"Now don't you go fretting on me," Elizabeth ordered. "You men go wash off and go on out to finish raising that barn. We'll be fine here."

"Are you sure?" Haakan looked nearly as white as his wife. "She's not going to bleed to death, now, is she?" His voice quivered on the last words.

"No. I know how to take care of this. You men go on."

Haakan took his wife's hand and looked into her eyes. "You vill listen to her?"

Ingeborg could tell how upset he was just by the deepening of his accent.

After the men left Elizabeth shook her head at her mother-in-law. "You should have told me before church how bad it was."

"I thought I was through with all this, but it started again yesterday. Worse than I've ever had. I was wishing Metiz were here to help me. I'm sure I have something that will—"

Elizabeth laid a gentle finger on her mother-in-law's lips. "Who was here to help me give birth to my beautiful little daughter?"

"That was different."

"Not a lot if we're to get to the bottom of this."

Ingeborg felt another gush of the wet warmth, as though her entire insides were flowing out. She watched carefully as Elizabeth took pestle and mortar, dropped several spoonfuls and pinches of something into the bowl, and began to mash them together. *I've seen women bleed out after childbirth. I've had to stanch the flow—and failed. Lord, if she doesn't come up with something that works, will I lie here and bleed to death?* The thought brought another rush, this time to her eyes. *I'm not ready to die.*

Dear Ellie,

I know you believe you have good reasons for not coming when you said you would. You felt you had to stay in Grafton, but I can't tell you how much I miss you. I wish you could have been here to see our barn go up—we're putting on the siding now, and the boys are spending every moment splitting shakes. Until I saw it up, I didn't realize how big it would be and how many shakes it would take to cover that roof. We are working as many hours as there are light, for haying will soon be upon us. Trygve is getting really good with a hammer. He said he'd rather pound nails than split shakes any day of the week.

Ellie reread the first lines. Andrew was angry that she hadn't come back to Blessing. *The nerve.* Had he no idea how difficult this was for her? After all, he didn't have to leave *his* family behind. She read the lines again. *It's a good thing you're not here right now, or I'd tell you exactly what I think.* She continued reading.

My sow ended up with twelve piglets. Astrid tried saving
the runt, but he died during the night. I warned her not to
get too attached to him, but you know Astrid. Other than
you, there is none more tenderhearted.

Ellie stopped reading and watched Rachel swinging on the swing
at the schoolhouse. They'd stopped by there on their way home from
the post office. As if anyone could be more tenderhearted than
Andrew.

I thought you were mad at him.

I am.

She remembered the time she fell and ripped her leg open on a
stick. He'd held her hand and cried with her while Ingeborg stitched
her up. Then while she'd had to lie with it up on pillows with hot
poultices to stave off the infection, he'd read to her and brought her
cookies. No wonder she loved him so. She'd always loved him. At
the thought of love, her mind flitted back to the kiss that changed
her world. The now familiar heat started in her middle and crept
up to her face, forcing her to use the letter as a fan. She smoothed
the sheet of paper and started to read again. *Oh, Andrew, how I miss
you.* She almost chuckled. She was mad one minute, pie-eyed the
next.

"Look at me!" Rachel called. "See how high I can go."

Ellie dutifully looked up, knowing that if she didn't, Rachel would
keep after her until she did. She caught herself from saying, "You be
careful now." She would sound just like her mother. Not that her
mother sounded bad, but she did have a tendency to worry. She reread
the part about Astrid being tenderhearted and smiled again. *My dear,
dear Andrew.*

We are going to have to make up our minds on the colors
of paint. We can paint the house and barn to match—not red
for both—or paint the house white, the barn red, or paint
both white with colored trim. I'm partial to a red barn myself,

but as Mor has said more than once, "A man is wise who defers to his wife at times."

Oh, I nearly forgot to tell you that Mor fainted in church last Sunday. She is staying over at Elizabeth's surgery for a while. I think Dr. Elizabeth just doesn't trust her to stay off her feet. This way she can make sure. That gave us all a bad scare, but they say it is nothing time won't take care of. Far as I can tell, that means some female something they don't want to talk about in front of the menfolk.

Ellie tried to swallow. *Not Ingeborg. Please, God, make her well again.*

I'd best get to bed so I can be up early to check on the barn before milking. We had a big windstorm Saturday night when we had the barn frame only partially up. You can imagine my relief when I went out there before sunrise and saw that it was still standing.

That is all the news I can think of. I am counting the days until you come back here where you belong.

All my love,
Your Andrew

Ellie dabbed at her eyes. All his love. And yes, he was hers.

Rachel dropped down on the grass beside her. "I made a line to mark how far I jumped when the swing was still high enough to give me a good push."

"If you break your leg, I won't be here to take care of you, so you might want to be a bit careful." There, she'd given a remonstrance without sounding like her mother.

"Pish fish, I won't break my leg." Rachel held one straight out and pumped it up and down. "Harold sprained his ankle real bad jumping off their barn roof. He thought the sheet he tied to his suspenders would help him fly."

119

"It didn't, I take it."

"Nope."

Ellie tucked the letter into her pocket. "I'm going to spend the afternoon sewing your dress. You need to stay around so I can try it on you."

"All right." Rachel stretched the words out on a prolonged sigh.

"If you'd rather sew it yourself . . ?"

"I helped you cut it out."

"That you did. When I'm ready, you can help me hem it too."

Since her mother was so busy with Arne, Ellie had been teaching Rachel to sew, just as Goodie had taught her, starting with hemming dish towels and napkins. When the young girl paid attention, her stitches were very neat and tiny.

Although, if Ellie thought about it, hers were that way when she was ten. She'd started learning to sew at five at her mother's side. Ellie stood and reached down to take Rachel's hand. "Come along. We should have brought Arne with us to play in the park."

"Tante Goodie said that Hans is coming home for a visit."

"He was coming for my wedding, but I forgot to write and tell him it was postponed. By the time our wedding comes around he'll be back in college again. One more year, and he'll graduate."

"I don't want to go back to school."

"Whyever not?"

"That mean Claus—he stuck my braid in the inkwell."

"That's because he likes you."

Rachel stopped walking and stared up at Ellie openmouthed, horror filling her round blue eyes. "Likes me? He hates me."

Ellie took her hand again. "We'll see."

"Are you excited for the party tomorrow?"

"Yes, are you?"

The women of the church were giving a party for Ellie. She didn't know what to expect, but she was looking forward to the gathering.

By evening Ellie had Rachel's dress ready to be hemmed, so she stood her cousin on a box to mark the hem.

"You cut it long enough so you can put in a deep hem that we can let down." Goodie kept the knitting needles flying while she watched Ellie and Rachel. "Land sakes, that child is sprouting up right before our eyes."

"Of course, Ma. Three inches, at least." Ellie folded the hem up to show the depth and took another pin from her mouth to pin the hem in place.

"You be careful you don't go swallowing one of them pins, missy."

Ellie rolled her eyes and made Rachel giggle.

"That's what pincushions are for."

"Could you move that lamp a bit closer to the edge of the table, please?" Ellie asked.

Goodie did so and nodded her approval. "You look nice in that dress, Rachel. Make sure you don't outgrow it before school starts."

"Tante Goodie, I'm not growing that fast."

Ellie's mind flipped back through the years, hearing her mother say the same things to her. Was that what having children of your own was like? Replaying your own childhood over again but from a different angle? Was that how one learned to live and love, by watching those ahead and doing what they did? But things were changing, and how did one learn to make wise choices? She knew if she asked her mother, she would say that you had to depend on the only source of real wisdom—God's Word—and you must ask for His help and listen for His answers.

Ellie slipped the last pin in place and stood to help Rachel step down without dislodging any of the pins. "I'll iron that in, and then we can begin hemming it. Oh, pish fish"—she grinned at her cousin—"I forgot to put the sadirons on to heat."

Rachel walked carefully into her aunt's bedroom to take off her dress. "I'll put them on as soon as we're done here." She stood perfectly still while Ellie lifted the dress over her head, only snagging one pin on her hair.

"Ouch."

"Sorry." Ellie untangled it and hung the dress on a hanger.

"This is such a pretty dress." Rachel stroked the red and white gingham, trimmed with a white collar and cuffs on the sleeves.

"We need to make you some warmer ones for winter." Ellie found a thread hanging and took the scissors out of her apron pocket to cut it.

"I'll never get my sweater all knitted."

"I'll help."

"But you're going to move away."

Ellie nibbled on her lower lip. While going to Andrew was the dream of her life, leaving her family behind was getting to be a terrible wrench. She already felt it, like some part of her inside was being torn from the rest, leaving a suppurating wound. If only Pa hadn't moved them to Grafton. It would be so much easier if they all still lived in Blessing.

She turned at the clang of the heavy flatirons hitting the stovetop. "Did you put fresh wood in first?"

"No." Iron scraped on iron as Rachel pushed them back, opened the front lid and set it aside, then shook the grate and added more wood, setting the lid back in place and moving the flatirons forward to the hottest part of the stove again. Just listening to the familiar sounds made Ellie see what was going on. One day soon she would be the one doing all of this. Fixing the meals, baking, sweeping and scrubbing, putting by food for the winter.

"I hope Andrew is taking care of my garden."

Olaf looked up from reading his paper. "If he is building the barn from dawn to dark, I doubt he has time for a garden."

Ellie heaved a sigh. She would have to go before the weeds made it impossible for her vegetables to grow.

"Sure hope Andrew has built a coop for the chickens I promised you." Goodie looked to Olaf. "Do we have a crate for them?"

"We will by tomorrow night. Shame you can't get them there overnight so they don't quit laying."

Ellie knew what he meant. Chickens moved during the night and settled before dawn kept right on laying.

"I'll send a couple of pullets that aren't laying yet and a young rooster. That should get you started."

Ellie sniffed back tears. These parents of hers were so dear. Olaf had made a bed, a dresser, and a table and chairs for them, and he was just finishing a rocking chair for her. He said every woman needed a rocking chair. She and Andrew were starting their married life so rich, thanks to their families and friends.

Late the next morning the three of them left Arne with the neighbor and strolled six blocks to the church, where the women were gathering for a special dinner and party for Ellie. Rachel carried a gift she had made and wrapped in secret, Goodie had a basket over her arm, and Ellie carried her parasol to keep the sun off all three of them.

"You both look so lovely." Ellie glanced from her mother to her cousin. All three of them were wearing straw hats with ribbons, new dresses, and both she and her mother wore cameos pinned to ribbons at their throats. Rachel skipped a couple of times and twirled once to see her red and white gingham skirt swirl about her.

"Ladies don't swirl and twirl. They walk properly." Goodie shifted her basket to her other arm.

"Let me carry that, Ma. You take the parasol." Ellie winked at Rachel, now walking primly beside her. She handed the carved wooden handle to her mother but had to tug a trifle to get the basket.

"Don't look inside it."

"Of course not." Not that she could see anything beneath the neatly folded dish towel anyway.

"Ellie, stop a moment." Goodie pulled on the edge of the basket.

"Of course. Is something wrong?"

"No, no. I just wanted to thank you for staying for this party. I know you'd rather be with Andrew, but . . ."

Ellie bit back tears. "I'm glad too, Ma."

"We better go on before we all start to cry." All three of them sniffled and picked up the pace again.

The pastor's wife stopped them at the door. "Please wait a moment," she said after greeting them. "Goodie, you and Rachel go ahead. I'll bring the guest of honor in a few minutes."

Curiosity swelled like a beesting. Ellie smiled at the woman, who reminded her of a mama bunny. "And how are you today, Mrs. Washburn?"

"Just fine, dear. We are going to miss you so much. It seems like you have been here all your life, not just a couple of years."

"Thank you." Ellie heard laughter and some giggles from behind the door. What was going on?

"Oh, ignore that." Mrs. Washburn glanced at the door and turned back to Ellie. "How is that young man of yours?"

"He's building our barn right now. I don't believe the house has come yet. He ordered one from Sears and Roebuck." Was she bragging on Andrew? She hoped she didn't sound prideful, but how could she help doing so when Andrew was so wonderful?

The door opened and one of the other women peeked out. "We are ready now." She pushed the door open all the way and motioned for them to go before her. Women and girls of the congregation lined the stairs going to the basement and each one shook Ellie's hand as she descended the steps. She paused at the doorway to the parish hall and put her hand to her throat.

"Oh, how lovely."

White cloths draped all the tables, and pink ribbons decorated the pint jars holding sprays of white bridal wreath, purple irises, and lilacs. Pink paper hearts and pink napkins lay at every place. The room smelled as sweet as it looked. A table off to the side held gifts wrapped in paper or dish towels or colored fabrics.

"This is too much."

"You and your mother and cousin will sit up there, with me and Mrs. Saunders." Mrs. Washburn pointed to the front of the room. Most of the other chairs already had women standing behind them.

She followed her hostess down the center of the room between the two lines of tables, smiling and nodding to all those present. Some had been her teachers in church school, some were her friends, like Maydell, some the mothers of her friends—not all members of the congregation—and some were from school.

I never knew I had this many friends here, Ellie thought as she made her way forward. *If only Andrew could see all of this.* She took the chair indicated, and after they all sang the table prayer, they sat.

Women brought out plates already filled with small sandwiches cut in triangles and squares, two kinds of salad, and rolls, each with a tiny heart of extra dough baked on top. One woman poured tea into cups on saucers in front of their place settings, while another woman wheeled in a white-draped cart with a pink-frosted sheet cake in the center.

Ellie could not quit shaking her head. This was too much. What had she done to deserve a party like this? She turned to her mother. "Did you know of this?"

"Some. But I am as surprised as you, although much of the lilacs and bridal wreath are from my bushes out by the fence."

The meal passed swiftly, visiting and laughter filling the room with a scent as sweet as the flowers on the tables.

Mrs. Saunders, head of the Ladies Aid Society, stood and tapped her cup with her spoon. "I want to welcome all of you this fine summer's day as we honor one of our own dear daughters about to embark on the sea called matrimony. Ellie Wold has come into all our hearts, and today we will bless her as she begins her new life. While the ladies are clearing, Misses Beth and Mary will share some of their songs with us."

After the lovely music ended and everyone had clapped their appreciation, Mrs. Washburn continued. "Now if any of you have something you'd like to say, please raise your hand."

Mrs. Wilson, who'd led the high school girls in music, stood. "Dear Ellie, I just want to tell you how much your willing heart has meant to me. So often you saw what I needed before I did and took care of it, like finding the music or setting out the chairs. I will miss your smiling face next fall." She sat down to applause. Ellie knew her face would either crack with smiling or the tears would burst forth.

Another woman stood. "Ellie, I still have the handkerchief you made for me when I was sick. So often you and your mother brought over supper or fresh bread or pies. You seemed to show up when I was most despondent. I'll always think of you as an angel of mercy. Thank you."

Ellie reached for her mother's hand. While she'd been the deliverer, her mother had done most of the fixings. Nodding and smiling, she bit her lip to keep the tears from brimming over. *But, Lord, none of these things were big things. I never did big things. It's Mor who needs these thanks more than I do.*

Ellie smiled and nodded again. Then when Mrs. Saunders sat down, she stood up. "Thank you all for the lovely things you have said, but I have to tell you something. My mother here is the one behind all the things I did. She would fix something and say, 'Take this over to so and so.' And I would. I . . . we thank you from the bottom of our hearts." She sat down to nodding and smiling, and a glance at her mother showed what she knew it would. Two fat tears slipped down Goodie's cheeks.

"Thank you, Ellie, and now what we've all been waiting for—the gifts. Small things that we know every young woman, or old one for that matter, needs in her home. Rachel and Julia, will you two please bring the gifts to Ellie, and then we'll pass them around the room so everyone can see."

Giggling, the two girls did as they were told.

"Make sure the tags stay with the gifts so you know who to thank," Goodie whispered.

Ellie nodded and began opening the parade of packages. Flower and garden seeds, a cutting of a rosebush, a start of a lilac, knitting needles, sewing needles and pins, pieces of cloth for future quilts, dish towels, embroidered pillowcases, an embroidered tablecloth, hemmed napkins, a sadiron dressed in calico, clothespins, jars of pickles and jams, three strawberry plants, a note that said *Come to my house for two hens,* an oval braided rug, potholders, crocheted doilies and antimacassars, a carved box for her personal things, a cast-iron skillet, six teaspoons, and a lovely blue vase.

Ellie stood after opening all the packages and smiled at each woman there. "You have blessed me beyond measure. I thank you, and I know Andrew will thank you." She sniffed back tears. "You have been so good to me." More tears. She wiped them with her napkin. "Thank you and thank you again."

Olaf drove up to the church door just as they'd finished putting the many gifts into boxes. "They said I would be needed."

"Ja, you are." Goodie handed him a box.

"Looks like I better build another trunk."

Ellie threw her arms around him and whispered in his ear, "You've been too good to me already. Thank you."

That night, after writing a letter to Andrew, she knelt at the window. Staring at the azure sky, she whispered, "Father, thank you. I cannot say it often enough. And take care of Andrew, please. Let him know how much I love him. Amen. And thank you for caring so much, even to giving me a blue vase." And here she'd been concerned about having the things necessary for her house, the one Andrew might be building right now.

June 2, 1900

Dear Andrew,

I'm so sorry I was unable to come when I had said I would, but Ma really wanted me to stay for the party the church ladies had for me today. It was for us really, as everything they gave me will make our house more a home. The tables were set with white cloths and flowers down the centers. I think everyone from the church came—that is, the women and older girls, and many others besides. Every time I think of the nice things they said and the lovely gifts, I tear up all over again. Pa said he would have to build another trunk to carry all our housewares.

So who is more important to her? Me or her mother? Andrew chewed on his lower lip. Waiting was never comfortable.

I will plan on arriving on Wednesday. I hope Penny didn't mind that I held off my arrival for almost a week.

Have you looked at our garden? I know you are so very

busy, so I hesitate to even ask. I never dreamed that leaving my family would be so difficult. Rachel cries about it at least once a day, and Arne mopes along with her. I catch Ma watching me, as if trying to memorize my every word and action. I have to confess to having some anger at Pa for moving us all here, yet I know he did what he thought best for his family and the furniture business. His business is growing all the time, so on that count he made a wise decision. I pray you and I will always make wise decisions. Although wise and painless certainly do not go hand in hand.

Andrew looked up from reading the letter to study his barn. Their barn. But at home it was his mother's house and his pa's barn. And Ingeborg's cheese house. He returned to his reading, knowing that he better read quickly because the others were coming across the field to continue nailing on the siding. He needed to order the glass for the windows too. If they made as much progress today as the last three, some of the men could start with the roofing.

Two more days and he would be able to see Ellie's sweet face every day, touch her hand, walk with her in the evening. His insides warmed.

A cool breeze tugged at his hat brim. He glanced up to see clouds gathering on the western horizon and sniffed the air. Sure enough, it smelled like rain. The gardens needed rain, the wheat fields needed rain, and the hayfields needed it too, but heavy rain might beat the stands down. A gentle rain would be a wonderful gift to all except the barn building.

Not that they couldn't work in the rain, but lightning would bring the work to a stop.

He finished reading the last lines of the letter.

I can't wait to see your smile and touch your face.

Love always,
Your Ellie

His face warmed at the thought of her hand on his skin. Andrew folded the letter and put it back into his pocket. Right now he didn't want the men teasing him. He'd been the butt of their jokes for longer than he cared. Time they found someone else to torment, although he knew it was all in good fun. And laughter made the work go faster.

How would he ever pay them all back for the time spent here? The Baards, Pastor Solberg, Hjelmer, even the Valderses all took time away from things needing doing at their own places.

He took his tape measure out and set the cedar board across the sawhorses. Measure twice, cut once. One of the proverbs his pa had drilled into him from the first time he cut a board.

"If that rain drives us off, we'll need to get those first two litters of pigs cut. We can do that in the barn. Sheep need to be sheared too." Haakan moved the ladder over to start a new section. There were more board cuts to be made, since they were working on the front of the barn, around the big double doors on the ground floor, and the opening to the haymow on the second floor.

"Did Mor come home yet?"

"No. She should be coming home later. Astrid set dinner to cooking and went on over to Thorliff's. I know he has to work on the newspaper today." Haakan checked the edge on the saw. "Need to do some sharpening too."

Thunder grumbled in the distance. Andrew checked the sky. While the sun shone immediately over them, to the north and west the sky already wore dark gray clouds, billowing like sheets before a wind. Rain veils slanted in the west.

"Might blow on by us." Haakan reached down for the board Andrew had cut. They took turns nailing from the ladder or cutting at the sawhorses. They could hear the others talking as they worked on the east side. The slam of the mallet on the froe, the screech of the shingles splitting away, hammers on nails, the rasp of saws—all the sounds of building sang like music to Andrew's ears. Thunder rolled, closer now. The first fine rain mist blew across his face.

The men climbed down from the ladders as lightning forked the sky to the north.

"Here it comes."

"Shame we don't have even a part of the roof on."

"We could sit under the wagon. Wait it out."

"How about a cup of hot coffee?" Haakan slammed the lid of the toolbox so all would be kept dry. "Let's go."

"Bet I can beat you." Trygve sent a dare to Andrew.

"No, I can." Samuel started off running without waiting to see who would pick up the challenge.

Andrew glanced at his father. Haakan's eyebrows raised. Trygve yelled, "Go," and they all pelted across the field. Andrew let the others get ahead, pacing himself so he wouldn't run out of steam. Haakan matched him, stride for stride.

Hjelmer tried to keep up with the younger ones but fell back, his chest pumping like Samuel's legs. "I-need-to run-more often."

Past Lars and the Baards, leaving Reverend Solberg panting, Haakan and Andrew kept on, boots slamming into the ground. Andrew's chest started to hurt, a stitch caught his side. They didn't catch Trygve but passed Samuel, spraddle-legged and bent over to catch his breath.

"I won." Trygve hit the Bjorklunds' porch and turned, throwing his hands into the air.

Andrew and Haakan collapsed on the steps at the same time.

"You shoulda outrun me." Haakan spoke between sucks of air.

"I tried. You wouldn't give up." Andrew gulped in air.

Rain pelted them all, running from the hat brims of the others as they trotted up.

Lightning split the sky, and thunder crashed so close their ears rang. They all followed Haakan inside the house and stood dripping on the rugs while he rattled the grate on the stove and lifted both round lids to add sticks of pitch, and as they caught, laid split wood on top, setting the lids back in place and turning the draft on full open.

"Andrew, how about grinding us up some coffee?" He nodded to the grinder and the jar of beans next to it. "Come on, gather round. There's enough room for all of us. Crazy fools we are, running across the field like that during a lightning storm."

"I won," Trygve stated. "And most of us got here before the lightning started."

"That you did, son." Lars clapped his boy on the shoulder. "Left all us old codgers far behind." He turned to his other boy. "What happened to you, Samuel?"

"I tripped and fell." Disgust made him shake his head. "Like a dumb little kid."

"I almost fell." Hjelmer nudged Samuel with his elbow. "Sitting in meetings for the legislature and running across a field are two different things. I thought my chest would burst out there."

"Then you'd bleed all over." Samuel grinned back at him.

"We can't have that, you know." Lars shook his head and stared at Hjelmer as if mortally worried about him.

"It would hurt?"

"Ja, but you know, when men turn into politicians, their blood turns color, from good red to . . ." He paused.

"To what?"

"To green, 'cause all they talk about—think about—is money."

Hjelmer laughed first, and the others joined in.

Andrew caught his pa's eye and enjoyed the wink. He knew Haakan's views on those in government. He'd heard the discussions often enough. Far always felt the farmers got the short end of the stick.

"A good day's labor never hurt anybody."

"You didn't see my hands Saturday night. Hurt was real there." Hjelmer took off his leather gloves and held up his hands that showed the bandages his wife had wrapped around his palms.

"A few more days, and maybe you'll be worth something again." Lars looked all innocent as he sent the barb zinging Hjelmer's way.

Andrew turned the crank on the square wooden coffee grinder

with more force to keep from snorting. Everyone got blisters at one time or another, especially in the spring, but not that bad. At least Hjelmer kept coming back. Andrew measured the grounds into the coffeepot that Trygve filled from the reservoir and set the gray enameled pot on the front of the stove.

How strange it seemed to be in the kitchen like this without his mor making the coffee and cutting bread and cheese. He looked in the breadbox, but the half loaf of bread wouldn't feed everyone.

"See if there is more in the pantry." Haakan was getting cups from the cupboard.

The beans baking in the oven flavored the room, but they wouldn't be done until supper. No bread, but a half full pan of gingerbread would work if he cut the pieces smaller than usual. That and the cookies in the cookie jar. Andrew glanced around looking for anything else. Mor would have had bread rising while she and Astrid washed the clothes. Today she would have hung the clean clothes on the porch or left them in the basket to hang when the rain ceased. He glanced outside to see fat drops plopping into the mud puddles. White lightning forked—it and the thunder had moved farther east, leaving a steady rainfall to nourish the earth.

"You can hear the ground sighing in appreciation." Haakan stood just behind Andrew's shoulder.

"Mor always says the trees clap their branches and leaves for joy when the rain comes."

"She's right. I've heard them."

Andrew's smile tripped on a sigh. "I can't wait until Mor gets home."

"Ja. The house just gets all cold and lonesome without her."

Is that what being married is like—even the house knows when the wife is not there? Andrew never had liked empty houses. They didn't even smell right.

But the aroma of boiling coffee smelled like life itself. The crackle of wood in the stove, the laughter of the men settling around the table, all spoke of home and friends who pitched in to work together—and when the rare times came for play, knew how to do that too.

In my house one day, I want this, with Ellie cooking and making us all feel welcome. Even when we come home in the middle of the morning because we got rained out. Please, God, make my mor all right again. Andrew took another sip of coffee. Ellie had asked him if he prayed about things. He'd not answered her. *But I do,* he thought. *And I think I've been doing so more often.*

༄

"I should be at home baking bread," Ingeborg said. She'd spent a whole week under the watchful eye of her daughter-in-law.

"You must be feeling better." Elizabeth checked her patient's pulse. "Time for your medicine again, and if we don't see a new surge of bleeding, you can go home tonight, but with strict orders to take it easy."

"Ma doesn't know how to take it easy. You better tell her exactly." Astrid looked up from the log cabin quilt block she was piecing.

"Astrid." Ingeborg stared at her daughter.

"Well, you wanted to be home making bread, and while I set the beans to baking, you would find all kinds of other things to do." She flinched. "Ouch." She stuck her finger in her mouth so as not to spot her block with a drop of blood.

"What is wrong with that?"

"Tante Kaaren and I have been doing it and can continue to do so for as long as needed. I started the supper. I'll go home and bake some molasses bread to go with the beans, and there is gingerbread for dessert. I took care of it all, except I didn't do the wash. It looked like rain." She nodded to the water dripping off everything out of doors.

"I'm sorry, Astrid, for not being more grateful. Just this lying around makes me feel like a useless old woman."

"Mor!"

"Don't worry, Astrid. Being sick does that to people who usually take care of everyone else." Elizabeth held out a cup. "Drink this."

"It tastes terrible."

"I know. I made it that way just for you. For others I might add honey." Elizabeth's lips curled upward.

"What is in it?"

"I'll give you the list of ingredients one of these days. A doctor should have some secrets, don't you think?"

Ingeborg swallowed and made a face that made Astrid snicker.

Over in the corner in a basket baby Inga woke up, stretching and making little noises that told them she'd be ready to eat soon. When she was ready to eat, if her mother wasn't right there, the whole world, or at least those in this house, would know of her displeasure.

"I'll change her." Astrid put her sewing down and went to pick up the baby.

"When the day comes that you have your first baby, you'll be such a good little mother." Elizabeth sat down in the chair Astrid had vacated and began to unbutton her waist.

"Could I rock her when you finish feeding her?" Ingeborg asked.

"I think so, but we don't want the flow to start up again. Although by now all the medications should keep that from happening." They smiled at each other, listening to Astrid coo and talk with the baby.

"She is as good with babies as Andrew is with the animals."

"Speaking of Andrew, when will Ellie be coming?"

"I'm not sure. She had to stay for a party the church ladies were giving for her."

"How nice. Speaking of parties, how's the wedding-ring quilt coming?"

"The frame is set up at the Solbergs'. Anyone who can find time to stop in and work on it is welcome. That's another thing I should be doing."

"Ingeborg, you are forty-two years old. You don't have to do everything for everyone anymore."

"Now you sound like a doctor."

"I am a doctor."

The wail preceded Astrid's entry with the baby. "She sure gets upset when she can't eat immediately."

"She's a little pig." Elizabeth set her daughter to nursing and flipped the baby blanket over her shoulder.

The bell on the surgery door chimed.

"Oh no. Why does this always happen?"

"I'll go." Astrid whirled out the door before Elizabeth could even respond.

"She is such a good help. I don't know what I'd do without her." Elizabeth leaned her head against the back of the chair and set it in motion with her foot. The squeak of the rocker and the nuzzle and slurp of the nursing child sang of comfort and home in the quiet room. "Between her and Thelma we manage."

Ingeborg settled into her pillows, her eyes drifting closed again. *My word,* she thought, *I sleep both night and day. What would my mor say if she saw me like this?*

She heard Astrid whisper to Elizabeth but faded out before the answer.

Sometime later Ingeborg sat in the chair, rocking the baby and telling her how much God loved her, as did her bestemor. "She smiled at me."

Astrid nodded. "She likes to smile. Soon she'll be answering you. I think she'll be a chatterbox."

"You talk like the two of you have been sharing secrets already."

"Remember Penny's Linnea? She acted just like this one. That's how I know. And Gustaf would hardly smile for the longest time. He's still all serious."

"You're right. Astrid, you are so observant for someone your age."

"I must be related to you and Thorliff."

"Is he done with the paper?"

"Not quite. He said he should have the press running this evening.

He had something to fix on it again. That press is broken down more than it is running." Astrid peered out the window. "It looks like the rain finally stopped. I better get on home and get the supper on the table. Andrew came by while you were sleeping, said the house is lonely for you."

"Well, I'm lonely to be there too. Tell your pa to come get me after supper. And you better go get Elizabeth before you leave. Her daughter is screwing up her face and making sucking motions again."

"Bye, Mor. I'll see you at home." Astrid kissed her mother good-bye and headed for the kitchen, where Thelma had started making supper.

"Why don't you bring your baked beans over here, and we can all have supper together?" Elizabeth asked.

"I think the men will want to stay close to home so Andrew can head right back to the barn." Just then a howl made them both smile. "You better go see to Inga."

"It seems that all I do is nurse this baby and take care of patients." Elizabeth was settled in the rocker, with Ingeborg sitting up in the bed, pillows propped behind her against the headboard.

"I should be out there helping Thelma make supper at least."

Elizabeth rolled her eyes. "I have it all ready for whenever Thorliff manages to fix that machine and come home to eat."

"Haakan said he would go look at it one of these days."

"How could he fix a machine he's never worked with?"

"I don't know, but he has a gift for understanding machines. When I was having trouble with my sewing machine, he studied it, took it all apart, cleaned and oiled it and fixed a spring, and it's worked fine ever since. He'd never sewed on it, mind you, but he figured out what each piece did and put them all back together right." Ingeborg picked up the quilt block that Astrid had been piecing and, laying two edges together, began to weave the needle in and out of the material and pulling the thread through.

"Your stitches are so perfect. Why is it that I can sew just fine on people, but give me two pieces of cotton and one always ends up longer than the other. And the stitches make up their own design."

"I don't know. I've seen your human handiwork. It hardly leaves a scar."

With a needle and thread in her hands, Ingeborg felt like she was accomplishing something at least. "I have a question."

"It must be medical if you feel the need to ask."

"It is. Do all women in the change of life get crabby and short of temper?"

"Not all, but many. Why?"

"I've never been so cantankerous in my life. I remember when I was in the pit, that was bad, but I didn't want to bite someone's head off." *Especially not my husband's.*

"This too shall pass."

"I surely hope so. I don't suppose you have a receipt for a grumpy woman?"

Elizabeth chuckled. "If I could come up with something like that, I'd be the richest woman around. Every man would come to me and purchase it for his wife. Let's see, we could call it Dr. Bjorklund's Happy Medicine."

"Or Dr. Bjorklund's Better Way."

"Dr. Bjorklund's Guaranteed Bliss." The two laughed again.

"Now that is a good sound to come home to." Thorliff stopped in the doorway. "Do you mind if a mere man enters the sickroom, which, by the way, doesn't sound sick at all."

"The room isn't the sick one. Your mother is, and she's getting well."

Thorliff chuckled and shook his head. "I know how to make my mother well. Buy her a few more cows so she can work harder in the cheese house."

"Thorliff, what a thing to say." Elizabeth held the baby to her shoulder and patted her back for a big burp.

"She burps as loud as a drunken logger."

"Thorliff Bjorklund, what a thing to say about your dear little daughter." Ingeborg stared at her son, her mouth half open.

"Dear demanding little daughter." He glanced down at his hands. "I better go scrub again. How long until supper?"

"Ten minutes. I just need to serve it." Elizabeth handed the baby to Ingeborg. "If you will rock her back to sleep, I'll set three places. You can join us in the dining room for supper, and if everything goes well, I'm sending you home."

"Good." Ingeborg threw back the sheet with her free hand and, cradling the baby in her other arm, took over the rocker. At least Elizabeth had allowed her to get dressed.

Amazing that her daughter-in-law could give her orders and she obeyed. But fainting and bleeding like that? She shook her head. Never again. *Please, Lord, never again.* She felt the two stitches under her chin. And to think she'd fainted in church. *Uff da.*

15

"I'LL COME BACK to visit, and you can come to Blessing." Ellie hugged her mother.

"I know that, but we won't see you for months at a time." Goodie wiped her eyes again. "I was hoping you would wait until Hans came home."

"But he won't be here until July. I have to be with Andrew to help put the house up and take care of my garden." *And if I don't see Andrew pretty soon, I think I'll just faint away.*

Ellie hugged Rachel and then Arne. "Now, you behave yourselves, and no more falling out of trees, Rachel."

Rachel stared at her bare toes. The cast on her right arm gleamed white in the sunlight. "I won't."

"Of course, that means you can't climb them, at least not until the cast comes off." Ellie grinned at her pained look. She knew the accident had scared her cousin pretty badly—for a while. Rachel had come screaming into the house, clutching the broken arm to her chest. Goodie had splinted it, and they made a trip to the doctor. He'd set the arm, put on a cast, and warned the little girl that if she fell on it, there would be real trouble.

Handing her little brother back to Goodie, Ellie watched while

Olaf and one of his workmen took her trunks from the wagon. The crate of chickens was the last to be unloaded. The rooster crowed as if in defiance of the indignities imposed upon him. Sometimes she felt the same. None of this had gone the way she and Andrew had dreamed and planned. Her mother had reminded her that God's plans were not our plans but His were always for our good.

She tried to concentrate on finding the good in the plans while Rachel strangled her middle and cried into her traveling dress. "Shh now. It will be all right. Once we have our house and after the wedding, you can come visit."

"But then there will be school, and I'll never get to see you." Rachel looked up with a tear-stained face. "Besides, it will never be the same again."

"No, it won't. But if what Ma says is true, and we know God's Word is true, it will be better." *Please, Lord, help me believe that right now. I thought we were doing right, but this is so hard. I could stay here for the rest of the summer, but Andrew wants me there. I feel like I'm being ripped in half.*

The train chugged into the station, the wheels screeching as the engineer braked to a stop. After several people stepped down to the plank platform, the conductor helped a lady up the steps, then looked toward the Wolds.

"Time to board."

Ellie sucked in a deep breath, kissed Arne and Rachel one last time, and hugged her mother. "I'll write."

"I know. We will too."

"All your things are loaded." Olaf stopped at her side.

"Thank you, Pa."

"I'll bring your furniture in time for the wedding."

"How can I ever thank you enough?"

"Just love that young man and never turn your back on our Lord. That's all I ask."

"I will." She rested in his loving arms for a moment longer, then took a deep breath and stepped back. "I love you all." She turned and took the hand the conductor offered to help her up the steep steps. At the top she waved again, seeing them all through the sheen of moisture that threatened at any moment to overflow. She found a window seat on their side so she could wave again and smile bravely, but all she wanted to do was plaster her nose to the glass and let the tears flow.

The conductor called, "All aboard," and the train pulled slowly from the station, each turn of the mighty wheels taking her farther from this family and closer to the next. Was life always like this? Leaving and arriving? She mopped her face and collapsed against the back of the seat with a sigh that drained the starch from her shoulders and added a quiver to her lips.

"Lord, keep them safe," she whispered into her handkerchief, then dried her eyes again. Would the well of tears never dry up?

The *clackety clack* of the wheels lulled her into somnolence, her eyes and nose burned from all the wiping, and her mind floated, drifting between Grafton and Blessing, flashing vignettes of her two lives onto the backs of her eyelids. Laughing and playing with Astrid, Sophie, and Grace those years before; sewing with her mother, then teaching Rachel; sitting in the Grafton church with the sun streaming through the stained-glass windows, reminding her of the beauty of heaven; studying in the one-room school of Blessing, listening to Pastor Solberg read to them from *Pilgrim's Progress, The Adventures of Tom Sawyer,* stories from the Bible, and *Robinson Crusoe.*

Sometimes she felt like a young lady, and other times she wanted to hide behind her mother's skirts. *Hide yourself in me.* The words kept time with the train wheels. *Hide yourself in me.* She knew where the words came from, but why now? Why did she need a hiding place? She was on her way to living her dream of being with Andrew. *Lord, I love him. I've always loved him. You say there is no fear in love, but there is. Perfect love casts out all fear. What if I have a baby born dead? What if I can't have any babies? Perfect love. Only you have perfect love. Oh, please teach me to love the way you love. Thou who art the Alpha and Omega, the beginning and the end, the one who never changes.* The rocking of the train carried her into a sleep that allowed the healing of her tear-swollen eyes and raw throat.

She woke as the train slowed, the conductor stopping by her seat. "Your stop, miss. Blessing."

"Already?" She stretched and hid a yawn behind her gloved hand. She touched her hair to make sure it was still tucked under her hat and repinned the straw to straighten it.

"You look lovely, miss. I know your young man will be overjoyed to see you."

"You know Andrew?"

"Of course. I've had this run for years. Many a meal I've enjoyed at the boardinghouse. Henry and I go way back."

"Oh."

He tipped his hat. "You take care now, and welcome back to Blessing."

Andrew was standing on the platform, tall, tanned, and studying each window. She waved, and he broke into a smile that blew away all her doubts and fears. Andrew was waiting for her. She picked up her valise and looped her reticule over her wrist. Welcome to Blessing, indeed.

She never took her eyes off his as the conductor helped her down the stairs and reached in for her valise and set it on the platform. But instead of flying into his arms like she'd dreamed of, she walked straight and sure, treasuring the way his smile creased his cheeks, glinted from his eyes, eyes that matched the sky above, a Dakota sky of a blue that deepened the more you looked into it.

"Ah, Ellie." His chin quivered, and he blinked once to clear the moisture that made her sniff as her own eyes needed clearing too. She stepped into his arms and sighed.

"You've come home."

"Indeed." She clapped one hand onto her hat to keep it from being knocked askew as his lips met hers in a kiss of welcome, of promise. His arms encircled her waist; his heart beat against hers. He smelled of sun and clean wind, starch in his shirt and shaving soap on his cheek. *Andrew*. Stepping back, she laid a hand to her throat. Ah, the pounding of her heart and the warmth of her face.

He grabbed her again, this time swinging her around. "I have so much to show you, to tell you. The house came. The barn is nearly done. Tomorrow we start haying, and you're here. You're finally here." He ripped his straw hat from his head and waved it at the leaving train. The conductor waved back.

Ellie clung to his arm. *I'm here. I truly am here.*

"Let's go look at the house and then go home."

"All right." She tucked her arm through his as they strolled down the platform, watching the train shrink while it headed down the tracks. She felt like skipping and twirling, as Rachel did, enjoying the swirl of her new gingham dress. Up ahead huge stacks of lumber, siding, and trusses took up all the platform and spilled onto the dirt. "There's so much."

"I know." Andrew laid his other hand over hers and squeezed. "Big enough to have several children before we have to add on."

Babies. Why did he bring up babies today? When can I talk to him about my fears?

Andrew didn't seem to realize her withdrawal. He bent over to pick up a packet. "This must be the plans." He turned it over to find a line drawing of their house.

Ellie stared at it. "Andrew, that isn't the one we chose." *I didn't like this one nearly as well.*

He shrugged. "I know, but I figured this one would be better."

"How could you make that decision without asking me?" She knew a note of querulousness colored her voice, but really—the nerve of him to do that.

Andrew assumed patience like putting on a cloak. "You weren't here, remember? And I decided this was a better deal. After all, it was fifty dollars cheaper." He spoke slowly, as if trying to explain something to someone who was a bit slow.

"But you didn't even tell me."

"I didn't think it was that important. It's a great house, and it's all ours." He took her hand and tried tucking it back into his arm.

While she resisted for a moment, Ellie gave in and let him have his way. *You should be grateful you'll have a brand-new house,* the little voice inside chided. *Most people don't start out with a brand-new house and barn.*

"Let's go home."

She nodded. Home was with Andrew. Ignoring the voice inside her head, she said, "Oh, my things."

"They've already loaded them into the wagon."

"My chickens?"

"If that squawking crate is your chickens, yes."

"Do we have a place for them?"

"Well, we can put them in with Astrid's chickens, or we can put wire over a stall in our barn to keep them in. I'll build an outside run as soon as I can." He helped her up into the wagon, then paused, looking up at her. "I am so glad you are finally here."

"Me too." *And while I can't wait to see all the others, I am so glad you came alone to pick me up.* She settled her skirts, glanced over her shoulder to make sure all her trunks and bags were there, and watched Andrew step up on the wagon wheel and take his place beside her. *I wonder if I will ever tire of watching Andrew.* The thought made her smile again. Not anytime soon, that was for sure.

They swung by the store, and Penny must have been watching for them, for she burst through the door as soon as the wagon stopped. "Welcome home, Ellie. I've been afraid you might not come until fall, and I need help so badly. Mr. Valders is home with the grippe, and Astrid is helping Dr. Elizabeth. I need help."

"And Hjelmer has been out working on our barn with the rest of us."

"Along with every able-bodied man in town. Ingeborg said she had room to store your things, so just bring what you need. You'll make a fine shopkeeper."

"I'll see you later this evening, then?"

"Right, and you'll stay in our spare room. I've moved the children up to the attic for the summer."

"Where are they now?"

"Out to Tante Kaaren's. Ilse is teaching the girls to sew, and George is teaching the boys about woodworking, just like Onkel Olaf used to do. Don't know what Kaaren would do without the two of them. George is so good with the students, being deaf himself."

Andrew flicked the reins and headed out.

"What are the twins doing?"

"Most likely hoeing and pulling weeds at Tante Kaaren's. Mor's strawberries will be ripe soon, and then the canning begins."

"I will make jam for us." *Us—what a wonderful word. Us—as in Andrew and me. I will spread the jam I made on bread I made—for us.* Ellie hugged the thoughts to herself. *Us.*

"Once I show you the barn, I need to go help with shearing the sheep. Mor said she would give us a fleece or two."

There it was again, the magic word—us. She tucked her hand through the crook in Andrew's arm. "How wonderful. Do you suppose she would let me use her spinning wheel too?"

"Oh, I'm sure. And the sewing machine, the loom, whatever you need."

"The women from church gave us a braided rug to put in front of the stove. Andrew, wait until you see all the lovely things we have."

"Not just chickens?" He turned his head and grinned at her.

Her heart turned over with love for him, but she poked him in the ribs. "Do not make fun of my chickens. I have plant starts too and both flower and vegetable seeds."

"I suppose you want me to dig up more garden space."

No, but I sure wish you'd told me about the house. All you had to do was tell me.

They waved at the children playing in front of one of the houses, and a dog ran barking at the heels of the horses. Out of town he clucked the team to a more lively trot.

As they drove past the home fields, he pointed out to her what was planted where, the wheat now tall enough to bend in the breeze. Bluebells nodded beside the road. "If the corn keeps growing like it is, knee high by the Fourth of July won't be a problem. I let the sow and her piglets outside today for the first time. The little ones ran and squealed, their tails curled tight. The first one to dig in the dirt with his snout thought he was some special.

"There it is." He pointed toward the north, where two men were up on the barn roof nailing shakes in place.

"Oh, Andrew, it looks huge."

"Not as big as the home barn, but that loft should hold plenty of hay. The hay stand looks good too. We had a little rain. Now if it just holds off until after the hay is in . . ."

The closer they came, the rounder grew her eyes. *How did we afford such a barn? Should I ask him about that?* She knew that both of their gifts from Mr. Gould went into buying the house.

"We're going to go pick up the house materials this evening. Now that will be a caravan of wagons almost like harvest." He stopped the wagon near the barn.

"Is that Toby Valders up there?"

"Yes, and Gerald too. They're both out of work until haying starts, so they've shown up every day."

Ellie turned to stare at Andrew. The tone of his voice said more than his blank face.

"What could I do? Tell him to go away?" He shook his head. "Someday I'll work on his house or barn. Half of Blessing has pounded nails or split shakes or carved pegs. Maybe we should just call it the Blessing Barn. Mor is planning a party if we have time between haying and harvest. Other than graduation, there haven't been too many parties around here, and a big empty barn works good for a dance."

"Empty but for my chickens." She thought a moment. "Maybe it's not a good idea to bring them out here until we are living in the house. If a fox or something gets in, we won't be here to hear it."

"I plan on moving out here as soon as the roof is on the house."

"Before we are married?"

He nodded and swung down from the wagon. "I'll ride back and forth for the chores at home, but I think someone should be here—just in case, you know."

"Oh." For some reason, the idea disappointed her. She'd dreamed of walking into their brand-new, unlived-in house after the wedding. *The other house. Not the one they now owned.* It would still smell of paint and wallpaper, and together they would decide where to put their new furniture. She would put away all the lovely things she'd made through the years and all the gifts so generously given.

He smiled into her eyes as he lifted her down from the wagon, and all thoughts of disappointment flew right out of her head. The feel of his hands on her waist and the muscles in his arms bulging under her hands all sent a shiver straight to her middle. It was a good thing he held her for a moment after setting her feet on the ground, for her knees might well have buckled.

Don't be silly, she ordered herself. *This is only Andrew, remember? Only Andrew, my right foot.* Even her fingertips felt like she'd touched a hot stove. A little voice inside snickered. *Wanton.* Where was a fan when you needed one?

"Welcome, Ellie," Haakan called from the board he was standing on so he could hammer shingles in place on the gambrel roof.

"Thank you. I can't believe how far along this is." She pulled the strings of her reticule over her hand and set it up on the seat.

"Come, I'll show you the inside." Andrew took her hand, and she had to almost run to keep up with him. They stepped in through where the main door would be.

Ellie stared up through the floor joists of the haymow, clear to the rafters, where shingles covered some of the one-by-fours, but most of the eastern side still showed blue sky. "Will you have enough shingles?"

"The boys are trying to keep up, but a square of shingles doesn't go very far up there. We should have been splitting shakes all winter."

"Did you really know it was going to be this big?"

"Well, we added an extra fifteen feet in length, but the width stayed the same. Far decided that since we were doing it, we might as well go the whole size." He turned to the western wall. "Over there in that corner is where we'll put the chickens at first. I doubt we'll get a chicken house built this year. The pigs will be over there too. The milking stanchions down the east side."

"So you won't milk over at the home barn?"

"Not if we get more cows like Mor wants. I thought at first I'd have all the hogs here, but the cows need to be inside in the winter, so we'll see. I can always add more stanchions later."

"Andrew Bjorklund, I am so proud of you I could just pop."

He turned to look down at her. "Why?"

"You are so sure of what you are doing. I've been dithering about leaving home, and here you talk like you've been farming for years."

"I have been. All my life."

"No, I mean with your own barn and livestock. It's different."

"Not really. Now if we moved west and homesteaded or bought a homestead someone didn't prove up, that would be different."

Ellie rolled her eyes. "You just don't understand."

"Come on, I'll show you the cellar for the house. We got part of that dug out." He took her hand, and she trotted beside him across the packed earth to a hole in the ground, squared off with strings tied to stakes pounded into the ground.

"Our own cellar." When she closed her eyes, she could see shelves against the walls, filled with jars of peaches, apples, green beans, corn, and pickles. The jams would glow like jewels. There would be bins for the potatoes and carrots, barrels of apples, crocks of pickles and sausages.

And if the tornadoes came, they would hide down there, safe from the storms above.

"Ah, Andrew, we must be grateful for all that God has given us." She turned to look back at the barn. "So much."

"Well, we work hard too, you know."

She stared up at him. "Yes, but still, all this comes from His hands."

He half shrugged. "I didn't get to the garden."

"Oh." She crossed the grass to her plot. Someone had been hoeing. The radish row was recognizable with carrots interspersed. That way when they pulled the radishes, it left room for the carrots, which were much slower to grow. Her mother had taught her that trick. She looked closely, checking the stakes at the ends of the rows, not that she'd forgotten what she'd planted where. The corn and potatoes were up, the beans struggling against the weeds. The opportunistic peas were using the weeds as climbing posts. She let out a sigh. She'd left the garden in Grafton without a weed.

Glancing down at her dress, she shook her head. She needed to change into a work dress and apron and get busy. With no place to change here, she strode resolutely back to the wagon.

"Do you want to take me back to the house, or shall I drive myself? There's work to do here, or we won't have anything to eat next winter."

"I'll take you. Sorry about the weeds. How about if we band your chickens and put them in with Astrid's?"

"Fine." She climbed up over the wheel without waiting for his assistance. She should be able to get much of the garden cleaned out before dark that night. How come the weeds grew so much faster than the vegetables? How come that little worm of discontent took up residence?

SO MUCH FOR SPENDING the evenings with Ellie.

"You're going back out tonight?" Ingeborg set the last platter of food on the table and took her seat.

"It would be a shame to waste the full moon." Haakan bowed his head, and the others followed suit. "I Jesu navn . . ." They joined in the table prayer, and at the amen all reached for the serving bowls, helped themselves, and passed them on around the long table. Both Toby and Gerald, along with two of the German young men who were working for the Bjorklunds for the summer, ate suppers with the family.

Astrid helped with the meal preparation, spending only part of her day at the surgery since her mother needed her at home too.

"I saw Ellie today when I went for the mail." She grinned at Andrew when he looked up. "She likes working at the store. Tante Penny said she's the best worker she's ever had."

Andrew nodded. Everyone saw more of Ellie than he did. Instead of going calling like he wanted to, he would dig the cellar by moonlight, and after the horses were put away, either Haakan or Lars would come to help him. Three men were the most that could dig without getting in one another's way. The night before, Haakan had backed the sledge down the dug-out ramp, and they had shoveled the dirt on that for the team to drag out. Tossing the dirt over the walls had taken too much time. Leave it to Haakan to figure a way to make things easier. *Now if only I could figure a way to add a few more hours of daylight. Or learn to get by on less sleep.* He and the men were already milking by lantern light before the dawn.

The girls were doing most of the evening milking.

Andrew shoveled the food into his mouth without taking part in the almost nonexistent conversation.

"Oh, Thorliff said he'd come over to help dig tonight."

Andrew nodded, finished chewing, and asked, "Did he say what time?"

"No, just after supper."

"Please pass the bread."

Andrew did as asked, even though the request had been in German. He'd never realized the Norwegian and German languages were so much alike.

He held up his cup when Ingeborg came around the table with the coffeepot. "Thanks."

She laid her hand on his shoulder and squeezed before going on to the next.

He watched her for a moment. She looked more like herself again, no longer pale. Had she lain down today like Dr. Elizabeth had ordered?

"Takk for maten." He drained the coffee and pushed back from the table.

"You don't want dessert?"

"Later."

"You go to dig?" Heinrich asked, again in German.

"Ja."

"I'll come."

"You don't have to."

"I know. You need help."

Together they walked out and headed across the field, their long shadows dark in front of them. As the moon rose, the world silvered. Andrew could hear digging before they got there.

"What took you so long?" Thorliff asked as he tossed a shovelful on the sledge.

"You didn't stop by the house."

"I know. I thought digging out dirt was more important than visiting."

Andrew pulled his leather gloves out of his back pocket, grabbed a shovel handle, and pushed the blade into the heavy soil. Six feet down and still the black riverbed soil lay beneath their feet. How deep did it go, he'd often wondered. Another two feet and the cellar would be deep enough. While he planned to pour cement walls, the floor would remain dirt with support posts for the house on poured concrete blocks.

The three dug until the sledge was loaded, then tossed more dirt over the banks surrounding the sides. Haakan arrived with a harnessed team, backed them down the ramp, and hooked the traces to the double tree. With the chains jingling, he hupped the team, and the two dug in to pull the sledge up the grade and out to dump it. Heinrich went along to help shovel it clear.

"One more night and we should be done." Thorliff leaned on his shovel handle.

Andrew wiped the sweat from his forehead. "I hope so. I think I milked four cows this morning before I woke up."

"Good thing none kicked you awake." Thorliff tossed a couple more shovelfuls over the bank.

"Would have been easier if the house came on time."

"Why? You didn't have this shoveled out then either." They continued digging.

"Did you and Elizabeth talk about Mor?"

"Of course."

"She'll be all right?"

"Yes. But she has to take it a bit easier for a while."

"Our Mor?"

"This scared her. She's trying to listen. She has to find someone to take over the cheese house, at least for a short time."

"But who?"

They could hear the horses returning, and the sledge backed down the ramp.

"That's it for tonight." Haakan unhooked the traces. "You can't burn both ends of the candle and the middle too. All this will get done in good time."

The men rammed their shovels into the dirt and followed the horses back to the barn.

"Good night."

"God nacht," Heinrich called back as he headed across the fields for home.

"You want dessert?" Andrew asked.

"Nope. I want my bed. I print tomorrow." Thorliff clapped his brother on the upper arm. "Get to bed before you fall asleep."

Andrew took his boots off on the porch and hung his hat on the peg inside the kitchen. All this work, and Ellie didn't like the house. She would like it when it was finished. The kerosene lamp on the table burned low, and a cake pan covered with a dishcloth and a couple of plates and forks sat beside it. The quiet house told him both Mor and Astrid had gone to bed. He paused at the table, cut himself a piece of cake, and ate it while he climbed the stairs to his room. *Thank you, God, for keeping us all safe today. Please . . .* His head hit the pillow, and he was out before he could finish the thought.

With three mowing machines, staggered so that they looked connected in tandem, the grass fell in wide swaths. They moved from one field to the next, leaving the long grass to dry in the warm sun. A gentle breeze assisted in the hay drying so that two days after cutting, two more teams went through with the rakes, leaving rounded tubes of drying grass across the fields. Thanks to the machinery, the real labor didn't start until it was time to haul the hay into the barns.

In the meantime, Andrew, Trygve, and the Geddick boys kept on shingling the barn so it would be finished in time to protect the hay. Toby and Gerald laid the decking on the haymow floor. Hammers rang and Samuel grew adept at running squares of shingles up the ladder and hoisting them to those on the roof.

The June sun beat down, burning the backs of the men and giving all of the gardens the energy needed for growth. Roses bloomed along the porches while the lilacs faded, and daisies raised yellow faces to the sun. The peas climbed high on the strings the girls strung between the posts and blossomed white. They harvested radishes and leafy lettuce, staked the tomato plants, and poured manure tea over every plant in the gardens. On the advice of an article in the newspaper, Ingeborg had stirred cow manure into a barrel of water and let it steep like tea before using it as fertilizer.

With the ripening of both the wild and garden strawberries, they had strawberry shortcake for dessert and fresh berries on pancakes in the mornings. Ellie worked in her own garden in the evenings, when she could get free, so she and Andrew rarely had time for more than the briefest hello. But even the sight of each other from a distance was better than the miles between them before.

Grace and Sophie drove the hay wagons, pulling the loader behind. No longer did the men have to fork all the hay up onto the loads. Instead, two men worked with hay forks to distribute the loads and pack them down sufficiently. When more hands were needed, the men left off roofing and headed out into the fields. Always the push to get all the hay in before it rained took precedence.

They filled the big barns at Haakan's and Lars's and stacked more not far from the barns. The mowers moved on to the Baards' and Solbergs', while those hauling kept the wagons rolling.

"We're taking Sunday off," Haakan decreed on Thursday. "Everyone needs a rest, and so do the horses."

"How about going fishing and having a picnic down by the river," Ingeborg suggested. The men were eating in her kitchen today. She and Kaaren were switching off days so they could make strawberry jam and can some for sauce.

"Good idea."

"I thought to get the forms for the concrete started on the house," Andrew said.

"We'll get to that in time. Most likely put it up between haying and harvesting. We'll all help then. Makes more sense."

Andrew stared at his plate. He knew his pa was right but . . . He heaved a sigh. "I'll ask Ellie to come too."

"Of course. Then if the fishermen—" Haakan glanced up when he heard his wife clear her throat. "Er, those fishing in contrast to those swimming and playing ball or just plain visiting, if they catch fish, we could have a fish fry for supper."

"Let the others know. The more the merrier." Ingeborg smiled at her husband. "We do need a day of rest. The good Lord knew that when He planned the Sabbath."

Andrew could feel her gaze on him. While he wanted to smile and join in the plans, all he could think was to get the barn finished and the house up. Already a month nearly gone of the three Haakan asked them to wait. And once harvest started, he'd be expected to move on with the threshing machine after they finished their own fields and threshed those around the area. All those years he had pestered his pa to go along, and now all he wanted to do was to stay home and keep building.

Ingeborg refilled his coffee cup. With her hand on his shoulder, she whispered in his ear, "It will all get done and in time, God willing. Never fear."

Andrew nodded. With all the delays that had gone on, they were already running later than he'd planned. Of course the house didn't need to be done before the wedding, but he wanted to carry

Ellie into their own house. While finished would be best, the roof on and the doors and windows in would be more of a possibility.

Even though the barn roof wasn't finished, they hung the pulleys and strung the ropes to lift the loads of hay into Andrew's barn. Setting the tines into the load, he stood back and watched the first load rise and swing into the maw of his barn. When it reached the back, he pulled the trip cord, and the hay dropped to the floor.

"We did it!" He slid to the ground with a thump, charged inside the barn, and climbed the slanted ladder to the huge mow. The one load of dropped hay looked puny against all the empty floor and space, but it was a start. Hay in his own barn. If only Ellie could be here to see this.

"Ready up there?" called Knute Baard.

"Sure enough. Let it come." The pulleys at the outer side of the long metal track that ran under the beam of the roof squealed and the ropes moved, sending dust motes to dancing in the light slanting through the still open roof and the window spaces in the back wall. He watched to make sure all the ropes and pulleys were doing their jobs, a sigh of satisfaction greeting the load of hay that paused before swinging along the track to the rear of the barn. With a *whoosh* the heavy iron jaws released their load and the hay fell to the floor. Andrew took a fork and spread the hay so they could pack it well. The more they got in the barn, the less spoilage they'd have from the weather.

He sneezed in the dust and removed his hat to wipe the sweat from his forehead, then, using both hands, he set his hat back on his head and continued moving hay from the center drop into the corners. With three hay wagons running, the hay loads kept rising to the mow door, swinging in and dropping.

"Hey, Bjorklund, time for a break!"

"Coming." Andrew jammed his fork into the hay and headed for the ladder. At the bottom of the ladder, he turned at the sound of a whisper. A feminine whisper. And a giggle.

"Ellie."

Framed in the door, she laughed in delight. "I wanted to surprise you."

"That you did." He strode to meet her. She launched herself into his arms, and he swung her around. "I'm getting you all dirty."

She kissed him, then stepped back. "You do look like a walking hayseed stack."

"Food's out here," Astrid called, "if you two can break away and join us."

They'd set baskets up on the empty hay wagon—jugs of strawberry swizzle to drink, sandwiches, and cake.

"There's even ice in the drink." Astrid held up the pitcher, then poured red liquid into tall glasses. "Come on and help yourselves."

The men gathered around and downed the drink as fast as the girls could pour. As the men found places to sit in the shade, Ellie took the pan of sandwiches around, then the chocolate cake, cut in three-inch squares, all of which disappeared in big bites.

"How did you get out here?" Andrew asked when she brought him more to eat.

"Astrid kidnapped me."

He arched an eyebrow. "Kidnapped you?"

"She brought in a load of cheese for shipping, came by for the mail, delivered cheese to the store, and the next thing I knew I was sitting up on the wagon seat and we were trotting out of town." The two girls swapped laughing looks and continued serving, teasing the men and getting teased in return.

"Sorry, the food's all gone." Astrid swung a basket over her arm and handed one to Ellie.

Andrew watched the other men watching the girls, their teasing, the laughter. Was Toby being too forward? Did Heinrich watch Ellie too closely? Was Ellie flirting? For sure Astrid was.

Or was he imagining things? Trygve climbed back up on the empty wagon and picked up the reins. He hupped the team, and the driver of the next wagon pulled forward. Andrew headed back to the haymow, the thought of others flirting with his Ellie itching around his collar like the hayseeds that sought to burrow into sweat-soaked skin creases.

He drove his fork into the hay with far more force than necessary. The first time he got to see her for days, and now this.

17

"WOULD YOU LIKE ME to wrap that for you?" Ellie asked.

"No. I have my bag."

Ellie smiled across the counter at her customer. "It's so good to see you, Anji." She leaned forward to smile at the little girl clutching her mother's skirt. "Melissa, would you like a lemon drop?"

The little girl looked up to her mother, then nodded shyly.

"You don't mind?" Ellie pulled the lid off the jar and, coming around the counter, bent over to hand the little one a lemon drop.

Melissa held the hard yellow candy between her thumb and first finger, then licked it, the tip of her tongue appearing and retreating as shyly as her smile.

"Put it in your mouth," her mother said.

She did as told, the candy bulging one cheek, her eyelashes feathering on slender cheeks.

"Did you say thank-you?"

She shook her head, rolled the candy around in her mouth, and tried to speak around it. The words came out garbled, a drop of drool seeping over her lip. She sucked in and wiped her lips and chin with the back of her hand.

"Here." Anji took a handkerchief from her pocket, spit on a

corner of it, and wiped her daughter's face.

Melissa tried dodging the hand on the chin and the dabbing cloth but finally gave up, her elfin face wrinkled in misery.

Ellie watched the byplay. It was hard to believe that Anji was the mother of two older girls, for the man she'd married had two daughters, and she now had two small children of her own—Melissa at three and a boy of two who'd stayed home with his father. Ivar Moen wrote articles about life in America for newspapers in Norway. Sometimes he wrote about events in Norway for Thorliff's paper and others here in America. Years ago Ellie had thought she and Anji would be related by being married to the two Bjorklund brothers. But Thorliff and Anji had gone their separate ways, and Ellie had never fully understood what happened.

"It is so good to have you back here in Blessing." Anji reached over and patted Ellie's hand. "And thank you for the treat for Melissa." She picked up her bag where she'd stored her purchases. "Come, Melissa, we must get home to make supper."

Ellie watched them go, then smiled and waved when the little one stopped, turned, and waved at her.

"She's precious, isn't she?" Penny came through the back curtain at her usual breakneck speed.

"She sure is. I hope you don't mind that I gave her a lemon drop."

"Not at all. I mainly keep them and the peppermints for just that purpose. I finished the last batch of jam. I see you got the mail all put away."

Square slots lined the wall behind the counter with family names on the lower lip. Whoever was working in the store when the train came through with the mail sorted it out into the boxes after making sure the outgoing mail was put in the pouch and hooked over the arm for the train conductor to snag. As soon as the new building was finished for the bank and post office, this would all be moved over there.

"There are some more boxes out on the platform for the store."

"Good. I'm due for bolts of corduroy and wool, as well as some heavier silks for winter wear. And we're about out of sugar. Everyone canning nearly cleaned me out." Penny tied a store apron about her waist. "I'll get the dolly, and between the two of us, we can surely bring it all in."

"Are you sure you should be lifting heavy things?" Ellie asked.

Penny snorted. "I'm with child, not an invalid."

For the next few minutes they loaded brown fifty-pound sacks of sugar on the dolly, brought those into the storeroom, and then brought in the cardboard boxes.

"That crate will have to wait."

"Do you know what's in it?"

"Pails, nails, and other building supplies. Keeping ahead of Andrew's need of nails has been interesting." Penny thought a moment. "I think I ordered fencing staples too."

"How do you keep track of everything?"

"I'll teach you how to enter the bills of lading and such." Penny cocked her head and, with a slight nod, continued. "You know, you could keep working for me, part time at least, after you and Andrew are married. You have a real aptitude for figures and for where things should go. That display you put up in the window? I've had more compliments on it."

"Thank you. I like to make things look pretty. It's interesting that when I suggest something else to buy, lots of times people do."

"The mark of a good storekeeper. You keep an eye out for anything we are running low on."

"What if you had the coffeepot on for when the mail is out— maybe some cookies or rolls? I think folks would stop and visit more, shop more too. They like to visit when they pick up their mail. Didn't you used to do that?"

Penny nodded. "We did, but I stopped when the trains put on dining cars. But it might be a good idea to set up a table by the stove. Maybe even charge a penny or two for the coffee and rolls."

"Ma?" Linnea stuck her head through the curtain that separated the home from the store.

"Yes?" Penny unwrapped the box with fabrics in it.

"Can I have a cookie?"

"May I?"

"Do you want one too?"

Penny rolled her eyes, and Ellie fought to keep from laughing.

"Make sure you share with Gustaf."

"You want one?"

"No, thank you."

The head disappeared, and they could hear the scraping of the stool being dragged over to the counter, then the clink of the lid removed from the jar, and a giggle.

"You can be sure they will each have more than one."

"I'll bake more." Ellie folded the wrapping paper. "They did a good job picking the strawberries this morning."

"I know. They love working alongside of you." Penny took the pencil she kept stuck in the knot of hair she wore at the nape of her neck and marked the prices on the ends of the bolts of fabric. "We better reorganize the fabric section so we can put these out. Mrs. Valders was looking for wool serge the other day."

"Is she still always way ahead of everyone else?"

"She likes people to think so." Penny rolled her lips together. "Sorry, that wasn't very nice." They both chuckled. Penny opened another package. "Oh, good. The new sewing machine needles. We ran out and couldn't get any more for a while." She handed the packets to Ellie. "Here, count these and make sure the count matches that on the packing slip. I've had a bit of trouble with this company a couple of times."

"They wouldn't try to cheat you, would they?"

"No, I don't think so, but mistakes happen. I've learned to be real careful."

"Are you going to the picnic tomorrow?"

"I'm sure we are. I haven't mentioned it to Hjelmer yet. I think he's getting restless to get back to Bismarck. Afraid something might happen there without him."

Ellie kept on counting. Was that a trace of resentment in Penny's voice? "We match."

"Good. We'll go bag the sugar next."

The bell over the door tinkled.

Penny looked up. "Why, Bestemor, how good to see you."

White of hair but still pink of cheek, Bridget now walked with a cane, carrying a basket on her other arm. "God dag. I decided I needed some of that glorious sun, so I came myself. Did you get any sugar on the train? I need both white and brown and some ginger. I can't make gingerbread without ginger."

"We were just going to bag the sugar. How much do you need?"

"Can I have a full sack of each?"

"Not today, but I'll order again on Monday. Will ten pounds tide you over?"

"It will have to. Raspberries are coming on fast. You better get a good stock in. Have you been out to see the Juneberries?"

Ellie enjoyed listening to Andrew's grandmother talk. While she spoke English, her Norwegian accent was so pronounced that one had to listen carefully.

Bridget looked over her spectacles to Ellie. "It is most surely good to have you back here where you belong. I never did see the need for Olaf to move his family away like he did." She raised a hand when Penny started to say something. "I know. I've heard all the reasons, and I know he is doing real good in Grafton, but still . . ." She shook her head. "Couldn't love that Goodie more if she was my own."

Ellie smiled. She would soon be related to this woman, and the thought made her want to hug Bridget. "How's the boardinghouse doing?"

"Fair to middlin'. Keeps a roof over our heads and us out of mischief."

Ellie smiled wider. Bridget had been saying the same thing for years. As if she would ever get into mischief. "I'll go measure out the sugar." She headed for the storeroom, where hundred weights of beans, flour, rice, and sugar were lined up, ready to weigh out. She set a paper bag on the scale and opened one of the sugar sacks. Using the scoop hanging on a nail on the wall, she filled the bag to exactly ten pounds, wrapped it in string, and did the same for the brown sugar.

"Here we go. Why don't I carry these back for you?"

"That would be fine. And maybe you could stay for a cup of coffee. I think Mrs. Sam would be taking bread pudding out of the oven right about now. Penny, shame you can't just close up the store and come too. We never get a chance to really visit."

"Monday at Solbergs'—I promise we'll sit together and catch up."

"I don't know if I can get away then or not."

"Yes you can. We need every needle we can get. Besides, Mrs. Sam said you should go out more. She can handle things just fine."

"That's what concerns me." Bridget picked up her basket that now had ginger and several other packets of spices in it. "You better watch out, or I'll steal this young woman right away from you."

Penny smiled and patted her mother-in-law's arm. "Oh, did you get your mail?"

"Henry came for it earlier. I forgot to tell him to get sugar."

Ellie walked with Bridget out the door and waited while she negotiated the three steps down to the street.

"So you're going to marry that grandson of mine, are you?"

"Just as soon as we are able." Ellie matched her stride to the slower one.

"I thought you'd be married by now."

"Haakan asked us to wait until after harvest."

"Now why did he do that?"

"We don't really know. He just felt it would be better, especially when the house didn't come when it was supposed to."

"Well, I just hope you don't find someone else in the meantime, like Anji did. Near broke Thorliff's heart, she did. Be a shame for the same to happen to Andrew."

"You needn't worry about that. There's never been anyone but Andrew for me." Ellie could feel her cheeks pinking up. *Even when he does something to— Leave that thought alone,* she ordered herself.

She should have put her hat on. She paused when Bridget stopped walking.

"Are you all right?"

"Ja, just got to get my breath a little."

"Is it too hot for you?"

"Nei." Bridget straightened her shoulders. "I forget sometimes."

"Forget what?"

"That I am an old woman and sometimes I have to slow down. Uff da." She leaned a little more heavily on her cane. "What it comes to when you need a stick to hold you up . . ." She shook her head slowly, as if pondering what she'd said. "I know I should be grateful, but . . ." She glanced over at Ellie. "I *am* grateful."

"I think we all forget to be grateful at times. I know I do."

"My mor always told us to count our blessings." Bridget patted Ellie's hand. "You are one of mine. You will make Andrew a good wife."

"I pray so."

"Come, we will have our coffee on the back porch, where the breeze cools me in the shade. I am like a lizard. I love the sunshine, but when it gets too hot, I hide in the shade."

Ellie made sure they didn't walk too fast the rest of the way, watching the old woman with sideways glances so she wouldn't be caught eyeing her. Bestemor had aged a lot in the two years Ellie had been gone.

When she got back to the store, Penny was busy with a customer, so she went back to the house to begin making supper. Since Hjelmer wouldn't be home, she decided to cut bread, put cheese in the middle of two slices, and fry the bread in butter. Both she and the children loved fried cheese sandwiches, and they could eat outside, where the breeze would be cool. Penny didn't much care what she fixed as long as there was plenty for everyone.

"What shall we take to the picnic?" Penny asked later as they finished the chocolate pudding Ellie had made to go with the sandwiches. She flinched when the mound under her apron bounced. "Easy, baby, your ma needs a bit of rest."

Ellie watched the apron move again. Penny was so nonchalant about being pregnant. *One of these days I might have enough courage to ask her some questions.* "I could bake a cake."

"That's a start. We have some potatoes in stock, so we could make potato salad. I'll sure be glad when the garden comes in."

"Not long until the peas will be ready." Ellie waved the fan she'd brought out, since the evening breeze had yet to make itself known. A mosquito whined in her ear, so she waited until it sat on her arm, then smashed it. "Do you think mosquitoes like some people better than others?"

Penny leaned against the back of the other rocker with her eyes closed. "Yes, they love me but don't bother Hjelmer at all."

"Did I hear someone taking my name in vain?" A deep voice brought the children running from the swing.

"Pa? Can you push me?" Linnea asked.

"I will if your ma will pour me some of that red stuff I see around your mouth." He swept his daughter up in his arms. "What do you say?"

"I'll get it." Ellie stood and stretched her shoulders before heading into the house. She filled the pitcher and broke off a couple chips of ice from the icebox, one of the latest conveniences that Penny had seen in a catalog and ordered. One thing for sure, Penny and Hjelmer always had the latest contraptions. A small pump with a handle sat on their kitchen sink, and when you pumped it, water came out just like out at the well. No more hauling water. Another pipe drained from under the sink and out to a bucket behind the house. They used that water for the garden and flowers. Hjelmer said many homes in the bigger cities had running water and even a toilet that flushed. No more outhouses.

"Mange takk," he said when she handed him a full glass. "Andrew said to tell you he won't be coming by this evening."

That's no surprise. Ellie shook her head to clear that thought from her mind. *Ellie Wold, that is not a very Christian or loving thought. What is the matter with you?*

"They are nailing the last shakes on the barn roof. Said he'd finish by moonlight or lantern if he had to. Good thing, because it looks like it could rain tonight." He drank half the glass without taking a breath. "Did anything interesting come in the freight or the mail?"

Penny shook her head without opening her eyes. "Some newspapers came for you."

"Ah, good. Bismarck and Grand Forks?"

"And some from Minneapolis."

"Pa, you said you'd swing us."

"You're right. I got my drink, didn't I?" He stood with a groan. "Keeping up with those young Bjorklunds is making me an old man."

"We can bathe the children in the tub of water I left out in the sun," Ellie said softly in case Penny had dozed off.

Penny nodded.

After the rest of the household was in bed and the potatoes cooked for the salad, Ellie took out her tablet and added to the letter she'd started to her mother. She told her of Bridget's comment about missing her.

I could hardly talk, it made me so homesick for you. I hardly ever see Andrew now that haying is in full swing. I know he uses every minute to finish the barn. The cellar is dug out, but the house still waits in all its packaging. Astrid kidnapped me yesterday, and we surprised the men while they were putting the first of the hay into Andrew's barn. He was so excited. He took me up into the haymow to see all the ropes and pulleys. The swallows have already built nests under the barn eaves, even though they're not finished with the roof.

She went on to describe what her days were like and then closed.

I'll write more tomorrow. We're all going to the river to fish and picnic. Ingeborg is feeling better.

> Good night,
> Ellie

While she undressed she thought of the corduroy dress goods that arrived today. Rachel would love a jumper out of the deep blue. Penny had said she could use the sewing machine any time she wanted. Any time she had time, that is.

After church the next day they returned home to change clothes, and Hjelmer hitched up the team to take them and all the food "out to the farm," as he called it. Half of Blessing seemed to be there. The boys already had a baseball diamond laid out, and the men had the tables set up and a fire going to make the coffee.

"Come on, Ellie," Astrid called. "Let's go see if we can catch more fish than the boys. Pa says there is a prize for whoever gets the most fish."

Ellie looked around for Andrew.

Astrid rolled her eyes. "He took the buggy in to get Bestemor and Henry."

"Oh." They must have just missed each other. "Where are Sophie and Grace?"

"They don't like to go fishing."

Ellie shrugged. "I don't either." She glanced down at her outfit. "I didn't dress to go fishing."

Astrid snorted and took her cork with a hook imbedded in it and string wrapped around it from her pocket. "Guess I'll have to go alone, then."

"Do you have another cork?" Ingeborg asked.

"Ma, you want to go fishing?"

"Anytime. What are we using for bait?"

"I dug some worms."

"Good girl. Ellie, tell Kaaren where I am, would you please?"

"Of course."

"She'd come fishing if Andrew asked her."

Ellie could tell that Astrid was a bit miffed with her. But even if Andrew asked her to put a worm on a hook, she'd tell him no. Besides, the mosquitoes would eat her alive. So instead she went over to the tables and helped spread the tablecloths, setting the pans and dishcloth-covered dishes in the center. That breeze they'd wanted the night before had delayed until today.

"Come sit with us, Ellie," Sophie called as she and Grace spread a blanket out under a cottonwood tree.

"Coming." Ellie made her way over and sat down, tucking her skirt carefully about her legs.

"Guess what?" Sophie whispered.

"What?"

"I got another letter from Hamre." She pulled it from her pocket and waved it in the air.

"You've been writing to him?"

"Once. He wrote to me last winter, so I answered. That's polite, don't you think?"

"I guess. Is he still fishing?"

"Ja, out of Seattle. That's in Washington State."

"Sophie likes the boys, you know." Grace smiled as she both spoke and signed. In spite of not being able to hear, she had worked hard on learning to talk and read lips. While she spoke more slowly than the others, her smile was always so gentle that no one minded waiting for her.

"I figured that out." Ellie smiled back at Grace.

"Well, why not?" Sophie leaned forward. "If you weren't so fixated on Andrew, you'd see we have some fine-looking young men around here."

"Andrew is the finest."

"Oh, Ellie, you need to play a little."

Ellie saw the buggy coming down the track with Andrew driving his bestemor and Henry. Her heart picked up its beat. "I don't think so." Her middle warmed as the buggy neared. This afternoon she would finally have some time to spend with Andrew. Perhaps they would go for a walk. Perhaps he would kiss her again. Now her neck grew warm too. She watched him help the older folks from the buggy, and then he stared right at her, his smile widening. That special smile he saved for her. As he wound his way through those gathered, she heard Sophie snicker. But she didn't care one whit. Her Andrew stood head and shoulders above all the other men, at least in her eyes.

"You're pie-eyed," Sophie whispered.

"So?" If they'd been alone she would have leaped up and run into his arms. How much longer before they could have the wedding? Would these feelings last forever, or would it be different once they were married?

WILL WE EVER *get time to be alone?* Andrew looked at Ellie.

Even sitting next to her was not enough. He leaned back so his left arm, rigid now like the other to hold him up, felt the warmth from her back. Now that was better. She slumped slightly instead of sitting straight, so her back touched his arm. Heat leaped between them.

"Would you like some dessert?"

"No thank you. I'm full."

"Hey, Andrew, come play on my team." Trygve waved at him.

"I thought you were going fishing."

"Ah, they aren't biting now. Baseball is better."

"That means Astrid got more fish than you did."

"Tante Ingeborg helped her. That's not fair."

"Well, if we are going to have a fish fry for supper, someone better catch more fish. Come on, Ellie, we'll show them how." He leaned closer and whispered in her ear. "That way we can be alone for a while."

"But I told Astrid I don't like fishing." *Why can't we just go for a walk and talk?*

"You don't have to fish. You can sit on a log and look beautiful.

The fish will jump right out of the river just to see you."

Ellie shook her head and rolled her eyes. "Andrew Bjorklund, you say the silliest things."

"That's not silly." He drew back and wrapped his arms around his bent knees. "You are the most beautiful woman around."

"Shh. You're embarrassing me." She could feel the heat all the way to her ears and climbing higher.

Andrew heaved a sigh. "Look, do you want to come fishing or not?"

"Not really."

"You used to."

"I know, but"—she gestured to the dress she was wearing—"I'm not dressed to go fishing. And besides, that was a long time ago."

Andrew stood in one smooth motion, pulled her to her feet, and hung on to her hand. "Come on. We're going fishing."

Ellie heard snickers, which she knew were from Astrid and Trygve. "Andrew, stop!" He didn't even look back at her. Whatever had happened to her easygoing Andrew? Here he was acting like a caveman, hauling her down to the river. She caught her foot under a root and stumbled. "Andrew Bjorklund. Ouch." She tried jerking her hand out of his, but at least she got him to stop.

"What?" The glare he gave her when he turned around made her clamp her teeth.

She bent over and wriggled her foot. "You were hurrying me so fast, I stumbled on a root." She put her weight on her foot. "Ow. Now look what you've done." *All I need is something sprained or broken so I can't work in the store or my garden.*

"What *I've* done! All I wanted was to be alone with you, and I thought you wanted the same." He was near to shouting, and the harsh words kept on coming. "Here we get the chance, and you don't even want to come, and—" He raised his hands and let them drop to his sides. "What's the matter with you?"

Ellie almost apologized, but the look on his face steeled her backbone. "With me?" She raised her chin and narrowed her eyes. "Right now, Mr. Bjorklund, I want to be anywhere rather than with you. My foot hurts, thanks to you, and I am going back to the others."

"Whatever you want. If you should just happen to change your mind, I'll be down at the river catching enough fish for supper. All Bjorklund women are good at fishing." He spun away, stomping the brush as if killing snakes.

"Well, since I am not a Bjorklund . . . yet, I'll go visit with your grandmother or someone," she yelled after him. No matter that her foot burned and ached, she turned and flounced up the path, pushing aside branches like they were the enemy. "And if you are going to act like this," she muttered, "I'm very glad I'm not married to you yet." She turned to say one more thing to Andrew, but this time she didn't yell. "And you bought the wrong house too."

She followed the cheering to the ball field, all the while in her mind calling Andrew every name she could think of. She'd as soon have shouted them to the trees. He'd looked more like that boy of years ago, the one who'd pounded Toby Valders into the dirt, his rage-reddened face a mask of fury. What had happened to the gentle man she'd grown into love with?

Sophie and Grace were sitting on a blanket under a tree with the other women, while the men and boys who'd divided into two teams took turns trying to whack the ball into the cow pasture. So far they hadn't gotten very far, but for all the shouting and cheering anything was possible.

"I thought you were going fishing." Sophie patted a place beside her.

Ellie sat down and rubbed her foot through her shoe. "He dragged me over a root, and when I said ouch, he got all angry and yelled at me."

"I do hope you yelled back."

"Sophie!" Grace sounded shocked.

"Well, Andrew needs to be taken down a peg or two. He's still angry at Onkel Haakan and is taking it out on all of us. He yelled at me when that crazy cow tried to kick the bucket over this morning."

"Andrew yelled at you?" Ellie could feel her eyes widen. Andrew never yelled at anyone, except for Toby Valders. And that not for a long time, or at least not that she knew. *But he yelled at me.*

"He's been grumpy lately." Sophie shook her head. "Really grumpy."

"He's been worried about the barn and the house," Ellie muttered into her bent knees.

"There now, you go sticking up for him. You've always thought he was Mr. Perfect, but if you'd been here the last month, you'd have seen what I'm talking about."

Ellie looked at Grace, who was studying the buckles on her shoes. She tapped Grace on the shoulder. "Is that true?"

"What?" She failed to meet Ellie's gaze.

"Oh, you know what we're talking about." Sophie poked her sister. "You just don't want to hear anything bad about anybody, let alone your beloved Andrew."

Grace's eyes darkened. "You are talking too fast. Please sign." Her fingers flashed faster than her words.

Sophie sighed. "I'm sorry." She signed as well. "I get frustrated with Andrew being so grumpy."

Grace tipped her head to the side and gave Ellie a gentle smile. "He'll be all right again after you two are married."

"If we ever get married."

"Ah, but you will. You know Andrew loves no one but you. Always has."

"I know." She thought back to the look on his face. "But right now . . ." *Like Sophie said, he was really mad. But then so was I.* "I think we just had our first fight."

"We could always sneak up on him and push him into the river."

Ellie laughed outright at the triumphant look Sophie gave her. "We could do that, and he'd pull us in like he did those years ago, and we'd all be muddy and wet."

A cheer rose from Trygve's team as he shouted, "A home run. Go, Pa, go before they get it."

Kaaren stood clapping and laughing with the others. "Come on, Lars, come on home."

"Pa hit a home run?" Sophie leaped to her feet and joined in the cheering.

Ellie wished Andrew were here playing ball rather than fishing down at the river. *I should go down there and apologize,* she thought. *It wasn't his fault I caught my foot on that root. All he wanted was for us to be together, alone for a change.* But while the thoughts sounded good, her foot still ached, and her feelings felt mashed into teeny-tiny bits.

"Where are you going?" Sophie asked when Ellie stood and started to leave.

"To find Andrew."

"Oh, let him stew awhile. It'll be good for him."

Ellie stopped, thought a moment, then started out again. "I'll be right back."

"Of course you will, and I'm a whistling duck."

"Sophie." Grace shook her head. "What has come over you?"

"Ellie, could you please come here for a bit?" Bridget waved as she called.

"Of course." Ellie made her way to Bridget's side. "Can I get you something?"

"In a minute, but right now please sit down so we can talk."

Ellie did as she was asked, but her mind wanted to head for the river.

Andrew's cork bobbed in the languid current. Nothing. No fish biting. He heard Astrid laugh just downriver from him. It sounded like she and his mother were bringing in fish hand over fist. He and Ellie could finally have had a long talk if she hadn't been so stubborn. Since when didn't she like to fish? He jerked his pole, the cork and grasshopper he'd caught flew past, and he grabbed the string. *Go back and see if Ellie is all right.* The voice had said the same thing three times now.

He ignored it and trudged up the path to the next place he'd always caught fish and tossed the cork and line out again. Perhaps she really didn't want to be with him after all. *What could I have done that made her so mad? Sure she stumbled, but that wasn't enough to make her mad. Or was it? I just wanted her all to myself for a change.*

His cork dove, he jerked the line, and a fish flew back over his head. He might as well have been a little kid again, fish flopping around like that. He grabbed the line and overhanded it until he held the flopping fish. Even the grasshopper was still good, although more than a little waterlogged. He wriggled the hook free of the fish's lower lip, tossed the baited hook back in the water, and broke off a stick to hold the fish.

At least he wasn't wasting all of his time. He could have been home working on the house. Not that that seemed to matter to Ellie. Why, when he'd shown her the hay coming into the barn, how beautifully everything was working, she'd hardly said a word. He jerked the line again—another nice fish. If Ellie were here, they would be catching twice as many. Maybe he should make a pole for her. Perhaps she'd be coming down the trail any minute to say she was sorry for disappointing him, that she wanted to be with him no matter what.

Four fish later, no Ellie.

Ten fish later, no Ellie.

Andrew deliberately unclenched his jaw. Fishing was supposed to be relaxing. From the sounds of it, Astrid and Mor were having a wonderful time. Amazing they caught anything at all with all that laughter and giggling. Maybe Ellie had joined them, but when he listened, he didn't hear her voice. He could hear the cheering from the ball game, though.

Everyone in Blessing was having a good time—except him.

And Ellie.

Wearing the baby in a sling across her chest, Dr. Elizabeth had joined Ellie and Bestemor.

"Aren't you afraid you'll bump her or something?"

"She's perfectly content this way. I learned of the sling like this from an old woman in Chicago. She brought her grandson in to see me when I worked at the hospital. She said in Ireland all the women carried their babies this way, so I decided that when I had children, I would do the same. It makes sense. The baby can still hear the mother's heart and feel her warmth, although on the outside now rather than safe inside."

"The things you young people do these days—so different." Bridget held out her arms. "Let me hold her, please. It's been too long since I've held a baby."

"We came to visit only a few days ago."

"Did you?"

Elizabeth handed over the baby. "This is your great-grandmother. Be nice to her, little Inga."

Ellie watched as the baby stretched and wriggled a bit, then settled back to sleep. "She seems a very contented baby."

"She is—most of the time. But when she decides it is time to eat, her mother better not be long about getting ready."

"She and I have a lot in common."

"Oh, really?"

"Sure. I graduated from high school, and she graduated into the outside world almost on the same day."

"True. I hadn't thought of it that way. When she decided to come, she wasn't waiting around long."

What will my baby be like? The thought made Ellie swallow. *Not a blue one, please Lord.* A baby. Why think about a baby right now when she was still upset with Andrew? She'd overheard snippets when women were talking about having babies, but they always hushed when they realized she was listening. After all, things like that were not for a young lady's ears. But oh, did she have questions. And who better to ask than Dr. Elizabeth? But not right now. Bestemor would be shocked. And appalled. And there were too many other ears close by.

"That's it! That's the ball game." The shout went up, and the victors pounded each other on the back.

The losers promised that the next game would be theirs.

"Do they always play the same teams?" Ellie asked.

Elizabeth shook her head. "No. It all depends on who shows up. I'm sure Andrew was missed. He's always good for a hit or two."

Thorliff dropped down on the blanket beside them. "I never got one hit."

"I'm sorry."

"No you're not." He leaned toward Bestemor. "How's the best baby in the world?"

"Go on with you. You'd think this was the first baby ever born."

"She isn't?" He sat up in mock surprise, only to earn a thump on the shoulder from his grandmother.

"Oh, you."

Inga stretched and turned her head from side to side.

"Now look what you've done." Bridget rocked the struggling baby, but the motion failed to bring the desired results. Another stretch, a frown, a twisted face, a sucking motion, a whimper, and then came a full-blown howl.

"See? What did I tell you?" Elizabeth reached for her daughter.

Ellie watched as two wet spots appeared on the front of Elizabeth's gown.

"As your father says, uff da." Elizabeth tucked child and blanket over her shoulder and glanced over to Ellie. "You want to come visit with me while I feed her?"

Ellie got to her feet. "Yes, I'd love to."

"What? Did someone pinch that baby?" Haakan joined them, wiping the sweat from his forehead with the back of his hand and shirtsleeve.

Inga screwed up her little face and screamed louder.

"Sorry," Elizabeth said. "Please excuse us."

"You want a ride up to the house?" Haakan asked. "We're heading up to the barn soon for milking anyway."

"I thought we'd just sit in the buggy."

"Whatever you want. Let me take her, and you climb up, then I can hand her to you." Haakan took the angry child. "Hush now, your grandpa has you. Ma will be ready in a minute."

The crying stopped.

"What did you do?" Elizabeth reached from the buggy seat for her daughter.

"Just explained things. That's all." Haakan handed Inga up, then gave Ellie a hand. He tipped his hat and headed back to the gathering, whistling as he went.

Elizabeth settled the baby under a blanket on her shoulder and leaned against the seatback with a sigh.

"So now. I take it you and Andrew had a bit of a spat."

"How did you know?" Ellie shook her head at the knowing look Elizabeth gave her. "I s'pose everyone figured that one out. It was our first fight."

"Don't feel bad. There'll be plenty more. Making up makes a good disagreement worthwhile."

"But I said . . . He said . . ." Ellie shook her head. "It was ugly."

"Arguments can be like that. You have to talk things out later, is all."

Andrew Bjorklund, when I get a chance, we're going to do some talking all right, and you might not like hearing some of the things I have to say.

19

I HAVEN'T HAD THAT MUCH FUN *fishing in a long time. Not that I've gone fishing recently.*

Ingeborg thought back over the day. If only they could do things like this more often. A picnic, a ball game, a fishing contest that she and Astrid won easily, and then a fish fry to top it all off. The only sour note in the day was the spat between Andrew and Ellie. She brushed her hair a few more strokes and paused. *Oh, my son, it takes a lot to rile you, but when you get riled* . . . She shook her head and went back to brushing. She still wished she'd not heard every word, but sound carries down by the river.

Haakan came in from the outhouse and paused in the doorway. "You look like a young girl sitting there like that."

"I was old when I married the first time. You never saw me when I was young."

He sat down on the bed beside her and took her hand. "You weren't old then, and you aren't old now." He planted a kiss in the palm of her hand. "We had a good time today, ja?"

"We did. I was just wishing we could do things like that more often. All you men have been working so hard, getting the barn done, the fieldwork, and the haying."

"Andrew finished up the last of the barn roof. All is weathertight now. And if the rain holds off a few more days, all the hay will be in. I been cutting at Solbergs', and Lars is over at Baards'."

"Like I said." She leaned into his shoulder while she loosely plaited her hair. "And before we know it, harvest will be here."

"The days go by so quickly. Is it because we are older, do you think?"

She shrugged. "And wiser, I hope." She tossed her braid over her shoulder. "Would you like to be young again?"

"How young?"

"Oh, in our twenties but know all that we know now."

"Ah, my Inge, you think too much about things that are not possible. The Bible says we are to live in the day, this day, not years before or years hence."

"I did live this day, and I loved every minute of it." She turned, her smile teasing. "Especially winning the biggest number of fish caught."

"Ah, but you and Astrid teamed up. That was not fair."

"No one said we couldn't." She kissed his cheek. "You and I need to go fishing more."

He nodded. "But who caught more? You or Astrid?"

She shrugged again. "I don't know. We didn't keep track, just kept on pulling in the fish. They tasted so good. Remember how Metiz used to dry the fish? That was one of her winter foods."

"She taught us many things."

"At times I still miss her so. I look over to find her cabin by the river and then remember that the flood took it away. Sometimes I wonder if she and Agnes are visiting up in heaven." She blinked to stop the tears that burned at the back of her eyes and nose. "I know I should be grateful I had them for friends as long as I did . . ." A pause lengthened while she sniffed again. "And I am." She heaved a sigh. "I really am, but I sure miss them."

"You have Kaaren."

"I know. And now we have Elizabeth and little Inga. Remember how for the first years Metiz would go home to visit her family in the winter and come back in the spring? But finally she quit doing that, and I think she counted us as her family instead. All the horrid stories that go around about the Indians. They make me sad."

Haakan nodded. "I wonder how Baptiste and Manda are doing."

"We haven't received a letter from her for a long time." Ingeborg scrunched her eyes to remember better. "Christmastime perhaps. Yes, that was it. But Deborah shares her letters when she gets them. Just think, they have three children now, perhaps four. It's hard for me to imagine Manda with four children. I only remember her as a child herself."

"Sometimes your memory plays tricks." He yawned. "I need to get to sleep. You'll blow out the lamp?"

"Ja." She stood and, cupping her hand around the chimney, blew out the kerosene lamp. Darkness made the moonlit square on the floor even brighter. She folded back the sheet and lay down on the bed. The breeze tossed the sheer white curtains and cooled her neck, kissing her toes as it passed. She stretched against the mattress, listening to the rustling and creaks of the rope-strung bed. Looked to be about time to tighten the ropes again. Haakan's lips puffed beside her, not deep enough in sleep to snore yet. Staring up at the ceiling, she found his hand with hers, loving the warm feel of it. Even in his sleep he squeezed back when she clasped his hand.

Once in a while lately, she'd seen the black pit yawning as it had so many years before, but now she knew what to do about it. The bigger the pit, the more she threw the Word of God against it, memory verse after memory verse. Had she only known that before, perhaps that year would not have nearly killed her. But as Haakan had said, you had to live each day as it came and dwell on neither the past nor the future. Most of the time she could do that, but banishing Elizabeth's warning was not easy. If she had more episodes of bleeding like she'd had, they might need to consider a hysterectomy. Even the word was ugly, let alone the procedure of cutting her open and removing her uterus. Not that she needed it anymore, hadn't for a long time, but the thought of such a thing . . .

Dear Lord, please, there has to be another way. But if it would help her not to feel so tired all the time . . . *Lord, whatever you will.*

Taking in a deep breath, she let it all out on a sigh and rejoiced as her eyes drifted closed. This time sleep would not be long in coming, not like some of the past nights. Not sleeping steady was another one of those aggravations of late. *Thank you, Father, for Elizabeth and that I haven't felt so crabby lately. Mange takk.*

෴

Who was that silent young man eating so fiercely, sitting in Andrew's place? It looked like her son but certainly didn't act like him. *Whoever took my boy, please bring him back.* She knew Haakan would laugh if she told him this. Today she and Astrid would pick the peas for the first time this year and maybe find enough baby potatoes under the plants to make creamed peas and new potatoes, another marker of the changing of the seasons for her. So far they'd had radishes and lettuce sprinkled with vinegar and sugar, always the first crops. And strawberries. They should be ready for picking again too.

"You think the dun cow will calve today?" Haakan spoke toward the eating machine at the end of the table. "Andrew?"

"What? Huh?" Andrew blinked as he looked up, his fork poised halfway to his mouth.

"I asked if you thought the dun cow will calve today."

Andrew shrugged. "I didn't check on her."

"I see." Haakan stared at his son, who'd gone back to eating. "Were you planning on doing that?"

"I guess."

"That means yes?"

"Yes, I'll check on her." Andrew's tone cut across the table. He never looked up to see the consternation on his pa's face.

Ingeborg forced herself to sit still and say nothing, though she wanted to go around the table and smack her son on the back. *What's the matter with him?*

"Andrew, you know what? You're being rude." Astrid glared at him. "And that's not like the Andrew we used to know."

He half shrugged and frowned.

"Just because you had a fight with Ellie doesn't mean—"

"I did not have a fight with Ellie."

"Oh, you're being mean on general principle?"

He ignored her comment and pushed his chair back. "As soon as it's dry enough, we'll haul from the north field first, right?"

"Ja, I am cutting at Baards' with Lars," Haakan replied.

Ingeborg watched her son leave the room, then refilled her husband's coffee cup, her other hand patting his shoulder at the same time. "All will be well."

"Ja, I know. But in the meantime, it might get harder."

After the men left for the fields, Ingeborg and Astrid hurried with the dishes and, setting the roast to cooking in the oven to be ready in time for dinner, hustled out to the garden, gently digging under the potato vines with their fingers for ones big enough to eat, all the while being careful not to disturb the plants.

"I feel like I'm taking eggs from a newly setting hen," Astrid said as she knelt in the dirt.

"Speaking of which, the hens Ellie brought—one of them was setting the other day. Is she still?"

"Yes. Won't that make Ellie excited to have a flock of chicks to go with her others?"

"Don't tell her."

Astrid chuckled. "I won't." Once they had enough potatoes, they moved to the pea trellises and sought through the leaves for the full pea pods.

"Hey, you're supposed to pick them now, not eat them." Ingeborg grinned at her daughter as she pushed on the curved side of a huge pod and popped the peas into her mouth. "Nothing is as good as new peas. These are so sweet, you'd think God dusted them with sugar."

They both munched at the same time, wearing the same amused expression.

"We could just put the pods out on the table and let everyone eat them raw."

"We could, but that would make it difficult to have creamed peas and potatoes."

"Right. Back to picking and not eating."

Ingeborg hummed a tune as she stripped the peas from the vines, making sure each pod was full before pulling it off. The crop looked to be heavy this year, with lots of blossoms and bees buzzing around, doing their pollinating job.

"Mor?"

"Ja."

"Do you think Andrew is always going to be like this?"

"No. Once the house and barn are finished and they get married, we'll see our old Andrew again."

"You sure? I really don't like him much right now."

"No, but we love him, and we will pray that God sees him through this."

"I saw Ellie crying one day."

"They will work it out. All young people have times like this."

"Maybe Pa shouldn't have asked them to wait."

"Astrid, your far is one of the most conscientious men I have ever known. He would not have asked that of them if he did not have a good reason. Ah, dear daughter, your pa listens to God better than anyone I know. He believes this came from God, and so do I."

"Andrew doesn't."

"Then that will be between God and Andrew, won't it?"

"I guess. I think I wouldn't want to be in Andrew's shoes."

"Reminds me of the Jonah story. He didn't like what God said, and he tried to run away."

"Until the whale ate him." Astrid stopped picking. "How could a man live for three days in the belly of a whale?"

"Only by the hand of God."

"Good thing there aren't any whales in North Dakota."

"God will use whatever He has to use to bring Andrew to the place He wants him to be."

"You want to pick the next row too?"

"Ja, get them all. We'll mix some with the lettuce for salad."

Barney's barking drew their attention to a man riding up the lane.

"Do you know who that is?"

"No. I'll go see. You keep picking. If you get done, start on the strawberries. Perhaps I'll get a batch of jam made this afternoon." Ingeborg carried her basket up and set it on the porch, then turned to greet the rider.

"Hello. Are you Mrs. Bjorklund?"

"Ja, that I am." She waited at the gate for him to dismount. "How can I help you?"

"I heard you was looking for milk cows."

"Ja. You have some for sale?"

"Two milking and a heifer due in a month or so."

"How old are the two and what kind?"

"Oh, three or four, I'd guess. Just milk cows. No particular breed."

"Why are you selling them?"

"I'm going back home. Lost my wheat to grasshoppers last year and got no money to buy seed. Better to go back to Iowa and work for my pa."

"How much do you want?"

He thought for a moment. "Thirty each?"

"That sounds about right. I'll think about it."

"If I could sell my place, it would be better than lettin' it go back to the bank."

"You want to take your horse down to the barn and let him loose in the corral? Stay for dinner? You could talk with my husband about the land." As soon as the words were out of her mouth, Ingeborg realized she'd made a mistake. Haakan would not be home for dinner. He would be eating at the Baards'. And yet she knew he would want to know about the land. Not about the cows, but the land.

"That would be right kind of you. Name is Joshua. Joshua Landsverk."

"I'm glad to meet you, Mr. Landsverk. You're welcome to sit on the porch here, and I'll bring you some coffee." After he nodded and reined his horse around, Ingeborg returned to the garden, where Astrid was bringing in her basket of peas.

"Please take one of the horses and ride on over to the Baards'. I think your pa will want to talk with this young man."

"Sure. You want me to see if we have mail at the same time?"

"Ja, and tell Pa to come home for dinner." *Or should I just send this man on over there? So much indecision lately.* Questions, always questions. More land to buy. Haakan would be pleased. Times like this were when she missed Goodie the most. They used to quilt together, can together, and do things together like snap beans and shell peas. Goodie had been her second right hand.

After Astrid left, Ingeborg stuck wood into the stove, pulled the coffeepot forward, and checked the meat baking in the oven. She should have put more wood in sooner. As soon as she served the coffee, she began shelling the peas. Her thoughts flew as fast as her fingers. With more land for hay and feed grain, they could have more cows. If that place could be planted to wheat, then more of the home farm could be used for hay and feed grain. Would Trygve want the place in a couple of years? Had she made a mistake in calling Haakan home? No. He'd want to know about this. Of course, he could have already known and not thought to mention it. At least not about the cows. He really did not want more cows to milk. But two cows and a bred heifer weren't many. She hadn't even had to go looking. God brought the man right to her door.

Since she'd not set bread this morning, she scrubbed the potatoes first and set them to boiling, then mixed biscuits for dinner. After she slipped the baking sheet into the oven and started the peas to simmering, she melted butter, stirred in flour, and added milk to make a white sauce for the peas and potatoes. What a treat that would be.

Barney barked, and she heard Astrid call the dog as she loped the horse to the barn. When she glanced out the door, she found the young man sound asleep in the rocking chair. His hat was tipped so far back on his head, a bit of breeze would lift it right off. A shock of dark brown hair fell over his forehead. He looked more like a rancher than a farmer in his Levi pants and full-sleeved shirt with no collar. No overalls with suspenders like most of the men she knew wore.

She watched as Astrid came into the yard, the squeak of the gate waking Mr. Landsverk. He started, grabbed his hat, and rose to his feet, hat clasped to his chest.

As soon as she saw him, Astrid stopped and a smile broke over her face as if she'd just seen an old friend. She mounted the stairs, her smile growing wider. "I'm Astrid Bjorklund."

When he introduced himself, Ingeborg knew they were in for a problem. The awe in his voice said it all. *I should have just sent him on his way.*

20

SHE WASN'T A WANTON.

Thank God for Dr. Elizabeth, who was willing to answer all her questions without making her feel embarrassed or like a ninny, as her mother had. But then, her mother had been embarrassed too, if the red on her face was a good indication. Elizabeth had been so matter-of-fact that Ellie felt perfectly comfortable. Relief flowed sweetly through her like the best spring water. She climbed the stairs to her room and slowly undressed.

The picnic last Sunday had been one of the most confusing days of her entire life. But one thing she knew for sure. Andrew Bjorklund could be a pain in the neck. Or as in this case, in the foot. When she took her shoe off, she saw that her foot was still bruised. No wonder it hurt. Although she'd not shown it to Elizabeth, she'd suggested she go home and soak it in cold water, which she had done, but the bruising and swelling had formed quickly.

Ellie hung up her clothes and slipped a nightdress over her head. Another two months and she would be in her own house, getting ready for bed, and getting along with Andrew. Surely all this would straighten out when they were married.

"I should have gone to him and apologized," she told the face in the mirror as she untied the bow that kept her hair back. Shaking her head, she ran her fingers through her hair, then reached for her hairbrush. One hundred strokes a night. Andrew loved her hair. He'd said so more than once. She let her mind rove as she brushed, thinking of Andrew at graduation, Andrew sticking up for her years earlier, Andrew showing her his barn, herself holding baby Inga, dreaming of having a baby of her own with Bjorklund blue eyes, yet being terrified every time she thought of a baby.

She glanced again into the mirror. *What would I look like with a fringe?*

"If the haying keeps on as it is, Haakan said we will have time before harvest to get your house up," Hjelmer told Ellie the following evening when they were sitting on the back porch enjoying the breeze that came up just in time to discourage the mosquitoes.

"Really?" Joy rushed from her toes to the tips of her fingers.

"Of course no rain during haying means the wheat fields are in bad need of moisture. That's one thing about farming. There's rarely enough of everything."

"According to the newspapers, the legislature figures the same." Penny closed her accounts book. "I sure wish they'd get after the railroads. Shipping costs are far too high, and if I'm feeling it, what about the farmers?"

"Haakan gets tight-lipped every time someone brings up the subject. You know the flour mill they've set up down by Valley City? He's talking of doing one here. Said if we can have a cheese house, why not a flour mill."

"Using river power? That's why the mills were built by the rapids in Minneapolis."

"No, steam engine. If steam can pull the trains, why not run the mill? That's what all milling will be based on one of these days. When

I was back in Minneapolis, I went and looked at the flour mills. I was thinking since many of the grain elevators were built by co-ops, why not a flour mill?"

"Who would have the money to do such a thing? It would cost thousands."

Hjelmer set his chair to rocking, his eyes narrowed, lost in thought.

Penny smiled at Ellie and raised one eyebrow as if to say "Men."

"How does a co-op work?" Ellie kept her voice down.

"Everyone contributes to the cost," Penny explained. "Our bank started that way. Many of the people of Blessing got together and pooled their money. Actually, the women started talking about it first. Hjelmer ran it for a time, and while he is still in charge, Mr. Valders runs it on a day-to-day basis. We used to vote on applications for loans, but now that there are so many more people around here, the board of directors makes those decisions."

"Who's on the board?"

"Haakan, Lars, Pastor Solberg, Mr. Moen, Hjelmer, and Mr. Valders. I think we should have a woman or two on the board, but so far that's not happened. All the shareholders elect people to the board."

"Is Andrew a shareholder?"

Penny nodded. "Anyone who has a savings account at the bank and is eighteen and over is a shareholder."

Ellie thought to the small amount of money she had saved in a leather drawstring bag and kept under her bed. Perhaps she should have that in the bank. "So women are shareholders too?"

"Yes. I am one because I own this store. Ingeborg owns her cheese house, and Bridget owns the boardinghouse. We have a good number of female-owned businesses here in town."

Hjelmer rejoined the conversation. "I think we should call a meeting of the grain elevator co-operative and do some real talking about a flour mill. Soon as haying is done and I get back from Bismarck, I'm going to Valley City and look over their mill. I heard they're thinking of building one in Dickinson too. There's enough wheat shipped out of the Red River Valley to run another mill."

"Right. One more reason for you to run off someplace." While Penny smiled, her tone wore a bite.

Ellie stared at Hjelmer. "You're not just fooling around with this idea, are you?"

He shook his head slowly. "Anything we can do to make things better for the farmers here, I'm in favor of."

"Where would you sell the flour?" Ellie squirmed inside, never liking it when people took potshots at each other.

"What's wrong with right here in the Dakotas? A lot of new people are coming in, and everyone needs flour." He nodded in time with the rocker. "If that Marquis de Mores could set up a beef-packing plant in Medora, we ought to be able to do a flour mill here."

"But remember he lost his shirt and the shirts of some heavy investors in all his schemes."

Hjelmer ignored his wife's rebuttal. "I think he was a man before his time. I talked with Theodore Roosevelt on one of his trips out there. He says more of us need to be far thinkers like de Mores. Shame the man didn't get along better with the local people."

"I read about how he named the town for his wife. I thought that was so romantic." Ellie sighed. "But I wonder if he really liked it when she went hunting with the men."

"She's known to be a better shot than he was, just like Ingeborg can outshoot all of us. That woman has an eye for shooting. That's for sure."

"That woman, as you so inelegantly put it, has an eye for all kinds of things. Who would have thought her cheese house would make Blessing known across the country, in spite of all the male naysayers? She sends cheese clear to New York and west to Seattle, where so many Norwegians have settled. Since she started making gammelost, she can't keep up with the orders."

"Next thing I know, you'll be keeping goats to make goat cheese."

Penny's laugh burst out, making even the children look to see what was happening. "Why do you think I started the store? I don't like milking cows, I don't like shoveling cow manure, and I don't want to do the same for goats either."

"Less to shovel."

"Hjelmer Bjorklund, if I have to have goats, you have to stay home to milk them." She muttered under her breath, "And that would be the day."

"Ellie could milk them."

Ellie shook her head. "Never did care for the smell of goats."

"Don't tease her, you big lug. You know that's why you went into blacksmithing and selling machinery."

"Not all of us are cut out to be farmers." He scratched his neck. "I'm helping with the haying only because of my good heart."

"Oh, please." Penny swatted his arm as she stood to call the children in for bed. "You are such a tease."

"Would you rather I went gambling again?"

"Just try it."

"Ah, Penny, my dear, all of life is a gamble, especially if you're farming or running a business—"

"Or running the state. Come on, Gustaf, Linnea. Bedtime."

Ellie went inside to light the kerosene lamps. A moth fluttered around the chimney, quickly joined by another. June bugs climbed the window screens and committed suicide against the doors. Big as they were, Ellie remembered the boys tying strings to the bugs and having pulling contests of tiny boxes of folded paper and tiny bits of wood. Andrew's bug always seemed to win.

He hadn't come by to apologize today either. Was he still mad at her? If it wasn't so late, she would walk out to the farm and tell him how sorry she was. But then, walking that far would make her foot hurt even more. She'd been limping around for several days as it was, and with every twinge she alternated between anger and sorrow.

After the children were in bed and Penny and Hjelmer were reading in the kitchen, Ellie said good-night and went upstairs to finish the letter to her mother. Taking tablet and pen, she sat down at the small table she used as a desk and let her thoughts roam. Would she and Andrew ever sit on their porch with company and have pleasant discussions like this one tonight? Who knew? She picked up the letter where she'd left off.

We had the most delightful, well, mostly delightful picnic out by the river Sunday. What wasn't delightful was that I caught my foot on a root across the trail and if Andrew hadn't saved me, I would have fallen flat on my face.

She decided not to include the argument with Andrew. After all there was no reason to upset her mother too.

Astrid and Ingeborg won the fishing contest, much to Trygve's disgust. He says they cheated by fishing together. It wasn't supposed to be teamwork. The ball game was fun to watch.

Even though Andrew had not been playing. Did thoughts of him have to intrude on everything?

The men and boys around here have turned into baseball fans, reading about the national teams that are playing and playing themselves, the few times they take off work. If the women have their way, there will be no more farming on Sundays. After all, that is the Lord's day. "And if He saw the need to rest, so do we." I'm quoting Ingeborg here, as if you didn't know. She told me again how she misses you and wishes you still lived here. As do I. That would make life about perfect.

Other than Andrew being so overbearing. *Has he always been like this?*

I enjoy working at the store and helping Penny with the house and children. I think I told you that before. Today the women met for quilting. I stayed at the store so Penny could go. I'm thinking they are working on a wedding-ring quilt for Andrew and me. No one said anything, but I caught the looks they gave each other. I'm sure I will be invited to the quilting bees when I am married and no longer one of the young girls.

I must say good-night and go on to bed. Oh, something interesting. Hjelmer and Haakan are thinking of starting a co-operative flour mill here. Pretty soon you won't recognize Blessing with all the new things going on. I love you, and give my love to the little ones. Pa too.

Your loving daughter,
Ellie

P.S. If Hans doesn't stop here on his way to you, tell him to make sure he does before he leaves again. I want to see him too.

EW

☙

She could have made it out here if she had wanted to. Andrew pushed his forehead into the flank of the cow he was milking. When it twitched its tail and caught him across the cheek with the brush of it, he huffed a sigh and lightened up on the pulling and squeezing. No sense taking his bad mood out on the cow. If she put her foot in the bucket, it would be his own fault.

Perhaps the fight with Ellie was all your fault. The little voice had whispered those same words more than once since Sunday. He'd heard them first thing every morning when he opened his eyes before daylight. He needed to ask his family's forgiveness too. Surely that had been drummed into his head often enough through the years. Maybe he needed a few hours at the woodpile to remind him.

He stripped the last milk from the cow's teats and rose from the three-legged stool, swinging the full bucket away from her feet as he stood.

"One more to go. You want her, or should I take her?" Trygve looked up from pouring the milk through the strainer and into a milk can.

"I will. You go on home."

"You going to work on the forms for the basement tonight?"

"For a while."

"I'll help you."

Andrew emptied his foaming pail. "Thanks, but you don't have to." He'd snapped at Trygve today too, and here his cousin was offering to help some more. Why did everyone have to be so good to him? They made him feel even worse.

"I know, but I like building things. You'll help me with my house someday."

"That I will." *I'll never be able to repay all the help people have given me. Now if only Ellie would come through that door.* He sat himself down at the final cow and, after washing bits of grass and leaves off her udder, planted his head in her flank and picked up the squeeze-and-pull rhythm again. One bad thing about milking cows, it gave one too much time to think. When guilt weighed heavy on his soul, thinking time was not comfortable.

Just apologize and get it over with. How many times have you heard Mor say that through the years?

"All right! I will! Just as soon as I finish here."

"What'd you say?" Trygve stopped pushing the flat shovel that cleaned out the gutter.

"Nothing. Just muttering." As soon as he finished, he poured the milk into the milk can, saving the last in the bottom for the barn cats. Barney sat wagging his tail in anticipation, so he set the pail down and let the dog lick out the bottom. Mor would scold him for that, but the cats did not appreciate the dog lapping out of their dish.

He and Trygve each took a side of the barn and, one by one, released the cows from their stalls. Head to tail they paraded out of the barn and over to the watering trough, got their drink, and ambled on out to pasture, limp udders swinging from side to side as they walked. Andrew watched them go. Always the same routine except in the winter when they were kept inside overnight. Did they ever get mad at each other and carry a grudge?

All the talk at the supper table circled around the visit from Joshua Landsverk.

"How many acres?" Andrew asked.

"Half a section, between five and six miles south of here."

"Beyond the Peterson place?"

"Ja, another two or three miles. He's not planted it this year. We could go cut the hay if we buy it."

"Why didn't he cut the hay?"

"Started to and just gave up. He's going to walk away from it."

"What did Lars say?"

"Buy it. We could split it, all kinds of ways to go."

"We can afford it." Ingeborg passed the meat platter around again. "Is it fenced?"

"I don't think so."

"How much does he owe the bank?" Andrew propped his chin on the heel of his hand.

"Not real sure. He paid the owner what he had in it and took over the mortgage."

"So we will buy the cows too." Ingeborg's tone made Andrew smile inside. His mor wasn't arguing on this one. More land, more cows.

"Is there a house?" Astrid joined the conversation.

"A shack more than a house and the same for the barn. I've seen the place. It will take some work. There's still sod that's not been broken. Will make good hay, but that's a long way to haul hay. We'll get it planted to wheat next year, then just go harvest it."

"It sounds to me like you've decided."

"If he will take a lump sum, and we take over the mortgage," Haakan said. "We could pay it off after harvest if all goes well."

"If all goes well." The same phrase one heard time after time. That and *Lord willing.* Andrew thought on them both while he chewed his

meat. Fried rabbit, thanks to Trygve and his snares. Tending the snares used to be his job before Trygve took it over, and soon it would pass on to Samuel. He was surprised Trygve hadn't given it up already.

Andrew cleaned the last of the gravy off his plate with a piece of biscuit. When he finished chewing, he cleared his throat. "I have something to say." His throat muscles tightened as the others looked at him.

"Ja?" Haakan nodded slowly.

"I ask you all to forgive me for the way I've been acting." His voice broke, but he kept on going. "You were right, Astrid. I have been rude and mean, and I'm sorry." He looked from face to face, and all he could see was love shimmering back at him. Tears glinted in his mother's eyes as she nodded her approval.

"Of course you are forgiven." Haakan was the first to answer. "That is good."

Astrid winked at him, raised her shoulders, and dropped them again in what was meant to mime surrender. "I guess so, but I sure hope you plan to ask Ellie's too. I hate it when people are mad at each other."

"Me too. Thank you." He pushed back his chair. "And now I better get over to work on those forms before dark falls. Trygve is coming to help."

"I am too, and I'm sure Lars will be there." Haakan drained the last from his coffee cup. "We buy that place, and it will mean another wait on your house."

"I figured that, but there isn't much land left to buy around here. Have to take what we can get."

Haakan clapped a hand on his son's shoulder. "Spoken like a true farmer."

"Don't forget Ellie," Astrid called as Andrew turned toward the door.

As if I could, just like I'd forget to breathe. "I won't."

The moon shone bright by the time he'd finished working and had walked on into Blessing. The lights were all out at the store. He'd been hoping she would still be up. Standing under her window, he whistled. Nothing. He picked up a couple of pebbles and tossed them gently to rattle against the windowpane. He waited—nothing.

"Come on, Ellie, please wake up. I couldn't come earlier." He tossed more pebbles. One went through the open window and clattered on the floor. "Hjelmer will never let me live this down if he comes out."

He leaned over to find some more small stones when a giggle floated down. He straightened and smiled up at her.

"What are you doing here at this hour?" Her whisper drifted on the breeze.

He swallowed hard. "I came to ask you to forgive me. Will you please?"

"Oh, Andrew."

"Well?" Dare he ask her to come down?

"Yes, I'll forgive you if you forgive me."

He could hear the tears in her voice. Had she had as bad a time as he? "For what? You weren't the one being so contrary."

"I could have agreed to go fishing."

"Ja. How is your foot?" To think he had let her limp off that way.

"It's getting better."

"Forgive me for that, too?"

"Oh yes, Andrew. Don't let's ever argue again."

"We won't."

"Yes, you will." Hjelmer's voice cut into their whispers. "Andrew, go on home. It's late."

"Yes, sir." Andrew blew his love a kiss and took off running. Ellie forgave him. Her laughter floated right over his shoulder. He leaped into the air and whooped his joy.

Now if he could just get that house up so they could be married.

21

Mixing cement was a grimy job.

"Last batch for tonight." Haakan raised his voice to be heard over the rush and scrape of cement poured from the wheelbarrow into the wall form for the cellar of Andrew's house. All they could get poured each evening was half a wall.

"Good thing you built these forms in smaller sections." Lars tamped solid the last of the pour.

"Pa said to." Andrew scraped the drying cement from his shovel, then rammed it up and down in a pail of water to wash the residue away. They had two walls finished and needed to bring in some more rock and gravel.

"Amazing thing to have to travel west to the gravel quarry." Haakan raised his hat to wipe the sweat away with his handkerchief. "Most people have to haul away the rocks or at least pile them up so they have enough good soil to plant in. When they homesteaded here, all they saw was miles of horse-high prairie grass. No idea what kind of soil lay under it. That's what Ingeborg told me."

"Talked with a man from out west. He said those smart Norwegians took all the good soil, left the rocky land for the others."

"I don't know so much about smart. We just got here first. Or at least Roald and Carl did. I'm ever grateful to those first Bjorklund men who homesteaded so wisely." Haakan washed off his shovel and the heavy iron bar they used to tamp the cement in amongst the gravel.

"And the wives they left behind." Lars followed Haakan as he strode up the ramp to ground level. Andrew knew the stories of the terrible winter that took both his far, his onkel Carl, and the two babies, because Ingeborg had told them many times. He'd been a baby, but Thorliff, at five, remembered, too.

"Thorliff said he put so many windows in his house because he never wanted to live in the dark again like the soddy."

"Better than that tar-paper shack Landsverk is living in. Don't know how he kept from freezing to death last winter."

"Or burning it down like that fellow over at Park River. Got the chimney so hot the roof caught on fire, and it was gone in a minute. The soddies were cooler in summer than most of our houses today—when they were built right."

The three men walked across the fields to their houses, going around the wheat fields instead of through them.

"What do you think of this new scheme of Hjelmer's?" Lars asked.

"Be a good thing if we can find a way to pay for it."

"He's convinced it will pay for itself in five years or less."

"I know, but you still have to have money to build it. You want to run it?"

"No." Lars nudged Andrew with his elbow. "What about you?"

"All I've ever wanted to do is farm. You know that."

"We need someone real experienced in milling and someone real good with a steam engine. You could run that engine, Lars. You've kept ours humming for years and rebuilt them when they needed it."

"I know. I thought about it. Where do you think we should put it?"

"Near the railroad track in Blessing would be central. Right by the elevator, I'd imagine, if there's enough room there. But I don't think our bank has enough money to handle an undertaking like this. Hjelmer says he'll find the money, but at what kind of interest?"

Andrew listened to the discussion but had nothing to add to it. Providing milk for his mother's cheese house was more to his liking, along with raising the hogs on the leftovers from the cheese process. He had four sows so far with two more to farrow. They should have a good crop of butcher-sized hogs come fall. Which reminded him—it was getting past time for cutting all the boars.

"How much more hay to cut?" he asked.

"Another ten acres at Solbergs' and we should be done. Unless we buy that new piece."

"I thought you made up your mind." Andrew leaned down to pet Barney, who'd come running to greet them.

"Guess I have, but doubts still creep in. Told Landsverk I'd let him know tomorrow. All Ingeborg can think about is more cows and land to grow grain and hay for them. Night, Lars."

Haakan and Andrew stopped at the wash bench and, after cleaning up, left their boots on the porch before pausing at the water bucket for a long drink.

"The coffee can be hot in a minute if you'd like." Ingeborg's voice came from the parlor, where the sound of the spinning wheel announced what she was doing. "Do you want some strawberry and rhubarb pie?"

"Does a cow moo?" Haakan continued on into the parlor and settled into his rocking chair. "Ah, now this feels mighty good."

Andrew stuck some wood into the fire and pulled the coffeepot forward. "Hey, isn't Samuel supposed to be keeping the woodbox full?"

"He filled it earlier, and then I made the pie."

"Where's Astrid?"

"Over to Elizabeth's. And don't ask why."

"Why not?"

"Just because."

Andrew wandered into the parlor. "Is Ellie there too?"

"I don't know." She frowned at him. "Sometimes it is better not to ask questions."

"Give it up, son. She's not going to tell you. You're going to have to learn that at times, especially when an important event is coming, you don't question anything. You just eat your pie and go to bed."

Andrew started to ask what important event, then clamped his mouth shut. *The wedding.* "I'll get the coffee."

"Half a pie is not considered a piece," warned Ingeborg.

"There are two of them."

"I know. I want some for tomorrow too."

"Fours?"

"Fives."

Andrew threw his father a glance and returned to the kitchen. Nobody made pies as good as his mor. Maybe Ellie should take lessons. Not that her pies were not good. They just didn't quite measure up to what he was used to. Astrid had learned well, so he knew Mor could pass on the knack.

He cut the pie and, sliding each piece onto a plate, took them into the parlor. "I'll get the coffee as soon as it's hot." He handed his mother hers.

"Thank you, Andrew. That was kind of you."

"You look pretty busy. This year's wool or last's?"

"Last. I washed the first of the fleece today. Wish I had some sheepskins with the wool on. We haven't kept any like that for a long time."

"Come butchering time we'll have some. What do you want to make?" Haakan scraped the last of his pie from the plate. "Mange takk, wife. That hit the spot."

"Oh, the coffee." Andrew headed for the kitchen. "Don't touch my pie."

"Now, who would ever do that?" False innocence dripped from Haakan's voice.

"Mor!"

"You better bring yourself another piece."

Andrew delivered the coffee, giving his father a stern but entirely useless glare.

"Mange takk," Haakan responded with a chuckle. He raised his cup in salute.

Andrew rolled his eyes and shook his head. "I think I feel a *tsk* coming on." He sat down to finish his new piece of pie, not a bad deal since he'd eaten more than half of the other piece. Then holding his coffee cup in both hands, he let his gaze blur over the rim so he could imagine his finished house and barn—Ellie hanging clothes on the line, Ellie with her golden hair blowing in the wind that dried the sheets almost as fast as one hung them up. He knew she left her hair down for him while many of the young women wore theirs braided in a coronet like his mor's or tucked neatly into a bun at the base of the neck, or at least tied back along the top. He liked Ellie's best with combs picking up the sides. How beautiful she was, slim like a willow branch that bent and danced in the wind. Ellie. His Ellie.

He pushed himself to his feet. It seemed their wedding would never come. For the first time in years, he couldn't wait for harvest to start. But they had to get through haying first.

Haakan sat in his chair, chin on his chest, the coffee cup on the floor beside him. Ingeborg continued to hum along with her spinning, the spindle filling with yarn, even and strong. Like everything she did, his mor spun the nicest yarn. Not that he was any judge, but he'd heard others complimenting her.

"Good night."

"Good night, Andrew. It's so good to have you back."

He leaned over and kissed her forehead.

"Why, how nice. Thank you for that too." Ingeborg patted his cheek.

"I'm the one who has much to be thankful for. I'm sorry I don't say so more often. That pie was the best."

He'd planned to write Ellie a note. Funny, or perhaps not funny but strange, here they were living only a mile from each other, and they hardly had any time together at all. Unless he went there now and called to her window like he had the night before. Instead, he crawled into bed. There was too much to do to go out again tonight. Eating pie had taken the time away.

❧

As soon as they finished up with the Solbergs' hay, they headed on over to the newly purchased farm. What had been sowed to wheat the year before was nothing but weeds, needing to be plowed again for the next spring. The hayfields were almost too dry. Sophie and Grace drove the cook wagon to see if they could handle the work. With Mrs. Sam cooking at the boardinghouse, she would not be able to cook for the threshing crew this year. The girls' laughter and teasing almost made up for the food—almost but not quite.

"If you two want to drive the wagon for the threshing crew, you're going to have to get up earlier and cook longer. We'll have three times as many men along then as now." Lars mopped the gravy up with a piece of bread.

"I know that now." Sophie sat on the wagon tongue, her elbows on her knees. "It sounded pretty simple when Ma told us about it."

Grace leaned against the wheel. "I'd rather be home milking cows."

"Ilse said she'd do this."

"But she can't for harvest."

Andrew listened to the discussion. He'd been on the rake, and his rear hurt from the metal seat. He'd rather be home milking too. Now that was a chore he enjoyed. While the yield on this place didn't come up to that at home, it would be a good addition after some plowing and fertilizing.

They'd been lucky to get it.

He could have finished pouring the cellar walls had he been at home. Only half of one to finish. Patience. Easy to say and difficult to do—especially at a time like this.

"We'll announce the house raising for Saturday, if that's all right with you." Haakan rode beside Andrew on one of the loaded hay wagons, pulling the mower behind.

Andrew grinned over his shoulder. "You mean it?"

"Ja, we got a break here. The wheat's not ready yet."

Andrew nodded. *Do not leap off the wagon and run all the way home,* he ordered himself. But three more days.

He glanced to the west to catch heat lightning fracturing the sky. "Storm's coming."

"I know. You can smell it. We sure need rain, but I'm hoping for a gentle two-day pour to water everything good."

"But not knock all the wheat down." Or hail. The last thing they needed right now was a hailstorm. They drove into the yard in front of his barn at the same time as the first drops fell. Thunder rolled far off, the earth grumbling for a faster drink.

"Let's get as much up into the barn as we can." Haakan swung down and unhitched the mower. "Take that team around to the back to pull the loads up."

As soon as the prongs came within reach, Haakan sunk them into the hay and hollered, "Take her up!"

The first load shifted, then lifted in the giant teeth and creaked its way to the top pulley before whooshing into the loft. Andrew pulled the release line, the load dropped, and the prongs clanged together again as the ropes hummed to start all over again.

Miraculously, the rain held off after the first spatter. They emptied the one wagon, and the waiting team pulled the next wagon into place. Lightning flashed closer this time, and thunder waited before answering. But when it crashed instead of rumbled, Andrew knew it was close. He could see through the haymow door that the sky had darkened. Another load whooshed in and dropped.

The clouds opened and rain poured down. The men on the load straightened the hay as much as they could to provide run off and slid to the ground. They all gathered inside the barn door and watched.

"Most likely have to unload that and let it dry out." Lars leaned against the doorjamb.

"I'm grateful it isn't hailing." Haakan took off his hat and lifted his face to the mist blowing in. "We'll let it dry and restack it later. We can bring those two stacks home after harvest or during the winter. Be easy to do on the sledge."

Leave it to Haakan, always putting the best face on things. Andrew studied his pa standing so easy in the doorway. Here he'd been thinking how bad it was the load was getting wet, and Haakan was counting his blessings—no hail, extra hay, they got most of it in, gardens needed rain. The rain let up as the thunder and lightning moved off to the east. They weren't going to get the soaking they were hoping for. One of the horses snorted and stamped a foot.

"I'll unhitch the team and take them on home."

"Yeah, we'll get the others." Haakan stepped outside and looked to the west. "Might drizzle a bit longer, but the main storm's beyond us. Let's get going."

If I'd gotten the corral built, they could stay here. Another one of those pesky ifs. He hooked the traces up on the rump pad and hupped the horses forward, away from the doubletree and wagon tongue.

"I've got the other team," Trygve called from the back of the barn. "Let's go."

Andrew swung up on one of his team. "Come on, Pa, let's ride 'em home."

"You think I'm too old to mount a horse anymore?" Haakan asked.

"Well?"

Haakan grabbed the horns on the collar and swung up. Or rather tried to. His feet slipped, and he straightened back up.

"You want a leg up?" Andrew grinned at his pa.

"Just give me a minute. I'll make it."

Lars rode up with the fourth team. "Need some help?"

Haakan glared at them both and swung again, this time hooking his heel in the rump pad and pulling himself up. "Gotten out of practice, I guess."

"I guess so." Andrew ducked as Haakan swatted at him with the end of the lines.

Three more days and they'd get the house up. Andrew glanced back over his shoulder. The half load of hay stood forlorn in front of the barn, the only indication someone would be living there soon, other than the hole in the ground with almost all the cellar walls in. For certain he wouldn't be pouring cement tonight.

"Wonder if they started milking yet." Haakan pulled his hat farther down on his head as the breeze kicked up.

While at first the rain had felt good, now Andrew shivered from the chilly wind. His shirt lay plastered to his skin. He nudged his team to a trot. "Come on, boys, let's get on home."

Three more days and the house goes up. His thoughts kept time with the clippety-clop of heavy hooves. Three more days and he'd see Ellie. Unless, of course, he unharnessed the team and rode one on into Blessing. But there were cows to milk. Always something needing doing. Keeping him away from Ellie.

The sun was out by the time they'd finished milking.

"Well, it was better than nothing," Haakan said with a sigh, "but that didn't do a whole lot more than wash the air clean."

"At least it didn't hail," Andrew added, his thoughts jumping back to Ellie. What was she doing right now? Thinking of him as he was thinking of her?

22

I WONDER IF THEY GOT BACK *from haying before the rain hit.*

Ellie stared out at the rain-washed streets. It was well into July, and this was the first rain in over a month. Had it lasted long enough to do her garden much good? She'd not paid a lot of attention to the rain before, but she'd never had a garden of her own before either. Even though she'd helped her mother with the family garden, this was different. It was hers, or rather *theirs.* Hers and Andrew's. She'd been out hoeing the corn the night before and picked the peas, although there weren't enough to do more than eat right in the garden yet.

"Ellie, could you please take the cake out of the oven for me?" Penny called from the store.

"Of course." Ellie plucked a straw from the broom and broke it into smaller pieces. Then opening the oven door, she stuck the bit of straw into the cake, which had risen nicely. Nothing on the straw when she checked it. Using her apron folded over to keep from burning her hand, she pulled the cake pan out and set it on the reservoir, then closed the oven door. She dug out the cooling rack and set the pan on it on the table. Ah, nothing smelled better than a cake just out of the oven, except perhaps bread or cookies, but right now the cake held her attention.

She slid the stew, which had been cooking on top of the stove, into the oven and started the biscuits. Since Hjelmer had left that morning for Bismarck, supper would be a more simple meal—chicken stew with a biscuit topping. The last of the strawberries would go over the cake.

"Ellie, will you fix Gertie?" Linnea held up the cloth doll her mother had made.

"What's the matter?"

"Gustaf ate her eyes."

"Ate them?"

"He said he did."

"Tell him to come see me."

The little girl scampered off.

Ellie stared at the doll. Sure enough, the button eyes were missing, and the yarn hair needed rebraiding.

When Gustaf charged into the kitchen, she held up the doll. "You didn't really eat the buttons—did you?"

He stared at his big toe, then grinned up at her. He shook his head and dug into his pocket, producing the two buttons.

"So why tease her like that?"

He shrugged, his eyes big, and shook his head.

"Promise me you won't tease her like that again."

He sighed and twitched his mouth from side to side. "All right."

"Go get my sewing kit and, to make her feel better, push her in the swing."

"Do I hafta?"

"Yes. Perhaps it will help remind you to not tease your little sister."

He gave her a kicked-puppy look, one he was very good at, and turned toward the stairs.

"Where are you going?"

"To get your sewing box."

"It's in the parlor by the rocking chair. And when you get done swinging your sister, I need more wood in the woodbox. She can help you do that." Ellie knew that would cheer him up. Any chance to boss his little sister made him puff up like a rooster. Most of the time she didn't blame him for teasing Linnea. She always got really upset, fun for any older brother to see. Hans used to tease Ellie until Andrew told him he mustn't do that anymore. Both Thorliff and Hans had teased Andrew for that, but he never backed down. Andrew—always her champion.

"Thank you." She took the sewing box and, after laying biscuits on top of the stew, sat down to sew the eyes back in place. Gertie needed a bath, that was for sure.

"You are so good with them." Penny slumped into the chair beside her. "I don't know how I will take care of a new baby and these two and the store." She laid a hand on the small mound under her apron. "That is, if I can carry this baby to term."

Ellie wanted to ask how many babies Penny had lost, but knowing what a painful subject that was, she kept her own counsel. "Perhaps I will be able to help through the fall anyway. Surely there is someone else in the family who wants to come from Norway. Or maybe Rebecca Baard would like to help you."

"She's pretty busy helping Dorothy and Knute. Their little Swen never has done good. He's two and can't even sit up yet. Good thing Rebecca and Gus are living with their brother. Makes it easier for everyone."

"How come Mr. Valders never helps you in the store anymore?"

"He's busy with the bank, and he keeps accounts for more people all the time, especially the grain elevator. He likes bookkeeping, and he's good at it. Of course Hildegunn likes it better that he manages the bank rather than clerking in the store." Penny's grin took the sting out of her words.

"No changes there, eh? What about Gerald? Couldn't he help in the store?"

"Possibly. But ever since he came back from the war, he's been sickly. The malaria hits him again and again. Puts him back in bed, which makes him undependable. I feel sorry for him. He's a good man. I think you've spoiled me."

Ellie tied off the last knot on the button and began finger combing the doll's yarn hair so she could braid it again. "Supper will be ready pretty quick."

The bell tinkled over the front door of the store, and Penny heaved herself to her feet. "I'm putting out the Closed sign as soon as this customer leaves."

Ellie went ahead setting the table outside and keeping an eye on the children as they hauled in wood for the woodbox, Linnea one or two sticks at a time, Gustaf handing her light pieces.

"You got to be careful." Gustaf's voice came through the open door.

Hearing Linnea screaming, Ellie went to check. "What happened?" She scooped Linnea up into her arms.

"She dropped a piece of wood on her toe. I warned her."

Ellie inspected the abused toe and comforted the little girl. "It's not bleeding. You'll be all right."

"Gustaf hurt me."

"I'm sure it was an accident."

"Where's Ma?"

"She's busy in the store right now."

Linnea sniffed again and scrubbed away her tears with balled fists. "Put me down, please."

Ellie set her down again and handed her the doll that once again had two button eyes, its braided hair tied with a piece of yarn.

"Oh, look." Linnea held up the doll. "You fixed her." Her head nodded up and down while a smile beamed from eyes still damp with tears.

"Go tell your brother to wash up for supper, and you wash too."

"Will you help me?" She tucked her doll under her arm and headed for the washing bench. "Gustaf, come eat."

They were just drying their hands when Penny came out the door. "Now, that was one nice young man."

"Who?"

"Joshua Landsverk. He sold his place to Haakan and, once he got his money, came by to pay off his bill here. When I heard he was leaving, I sort of wrote it off, thinking there's another bad debt. But he came by and paid up."

"Where's he going?"

"Said back home, to Iowa or Ohio, I think. His girl was supposed to come out so they could get married. But she never showed up, and then the grasshoppers got his wheat. He sold his cows to Ingeborg." Penny grinned. "He's one fine-looking man, that I can tell you."

"Penny!"

"Well, I've got eyes God gave me to see with. And when He made beautiful men or women, I think we should appreciate His creation, just like we would a fine sunset or a gorgeous flower. Loving my husband doesn't affect my eyesight."

Ellie smiled back, then chuckled. The two looked at each other again and burst into laughter.

"What's so funny?" Gustaf asked.

"You wouldn't understand." Penny tried to be serious, but Ellie's giggle did her in. They finally figured they'd better not look at each other so they could quit laughing. So they each looked away. "My," Penny said at last, "that was better than a good cry." She wiped her eyes. "Not that I'm not crying anyway."

"Me too. I'll get the supper on the table. You just sit there."

As dusk softened the edges of the land, Ellie kept hoping that Andrew would come by before dark. Then she hoped he would come before bedtime. Then she fell asleep so fast she had no more time to hope.

❧

In the morning as she was fixing breakfast she heard a horse lope into town and stop at the store. *Please, Lord, not an emergency.* But when Andrew's face smiled at her through the screen door, she pushed the door open and stepped into his hug. "I was hoping you'd come last night. Of course I've hoped that every night, but I know you are so busy."

"We didn't get back until just before the rain—got one wagonload up into the haymow and part of the other."

"I know . . . then you had to milk cows."

"Ja, and then I wanted to come, but . . ." He paused and kissed her forehead, then her lips. "I have such good news."

"What?" She leaned her cheek against his chest so she could hear his heart.

"Three more days. Well, just two more now."

"And what?"

"Guess."

"Andrew Bjorklund, I hate guessing games."

"You'll like the answer."

"We are getting married next week."

"No." He shook his head. "Not that I don't want to, but I agreed."

"I told you I don't like guessing games. Now what?" She stamped her foot just the slightest.

"Saturday we are having a house raising. Our house. I'll finish the last wall of the cellar today."

"Oh, Andrew, really?" She stared up at him to see if he was teasing. He wasn't. "Our house. We're going to have a house right soon."

"What's that I hear?" Penny asked.

"Saturday we're having a house raising. Everyone is invited." Andrew tucked Ellie under his arm. "Where's Hjelmer?"

"He left for Bismarck yesterday."

"He said he'd help."

"You know he's all excited about the flour mill. He went to see if he could find investors. Have you had breakfast?"

"Yes. I'm going around to let everyone know about the house raising."

"We'll be there. Wouldn't miss it. I'll see if I can get Mr. Valders to mind the store, or else I'll just put up the Closed sign."

Ellie stared at Penny, sure her jaw was dropping open. Penny never closed the store except on Sunday.

"I need to go. Lots of people to call on." Andrew kissed the tip of her nose. "See you Saturday." With that he leaped off the porch and ran around the house, waving to her as he went.

"I'd say that is one happy young man."

Ellie stared after him. "I'd say you are right."

The church bell ringing jerked her out of a sound sleep. Fire. It had to be a fire when dark still reigned. She leaned out the window to hear someone yelling, "Prairie fire! Prairie fire!" While she couldn't tell from which direction the fire was burning, she could smell the smoke.

Pulling her nightdress over her head, she dressed in two minutes and headed down the stairs, braiding her hair as she went.

Penny met her at the bottom of the stairs. "Get the rugs. I'll grab the shovels."

"What about the children?"

"Oh! I forgot about them."

"You stay here. You needn't be out beating out a fire. I'll get a ride with someone." Ellie wrapped a cloth around her hair.

"But . . ."

"No, listen. You shouldn't be inhaling all that smoke. Everyone will be needing coffee and food."

"True."

Ellie dug leather work gloves out of the basket.

"Take a jacket to protect your arms from sparks."

Ellie did as she was told and, carrying her tools, stepped out into the night. She could hear a wagon coming and ran around the building to flag a ride. "Thanks," she said and climbed into the back of the wagon with the Lincolns.

Sam clucked the horses into a fast trot, and they headed west.

"You ever fought a prairie fire?" Mrs. Sam asked over the racket of the wagon.

"No, but I know that every hand is needed. I made Penny stay back."

"Good girl."

Other wagons joined them along the road, and riders on horseback galloped on by. The smoke billowed up ahead and already stung their eyes. Flickering red and yellow showed the fire line, with people already outlined against the light, flailing the ground, tossing dirt with shovels. A team pulling a drag worked on the area the men had plowed earlier.

"Over here," a voice hollered off to the north.

They all bailed out of the wagon and ran across the prairie.

"If we can stop it before it gets to our fire break, we can keep it from jumping."

The wind blew sparks that blazed in the dry grass. Ellie took her rug and slammed it against a small blaze. A couple more hits and the flame was out. Paying no attention to those around her, she concentrated on beating out flare-ups. Her arms weighed a hundred pounds each and her back screamed in agony, but like the others, she coughed and kept on.

"Ellie, over here," Andrew called from behind her. Good thing she could hear him, because her eyes were running so, she could hardly see. She turned and stumbled into his arms.

"Stay by me." He spoke right in her ear.

A nod was all she could accomplish.

Back, ever backward, the wind, smoke, and flames drove them. Word came down the long line of firefighters to go east of the firebreak and try to keep it from jumping the firebreak. Off in the west they could see a haystack burning—and a building. Ellie stumbled over the rough clods of the area disked to kill off the vegetation. Sparks landed all around them, igniting the dry grass almost immediately, but here they could stamp those out before they flamed.

"Ellie!"

She looked off to her left. Andrew came running and brushed off her back. "You were smoldering. You've got to be careful."

She coughed and nodded and continued swatting flare-ups with the rug and stamping out the smaller ones. If only it would rain. *God, send us rain.* Someone had said heat lightning most likely started the blaze.

Even with the smoke, the sky looked lighter, and with dawn the wind dropped.

The fire gobbled and grabbed every blade on the west side of the firebreak, but only bits and pieces of gray showed on the east. The railroad line stopped the inferno from going farther south.

A team and wagon came trotting from town, Penny and Bridget waving from the wagon seat. "Water, coffee, sandwiches—any takers?"

While a few men remained to guard the line, most of the fire-fighters congregated around the wagon, chugging water and coffee, wolfing the sandwiches, then moving back to let those guarding have a break and a chance to eat.

"Thank God we took the time to plow and disk the firebreak" were the words heard most often.

"Haakan, you gave wise advice." Pastor Solberg clapped him on the shoulder.

"Read it in a newspaper, and since we didn't have a really large area to protect, it made sense. I'm thinking we should make it a yard or two wider. That wind sure was pushing sparks."

"Since my place would have been one of the first to go, I can't thank you enough."

"Well, Pastor, like you've said so many times, God's family has to pull together. And we do." Haakan wiped his blackened face with his shirtsleeve.

"If we'd gotten that fire wagon instead of just talking about it, we could have saved that shed," Lars put in.

"I'll look into it," Haakan promised, "but everyone is going to have to donate to pay for it."

Ellie's gaze followed what her ears heard. Gerald Valders was coughing so hard he collapsed and had to be loaded into the wagon to go back to town to see Dr. Elizabeth.

While she felt lightheaded from the smoke and from coughing, she stood drinking her coffee with the others, all black of face and filthy with smoke and dirt.

"If we aren't a sight." Sophie pointed to Ellie. "I must look just like you, and that's pretty bad."

Penny handed Ellie a sandwich. "I have plenty of warm water at home. We'll stand you in the washtub and pour it right over you."

Ellie nodded and took a bite of her sandwich. She could see Andrew with other men back prowling the fire line. What if no one had wakened and rung the bell? Would the firebreak have held all those flames back?

～✑

The prairie fire was the main topic of conversation on Saturday, when those who could gathered to raise Andrew and Ellie's house.

Ellie wished her ma and pa were there to help with the house raising, but she'd have had to send them a telegram, and she figured the scare of that would take all the pleasure from it. Besides, they couldn't get there until afternoon anyway.

The walls went up so fast the women didn't have dinner ready when the men said it was time to eat. Before they needed to leave for chores, the entire two-story house was framed, the roof ready for shakes, the windows in, and some of the siding on.

"Thank you, everyone," Andrew said to each as the families loaded into their wagons and headed on home, everyone amazed at the progress.

"Well, son, I never would have believed it if I didn't see it." Haakan clapped Andrew on the shoulder.

"Me either. Two stories and the cellar. We can start adding the porch on tomorrow."

"As many as can will be coming back. You should be able to move in soon. Where's Ellie?"

"She took Penny and the children home. I don't think Penny was feeling well."

"As well, let's get the tools put away and get to the milking. Cows wait for no man."

"I'll be right there." Andrew picked up a couple of pieces of siding and threw them on the trash pile, as they were too small to be used. With most of the pieces cut in the factory, there had been little sawing this day. He walked through the house one more time. Tomorrow they'd build the stairway. Whoever would have thought a house could go up so fast? Shame that Ellie couldn't be here to enjoy this moment with him. He smiled to himself. He had a couple of pictures of kitchen stoves. He would leave it up to her to pick the one she wanted. They'd order that together. He'd learned his lesson about ordering anything for the house before asking her. He leaped to the ground and joined his pa, gathering tools and putting them in the boxes to keep the dew off.

As they walked across the fields to the homeplace, he looked back once. *My house. My own place. Mine and Ellie's.* Someone had brought her an apple tree sapling. She'd planted it on a corner of the garden, the garden now entirely free of weeds thanks to some enterprising women.

"It's only a house, son," Haakan said gently. "It'll be up to you and Ellie to make it a home. You know what I mean?"

"I guess so." Andrew paused. "But if I don't, I sure expect I'll be learning it soon." *And moving in can't come soon enough.*

23

"Mor, you need to come."

"What? Astrid, what is it?" Ingeborg blinked and tried to focus. "I thought you were staying at Elizabeth's tonight."

"I was. But I came home to get you. Penny is having a problem, and Elizabeth is over there. She wants your help too."

Ingeborg's feet hit the floor, and she was dressing as Astrid finished speaking.

"What's going on?" Haakan asked, his voice soft in the darkness.

"Elizabeth has gone to care for Penny, and she wants Mor."

"I'll harness the buggy."

"I have Thorliff's buggy here. I'll take Mor."

"Can I get you anything?"

"No. Go back to sleep. I'll let you know what's happening." Ingeborg's prayers circled higher as she left the house and climbed into the buggy. "What time is it?"

"I have no idea." Astrid clucked the horse into a trot and out the lane. "We'd all gone to sleep, and sometime later I heard a pounding at the door. Thorliff answered and away we went."

"She's losing the baby?"

"I'm thinking that's it. Penny never said anything about an injury, but they left early from the house raising. I feel so sad for her."

"I know. She's lost so many." Just the words brought back Ingeborg's own pain at losing her baby. And after Astrid she'd never had any more. But Penny had two children, so what was causing her to lose so many? She was healthy, strong. Why could some women carry babies with no trouble and others couldn't? And so many died in childbirth. Metiz had said that more white women died in childbirth than Indian women. Why was that? It was easy to get overloaded with questions that seemed to have no answers in the middle of the night. Like weeping that tarried for the night, but the promise said joy comes with the morning. There would most likely be no joy for Penny come morning.

As soon as they walked in the door, Penny held out her arms. "Oh, Ingeborg, I'm losing another one. Why does God want my babies in heaven before they can grow up to be people?"

Ingeborg, tears streaming down her face, held the younger woman in her arms, and they cried together before another spasm wracked Penny's body. *I don't know why. All I know is how much it hurts.* Two or three more contractions, and the tiny baby slipped into a world it would never know.

While Elizabeth went about her doctoring duties, Ingeborg rocked Penny in her arms as if she were holding a child. Glancing over, she saw Ellie, both hands clamped over her mouth, her eyes wide, face white, even in the dim light. Something was wrong. Was it more than Penny losing the baby?

"I want Tante Agnes, but God took her too. Doesn't He want me to have anyone?" Penny moaned.

Ingeborg looked over their patient to see Elizabeth shaking her head and sniffing back tears too. There was no need to remind Penny she had two healthy children, a husband, and all the rest of her family. All she needed right now was someone to hold her and cry with her.

"And Hjelmer, he's never here when I need him." She was sobbing so hard that the bed shook.

"Astrid, help me change the bed now," Elizabeth ordered. "Ellie, please go make sure the children are still asleep and heat some milk." While Ingeborg helped move Penny around, they changed the sheets. Ellie returned with some heated milk, and Penny drank it when told to and collapsed back into Ingeborg's arms.

"I added a bit of laudanum to that, so she should sleep soon. That will help take the edge off." Elizabeth spoke softly.

"Was my baby a boy or a girl?"

"A girl."

"Her name is Agnes. And I want her to be buried next to my tante Agnes."

"We'll take care of that." Elizabeth looked at Ingeborg.

"Haakan will build a little box," Ingeborg said, nodding.

"Mange takk, Ingeborg. You are so good to me." She buried her face in her hands. "I want my baby."

Ingeborg shifted to the chair that Astrid placed beside the bed and held Penny's hand until she slept. "Is there any answer to why?"

Elizabeth shook her head. "I'm sure there is, but I don't know it. Someday I hope we know more about these things, but right now all I can say is 'The Lord gave, and the Lord hath taken away; blessed be the name of the Lord.'"

"The Bible says He weeps with us in our sorrow." Ingeborg stroked the hair back from Penny's face, which no longer dripped with perspiration.

"But, Mor, there has to be a reason." Astrid knelt beside her mother and laid her cheek on her mother's knee.

"My mother used to say, 'God made it so, and so it is.' I was never happy to hear that, because I knew she'd offer no other answer." Ingeborg beckoned Ellie to come join them.

"You've always said that to me too, but I don't think God does things without a reason."

"I know. But I don't believe God does all this. Sin and evil are loose in this world."

"But we have Easter. The Bible says Jesus defeated sin when He rose from the dead."

"I know, but think how often we choose to sin anyway." Ingeborg leaned over and kissed her daughter's temple. "God promises to always be with us, to walk through the valleys with us, to be our shepherd, our comforter."

Ellie sat on the edge of the bed, her arms wrapped around her middle, as if holding herself together. "But He could have stopped this baby from dying. He could have done so for my mother too."

"He could have, but He didn't. And we don't know why. People have been asking that same question since time began. I did when I lost the baby. I did when I never had any more. I do now, too, but I know for certain God is welcoming that baby home at the same time as He is comforting us who remain behind."

"How is He comforting us?"

"With each other. We hug, we cry, we hold each other. We're here to listen and to love. We're God's hands right here in Blessing." Ingeborg wrapped her arms around both Astrid and Ellie. "And we rejoice for all the babies who live and grow up fine and strong like you."

Astrid turned to look out the window. "Dawn is coming."

"Ja, the night tarries, but the sun always rises. That's my daily reminder that God overcomes the dark. Like the sun, He is here always. Even when we can't see Him, we know He is here and that, if we wait, we will sense and feel Him again."

Elizabeth went to stand at the window, her hands cupping her elbows. "We're having a pink and gold sunrise. Thank you for coming, Ingeborg. I need to be reminded of the sun in the sky and the Son of our heavenly Father. And that I'm not the one defeating death. He is. I'm just one of His servants, doing the best I can and leaving the rest in His hands."

Ingeborg rose and, taking Astrid and Ellie with her, went to stand by Elizabeth. She wrapped her arms around them all, and they stood for a while, arms entangled, watching the gold rim of the sun inch above the horizon and then spring into the air, heralded by birdsong.

"My dear daughters, I prayed for years for more babies, but He gave me full-grown daughters instead. I thank Him daily for each one

of you, and I pray that you will grow to know Him better day by day."
Tears slipped down her cheeks, matching the ones on their faces.
"And now, Lord God, fill us with your peace and bring healing to our
dear Penny. In Jesus' mighty name, amen."

Elizabeth stepped back to the bed to check on her patient.

Ellie hugged her soon-to-be mother-in-law one more time. "I'll
go make breakfast."

"I need to get on home," Ingeborg said. "Astrid, you want to take
me? Or I could walk."

"You take her, Astrid," Elizabeth said. "Then take the buggy back
to our house. I'll go feed Inga and come back later to check on Penny.
Thorliff's probably ready to bring her over here by now."

"I'm surprised we haven't heard her screaming." Ingeborg patted
Elizabeth's cheek. "You have a beautiful daughter. I hope I can come
by in the next day or so and be with her for a while. Or you can bring
her out."

"We'll see. Ellie, any questions?"

Ellie shook her head. "Can Astrid take care of the children while
I open the store?"

"I'll be back to do that." Astrid followed her mother out the door.

After they climbed into the buggy, Astrid set her basket on the
floor.

"Mor . . ."

"Astrid, please don't ask me why again."

She gave her mother a wounded look. "I wasn't going to. I just
wondered if we should send Onkel Hjelmer a telegraph or wait to
write a letter."

"I'm sorry, Astrid. Let me think. Will it help her to have him
come home or will it cause dissension?"

"Dissension?"

"An argument or fight."

"Why would his coming home cause a fight? I thought she said
she wanted him there."

"No, she said he was gone again. It seems that Hjelmer is always gone when Penny needs him the most."

"And that makes her mad?"

"Sometimes."

"Then she should tell him to stay home."

Ingeborg snorted at the simplistic answer. "Astrid, wives don't go around telling their husbands what to do."

"Some do. Mr. Valders never says much, but Mrs. Valders tells him what to do."

"True."

"But you don't tell Pa what to do. You ask him nice. Is that the difference?"

"About as well as I could explain it." A wave of weariness nearly swamped Ingeborg. She didn't have the stamina of a few years ago, that was for certain. Especially since the big bleed, as she referred to her illness. The scary thing—what if it started again?

"You all right?"

"I will be."

"Do you need a nap?"

Ingeborg chuckled. "That's what I used to say to you when you turned cranky when you were little."

"You're not cranky anymore. You just have that gray look about your eyes again. Elizabeth asked me if you were still taking it easy."

"And what did you say?"

"I said, 'Easier, but she don't sit down much.'"

"Doesn't."

Astrid heaved a sigh. "You don't, you know."

Ingeborg waved at Andrew, who was already up nailing shakes on the roof of his house. He used the hammer to wave back and returned to his work.

"I'd hammer on shakes if they'd let me," Astrid declared.

"I know you would, but I'd rather you didn't."

"Because I'm a girl?"

"Because there's too much work to be done on the ground or in the house for you to be climbing up on his roof."

"What is it like, Ma, wearing men's britches?"

"Like walking around in your bloomers, only heavier. But they sure are handy for working in the garden and for milking cows. And for riding horseback."

"Maybe we should wear them and start a new style."

Ingeborg glanced at her daughter. "Your pa would have six fits from Sunday."

"I've been thinking."

"About what?" Ingeborg always knew that things were about to break loose when Astrid said those three little words. *Please, Lord, don't let her shock me too much.*

"Well, Elizabeth and I've been talking about what I will do when I graduate." She glanced sideways at her mother. "And since there is no man in my life . . ."

Thank you, Lord, for that.

"Not that that would make a real difference anyway. I for sure want to go to school."

"I think that's a fine idea. What school?"

"Oh good. I hoped you'd say that. Nursing school."

"I'd think you could get far better training working here with Dr. Elizabeth."

"She said I could do that, but she would like me to go to Chicago to train at the same place she did. To be a doctor, I'd need a college degree, but I could go right into nurse's training after I graduate." She paused a moment as she stopped the horses at the fence around the house. "I don't think I want to be a doctor, but I like taking care of sick people. You do too, Ma—so I take after you."

"I'm not so sure that I like it, not all the time, at least, but it's something I'm good at. God makes sure of that. People trust me and I trust God, and it works pretty well." She turned to climb down from the buggy. "Thanks for the buggy ride."

"You're welcome. Should we send Hjelmer a telegram?"

"Let Penny decide. She'll be feeling better by tomorrow."

Ingeborg paused at the gate to watch Astrid back up the team and buggy and turn around to head back to Penny's. While so many girls were marrying at fifteen and sixteen, she was glad to hear that her daughter wanted to go on to school. "Good thing we bought those extra cows," she told Barney as he wriggled at her feet. "We're going to need money for her to go to school." She paused and watched the dust swirling up behind the spinning wheels of the buggy. "But I hope not clear to Chicago."

Later that week Ingeborg breathed a sigh of relief when she realized it had been almost two months since her episode in church. Better to be done with the monthlies than to have a repeat of before. Ingeborg had set the bread to baking early, and after breakfast, as soon as the dew was off the plants, went out to pick beans. While they'd had one mess for supper, this time there were enough to can. The last of the peas needed picking too, but she'd do that later. With the men eating at Kaaren's today, she should be able to get it all done. The curds were ready to be drained and poured into the molds over at the cheese house on the morrow. And the raspberries that grew along the back fence of the garden would be ready to pick any day now.

Since Penny was back on her feet and Elizabeth had no one staying in her surgery, Astrid would have to come home to help her mother.

"Tante Ingeborg?" Sophie's voice made Ingeborg smile.

"In the garden."

"Mor said I should come help you for a while."

"Bless your heart. I was about to send for Astrid."

"What do you want me to do?"

"The beans and peas need picking. I'm thinking of drying the rest of the peas."

"Mor has a full tray of them drying. I like fresh better, or canned."

"Don't we all? Right from the garden is the very best."

"Why don't I pick the beans and you take the peas?" Sophie suggested.

"Good." But all the while she dropped fat pea pods into her basket, Ingeborg thought back to her future daughter-in-law. Ellie had looked so shocked when Penny's baby was born dead. What had been going through her mind?

24

"THORLIFF, WHEN YOU WERE AWAY at school, did you sometimes get so homesick you thought your heart would break?" Ellie asked. She'd been snagged to help Thorliff as soon as she'd arrived from Penny's.

Leaving off cranking the ice cream machine for a minute, Thorliff smiled down at the girl feeding the ice chips into the bucket surrounding the canister of cream, sugar, and egg mixture. "Ja, that is to be expected. But I thought Blessing was more your home."

"It is, or I thought so too, but I really miss Ma and the little ones."

"Why don't you go for a visit?"

"I can't leave Penny right now. She's not over the birth and loss of the baby. This one hit her real hard. And everyone is canning, so the other women don't have time to come help her either."

"I think we should have a party before harvest starts." Andrew sat on the top step. "Do they have barn warmings . . . like house-warmings?"

Ellie smiled at him. "We've had barn dances lots of times."

"A barn dance. Good idea. Saturday night would give everyone time to get ready." Thorliff gave the ice cream freezer another crank. "This feels like it is done. Let's pack it good and put the sacks over the top."

"I'll go see if the sauce is ready."

Astrid leaped off the porch. "Oh, I forgot to pick the eggs. Come on, Ellie, you can help me and visit your chickens." Grabbing a basket off the railing, she waited.

"Coming," Ellie said, and together the two headed for the chicken house. "I saw the chicks earlier. They are so cute and already getting their feathers."

"I was going to surprise you. When do you think you'll move them to your barn?"

"Andrew said anytime, now that he's living at the house."

"Sleeping, you mean, the little he sleeps. I heard him pounding nails last night just before I fell asleep."

Ellie turned the handle and held the door open for Astrid to go in first. The two girls stood and watched the hens cackle their way in from outside, sure there would be grain scattered soon.

"Sorry, ladies, no food this time. Just give us your eggs." Astrid made her way to the row of nesting boxes and removed the eggs from the straw to her basket.

Ellie watched her mother hen come in with five chicks following her and pecking about her feet. "Wish I'd brought some oats. Aren't they cute?"

"She lost three. One drowned in the water pan." Astrid straightened. "Two dozen eggs. Penny will be glad when you take eggs back with you."

"Oh, I didn't know I was doing that."

"You weren't until now. Say good-bye to your friends and come on. I want some ice cream before it's all gone."

"Just think, my own chickens."

"I'll give you a couple more. Then you'll have an even half dozen, not counting the chicks."

Ellie closed the door behind them. She'd never had chickens of her own before. Come to think of it, she'd never had any animals of her own before.

A while later the Bjorklunds, the Knutsons, and Ellie gathered on

Ingeborg's porch to open the ice cream canister. "Two flavors of syrup—raspberry and chocolate." Ingeborg set the bowls on the table. "Three if you mix them."

"Raspberry and chocolate?" Astrid wrinkled her nose.

Thorliff thumped her on the head. "Don't denigrate something if you haven't tried it."

"How can I do that—whatever de . . . de . . . that word is."

"Denigrate. To make fun of, to criticize."

"Why didn't you just say that?"

"Because you need to learn new words. A good vocabulary is the mark of an educated person."

"One of the marks." Elizabeth sat on the two-seater swing attached to the beams overhead, using one foot to keep the swing in motion and the baby in her lap content.

"What's another?" Astrid laid the spoons on the table next to the bowls.

"Oh, what books you are reading, the variety of things you are interested in. Getting knowledge is an important part of growing up."

"Some people have a lot of book learning and not much sense." Andrew plunked the ice cream canister on the table and, picking up a towel, wiped the moisture and bits of salty ice off so they could open it.

"If you mean common sense, I think that is a God-given gift." Haakan leaned back in his chair.

"Proverbs says if we want wisdom, all we have to do is ask for it." Ingeborg smiled at Thorliff.

"Easier than reading all those books."

"If you want to go to nursing school, you are going to have to read a lot of books." Elizabeth shrugged at Astrid's frown. "I thought you loved to read."

"Oh, I do, but some of it is so boring, like Roman history and Greek mythology."

"Do you ever read newspapers?" Thorliff asked.

"Only yours. And when you used to send us the *Northfield News*.

You write about interesting things."

Ingeborg scooped out the first bowlful. "Thorliff, since you did all the cranking, you get the first one."

Andrew took the second dish and eyed the syrups. Should he combine the two, just to make Astrid upset? He agreed with her. Who cared about all those big words? Leave them to Thorliff and Elizabeth. He poured his favorite, chocolate, then spooned on some raspberries, smashed and sugared.

Astrid rolled her eyes.

He took a bite and grinned at her. "You ought to try it. It's really good."

"You're fooling me."

"Nope." He held out his bowl. "Take a bite."

Astrid shook her head, twisted her mouth around, and reached for a spoon. "If you're lying to me, Carl Andrew Bjorklund, you will be in bad trouble."

He shrugged and held his bowl steady.

She dipped a tiny bite, then had to dig again to get some chocolate.

"Our brave Astrid." Thorliff had his tongue planted firmly in his cheek.

"Don't tease her, you meanie." Elizabeth nudged him with her toe.

Astrid waved her spoon in the air. "That is really good. Here, let me have another bite."

"Go get your own." Andrew clutched his bowl close to his chest, half turning away.

Ingeborg chuckled. "You two. Here, Astrid, hand this to your father."

"How come I didn't get both?" Haakan asked when he took his bowl.

Ingeborg sighed and shook her head. "You didn't ask for both, so I put on what I thought was your favorite." She took the bowl back and made a great to-do of adding chocolate.

When everyone was served, she sat down and ate her ice cream plain.

"How come you didn't try both?" Andrew sat down next to her.

"I like it this way." She glanced across the table at Thorliff's chuckle. "And no, I don't have to try something new all the time. There's value in the tried and true, in keeping things simple."

"I didn't say a word."

"No, but you thought real loud." Elizabeth put in her two cents.

Andrew leaned back in his chair, back so far it teetered on the back legs. When Ingeborg thumped on his arm, he brought the chair back down and caught a laughing look from Ellie.

"I'd rather train ten cows any day than one of you stubborn Bjork-lund men," Ellie said between chuckles.

"Cows don't train easy." Andrew reached for the ice cream canister.

"I know. That's my point."

"Anyone else want more?" When they all shook their heads, Andrew poured the last of the mostly melted ice cream into his bowl, scraping the sides with his spoon. "If my tongue was long enough, I'd lick it clean."

"Oink, oink."

He gave Astrid a teasing glare and spooned the cold treat into his mouth. Plain, or with one syrup or two, ice cream was his favorite dessert. Maybe worth more because of all the work to make it.

"Remember all the choices there were at Mrs. Sitze's Ice Cream Parlor?" Thorliff looked over at his wife.

"She made the best sodas anywhere."

"What's a soda?" Astrid asked.

"You put scoops of ice cream in a tall glass, along with a flavored syrup. Then you add soda water to make it fizzy," Elizabeth explained. She turned to Thorliff. "Maybe we should open a drugstore with a soda fountain next to Penny's."

Thorliff groaned. "Good idea; wrong investors."

Half listening to the conversation, Andrew's thoughts skipped across the field to the house he should be working on right now. But the siren call of ice cream and Ellie's presence had lured him away. "So are we having a barn dance on Saturday?"

"You mean the celebrate-the-new-barn dance that we've all been talking about?" Ingeborg's teasing tickled Ellie.

"I thought we were going to wait until after harvest." Haakan leaned back against the porch post.

"I just thought we needed a party now. Ellie and I, we thought that it would be fun." His comment brought a smile from his intended. He looked to his mother. "After all, you said we needed more socials like the fish fry and the ball game."

"I did." Ingeborg nodded and smiled at Haakan. "And some play before you all leave for threshing would be good."

"I'll finish letting everyone know," Astrid said.

❧

By the time Saturday and August rolled around, the men had already cut and shocked a good part of the Bjorklund wheat. Lars had the steam engine fine-tuned, repaired, and greased. The binder was another matter. It broke down the afternoon of the party.

Lars crawled out from under the binder and held up a part. "I don't know if Sam can repair this or if Hjelmer has one to sell."

"I'll go find out." Haakan took the part and studied the broken piece. "I know I can't repair it. That's for sure. Andrew, saddle me a horse."

Andrew did as asked, all the while calling the machine several uncomplimentary names. He led the saddled horse out to the men.

"You better see if Penny has any more twine. This should finish ours up but won't do all the Baards'."

Haakan mounted and waited. "Anything else?"

"Not that I can think of."

Andrew shoved his hands into his pockets and kicked a dirt clump.

"Don't fret, Andrew, this won't affect the party tonight. We'll start cutting again on Monday."

"I've never had a party at my own place before."

"I know. It's different. Hitch the team up and let's pull this thing back to the machine shed. You just can't catch all the problems no matter how hard you try."

Andrew swung aboard one of the horses after he'd hitched them to the binder, and they headed on home. Two hawks flew an aerial ballet against the deepening blue of the sky. The harness clanked and jingled, and the binder squeaked and squawked, thumping behind them. Letting his mind run free, Andrew thought to the dancing that night, when he would hold Ellie in his arms, see her laughing up at him, feel her head against his shoulder. Harvest had started, and it couldn't get over soon enough for him.

❧

"Hey, Andrew, some place you have here."

"Thanks. Lots to finish yet."

"There's always more to do. You never get ahead."

"Caught up would be good."

The banter between the young men continued, but Andrew paid it only half an ear. Where had Ellie gone?

"If you're looking for Ellie, she's giving a tour of the house." Haakan spoke for Andrew's ears only.

Ears turning hot, Andrew nodded. Was he that obvious? He turned back to join the others.

"Andrew, where do you want the punch table?"

"On the back wall, I guess." So many decisions. In the past he'd just done what he was told. "Over by the stall with the chickens would be good." Since he was staying at the house, he and Ellie had moved her chickens into their new home the night before.

The memory of the kiss she'd given him after he showed her the small door he'd cut at floor level so the chickens could go outside warmed him top to bottom. Ellie sure knew how to show her gratitude.

When the musicians had tuned up their instruments and the square-dance caller announced the Virginia Reel, he joined the rest of the men in a long line down the center aisle of the barn, women across from them. The musicians hit the beat, and away they went.

"Ladies and gentlemen, forward and back, forward again and left arm around . . ."

While the dance continued, Andrew forgot his responsibilities and gave in wholeheartedly to the beat of the music, the laughter of the dancers, and the giggles of the young girls and boys who were joining the older dancers for possibly the first time.

"Gents go left; ladies go right; form that arch and pass on through."

Andrew and Ellie ducked to get under the hands of two youngsters and on down to the end of the line and back to their positions.

Everyone mobbed the punch bowl in between dances. When the musicians took a break, Andrew wandered over to where the men were gathered around Hjelmer.

"You think the mill has any possibility of happening?" someone asked.

"A real good possibility. We aren't the only farmers tired of paying such exorbitant fees for shipping. Russell-Miller down in Valley City is thriving. Even bought up the ones in Dickinson and Minot. There's room for more, as only ten percent of Dakota wheat is milled here in the state. The rest goes east."

"Not to change the subject, but did you see the belt buckle Olson found in the dirt where the fire had been?" Pastor Solberg asked.

Haakan shook his head.

"Had a KL engraved on the back."

"Definitely not an Indian, then. Sure wish we knew who to send it to."

"Better keep it, just in case."

Andrew glanced around and noticed that most of the younger men were not in the circle. Nor in the barn. Had not the invitation made it clear that there would be no liquor at this party, just like all the parties at the Bjorklunds'? He stepped back and ambled outside, as if he were only needing a breath of air. Hearing male laughter off to the west, he followed the sound. But by the time he got there, no one was passing around a bottle or a flask. While the jokes were slightly off color, nothing unusual was going on other than a couple of the young men smoking.

As he approached the group, Andrew said, "The music's starting up. Let's get on back. Make sure you put out your cigarettes." He turned to leave, hoping the others would follow his lead.

"We're going to spend tomorrow night here at our house," Ellie told him sometime later.

"Ah, we?" His heart leaped into his throat.

"Me and the girls. That's all right with you, isn't it?"

He didn't dare answer for a moment, his throat had gone so dry. The picture that had flashed through his mind was not of Ellie and the other girls, but of him and Ellie. He ordered his thundering heart to slow down and took another deep breath. "Of . . . of course. I'll stay with my folks, then, tomorrow night."

"Good, let's go dance. I think there's a waltz coming next." She took his hand and dragged him back onto the dance floor.

When the dancing ended, Andrew and Ellie stood together thanking everyone for coming and waving them all good-bye. As each wagon drove out the lane, Andrew was even more pleased that he had been staying here. Sleeping in his own house brought more pleasure than he thought it would—even though all he had was a pallet on the floor. *If only we were married and Ellie were living here with me.*

"OH, ELLIE, I LOVE YOUR HOUSE," Rebecca said the following afternoon when the girls gathered to measure the windows for curtains.

"Me too, Rebecca. I have to pinch myself sometimes to make sure all this is real." Ellie surveyed the empty kitchen. And to think she had been so angry over Andrew's ordering this house instead of the one they had chosen together. They hadn't even ordered the stove yet, although Penny said if they didn't have the money, she'd order it anyway. Ellie could pay it off with her wages. Her pa was making cabinets for the kitchen and would send them on the train when he finished, along with the other furniture he'd already made for them.

She led the girls through the kitchen to the parlor. "When we looked at the plans in the Sears and Roebuck catalog, we could choose how many windows we wanted. Andrew said that windows let the heat out and the cold in, but if I wanted another window, I could have it." She turned in a circle. "I love the way the light comes in." She stopped and giggled.

"Our dining room is empty, but I hope to put wallpaper up someday, with wainscoting on the lower part of the walls." She waved her hand around the room. "I saw it in a book, and it was so pretty.

Elizabeth said it would look nice, that her mother's house had it." As they walked through another door, she paused. "This will be my sewing room."

"Until you need it for a nursery," Deborah teased, and Ellie could feel the heat come up her neck.

Rebecca shook her head. "Such a big house. My mother wanted a house this size, but they never could afford it. Now the little house is just fine. I'm thinking I might like to move back there."

"I saw you dancing with Gerald Valders a couple of times." Sophie poked their friend in the arm. "I think he is sweet on you."

"He is nice, but his brother is so much better looking," Rebecca said with a sigh.

"And a better dancer." Sophie twirled around, her arms in the air as though she were dancing with someone. "Show us the upstairs, Ellie."

They all trooped up the stairs that had no banister yet.

"Four bedrooms, and Thorliff says that we must keep a place for a necessary."

"Inside the house?" Astrid asked

"Yes. He says that is the latest thing. I don't understand how it works, but if it means no outhouse, I'm all in favor." They looked into all the rooms—two of which had only two-by-fours for walls.

"We have a lot to finish. I'm thinking we might close off the upstairs for the winter to make heating easier."

"Ellie, you sound like an old married woman already." Sophie led the way downstairs. "I kept back part of one cake and some punch for us, so let's eat."

"I'm not hungry," Grace signed and said.

"We can spread out our quilts and get into our nightdresses, then eat." Sophie seemed to be taking charge, but that was no surprise to anyone.

"Anyone need the outhouse? I'll light the lantern," Ellie said.

Sophie snorted. "There's enough moonlight. We don't need a lantern."

"What are we going to do? Leave the door open?" Deborah whispered.

"You need a light to use inside the outhouse?" More giggles.

"Well, you never know what kind of animal took refuge in there."

"All right, take the lantern." All six trooped to the outhouse, laughing all the way.

"Do you hear that?" Ellie stopped walking.

"Hear what?"

"Listen."

Everyone held their breath.

"I don't hear a thing, other than that pesky mosquito that's buzz-ing my ear." Sophie swatted at her hair.

"No, listen," Ellie insisted.

More silence. A dog barked off in the distance.

"That's Barney." Astrid shrugged.

"How do you know?"

"Came from the direction of my house."

"I wish we had brought him here." Ellie tried to ignore the hairs standing up on her arms.

"Why? What's there to be afraid of?" Deborah took her turn.

"It's like every once in a while I hear a hammer." Ellie held her breath to listen more closely.

"A hammer?"

"You heard me."

"Who'd be hammering tonight? Maybe it's a woodpecker."

"Woodpeckers are birds, and birds only fly around during the day."

"Oh yeah. Hear that owl?"

The *whoo-whoo* made shivers run up and down Ellie's spine. When they heard the beat of the wings, they all giggled again. And trooped back to the house.

Ellie set the lantern in place. "We can put the lantern in the middle of the floor and spread our quilts around it like wheel spokes."

"You spread the quilts. I'm fixing the cake and punch," Sophie said.

By the time they'd gotten the beds fixed, their clothes changed, and sat cross-legged on the pallets waiting for their food, Ellie was wishing even more that they'd brought the dog over. Something was bothering her, and she had no idea what. Just that hammering she thought she heard every now and then, but no one else seemed to hear it. Must be someone working late, and sound traveled better at night than during the day.

Ellie listened as the others talked about boys, the dance from the night before, boys, the latest gossip, and boys. She already had her man. Never would she refer to Andrew as a boy again. She smiled as she thought about her house, her chickens, all safe in their pen in the barn, and her garden. Once she and Andrew were married, what more could she want? She tuned back in to the conversation.

"But what do you want to do?" Astrid's voice wore all the passion of her body, leaning forward, imploring with her hands widespread.

"What is wrong with wanting to get married to a good man and having a family?" Sophie responded. "After having a few boyfriends first, you know, tasting the blossoms like a butterfly does. Flitting from one to another, now I think that sounds like—"

"Like trouble," Grace broke in.

Sophie shrugged. "Heinrich Geddick is a great dancer, and"—she leaned forward and lowered her voice—"he's a great kisser."

"Sophie Knutson, you haven't allowed him to kiss you?" Grace nearly collapsed in horror.

"Just a little kiss." She held her thumb and forefinger apart an inch or so.

"But he will think he is courting you."

"No he won't. Grace, calm down. Don't get so frazzled. After all, I'm not going to marry him." Sophie flopped back onto her quilt. "All right, fine. I won't let him kiss me again. I shouldn't have mentioned it."

"You shouldn't have done it. What if Pa finds out?"

"How would he find out unless someone tells him?" Sophie's eyes narrowed. The lantern threw shadows on her face that gave Ellie the shivers. She'd always known Sophie dared to do anything, but this was serious.

"I thought you said you were writing to Hamre?" Rebecca nudged Sophie's arm.

"So I'm writing to Hamre. That doesn't mean he's courting me or anything. We're just friends. I think I've become his way of keeping in touch with home."

"Hamre has never thought of Blessing as home. All he wanted was the sea again," Astrid said. "I think he'd have gone back to Norway if Onkel still had his boat."

"If it wasn't so expensive. When I asked Anji how much the tickets for her and Mr. Moen were, I nearly fell over backward." Ellie leaned backward as if falling.

"He must be a wealthy man to go back and forth so often," Deborah said, her eyes wide.

"I think the newspapers that he writes for pay his way," Astrid offered.

"How do you know that?"

"Thorliff said so, and he should know. Sometimes magazines pay his way to go write a story for them."

"I think I want to be a writer like Thorliff, then. I want to travel all over the world." Sophie flung her arms out as if to embrace the globe.

"You better marry a rich man instead, as much as you like school and reading and writing."

"Mor said I had to finish, that graduation was important to show that I finished something," Sophie said with a careless shrug. "Only two more years. Two l-o-n-g years."

Ellie grinned into her raised knees, burying a chuckle in her nightdress. While Sophie had grown taller and more lovely, she still started many things, like sewing a quilt or knitting a sweater, and Grace finished them for her.

"You have to admit I am a good cook."

"True, if you don't forget and leave the cookies in the oven." Grace snuck that one in, making all the girls giggle.

"When she has a baby, she'll most likely put it down somewhere and go off to do something else and forget where she left it." Astrid's comment brought forth another spate of giggles.

Sophie tossed her hair over her shoulder. "I'm not going to have babies until I'm at least twenty-five."

"You'll be an old maid by then."

"I didn't say I wasn't getting married, just that I won't have babies right away."

"I want babies, lots of babies," Ellie said softly, "but I want them all to live. I don't think I could bear it if my baby died."

"Like Penny's?" Grace asked.

"Ja, like Penny's. That baby was so tiny and so perfect, but . . ." Tears clogged her throat and burned her eyes. She wiped them with the hem of her nightdress. "And Penny is so sad."

Astrid sniffed too. "Mor was sad for a long time too. She wanted more babies, but no more ever came after me. When I see all the times that babies die, it makes me afraid."

"Terrified is a better word. It makes me afraid of loving Andrew, you know." Ellie shuddered as she finally admitted it to herself and the others. She sighed, a deep hurting sigh. *Blue or dead.* "If babies are a gift from God, why does He take them back before they even live?"

"I don't know," Astrid answered. "Mor says she just trusts that God loves us no matter what and that He works out all things for our good. I remember that Bible verse, but sometimes . . ." A stillness stretched.

Ellie cocked her head. There was that sound again. She turned back when Astrid continued.

"Sometimes it is easy to doubt."

"But is doubting wrong? A sin? I mean there is the story of Thomas—he was even called the doubter. Why would that be in the Bible if it wasn't to help us?"

"I don't know, but I remember Thorliff telling us about the discussions he had in college. He was on the debate team for a while."

Astrid waved her hands as she spoke. "I want to have discussions like that."

"About the Bible?"

"About all kinds of things. Like the women in the temperance movement, about women owning land and being able to vote."

"Remember? We talked about that in school," Grace added. "Pastor Solberg says to ask all our questions because God has all the answers."

"I know he said that, but when I ask a question, God seems to be really silent." Sophie leaned forward, elbows on her knees.

"What did you ask?"

"I asked if I should let Heinrich kiss me, and when He didn't answer, I decided it was yes." Sophie fluffed her hair with her fingers, undoing the remainder of the braid so her dark hair hung free.

When the others laughed, she picked up her hairbrush and began her hundred strokes.

"Would you like me to do that for you?" Ellie asked.

"Oh yes."

"I know. We could form a circle and brush each other's hair. That way we'll all enjoy having our hair brushed."

They all scrambled to kneel in the circle, each of them undoing her hair and handing the one behind her hairbrush. Silence but for the oh's and ah's that tickled the corners of the room.

"This will be a happy house," Rebecca said finally.

"Why?"

"Because the first gathering here is a party of good friends, and we've been laughing and talking of good things—well, mostly."

"I like that," Ellie said around a sigh.

"Hear that?" Sophie sat straight up.

"What?"

"Fire." The word came faintly through the open window.

"Fire!" The girls leaped to their feet and ran out the door. Even in the light of a half moon, they could see smoke coming from the barn.

26

"SOPHIE, YOU CAN RUN the fastest. Go for Andrew," Ellie hollered over her shoulder. "Deborah, you and Grace go ring the church bell." Sophie took off before Ellie could finish her instructions.

"Where are you going?" Rebecca screamed.

"To save my chickens."

"Ellie!" Rebecca ran beside her. "That's crazy. Don't go in there. Look, the fire is in the haymow."

"I have to save my chickens. My mor and others gave them to me." When Rebecca grabbed her arm, Ellie gave her a hard shove. "Leave me alone. I have time."

She paused a moment before diving into the smoke. Already the church bell was ringing. Grace hadn't had time to get to the church yet. Who rang it? She dove into the swirling smoke, immediately wishing she'd tied a wet cloth over her face. Hoping she was staying on track, she headed to the right toward the back corner. If she could get the trapdoor open to the outside, perhaps she could shoo them out. *All those gifts from Mor and our friends. Lord, help me save the chickens.* The heat from overhead beat upon her; the roar of the fire took over her heartbeat. Coughing and choking, she finally felt the wall of the pen. Her eyes burned beyond anything she'd ever felt before, even worse than the prairie fire. Gasping and choking, she dropped to the floor, where the air was better, and crawled to the pen door. She could hear the chickens clucking and screeching. Would they be like horses and refuse to leave?

Opening the pen's door, she crawled toward the outside wall. The heat was getting worse.

"Come on, chickens, I'll open the door and chase you out." Manure squished beneath her knees and under her hands, but a chicken flew past her. She reached the trapdoor and, after fumbling along the wall, drew out the peg to the hasp. The door fell outward, and she gulped the fresh air streaming in, then coughing and with tears streaming, she turned to find her chickens. "Come on. Come to the fresh air." How long had she been in the barn? How long would the ceiling hold?

She grabbed the legs of a chicken and dragged it to the door and threw it out. She grabbed another one and threw it out. She could see red streaks of fire off to the side, back toward the main door, the one she'd come in through. Two more chickens, out they went, but she couldn't find any chicks.

Get out! She wasn't sure whose voice she heard, maybe her own inside. *Get out that chicken door.* Dizzy beyond anything she'd ever known, she wanted to lie down but forced herself to find one more chicken. A burning board fell behind her. *Get out!* Using far more strength than she ever dreamed she had, she crawled back to the little trapdoor and tried to squeeze out. Air, real air, not smoke, filled her lungs. She coughed until she gagged, and then pushed, but her shoulders were too wide. Turning sideways, arms first, she inched herself through the little door and fell onto the ramp Andrew had built for her chickens to use to climb back into the barn in the evening. With one last burst of energy she staggered to her feet.

"Here, Ellie, come here!" Rebecca's voice led her away from the burning barn.

Ellie's eyes were so swollen, she could see only through slits, and that was like peering through water. But the voice she could follow.

"Oh, Ellie." Rebecca snatched her out of the smoke. "Run, we have to run. The barn could come down any second." Together they staggered, Rebecca half carrying her, out beyond the barn and toward the house.

"Water, water." Her throat burned. Her body felt on fire. Her head—the pain was fierce. She wasn't sure if she said the words or only thought them, but the coughing drove her to her knees.

"Here, let me help you." Ingeborg's voice choked on tears.

"Andrew?"

"They're fighting the fire. He went in to look for you."

Ellie collapsed into Ingeborg's arms. *Andrew* . . . The scream that never left her lips echoed in her head.

"Ellie!" He screamed her name over and over until the smoke made screaming impossible. He fought the arms that tried to haul him back.

"Andrew, she's out! She's all right." Haakan dragged him back. Andrew swung at his father, his fist slamming against a solid shoulder.

Haakan's fist connected solidly on Andrew's chin, and he heaved his son over his shoulder and staggered out of the barn.

"Save the house." Coughing and choking, he dumped Andrew onto the ground and headed for the bucket brigade.

"We are."

As more horses and wagons arrived, the firefighters drenched the house's roof with bucket after bucket of water. A giant crash, and the haymow burned through, bringing the entire barn down upon itself.

A tower of smoke and embers rose and feathered out, bits of burning board and hay seeking new fuel. Using water-soaked rugs and gunnysacks, the fighters beat out the embers. If it got into the drying wheat, they'd end up with another prairie fire to boot.

Ingeborg's tears bathed Ellie's face. "Oh, my dear girl, your hair is gone, but the burns are minor. How blessed you are."

"Andrew?"

"He's fine."

"Mor, where's Ellie?" Andrew whispered between coughing spasms. He rubbed his chin and sat up. "What hit me?"

"Your father." Ingeborg handed him a cup of water. "Drink slowly."

He shook his head and rubbed his eyes. "I can't see. Where's Ellie?" What he thought a scream came out a croak.

"She's right here, Andrew. Hear her coughing?" She guided his hands as he scooted closer.

"Ellie." He grabbed her hand. "Is she all right?"

"All but the smoke in her lungs, I think."

"Ingeborg?"

She heard Elizabeth calling. "Over here." She held the cup for Ellie to drink again. "Easy now."

Elizabeth dropped to her knees beside the two patients. "Are her burns bad?"

"No, not that I can tell." They both kept their voices low. "I'm more worried about their lungs."

Sitting on the ground, Andrew held Ellie close to his chest. While his words to her were soft, his face wore anger like a cloak.

Ellie coughed and gagged.

"Honey will help soothe that throat." Elizabeth moved her fingers gently over Ellie's head.

"I'll go get it," Andrew offered.

"No, you stay where you are. That's what you can do best for right now."

"M-my chickens," Ellie croaked.

"Ellie, it's you that's important. We can always get more chickens." Andrew clutched her fiercely, holding her hand against his cheek.

"How did the fire get started?" Elizabeth asked as she smoothed salve on Ellie's other hand.

"I don't know."

"Ellie thought she heard someone hammering but we decided it came from far away." Rebecca brought more water. "We were brushing our hair when we heard someone yell 'fire.' Or at least I think we did. It all happened so fast. Ellie told Sophie to get help, and Grace and Deborah ran to ring the church bell. I tried to keep Ellie from going into the barn, but she shoved me away. I'm sorry, Andrew. I tried to hang on to her."

"Shh, child, you did your best." Ingeborg gathered the now sobbing Rebecca into her arms.

Ingeborg glanced down at her son. Since she'd wrapped Ellie's head in soft bandages, he might not have realized her hair was mostly singed off. The salve she'd applied to the burns on her scalp would help the pain.

As the rising sun lightened the eastern sky, the firefighters stopped by to tell Andrew how sorry they were.

"Sure wish we'd had the fire wagon," one said.

"Wish we could have saved it." Knute Baard shook his head. "Fine barn. You think the hay wasn't dry enough?"

"No. I walked through there earlier in the day and didn't find any hot spots. Thank you for coming." Andrew shook his head from side to side. *Did I check closely enough?* The thought tormented him. *Surely I did.*

"Who rang the church bell?" asked Pastor Solberg.

"Grace and Deborah did. Remember? The girls were sleeping here last night," Ingeborg answered.

"No, I heard it ringing before we got halfway there, so we came on back," Deborah said.

Solberg shook his head. "Strange."

"Could someone have been working in the barn?" Rebecca joined the group. "Ellie heard hammering."

"But who?" Haakan wiped his sooty face with a cloth that had been drenched in the bucket. "We were all home in bed."

"I should have stayed here." Andrew held his sleeping Ellie close. He could hear her breath wheezing like an organ bellows with a leak.

"I thought about it but figured Mor would say it was improper or some such."

Sophie had tied a rag around her head to keep her hair back out of her eyes. Her nightdress gaped along the hem where she had ripped it running across the field. Smoke and grime stained all their faces and clothes.

"There is no reason anyone would have been working in the barn at that time of night—especially without Andrew," Haakan said.

"You think someone set the fire deliberately?" Sophie asked.

"Now, who would do a thing like that?" Ingeborg took the honey Sophie brought from home. "Mange takk." She knelt by Ellie and, pouring the honey into a spoon, held it up and said, "Wake her, Andrew. This will help." When Ellie stirred, Ingeborg moved the spoon to her lips. "Take this, dear one. It will soothe your throat."

"We need to get her breathing easier." Using her stethoscope, Elizabeth listened to Ellie's chest.

Haakan thanked those who came in from beating out burning embers. After everyone had gone but the family and the girls who had stayed overnight, Andrew sat back down beside Ellie.

"I know what my throat and chest feel like, and I wasn't in the barn that long." He gave his father a studying look. "I've sure got a sore spot on my chin, though."

Haakan flexed his hand. "Haven't had to knock anyone out for a long time. Guess desperation makes us do foolish things." He looked over the still smoldering barn remains. "What a shame."

"What a tragedy," Andrew said.

"No." Haakan half turned toward his son. "A tragedy would have been if someone had died in the fire. We can rebuild the barn."

"But what if someone did set it on purpose?" Andrew got up and stood beside his pa, hands in his back pockets, staring at some of the studs, now blackened spears against the brightening day. "Surely not. But if someone was pounding—what could that have been?" He turned to Sophie. "You didn't see any lights in the barn?"

"Andrew, we didn't look. The only time we went outside was to use the outhouse."

"Sound carries at night. Must have been someone somewhere else who couldn't sleep."

"Maybe Ellie will know more when she wakes up."

"That will be awhile. I've given her some laudanum to help relax her lungs." Elizabeth stood. "Let's get her over to my surgery so I can keep an eye on her." She turned to Rebecca, who held baby Inga and was trying to keep her from fussing but not succeeding much. "Here, let me take her. She's just hungry. We had a rather rude awakening."

A rooster crowed, greeting the rising sun.

"Ellie's rooster!" Astrid clapped her hands as the rooster and three hens came clucking from the other side of the barn. "Some of them lived. She'll be so happy."

"Sure, she almost gave her life for three stupid chickens!"

"Easy, Andrew. Right now be grateful things aren't a lot worse."

Andrew stared at his mother, shook his head, and knelt down to pick up Ellie. As he stood, the cloth wrapped around her head fell to the ground. When she whimpered in her sleep, he turned his head to comfort her. His eyes widened, his arms locked around her. "Her hair! Her hair is all gone!" He stumbled at the first step, then strode toward the wagon. "If someone started this fire and I find out who did it, I swear I'll kill him."

27

"ALL BECAUSE OF THOSE STUPID CHICKENS." Andrew paced in Elizabeth's surgery.

"Easy, Andrew, Ellie doesn't need your anger now. She needs your strength to survive this."

He watched as Elizabeth listened to Ellie's chest again and flinched at whatever sounds she heard. "Survive?" Andrew stared at the doctor. That first day Ellie had been coughing and sleeping, sleeping even while coughing. But yesterday and today she had seemed better—she'd smiled at him. His poor little hairless darling. He wanted to run, to smash someone, to find out who set the fire. He forced himself to not flinch when he looked at her, but Elizabeth had assured him Ellie's hair would grow back. He thought back to the night before.

"Andrew Bjorklund, don't you dare let her see how her hair being gone affects you." Elizabeth had backed him up against the wall. When he'd tried to sidestep her, she stepped right with him. "I believe you are a good man who loves this young woman, and right now she needs to know only that you love her and that she will get well. Do you understand me? Nothing about the chickens, nothing about someone who might have set the fire. All that matters is Ellie." She shook her finger at him. "Do you understand?"

He had nodded. No one in his entire life had lectured him like that.

Because you didn't need it before, the small voice inside now said, and it sounded far more patient than he felt. So many animals he'd nursed back to health, just like his mor with people. But this was Ellie! And she went into a burning barn to save her chickens. What was the matter with her? What had she been thinking? *You would have gone in for a horse or a cow.* That voice again. *But that's different. They are big animals of real value, with feelings and . . .* He didn't need help to see the errors of his reasoning.

If only he had been there. But he'd been over this ground too many times to count. After the scolding from Elizabeth he'd gone over to the station and sent a telegram to the Wolds, telling them that Ellie was terribly ill from the smoke, but she would be all right. *Please, God, that she will.* He leaned his head in his hands, his elbows propped on his knees. As Ellie fought to breathe, he fought to think clearly. But all he could think and hear was Ellie.

"Why don't you go lie down on the other bed, and I'll try to get her to take some broth." Elizabeth set her tray down on the small table by the bed.

"I'll feed her."

"All right. You sit on the other side of the bed and prop her up. Rub her back, pat her back, and we'll do this together."

Andrew did as she asked, holding Ellie so liquid could slide down her throat more easily.

"Ellie, you have to eat something. We have to get liquids into you to fight off the infection. Now open your mouth and swallow this." Elizabeth held a spoon to Ellie's mouth. She opened and swallowed. "Good, now again." Three times and then she broke into coughing, choking, and gagging.

Elizabeth set the cup and spoon down. Then with Andrew holding Ellie upright, she cupped her hand and thumped on the girl's back. "I saw this done once, the theory being to break loose the congestion in her lungs. Think of tiny sacs that hold air. Right now they are filled with fluid and infection, so they can't hold air. I saw them. The lungs work like bellows—inhale and the bellows expand; exhale and they deflate. With all that fluid in there, they can do neither. Right now she's breathing with a very small part of her lungs."

Ellie started coughing again and spit out a clump of phlegm.

"Good girl. Let's get it out." Elizabeth continued with the thumping. "At least there seems to be something I can do. Good thing you are such a healthy young woman, dear Ellie."

Ellie collapsed back against Andrew, her mouth open, struggling for every breath.

Elizabeth propped the pillows behind her. "I think she can breathe easier sitting up. Make sure she stays this way."

"I will."

"I'll be back in a while. Oh, Astrid said your mother will be coming over to relieve you in a bit. You should go get some sleep."

"But, I—"

"Andrew, I do not need another sick person on my hands. Ellie will need you even more later. Thank God your father got you out of the barn when he did, or you'd be in the same shape."

"Any change?" Ingeborg asked a bit later when she entered the room.

Andrew shook his head. "Elizabeth thinks so, but I don't know." He squeezed Ellie's hand. And when she squeezed back, he gave his mother half a smile. "She knows I'm here."

"I'm sure she does. She's not deaf, and it's a good thing if she doesn't try to talk."

"I know, but—"

"But nothing. You go get some sleep. I'll be right here." Ingeborg settled into the chair Elizabeth had vacated and stared at Andrew on the other side of the bed.

"Come on, Andrew, you heard Mor." Thorliff spoke from the doorway. "You'll sleep better if you take this other room. And my wife gave me this to give to you."

"What is it?"

"I don't know, but if I were you, I'd just drink it down. One thing I've learned, you don't want to get on the wrong side of Dr. Elizabeth." He emphasized the doctor part. He handed the glass to his brother. "Come along now."

"Did she send you in here after me?"

"Andrew, I need to explain something to you as one older and wiser brother to a younger and sometimes more bullheaded brother."

Andrew rolled his eyes, but he stood and followed Thorliff.

"Take your medicine," his mother called gently after him.

I've been taking it for some time now. But I'm not seeing that taking my medicine has had any effect on Ellie. He glanced over his shoulder. Ellie was smiling. Not a big smile but enough to make curves in her cheeks. If he had to dance on the ceiling, he'd do it if he could make her smile again. He took the glass Thorliff proffered and gulped it down. He hardly got his boots off before he fell back on the bed, sound asleep.

"He's sleeping." Elizabeth returned to the sickroom sometime later.

"What did you give him?"

"Let's just say he will sleep for a while. He needs it too. Smoke in your lungs like that is no joke. How's Haakan?"

"Still coughing once in a while, but I think he'll be fine."

"Let's see if we can get some more broth into Ellie."

Ingeborg laid the back of her hand on Ellie's cheek. "She's running a fever."

"I know, but so far she's holding her own. You prop her, and I'll feed."

The two women worked well together, almost reading each other's mind. While Ingeborg held Ellie upright and forward, Elizabeth thumped on her back again. After the coughing subsided, they bathed Ellie in cool water, changed the sheets, and settled her against the pillows again.

When Ingeborg took her hand, Ellie squeezed it. Her eyes fluttered as if to open, but with a slight shake of her head she drifted back to sleep. Ingeborg took her knitting out of the bag she'd brought and settled back in the chair. Picking up where she'd left off, she lent herself to the ancient rhythm of flying needles and yarn.

"What are you making?"

"A sweater for Andrew for Christmas. He's filling out in the shoulders so much that everything is getting tight on him."

Elizabeth adjusted the pillows behind Ellie again to keep her as upright as possible. "Watch that she remains like this. She'll breathe more easily."

"I will. I wish I'd known that for some of my patients through the years."

"I am so thankful that I insisted on going to medical school and then was able to work with Dr. Morganstein in Chicago. She was so wise in patient care, partly because she saw so many patients. I wish I could ask her what else we could do for Ellie."

"Praying is the most important thing we can do."

"You know, it is easy to overlook that. Thank you for reminding me."

"Pastor Solberg will be by, so we'll all pray together. But Jesus said 'Where two or three are gathered together in my name, there am I in the midst of them.'"

"You used a different verse another time. 'Where two or three agree'—wasn't it something about 'I will do it'?"

"Close. He said all we have to do is ask."

"But what if . . ." Elizabeth chewed her bottom lip. "I know too much. It is hard for me to have the faith to believe God will heal, and yet I know that He does. Does that make any sense?"

"He said faith as big as a mustard seed was all that was needed to move mountains into the sea."

"Sometimes I think mountains might be easier than lungs full of fluid."

Ingeborg laid her knitting needles down. "So we shall pray for your faith too, for faith for all of us, for peace for Andrew, for healing for our dear girl here. Lord God, you know us so well, inside and out. You see Ellie's lungs, and you know how to make her well again. We thank you that you said you would give us what we ask for." She paused and blew out a breath. "Holy Ghost, breath of life, breathe your life into Ellie's lungs and her entire body." The peace in the room settled like a benediction of love.

"Lord, help me to believe when I doubt. Remind me again what you've done in the past."

Pastor Solberg joined them from the doorway. "And help us, Father, to trust you with those we love. For you are our God and our King, our Father and our healer. To you alone we give all the praise and glory. Amen."

Ingeborg sat with her head bowed. *Father, my Father, giver of all good things. Thank you. Mange takk.* She heard Pastor Solberg cross the room and felt him by her chair. Felt him kneel beside the bed and take Ellie's hand in his.

"Ellie, we are believing for you, and if you can hear me, let me remind you of the faith you live by. The faith that says God is mightier than any sickness, that Jesus died and rose victorious so that we might live, both eternally and on this earth." He smoothed her hand, then her forehead. "Dear child, I've seen you grow into such a beautiful young woman, beautiful inside and out. Now we command that Satan take his attack away, that he leave you alone, for you are a daughter of the King of Kings. You are free of him and free of this illness, for Jesus said so." He stood and leaned against the windowsill. A breeze lifted the curtains and wafted across the bed.

Ingeborg opened her eyes and smiled up at her longtime friend. "Thank you. As always you know just how to pray."

"You were doing a fine job before I came. Are you taking turns tonight?"

Elizabeth nodded. "Andrew is sleeping now."

"I'll be back before daybreak, then, but if you need me, send for me immediately." He patted his pocket and withdrew a telegram.

"This came from Olaf." He handed it to Ingeborg, who read it aloud. "Goodie is sick Stop Can't come now Stop Praying Stop Olaf."

Elizabeth looked over at Ingeborg and then back to the pastor. "You know what? I have a feeling that all will be well. I believe Ellie is breathing more easily already. We'll let Olaf know, so they don't worry so."

"I'll be praying."

"Good night, and thank you for coming." Ingeborg listened to him leave, the screen door shutting softly behind him. "He and I've sat many a vigil."

"He's a fine man."

"Yes, he is. God has taken some and healed others. I finally had to realize that all were healed, just some on this side of the grave and some on the other side. You go on to bed, dear. I'll be here until you or Andrew come back."

"Or Thorliff."

"All right."

Ingeborg knitted until her eyes grew weary. She fixed Ellie's pillows and forced her to take spoonfuls of water. She laid her hands on Ellie's chest and prayed again for the loosening of the sickness in her lungs. She changed the warm dry cloths for cool wet ones every hour or so. Each time picking up her knitting again, she hummed along with the ticking needles.

"Ma?"

"No, dear Ellie. It is Ingeborg. Please don't try to talk."

Ellie nodded.

"Is there something you need?"

Another nod. "A-a-and . . ." she croaked.

"Drink this, and then I'll tell you all I can."

Ellie took several spoonfuls, her swallowing painful and slow.

"Good girl. Now, Andrew is sleeping. He has been coughing too, but he is well. Just worried about you."

Another half smile.

"This will make you laugh, I hope, but please don't. The rooster and four hens survived the fire. You saved them."

Ellie's eyes opened, not much, but she blinked her pleasure and squeezed Ingeborg's hand before falling back to sleep.

Andrew stumbled in sometime later, rubbing his eyes and scratching his head. He sank to the floor by the bed and took Ellie's hand while his mother told him what had happened. Laying his cheek against their clasped hands, he sighed. "I wish she'd be awake when I'm here."

"She will be." Ingeborg reminded him to change the cooling cloths and force Ellie to drink more water if she stirred. "And, Andrew, you must pray for her to be well. The Bible says the prayer of a good man availeth much. You are that good man, and you must continue to pray for her."

Andrew nodded, but she could feel something. His anger or resistance? *What is it, Lord?* She laid her hand on his shoulder, then made her way to the other room to lie down on the bed Andrew had left.

"Lord, she is either on the mend or . . ." She refused to consider the "or" and let her body and mind both drift into peaceful slumber, her prayers for Andrew floating heavenward.

Andrew kept his vigil just as his mother had told him, but every time he tried to pray, the words stuck in his throat. And in his mind. *Lord, I can't even pray!* He felt like running outside and shouting at the heavens. *Why can't I pray? I want Ellie to live. I want to pray.*

When Elizabeth relieved him, he went outside and sat on the front porch, his head in his hands. *I can't even pray for the woman I love. What kind of man am I?* When the sun lightened the horizon, he checked on Ellie one more time and headed home. At least he could milk cows.

OH, ANDREW, *if only I could talk with you.*

Through half-opened eyes Ellie watched him as he sat by the bed. Where had her Andrew gone, and who was this stranger—this man who was gnawing on his knuckles, watching her for any sign, his shoulders so tight, his voice still raspy? When he took her hand, she squeezed back and tried to smile. She started to say something, but Elizabeth's orders still rang in her ears.

"No talking." The slightest effort brought on paroxysms of coughing that ripped her throat and fired her lungs. She gagged and spit and spit and gagged. But she knew she was on the mend.

"Ellie?"

She nodded. *How could a nod feel like such an effort?* As did a smile. But she smiled anyway—sort of.

He held her hand against his cheek, his eyes bright with tears. "You aren't going to die."

I know that, but do you? What is it, Andrew? Elizabeth told you the crisis has passed. I am doing all I can to get better. Yes, I did a dumb thing, but . . . but I think more than that is troubling you. All the thinking and trying to understand made her fall asleep again. Everything was such an effort, and sleep was the only way out.

When she woke again, dusk had painted the outside dim, like looking through fine cheesecloth. The fragrance of roses drifted in on the breeze through the window. She wanted to inhale the perfume but sniffed gently instead, letting the rich scent linger in her nose. Elizabeth had told her repeatedly to breathe deeply, to get as much air as possible down into her ravaged lungs, but when she did she choked and coughed.

For a change she was alone. Usually she woke to find someone sitting in the chair by her bed, reading, knitting, even sleeping. A small schoolmarm bell sat on the table, and she was to ring it if she needed anything.

What I need are some answers. What do I know? I know that the barn is gone, four hens and a rooster are still live, and they saved the house. Thank you, God, for our house. No one else was injured, other than the crack on the jaw that Haakan delivered to Andrew. While I could have died in the blaze, all I lost was my hair. That will grow back. She touched the soft hat that Ingeborg had knit for her. Rubbing her hand over her scalp, she could already feel the peach fuzz. Her hair was growing back.

She let her mind float back to that night. Hammering. She'd thought someone was hammering. She'd heard someone yell "Fire." It wasn't one of the girls. She'd run outside. She saw smoke from the barn. *I saw someone come around the corner of the barn. But who?*

"I see you are awake." Thorliff stopped in the doorway. "May I come in?"

"Of course. I was just lying here trying to figure out what happened that night." She sounded worse than a frog with the croup.

"I brought you some honey water."

"Thank you. You don't have to force liquids down me any longer."

"Good. I'm not much for forcing." He handed her the glass. "Do you need to be sitting straighter to drink that?"

"No, I'm fine." She drank it slowly, sipping more than drinking so the honey would get a chance to do its job. Holding the glass with both hands, she asked, "Do you know what's wrong with Andrew?" Might as well leap right in.

"Other than losing the barn, you mean, and almost losing you?"

"Right."

"You think there's more?"

"I do." She sipped again, watching him over the rim of the glass.

"Hmm." Thorliff leaned back in the chair and crossed one ankle over his other knee. "Let's see. He's grumpy, testy, and driving himself harder than ever to finish the house and clear out the remains of the barn. Seems to be a family trait. When we have too much on our minds or things happen over which we have no control, we Bjorklunds seem to work ourselves into a frenzy and hope it will all go away."

"You do that?"

He nodded. "And Mor. I always thought Andrew was the easygoing one of the lot, but now I have to change my thinking. That's another thing that is hard for us."

"Changing your thinking?"

"Ja, and as a newspaper reporter, one is supposed to keep an open mind."

Ellie turned the glass in her hands, struggling with her next question. *Ask him.*

Don't be silly.

The voices argued back and forth.

"If I ask you something else, do you promise not to tell anyone?"

"If possible."

"Is that a yes or a no?"

"Sort of. It's keeping a track open in case I need to get you help of some kind and you don't want it."

"It's not that—it's more a silly question." She paused, watching her fingers clamp and unclamp. "Do you think Andrew does not love me any longer because my hair burned off?" She kept her gaze on the turning glass, trying to ignore the heat flaming up her face.

"Whatever gave you that idea?"

"I heard him crying about my hair one night, and now he hardly comes to see me." She tried to clear her throat but coughed instead, which led to wheezing, which drained her like she was a bucket kicked over by a cow. She handed Thorliff the glass and let her hands flop beside her, resting her now too heavy head against the pillows.

"You all right?"

"I will be. So?"

"So I know Andrew is sad about your hair, but he knows that it will grow back. He feels guilty because he wasn't there to protect you."

"That's dumb. I told him to leave us alone. We all did. Girls only."

"Ah, but Andrew has always felt it was his responsibility to take care of you."

She inhaled carefully. "I know. And usually I am so grateful for that, but this was a party, a girls' party." She waited, feeling her chest relaxing again.

"Someone said they thought they saw someone at the barn. Do you know who it was?"

She shook her head. "I close my eyes and try to see it again, but it's not clear. Someone did go ring the church bell, though. Surely it was the same person."

"I think you've talked enough for a week." Elizabeth swirled into the room. "Time to thump on your back again. Thorliff, perhaps I can teach you how to do this too, in case you ever have to do it for someone else. You cup your hand just so, then thump on her back, not hard, but hard enough to loosen up the congestion pockets inside so that she can cough them out."

"So coughing is a good thing?"

"Yes, it clears the lungs of unwanted fluid."

Ellie shuddered. More coughing, this time on demand. Three or four thumps, and she could feel it coming. Afterward she fell asleep, worn out by all the work. She'd never thought of coughing as hard work before, but it most assuredly was.

❧

Day flowed into day. Heat blanketed the land, broken only by a storm or two. The heat lightning promised others but failed to deliver.

The threshing crew worked the local area, and the vegetable gardens kept all the women canning and drying, preparing for the winter. On the outside Ellie tried to keep a placid smile in place, but inside she fumed at the restrictions Elizabeth laid out. Take it easy. No lifting. No walking up the stairs or across town. Walking around the house was permissible, but carrying baby Inga was not allowed. So she wrote her mother a long letter, not like the note she'd written as soon as she could.

Andrew took her for a buggy ride, but she couldn't sit up long enough to attend church. A buggy ride with Andrew should have been enjoyable, but it wasn't. He seemed to have nothing to say, and keeping up a conversation was beyond her. Besides, she didn't like her voice. Perhaps he didn't either. It sounded like mice scratching in the walls. When she'd mentioned that to Ingeborg, the woman burst out laughing.

"Now that is some picture, but I don't agree. Your voice is improving."

"Right. I say over ten words, and I run out of air." Ellie paused to grab a deeper breath and started coughing. When she could speak again, she whispered, "Forgive me for whining."

Ingeborg hugged her and kissed her cheek. "You have been so brave and gallant. Don't worry, Andrew will come around. I have something for you." She handed Ellie an envelope. "This came with mine. Goodie is much improved, praise God for that, but still frustrated she couldn't come."

"I told her I was getting better every day."

"I know, but mothers are like that."

One night Ellie dreamed of the fire again, of running out of the house, seeing the smoke from the barn, seeing the man come around the corner. She woke with a start! Toby. The man was Toby Valders. She could tell by the way he wore his hat, slightly off to one side, cocky, like him. And he was rather short and slender compared to the other men around. Both he and Gerald were short, dark haired, and good-looking in their own way, but totally the opposite of the tall, broad-shouldered Norwegians.

What had he been doing at the barn? Was he the one hammering? Who should she tell? Was the dream even real?

Of the last she was certain. It was a memory more than a dream. She lay awake for what seemed hours, going over the entire thing in her mind again and again. She remembered it all—running into the barn, crawling to free the chickens, opening the trapdoor and throwing the chickens out, Rebecca coming for her and dragging her away from the barn, the heat, the smoke. *Thank you, Father. I have not thanked you enough for my life, for protecting all the others. All I've been doing is fighting to breathe. Forgive me and heal my disease. Lord, I want to breathe with your breath, and I thank you for every breath I draw.*

She watched the sun come up, in awe that she lived through the barn burning and could greet the morning. She rubbed a hand across her scalp, feeling the new growth, rejoicing in the stubble that was new hair coming. *Like my hair is coming back, so will my strength.* She whispered the words aloud, "Like my hair is coming back, so will my strength. My strength is in God, my Father, creator of all things."

Elizabeth walked past the room and peeped in. "My, if you don't look chipper. All dressed and everything."

"I want to help you in the kitchen today."

"Ah, all right. But you must promise me to take it easy. Sit down if you get short of breath."

"I will." And for the first time since the accident, she held the baby, rocking her gently, talking with her, making Inga smile.

When Astrid came in with a basket of green beans, Ellie snapped the beans and filled the canning jars.

"I can't wait to tell Andrew how much better you are today."

"Maybe he should come see for himself."

"He's out on the binder, but I'll tell him."

"Who's been helping Penny?"

"Grace and Sophie and I have been taking turns. Rebecca is helping Mor in the cheese house. Mor is going to advertise for some more help. Everyone here is so busy trying to keep up with the gardens, feed the thresher crew— Oh, Hjelmer says he thinks he may have backers for the flour mill."

"Backers?"

"People with money who want to invest it here. Hjelmer is really excited. You should have heard him talking. I doubt anything else will happen now that harvest has started, but you watch—we just might get a flour mill in Blessing."

"But we don't have enough people to do the work here now."

"We have enough men, just not enough women. I think Mor will hire men to help in the cheese house. She's talking to Gerald today. He tried working in the wheat fields, but it made him too sick."

The mention of Gerald brought Toby back to her mind. All the while she and Astrid talked, their fingers kept snapping the beans. She could hear Elizabeth talking to a patient but could not understand the words. *Could I possibly do some bookwork for her to help out?*

Suddenly Ellie was so tired she could hardly hold the pan of snapped beans in her lap. She dumped the bean ends into the hollow of her apron and put one last bean in the pan. "I think I better go lie down. And here I was doing so well."

"Compared to last week, you're like a different person. Even your voice is better today." Astrid took the pan and set it in the kitchen on the table. "Do you need help?"

"No thanks, but I would like a glass of water, please." She drank the water slowly, as she'd learned, and reveled in the coolness flowing down her still sore throat. A light breeze lifted the back of the scarf she had tied over her head. If the chair wasn't so hard, she'd fall asleep right there. But she pushed herself upright instead and, after tossing the bean ends into the flower bed, walked down the hall to her room to lie down on the bed she'd made for the first time that morning. And without being terribly out of breath.

"Lord, what is the difference?" she whispered. "I don't understand it, but I sure thank you. Now if you could let me know one other thing. Who do I tell about Toby at the barn, or do I just keep that to myself? I'm afraid of what Andrew might do if he finds out."

29

HOT AND DRY. Perfect for harvest but hard on the garden.

Ingeborg carried another bucket of manure tea to her tomatoes. She'd watered the corn the day before. Potatoes would be tomorrow. She had been using this method all summer, adding extra water to the tea so it wouldn't be too strong and giving each plant both a meal and a drink at the same time. Haakan had teased her about her tea, but so be it.

She hurried so she could join the women—those who weren't cooking for the harvest crews—at the church to finish the wedding-ring quilt for Ellie and Andrew. Although why they tried to keep it a secret, she'd never know. The tradition had begun years before. Everyone who got married got a quilt. The quilters had gotten so they kept making one ahead in case someone decided to get married without giving them time to sew one. Then they embroidered the couple's names, the date, and Women of Blessing Lutheran Church down in the right-hand corner. The plan had been to have Ellie's finished earlier, but with the fires and all, things kind of got behind.

While Ingeborg rinsed out her bucket and tipped it upside down under the scrub bench, her thoughts turned to Andrew. He was driving himself far too hard. She understood trying to work off one's anger. She'd done it herself those long years before. As always, she found herself praying for her stubborn son. "Lord, you know him far better than I, and you love him far better than I. What can I do?"

Nothing.

Was it the wind or had she heard right? She nodded. "I don't think that was the answer I wanted." She returned to the kitchen to check on the bread baking in the oven. She'd leave for church when it came out, taking a loaf with her to share during afternoon coffee with the other ladies. She should take one over to Elizabeth too. She could never join the quilters because her medical practice now reached from Pembina to Warsaw.

Relishing the few minutes of quiet, Ingeborg took her Bible out to the front-porch rocking chair, where the shade already felt cooler than inside the house. *Lord, what is it you want me to hear right this moment?* Her Bible fell open to Ephesians, where the verse about Jesus already being victorious caught her eye. And because He triumphed over death and Satan, we can have the victory too. *"Put on the whole armour of God, that ye may be able to stand against the wiles of the devil. . . ."*

The shield of faith. *Can I hold the shield for Andrew right now?* The sword of the Word. *I don't think he wants to hear your Word. Like when Kaaren would come to me with a verse and all I wanted to do was to scream at her, "Go away and leave me alone. Can't you see I'm fighting to save this land for you too?" Thank you, Lord. You helped her persevere. For surely the pit that yawned always before me was of the devil, not of you. I know that now, but how can I help Andrew?*

Pray without ceasing.

Ah yes, another of those commands that seemed so impossible. But she'd learned that she could be praying inside while working outside, for Andrew, for Ellie, for forgiveness, for love to prevail. She could feel the anger in her son when he walked into a room. No matter how gentle he tried to be, it was there, smoldering underneath.

Could she sense it so well because she had been there herself? *Comfort one another with the comfort by which you were comforted* floated through her mind. *Lord, I'm trying to do that, but he sure doesn't make it easy. Talk about a stubborn Norwegian.*

She inhaled the wonderful aroma of baking bread and rose to check on it again. When she thumped on a loaf—a skill her mother had taught her so many years earlier—it sounded right, neither sluggish of the undone nor hollow of the too well done.

"This must be a day for remembering." She took the bread pans from the oven and turned the loaves out onto a towel that covered the wooden rack Andrew had built for her for Christmas one year when he was younger. Most of the wooden spoons she used came from his carving too. The Andrew who had always been so gentle and loving, taking care of everyone. And now he wouldn't let anyone, not even Ellie, take care of him.

Always back to Andrew.

Using her fingers, she dipped butter out of the crock and smoothed it over the crusts of the loaves, then covered all with a towel so the flies wouldn't get at them. Wrapping one loaf in a towel, she tucked it into the basket she'd prepared and headed out the door. Haakan had left a horse all harnessed and hooked up to the buggy for her.

Thank you, Lord. I am married to such a fine man. So many things to thank you for today and every day.

Since Kaaren had already left, Ingeborg drove to the church all by herself, wishing she could pick Ellie up. Being out with all the women would have been good for her, but it was her quilt they were finishing. When she arrived, the women were already stitching away two to a side, quilting the final end. Some were cutting pieces, and others at the sewing machines were piecing more quilt tops.

Kaaren looked up with a smile. "You finally got here."

"I know. Sorry I'm late. Hot as it is, you'd have thought that bread would rise in minutes." She set her basket on the table and took out the loaf of bread, unwrapping it so it would cool without turning the crust soggy.

"You can have this machine," Mary Martha Solberg said. "I'm

doing a crazy quilt in wools." She stood and whispered in Ingeborg's ear. "I was too lazy to cut small pieces. This goes faster."

"How are you?"

"Getting bigger every day, as you can see. I am so grateful that I've had easy pregnancies."

"Something to be grateful for, all right." Ingeborg sat down at what had become the traveling sewing machine. While it belonged to Penny, it showed up wherever there was sewing or quilting to be done. They'd often teased her that she should charge rent for it, or let people check it out, like a lending library.

The discussion of the day centered, at least for now, on the proposed flour mill.

"Mr. Valders says we must not bite off more than we can chew. This will be a monumental investment." Hildegunn Valders always quoted her husband as if he were an official.

"He said that back when we all formed the co-op and built the grain elevator too, and look how well that has turned out," Kaaren reminded them.

"Ja, at least we are not getting cheated at this end of the shipping of the wheat." Mrs. Magron, who rarely disagreed with Hildegunn Valders, spoke softly, as always.

"That Hjelmer always has big ideas," Hildegunn said with a sniff.

"Well, this time he has found other investors," Penny said.

"But then we won't own it like we do the elevator. That's brought money in for all of us." Kaaren looked up from her stitching.

"Mr. Valders says our bank hasn't the kind of money needed for such an enterprise, and we should not borrow money."

Penny stopped by Ingeborg at the sewing machine. "Mr. Valders. Why won't she ever use his proper name?"

"Why, Mrs. Bjorklund, what a thing to say." Ingeborg widened her eyes and looked innocent. The two chuckled. Hildegunn Valders was not an easy person to get along with, as Ingeborg had learned to her dismay a few years earlier. Forgiveness had been hard to come by. She wasn't sure Hildegunn had ever really gotten over their set-to.

Why was forgiveness such a hard thing to learn? She wanted to ask them all that question, but how could she do so without seeming to accuse anyone?

Laughter, even giggles, came from different parts of the room, conversations everywhere and questions too. The discussion on the flour mill died out, and they moved on to other events. Since Hjelmer was involved in politics, they usually looked to Penny for knowledge in that area, but today she kept on sewing without commenting.

"I read in the paper that Mr. Roosevelt claims his health was restored when he came to Dakota Territory." Hildegunn broached a new subject.

"You've got to admit, we have ourselves a good paper in the *Blessing Gazette*," Mrs. Nordstrum said. "That Thorliff, he finds all kinds of interesting things. Why, he said he is going to run a column with recipes and wondered if any of us would like to contribute."

Penny and Ingeborg exchanged looks of surprise. Ingeborg shook her head no. He'd not mentioned it to her.

"These men of ours, do they ever tell us anything?"

"Sure, what they want for supper."

Penny sucked on a finger she'd just jabbed with a needle. "Hjelmer's never home to tell me what he wants for supper. When he is home, all I ever hear is, 'When are you going to bake cookies?' He goes weeks without good cookies." She rolled her eyes, her tone biting off the words.

"Ja, that poor Hjelmer, staying at a hotel where they make sure he is comfortable." Ingeborg tried to lighten the talk. She knew how much Penny resented, even hated, having him gone so much, yet everyone had to admit that he managed to bring good things their way, like the quick approval of the grain elevator, help after the flood, and now the possibility of a flour mill. But then, Hjelmer always had been a gambler, and one who won most of the time. Now, as president of the bank, he gambled with bigger things. She'd never thought of it quite that way before. Farmers were gamblers in a way too. They gambled against the weather, bugs, accidents, prairie fires, hail—all the things that could wipe out what had looked like a good crop. Hard work and wisdom often were destroyed by fate.

"You're thinking mighty hard." Penny laid another stack of pieces to be sewn beside her.

"I know. I'm trying to figure out how to help Andrew, but God keeps telling me to do nothing." *Uff da.*

"Nothing but pray?"

"Ja, that is right."

"Ah, Ingeborg, that seems to be the fate of most of us women. These men go off and do all kinds of things, and we stay home and pray for them."

"Ja, and make sure everything keeps going on as usual." Ingeborg sewed two squares together, making sure the ends met perfectly. "We aren't complaining, are we?"

"I don't think so, more like discussing."

"Discussing what?" Kaaren left her chair at the stretcher bars and stopped beside the machine.

"Oh, men and life in general."

"Sounds interesting. Mary Martha asked me to help with the Christmas program this year. You think Thorliff might like to write us a new one?"

"You'd have to ask him. I didn't even know he was looking for someone to have a recipe column."

Kaaren smiled. "We're always the last to know. Someone asked me if we should find more chickens for Ellie."

"I planned on it. But not until they move into the house. Astrid said one of the hens she has is setting."

"Does Ellie know?"

Ingeborg shrugged. "Any time I mention her, Andrew goes real quiet."

"Uh-oh."

"Ladies, let us clean up here a bit and take our break for dinner," Hildegunn called out. "Kaaren, will you please read to us while we eat?"

Kaaren nodded. She'd been doing this for so many years now, it had become a tradition.

"I've got to slice the bread. It was too hot when I brought it." Ingeborg pushed back her chair.

"I sure wish you had time to bake bread to sell in the store," Penny said over her shoulder as she headed to the table to set out the cake she'd brought.

"That might be something for some of the new people to do. It would help until their farms get to producing."

"I don't need just any bread. No one makes bread the way you do."

As soon as the food was all set out, Hildegunn raised her hand for quiet. Since she didn't mind being in charge, the other women let her lead year after year. Actually, she loved being in charge, and they all knew it, no matter that each spring she said it was time for someone else to take over. She never asked twice, just sighed and said, "Well, if there is no one else, I will have to keep on. We must have a leader."

"Shall we sing the blessing?"

They joined her and split into harmony on the amen, holding it out, enjoying the blended sound.

"Does anyone have a special passage they'd like me to read?" Kaaren asked after everyone had filled their plates and found a place to sit.

"First Corinthians thirteen," someone suggested.

After Kaaren read the love chapter, she moved to I John and then to Psalm 139.

"You read so beautifully," Brynja Magron said with a smile and a sigh. "I never get tired of hearing you read."

"Thank you. I love to read aloud. Seems there's never enough time in the summer, only in the winter. Do any of you have any prayer requests before we begin to pray?"

"About the flour mill. That needs lots of prayer."

"I have a pain in my hip. Please pray it goes away."

"For Penny for losing her baby."

"For Ellie and Andrew too."

The requests came from all around the group. Kaaren nodded her encouragement. When the suggestions faded away, she closed her eyes and folded her hands. "I will begin, and then any of you who feels led to pray, please do so, for we know that where two or three are gathered in His name, Jesus will be right in the midst. Father, we come to you with all of our prayers, both of praise and of petition. I thank you that we can gather like this both to work and to draw closer to you." She paused and waited for the others to join in. One by one all the prayers mentioned were covered, along with many others, including wisdom for those who ran the country and a request for revival in the land. A sniff or two added even more depth as Mrs. Nordstrum confessed her feelings of despair over her son Robbie, who'd been injured badly a few years earlier and never grew anymore in his mind.

"And Father we know that you hear our prayers and that you have promised to answer. We love you and wait with faith. In Jesus' precious name we pray. Amen."

They all joined on the amen, several wiping their eyes as they did so.

"Sometimes I don't know what I'd do were it not for all of you." Mrs. Magron smiled around the circle. "All these years I've been coming, all the changes we've seen, I tell you, it is most amazing."

"So true." Kaaren smiled again. "I'd like to remind you that any time you feel led to pray for any of our concerns, please do so. And for all our men out on the threshing crews too, dear Lord, protect them."

"We better get back to stitching here, or this quilt won't be done before Christmas." Hildegunn called them back to work. They all found a place to work, and the cheerful hum of visiting and encouraging started up again.

Ingeborg took one of the chairs around the quilt frame and picked up stitching where someone else had left off. "I think this is the loveliest quilt we've made yet."

"You say that every time."

"Do I really?" She looked around the room to see others nodding. "Well, I never."

Amid chuckles and heads shaking, she laughed at herself. "Come to think of it, Haakan says I say the same thing about the Christmas tree every year."

Later, as the group was breaking up and Ingeborg was picking up the scraps of thread and cloth around the sewing machines, which they would load into the wagons to return to their owners, Penny knelt beside her.

"Thank you for praying for me."

"You're welcome."

"Do you ever forget?"

"No, never, though after a while the pain is not so great. But you always wonder who that child might have become, what her life might have been like."

Penny sighed. "I was afraid I was just being morbid. Agnes was the one I carried the longest. I was so sure." Her voice trailed off.

"You're not being morbid. It's not been very long."

"Thank you."

Ingeborg watched the young woman turn and smile at something someone else said, as if nothing was wrong. *Why are we like that? Hiding the hurts as if we're ashamed of them? When they're not even our fault? Like me with being so cranky, and I didn't want to tell anyone. Yet when I talked with Elizabeth, she was able to help me. Lord, how often have I not reached out to someone when I should have, when you've prompted me, and I said, "Later"? Even after all these years of knowing these women, there are too many secrets.*

ELLIE, HOW COULD YOU *do such a thing?*

Andrew let up the pressure on the cow's udders. "Sorry." Cows did not like force. They liked to be sweet-talked. Like women. He sucked in a deep breath and let the relaxation flow down his arms to his hands.

The cow quit switching her tail, and her restless hooves remained on the floor.

Why do I have the feeling Ellie knows more than she is telling me? That thought had been bombarding him all day. Had one of the cigarettes or cigars from those smoking out back been accidentally tossed into some dry grass and smoldered until it finally flamed? That was the only possibility he could think of, unless someone set it on purpose. He thought to the fire earlier in the spring. They finally decided some bum had sought refuge and went to sleep smoking. Burned himself up along with the machine shed. That the body was found back in a corner supported the theory. Sheriff Becker from Grafton said the same thing. Bridget said there had been a man asking at the boardinghouse if he could work for a meal earlier in the day. So that all fell into place. But this—there was no rhyme nor reason for the barn to go up in flames.

He finished the milking and hauled the full milk cans up to the cheese house to pour into the big flat pans in the morning.

"Astrid," Andrew asked at the supper table, "can you think of anything else from the night of the fire?"

She sighed and shook her head, giving him a look of patience pushed to the extreme. "We've gone over this a hundred times."

"I know. You said you all raced out of the house after Ellie. But didn't anyone see something? Please, I know this is repetitious, but I have to know." *Besides, I have a feeling Ellie knows something she's not telling me.*

How would you know? You don't see her much more often than if she were in Grafton. How could he ever tell her that the sight of her without hair had ignited his rage all over again?

Astrid shook her head, but she closed her eyes, the easier to replay the scene. "I was right behind Ellie. We saw smoke. Ellie took charge and sent Sophie home. She said, 'Sophie, you can run the fastest. You go get our families,' or something like that. Then Grace and Deborah went to ring the church bell. They took off. Ellie started for the barn screaming, 'My chickens.' Rebecca tried to stop her, but she pulled away, and . . ." Astrid stopped her singsong recitation.

"What?"

"Ellie said something else"—Astrid's eyes widened—"right when we ran out the door."

Andrew leaned forward. Biting his lip, he waited with all the patience he could muster.

Astrid frowned, scrunching her eyes closed. "'Someone at the barn. I see someone.'" She shook her head again. "Something like that, but Andrew, I wouldn't count on—"

The screen door slammed as Andrew dashed out.

He ran across the fields, climbing fences rather than following the longer roads, figuring he could run to town faster than catching a horse. He flopped down on the steps to Thorliff's house to catch his breath before going to find Ellie. To catch his breath and order himself not to flinch when he saw her.

"Well, look who's here, the long-lost suitor." Thorliff joined him on the steps.

"Is Ellie here?"

"Nothing like saying, 'Hello, how are you' or 'Good to see you.'"

"I need to talk to Ellie."

"Ah, but the question is, does Ellie want to talk with you? You've not treated her very well, you know."

Don't preach to me. I do enough of that myself. "I know and I have to apologize. Would you please ask her if she'll see me?" The thought of Ellie not wanting to see him made his stomach knot and his throat shut. "Please, Thorliff."

Thorliff laid a hand on his brother's shoulder. "Don't count on it." On his way into the house, he stopped and turned around. "You're not going to badger her again, are you?"

"What do you mean?"

"You know. Ask her the same questions over and over. If I were you, I'd apologize and ask her to forgive you, and leave it go at that. Talk about the wedding or something girls like to talk about. Just giving you a word of advice. That's all. A warning too. If Elizabeth thinks you are not taking good care of her patient, she'll string you up by your ears. I can tell you from experience, you don't want to have that happen."

"But—"

"I'm just warning you."

Andrew glanced down at his shirt. Bits of wheat straw and chaff clung to it; dust from the threshing grayed the material. *I should have changed, washed up good and changed my shirt, at least.* He took off his hat and beat the dust out by banging it against his leg, then smoothed his hair back with both hands before setting his hat in place again. Since when did he start acting before thinking? Since Ellie got him so tied up in knots, he didn't know here from there. He could feel the furrows deepening in his forehead, so he smoothed them away with his fingers. Afraid to turn his head and be disappointed, he froze when he heard the door squeak open.

"Andrew, would you like to come in?" Ellie said, stepping out onto the porch.

"Ah, it's nice out here. Do you feel like sitting down here or up on the chairs?" He had yet to turn and look at her. "I mean it is cooler out here, and—"

"Andrew, am I so terribly deformed that you cannot even look at me?"

"Why? Ellie, why would you say that?" He leaped to his feet, whipped his hat off with one hand, and turned to stare at her feet, her skirt, anywhere but her face, her sweet face that was no longer framed by long golden hair that glinted in the sunlight and glowed in the lamplight.

Her sigh tugged at his heart and set him to calling himself names, which made him chew on grump again.

"Here, take this chair. I'm going to get us something to drink." The door slammed behind her before he could get any more words past the lump in his throat. *I don't want something to drink. I want to talk to you.* He sat down in one of the rocking chairs and hooked his hat over his knee.

The door squeaked again, and he leaped to his feet. "I'll get that for you."

Ellie backed out of the door, tray in her hands. She handed him the tray and moved a small table in between the two chairs. "Set it here, please."

Andrew did as she said and took his chair again. She sat on the edge of the seat, as if ready to run at the slightest provocation. She handed him a glass of lemonade and held the plate of cookies until he took a couple. The crunch of cookies broke the silence.

Might as well get it over with. He took a swig of lemonade to wash down the cookie that stuck in his throat. And coughed. Glancing up, he caught her staring at him, her face frozen in a polite smile, the kind one wore when one didn't really care for the visitor. *Oh, Ellie.* He wanted to reach for her hand, but the thought that she might not let him take her hand scared him so badly he choked on another bite of cookie.

He drank more, cleared his throat, and forced out the words. "Please forgive me, Ellie. I am so sorry."

"Sorry for what?"

"Um, for being so angry at you." He rubbed the knuckle on his right hand. "I guess for being so angry at everything."

"Andrew, you've not been to see me for four days."

"I'm sorry. I just can't—"

"Can't what? Forgive me for doing something stupid? Yes, I know now I should not have gone into that barn, but I did and I've paid the price for that. I'm still paying the price for it." She paused to catch her breath. "Or are you sorry you can't look at me?"

"I look at you—" His voice tightened.

"No you don't. You look at my skirt, you look past me, but you don't look right at me."

Ellie had raised her voice. She was yelling at him! He stared at her, shock widening his eyes.

When she started to cough, he clenched his jaw and waited.

She took a sip of lemonade and sat back in her chair, her chest heaving with the effort of sucking in much needed air.

He stared at her hands, tightly woven in her lap. "Astrid said she thinks you saw someone at the barn that night."

"I might have."

"Do you know who it is?"

"I'm not sure."

"Well, who do you think it might be?"

His sarcastic tone brought her forward in her chair. She kept her voice low so she could breathe better. "Andrew Bjorklund, you better listen real good, because I'm only going to say this once. I'm not sure who it was, and you will not badger me to find out. I don't think for a moment someone set that fire on purpose, and you just better let it go, or you'll turn into some bitter, angry man with no friends because you drove them all away."

"Ellie, I—" He swallowed the fire that leaped in his belly.

"I will forgive you. I have forgiven you."

"It doesn't sound like it to me." His words could have been heard above a threshing machine. "I have to know if someone set that fire. He almost killed you."

"I almost killed myself. Can't you understand that?" She whipped the scarf off her head. "Look at me. My hair is growing back, my voice is coming back. Let it go, Andrew Bjorklund. Let God deal with it. He's given me a new life, and He'd give you one if you'd let Him." She doubled over coughing and staggered to the door.

"Let me help you!" He reached for her, but she slid past him and disappeared into the house. He could hear her coughing all the way down the hall. He reached for the door handle, stopped, and stared down at his hat, mangled between his hands. He stomped off the porch and toward the street, cramming his hat back onto his head, his arms pumping at his sides. *Let it go?* What did she know? *Why'd I bother to say I'm sorry anyway? That's the way she wants it, so be it. She knows something she's not telling me. I know she does.*

Staring at the ground, he almost bumped into Toby Valders standing in front of him. "What do you want?"

"Don't take it out on Ellie."

"Who do you think you are?"

"I was at your barn."

"What! Why were you there? You started that fire?"

"No, I was at the barn, but I—" Toby reeled back from the round-house punch to his jaw.

With a roar of rage Andrew followed that punch by leaping onto the stumbling man. He grabbed Toby by the throat, and they fell to the ground, Andrew on top. He banged Toby's head against the ground, knees holding him down.

"You nearly killed Ellie, you . . ." A string of names followed, accompanying the slamming.

"Andrew, no. Stop it!" Thorliff tried to pull him off but got an elbow in the gut for his trouble. He leaped onto his brother's back and locked an arm around his neck. "Andrew! Andrew! You'll kill him."

With a roar Andrew threw Thorliff off his back and staggered to his feet. "Get up, you slimy dog." Wiping blood from his nose, where Toby had landed a punch, Andrew leaned over to grab Toby's collar and drag him to his feet.

Thorliff tackled him from behind, catching him in the knees and slamming him to the ground.

Andrew lay there, one hand pounding the dirt. "Ellie! Ellie!"

Having already heard the fight going on, Elizabeth and Ellie were on the porch. At his scream Ellie ran to kneel at his side, coughing and choking but grabbing his hand.

"Oh, Andrew, what have you done?"

"I think he might have just killed Toby."

31

"Let's get him into the surgery," Elizabeth ordered. "Thorliff, you take his feet. Andrew, get up here and help carry him. Be careful with his head. If you broke his neck, there's no chance."

"I didn't mean to—"

"Of course you didn't mean to, but you did it. Now, let's see if we can keep him alive."

"Toby, you've got to live. I didn't mean to do this." Andrew leaned forward, his entire body shaking, fear forcing out any residual anger.

Ellie, tears streaming down her cheeks, stared into Toby's pale and bloody face. "Please live, Toby. Fight to live."

Thorliff and Andrew did as Elizabeth told them and carried the body around to the surgery door.

"Lay him on the table." Elizabeth put her stethoscope to his chest. "He's still alive." While she spoke, her fingers inspected the back of his head. "Mushy. Thorliff, is there any ice left in the icehouse?"

"Ja, some," Andrew answered.

"Get it here as fast as you can. We've got to keep his brain from swelling. Take the buggy." Thorliff and Andrew were out the door before she could finish speaking.

"Ellie, I need you to help me roll him onto his side and hold him there while I shave the back of his head and disinfect the wound. He could get violent if he starts to come to, so be prepared."

"You need more hands, I'm here." Henry Aarsgard came through the door. "We heard what went on."

"Thank you." Elizabeth showed them what to do, while Thelma fetched warm water from the reservoir.

"I'm here too." Penny joined them. "Tell me what to do."

"I need more light and these instruments soaked in carbolic acid. You'll find it in the bottom of that cabinet." Elizabeth snipped off the longest hair with a scissors, poured water into the soap mug, and stirred it with the bristles of the brush, then lathered the back of Toby's head. As soon as she finished shaving him, she nodded to Penny. "Hold a lamp here, so I can see better." With knowing fingers, she probed the area again. "I'm sure the cranium is at least cracked here. Might have to trephine him later, but for now I think bandages are about all I can do."

"That cut on his chin will need stitches." Penny raised the lamp higher so Elizabeth could see more.

"That's the least of his worries. I think we have cracked or broken ribs too. But at least his lungs are clear. That head wound is the worst. Why Andrew had to beat his head against that rock-hard ground is beyond me."

"What happened out there?" Henry asked.

"Andrew and I had a fight, and something happened when he saw Toby, I guess." Ellie rolled another towel and braced it against Toby's back.

"Do you know who was at the barn?" Elizabeth looked to Ellie.

Ellie nodded. "Toby. But I couldn't tell Andrew that. I'm sure he didn't set the fire. Toby and Gerald had a bad start in life, but they turned into hard-working men. He and Andrew just don't get along."

"Could be they had to chop too much wood together." Elizabeth finished her examination. "All right, we have him braced. Let's clean him up, and I'll put a couple of stitches in that chin. Henry, could you get his boots off?"

Ellie backed off to be out of the way, but her mind sent her pleas heavenward. *Please, Lord, don't let him die. Make him whole and sound again.*

"I want to see my son." Hildegunn Valders stepped inside the doorway, Mr. Valders right behind her.

"Give me a couple more minutes here, and then you can see him."

"I want to see him now."

Penny went to the door. "Look, Mr. and Mrs. Valders, let Dr. Bjorklund finish her work, and then you can see him. There isn't much room in here for this many people."

"Why didn't someone come and tell us right away?"

"We haven't had time. We're doing all we can to make him comfortable."

Please, Lord, get the ice here, Ellie prayed. *Calm this situation down.*

"That Andrew, he's always had it in for Toby. Likes to use him for a punching bag." Hildegunn Valders clamped her arms across her chest.

"Come this way, please." Penny took them both by an arm and led them into the waiting room. "You can help your boy best right now by praying for him. Sit down here. I will let you know when you can see him."

Ellie went to the window to see if the buggy was in sight yet. *I wish I could go get Ingeborg. If only I could breathe better so I could be more helpful.*

"There, Toby, you are going to have an interesting scar on your chin, but all the girls will think it fascinating." Elizabeth dropped her instruments back into the carbolic acid and lifted his eyelids to check his eyes.

Ellie watched Elizabeth's face, hoping for signs of hope, but the slight shake of the doctor's head told her to keep on praying. As soon as she heard the buggy, she went outside to wait by the door. Thorliff stopped the team, and Andrew leaped down before the buggy stopped rolling. Ingeborg followed them out of the buggy, basket over her arm.

"Oh, I am so glad you came," Ellie said.

"How is he?"

"The same. He's not regained consciousness."

Ingeborg nodded and turned to her son. "Just chop off a chunk about the size of two loaves of bread and beat it into small pieces. Cover the rest and get it in the cellar, where it's cooler." Without waiting for the ice, she went on into the surgery, with Ellie following.

"I'm glad you came." Elizabeth explained what she'd done and what she thought, then asked, "Do you know of any herbs that might reduce cranial swelling?"

"Not offhand, but a poultice of onions might help, unless there is an open wound. Then ice is best. Now I'm grateful I didn't make that last batch of ice cream." She took Toby's hand and laid her fingers across the inside of his wrist. "Pretty weak."

"I know."

Andrew brought in the gunnysack of crushed ice. "Where do you want this?"

"We'll lay his head on it and then wrap some in a towel to put over the top of his head. Kind of like an ice hat or cave."

"It'll soak those bandages."

"That's all right."

Ellie huddled in the corner, praying constantly, not only for Toby but for Andrew and for herself.

After they had him situated, Elizabeth called in his adoptive parents. "You can see him now. He hasn't awakened yet, but he seems to be resting comfortably."

Hildegunn Valders glared at Andrew, then took her son's hand, patting and stroking the back. Tears trickled down her cheeks. "Oh, Toby, don't give in to this. You got to fight the good fight. Your pa and I, we're praying. This wasn't your fault, you know."

Ellie looked up, but Andrew had left the room. He didn't need to hear those things from this woman. She had a feeling Hildegunn Valders didn't really understand forgiveness either. Least not from the stories she'd heard.

"We're going to move him now. Please go back to the waiting room, and when we have him comfortable, I'll show you the way to his room. You can sit with him for as long as you'd like."

"You be careful with him."

"Oh, we will."

"And don't you let that Andrew Bjorklund anywheres near him."

Henry harrumphed as they left the room. Elizabeth smiled at him. "Go get Andrew and Thorliff, will you please, Ellie?"

When they returned, Elizabeth assigned each of them a corner. "We're going to use this sheet to carry him. Each of you take a corner, and on three we will lift together and move him into the room next to Ellie's. Then once we have him settled, you can leave, and I'll bring his parents in. Ingeborg, could you please go pick up Inga? I heard her starting to fuss. How she slept through all this, I'll never know."

After the Valerses took their seats on either side of Toby's bed, Ingeborg entered the room. "May I bring a cup of coffee? I know how hard this waiting can be." She caught Anner's nod, but Hildegunn straightened to glare fire at her.

"Your son tried to kill my Toby."

Ingeborg thought of several things to say but instead backed out of the room. *Lord, help me. Help them. And please let Toby live.* She brought a tray back with two cups of coffee and a plate of cookies.

By later that night when Toby still hadn't wakened, Ingeborg took the seat by the bed. His parents had gone home an hour or so earlier, Hildegunn promising to return the next day.

"Can I get you anything?" Ellie asked.

"You can sit with me if you like. Conversation always makes the time pass easier."

Ellie sat down on the straight-backed chair. "Do you think he'll live?"

"Only God knows at this time, but he has a good chance."

"Where's Andrew? Gone home?"

"Ja. And how are you?"

"Tired, and my chest hurts some." Ellie touched the covering on her head. "The burns are better."

"Maybe we should have put you in ice too. All this excitement." Ingeborg picked up her knitting, moved the stitches toward the business end of the needles, and inserted the empty one into the first stitch of the new row. "When did you know?"

"Who was at the barn?"

"Ja."

"I dreamed the whole thing a couple of nights ago and realized it was Toby at the barn by his build and the way he always wore his hat. I couldn't tell anyone because I wasn't absolutely sure. And what good would telling have done?" She sighed. "I tried to prevent this."

"If there is an infection, one must lance it so the pus can drain out and the healing can begin."

"You mean for Andrew?"

"Ja. And perhaps for Toby too."

"But not if he dies."

"That is why we will leave this in God's hands, where it belongs. You go on to bed so you can get stronger too."

"I will. And I'll keep praying. I know all of you prayed for me and look how well I am doing." She leaned over and hugged Ingeborg. "Mange takk."

By the next morning, there was still no change in Toby. He lay as if only asleep, breathing easily but nonresponsive.

"Be grateful he is not having convulsions," Elizabeth said when Ellie asked her about it.

"I will."

"Keep spooning him water. That's important."

❧

When the train came from Grafton the next day, Sheriff Charles Becker stepped off the passenger car. He rented a horse and wagon at the livery and rode on out to the Bjorklund farm. Ingeborg met him at the front porch.

"Welcome, Sheriff, can I fix you a cup of coffee?"

"Thanks, but I think not. Mrs. Bjorklund, where might I find your son Andrew?"

"He's over to the Solbergs' with the threshing crew."

"Can you give me directions?"

Ingeborg told him how to find the place, then added, "What is this about?"

"It's about your son almost killing a man. We don't take too kindly to that kind of violence here in Walsh County. I'm sorry, ma'am." He touched the brim of his hat and returned to the wagon.

How did the sheriff learn about this? Poor Andrew.

Hildegunn, of course. She must have sent a telegram. Ingeborg clamped her teeth together. Leave it to that woman.

"Hello, Sheriff, welcome to Blessing." Haakan stepped away from the threshing machine so he could be heard.

"Sorry, this isn't a social call, Haakan. I come on business."

"How can I help you?"

"Could you point out your son Andrew to me?"

"I can, but you mind telling me why?"

"Don't go making this hard for me. I don't like this any better than you do. But I got to arrest your boy for beating Toby Valders near to death."

"I see." Haakan took a step back. "Toby didn't die, you know?"

"I know, but we can't have men going around and losing their tempers like that. Sets a bad example for the younger ones."

"There are a lot of circumstances to consider here."

"Be that as it may, I'm going to have to take him in." He looked around, studying the men. "That him in the blue shirt and straw hat?"

"Ja, it is. But I need him here for threshing. He's one of my crew."

"Sorry. But the law is the law. Since this is Friday, he won't go before the judge until Monday. You better be praying that the Valders boy don't die."

"We don't need a threat to do that, Sheriff. We've all already been praying." Haakan walked with the sheriff to where Andrew was forking wheat bundles onto the conveyor belt.

"Andrew Bjorklund, you are under arrest for the beating of Toby Valders. Will you come with me, or do I have to put handcuffs on you?"

Andrew looked to his father, who nodded. "Jail? Did Toby die?"

"No. Just come with me, please."

"Yes, sir." *Going to jail. I'm going to jail. Lord God, save me, please.*

32

I'M GOING TO JAIL.

Andrew stared out the train window, the train carrying him to Grafton and the jail. He glanced at the man beside him who gazed stoically forward. *How did he know I'd beaten Toby senseless?* Trapping any of the thoughts ricocheting through his mind took more than he had to give at that moment. *So quickly. This happened just yesterday. Toby is still alive. The telegraph.* He nodded. *Of course, someone sent a telegraph. Who? Who else but Mrs. Valders?* The way she'd glared at him the night before still sent chills up his back.

Pure hatred. Not just anger—she had a right to be angry—but hatred. Why? *What have I done to her?*

Other than beat her younger son into a coma and possible death. Oh, Lord, you know I didn't mean for this to happen.

But if he started that fire . . . Andrew ground his teeth and clenched his fists. The roiling in his stomach gave him a bitter taste. This whole thing gave him a bitter taste. The more he thought, the angrier he grew. *Toby! It is all Toby's fault!*

The sheriff cleared his throat and looked at Andrew. "Now, we're almost to town. You're not going to run or do something foolish, are you?"

Only if I had any chance of getting away. Andrew shook his head. "No."

"Good, because I got handcuffs right here if need be."

"I won't run."

"Sure sorry about this, son. Fine young man like you. What made you do it?"

"He started the fire that burned my barn down."

"You know that for certain?"

"He was there. Someone saw him."

"Don't mean he set the fire. Why would he want to do something terrible like that?"

"He and I . . . well, when we were kids in school, he'd pick on the younger, weaker ones, and I'd stick up for them."

"Meaning you two got into fistfights."

Andrew nodded. "Pastor Solberg always set us to chopping wood to work it off."

"And you think that this Toby bears a grudge?"

"Seems so." *He calls me Prince Andrew. He's jealous as all get-out.*

"You could say there's no love lost between you two?"

"You could say that."

The train slowed, iron wheels screeching against iron tracks.

"But you didn't set out to kill him?"

"No." *If I'd wanted to kill him, no one would have stopped me. But I did want to kill him. He hurt Ellie.* Back and forth his thoughts raged, ripping his insides with each volley.

He walked beside the sheriff to the jail and preceded him into the office. The door closing behind him made him flinch. When the cell door clanged, he stumbled forward and collapsed on a wooden cot covered by a tick filled with hay.

"Someone will bring you supper after a while. The slop bucket there is for your use. I'll bring you a jug of water."

"Thank you." Andrew ground the words past clenched teeth. If he kept his teeth together tight enough, perhaps he could keep from screaming.

That evening the Bjorklunds gathered around the kitchen table at Thorliff's house so that Ellie could join them. "So what can we do?" Haakan asked.

Thorliff looked over to his father. "There's not much anyone can do right now. I've sent a telegram to Olaf and asked him and Goodie to go visit Andrew in the morning. They'll let us know how he is."

"Should we take him some clean clothes? You know he went straight from the threshing." Ingeborg kept up her knitting, the needles flashing in the lamplight.

Elizabeth left the room to fetch Inga, who'd announced it was time to eat. For a change she'd let her mother have supper without any interruption. When she returned, Elizabeth asked, "Did the sheriff say anything more before he dragged Andrew off?"

Haakan thought a moment. "Just asked if he needed to use handcuffs and that he was arresting Andrew for the assault on Toby Valders. I tried to tell him of the circumstances, but he didn't want to hear anything else." Rubbing his tongue around his teeth, his eyes slitted as he thought back.

Ingeborg watched her husband, praying that he would remember anything that might help them. Her son, her dear Andrew, was in jail. *Lord, was there something we should have done about his temper? Did we fail him? I know we did the best we could, but what if the best wasn't good enough.* She held herself together through sheer force of will, wanting instead to throw herself into Haakan's arms and cry until there were no more tears.

"So there is nothing more we can do until tomorrow." Haakan looked each of the others in the eyes. "Except pray."

They all nodded.

Thorliff shook his head. "If this is anything like the cases I've sat through in Northfield when I worked for Mr. Rogers, the judge won't see him until Monday. He will either release Andrew at that point, possibly asking for bail, or will order him left in jail until there is some word on Toby."

"If Toby dies?"

"Then Andrew will be tried for murder."

The silence after Thorliff spoke seemed to suck the air out of the room. One after the other they coughed or cleared their throats.

Astrid broke the silence. "Andrew, I'm so mad at you I could beat you up myself. Why did he do such a stupid, stupid thing?" She stamped her foot on the *stupid*s, as if pounding on her brother.

Ingeborg laid down her knitting, one needle falling out of the last row of stitches, and gathered her daughter in her arms, where she cried on her mother's shoulder. "Shh, shh. I know. See how easy it is to be angrier than you ever thought possible?"

"Aren't you mad at him?"

Ingeborg nodded. "And at Toby, at all of it. But what does being angry do?" She paused to listen inside herself. *And at Hildegunn Valders. Why does she always make things worse? Will I have to forgive her again?*

Elizabeth returned from putting the baby in her cradle. "Mor, would you please go check on Toby? I heard his folks leave a bit ago."

"You are sure they are gone?"

Elizabeth nodded. "Why?"

"I don't want to see that woman right now." Anger flared inside Ingeborg in spite of her good intentions. Leave it to Hildegunn Valders to cause more trouble than was needed. When the good Lord was handing out compassion, she'd been somewhere else for sure. *Remember? She and Anner took those boys in?* Uff da, why did God always have to remind her of the good side of someone she really wanted to despise?

Sleep never brought Andrew a reprieve that night. Whenever he closed his eyes, all he could see and hear was Toby and the sound of his head hitting the ground. So he lay in jail staring at the heavy joists in the ceiling. The bars of his cage threw shadow bars on the floor until he felt them closing in on him, driving out the air. He leaped to his feet and stuck his face against the bars of the window opening.

In the morning he smelled the coffee before a woman arrived with the tray. "I brought this myself, since you're the only prisoner right now. Most likely that will change by the time midnight rolls around. Sheriff Becker always has to throw someone in for being drunk and disorderly." The woman, her gray hair knotted in a bun and a once-white apron covering her clear to her toes, held the tray in front of her. She peered at him through the bars. "You come and get this now." Bending over, she slid the tray through a slot near the floor.

"Thank you." His mother's drilling on good manners stood him in good stead, but he didn't change positions.

"You might want to eat while it's hot. I hurried it over right quick so you could have a hot breakfast. Might make your day go a little better."

Andrew nodded. The thought of food made him gag. The hours before him marched like soldiers in a line without end. Sitting on the edge of the bed, he propped his head in his hands and scrubbed his scalp with vicious fingers.

"Just slide the tray back out when you are finished."

"Ja, I will. Thank you." *Take it now before I kick it across the room.* Self-condemnation rode him with Spanish spurs and a merciless quirt.

"Can I bring you anything else?" She sounded like his mor, a Norwegian accent pleasant to the ear.

He shook his head. "No, nothing, thank you." He heard her say something to someone in the office, and then a door closed behind her. So many doors closing. All locking him in.

Sometime later a different man stopped at the cell door. "I'm Deputy Bronson. There's a man here to see you. Says he is Olaf Wold."

"No."

"He says he's a friend of your family."

"No. I mean, I don't want to see him." Andrew looked up from his study of the pits and rocks in the concrete floor. "I don't want to see anyone. Tell him no one is to come from Blessing either. I don't want to see anyone."

"Suit yourself, but that's kinda rude, being as he came over here and all."

"Just tell him." Andrew swallowed. "Please."

"You didn't touch your breakfast."

"I know."

"Push that tray on out, then. Shame to waste good food like that. Della is a good cook. She feels right bad such a fine young man as you . . ."

Get out of here! Andrew clamped his mouth shut before he said something he shouldn't. He glared at the deputy but got up off the bed to push the tray back. He could hear the discussion going on in the office, and before long, the door closed again.

Deputy Bronson returned. "He said I was to give you this and don't take no for an answer."

Guilt wore spurs too. After all the things that Onkel Olaf had made for him and Ellie, he should have . . .

"Olaf doesn't deserve to be treated like that," Ingeborg's voice whispered in his ear. Andrew stared at the man holding out a leather-bound book. A Bible. Olaf had brought him a Bible. *"Always remember, Andrew, no matter how bad things are, you'll find help in the Word of God."* Again his mother's voice. Andrew stood and walked across the cell to take the offered book.

"Thank you." He set it on the foot of the bed and took up pacing before he ripped the pages out. Three paces to the bars, three paces back.

You're not a destructive man. Why do you want to kick and rip and pound? The inner argument picked up again. One side against the other. Sometimes his mother's voice, sometimes Haakan's, sometimes his own. Even Pastor Solberg threw in his counsel.

When he turned down dinner, Della tsked and shook her head. "Ya can't fight to live if you don't eat."

What difference does it make? Toby dies, and they'll hang me. Or send me to prison. Dear God, let Toby live! Or has he died already?

Ellie held the spoon to Toby's lips again. "Please drink again, Toby." She set it between his lips and tipped the water in. She watched his throat, and sure enough, he swallowed. Never had she been so grateful for such a simple act. She repeated the routine until her arm ached. If only he would show some other sign that he was still in there.

Elizabeth would say she'd done well. Who'd have ever thought that she would be helping care for Toby Valders and Andrew would be sitting in jail? *Oh, dear Lord, please bring your love and compassion to work in this whole mess.* She touched the turban of bandages she wore. Even though she knew the burns weren't serious, she never would have dreamed superficial burns could hurt so much. Of course she remembered burning her finger on a sadiron one time. How badly that had hurt.

It must be time for her willow-bark tea again. Between that and the honey, her head and throat were both soothed. Just the thought of coughing made it happen. She took her cup and spoon out into the hall and leaned against the wall while she sucked in more air, forcing herself to breathe deeply, as Elizabeth insisted she do. Fighting to breathe reminded her of the fire and the fight. The fight and the fire. Both entwined with years of angry words and torment. Sometimes she wished she could knock their heads together. More violence. Violence begets violence.

Ingeborg joined her in the hallway. "You go on to bed now, and I'll sit with him." She motioned Ellie to the bed she'd just left.

Ellie nodded, her breathing easier again. "After I heat my tea."

"I'll do that. You go to bed. Do you need more pillows?"

Recovering from the coughing attack, Ellie just wanted to melt into a puddle and leak away, she was so weak. She shook her head and staggered to the bed, sinking down on the edge. After drinking the tea Ingeborg brought her, she lay back against the stack of pillows and tried to relax her breathing. *Lord, please help us all. Only you can do this.*

❧

"What do they mean, he won't have visitors?" Thorliff stared at his father.

"Here's the telegram; read it for yourself." Haakan handed the piece of paper to his son.

No one is to come Stop No one Stop Andrew said Stop Gave him a Bible Stop Olaf Wold.

Thorliff made a face. "What did he do—leave his brains at home?"

"Now, now." Ingeborg refilled their coffee cups. "I have a feeling Andrew is wrestling with more than we realize. Think how you would feel."

"What do you mean?"

"I mean, I believe God is answering our prayers but not exactly the way we think He should." Ingeborg looked up to see Ellie staring at her out of red-rimmed eyes. *You poor child. Father, hold her tight in your mighty hand.* She thought to the many prayers she'd sent up, the times in the night when she got up and sat with her Bible on her lap, leafing through it to find the verses she needed. Verses to give her strength for the new day. *Lo, I am with you always.* She would repeat that over and over until she fell asleep in the chair, where Haakan often found her at daybreak.

"I've been praying too, but sometimes I can't stop crying," Ellie whispered. "I am so tired of crying."

"I know."

"I was going to take the train over to Grafton." Thorliff propped his elbows on the table and sipped from his cup. "So the question is, do we abide by his wishes or do what we think best?"

Haakan and Ingeborg stared at each other. Haakan nodded. "We honor his wishes."

"If you say so."

"What about the court hearing on Monday?" Ellie asked.

"We'll cross that bridge when we come to it." Ingeborg glanced at the clock. "We need to be heading home soon."

"I'd best get over to Solbergs' to help with the threshing." Haakan stood. "Come, I'll give you a ride home."

Ingeborg kissed Ellie's cheek. "I'll be back later. See if you can get some sleep."

The hours stretched, measured by heartbeats and heels clanking the concrete. Late in the evening Sheriff Becker lived up to his reputation and threw two men in the other cells. "Sleep it off. That way you won't go hurtin' anyone else."

Andrew ignored their drunken questions and comments. Soon they were snoring on their beds, the fumes of alcohol overlaying the stench of despair that seeped from the cold concrete walls.

Dreams deviled him through the night, and he woke to the peals of church bells greeting the dawn of Sunday morning. The Bible lay clenched in his hand.

"Well, that's better," Della said when she came to retrieve the tray. "You don't go giving up hope, boy. Your life ain't over yet."

"Thank you. Mind if I keep the cup?"

"Not at all. I can bring you a basin of water if you want to wash up. Bronson'll be along later to empty the slop pail."

Andrew rubbed his jaw, finding a still tender spot from where Haakan had clobbered him. Wheat tares from the harvesting must have imbedded in his neck, the way it itched. Washing up sounded mighty good. "If it's not too much trouble."

Andrew scrubbed face, arms, and neck, dumped the water into the slop bucket, and settled against the wall behind his bed, the Bible propped on his knees. At least when he was reading, the voices in his head put an end to their argument.

He read of Joseph in prison in Egypt for something he didn't do. God brought him out of it. He read of the disciples in prison. They sang and worshiped, and God caused their release, Paul's more than once. He read the Psalms where David pleaded for God to show His face, to hear him, to never forget him. *What about me? I deserve to be in jail.* When night came, he tucked the Bible under his head again and slept deeply without the nightmares that had pursued him the night before.

ANDREW'S IN JAIL.

Ellie had to remind herself of that over and over. And over and over she heard the *thunk* of Toby's head against the packed dirt. If Toby died, Andrew would die too or spend the rest of his life in prison, which sounded far worse, in her opinion. It was as simple as that. Two days ago she was furious at him. Now she wept constantly, no longer on the outside, for she'd managed to gain some control. But on the inside the tears poured without ceasing, as did her prayers for him, for Toby, and for them all. When she had asked God to teach her to pray without ceasing, she'd never imagined this would be the way of learning.

"Ellie, time for you to go to bed. I'll take over." Ingeborg, with her ever-present knitting in her basket, stepped through the sickroom door on Sunday evening.

Ellie stood and stretched, remembering to breathe deeply as Elizabeth kept reminding her.

"Any change?"

"No, but how long can he live without eating?"

"That's not a problem yet if we can keep getting enough fluids into him. Has there been any response when you talk with him?"

Ellie shook her head. Each time she came in and talked to Toby, she prayed this would be the time that he would blink, would talk, would give some indication that he was still alive in the husk of a body. But if he wasn't alive, he wouldn't be breathing, so he was alive. If she understood what Elizabeth meant by coma, his brain was asleep. They'd run out of ice the day before, and he had not had any convulsions. She'd been afraid he'd have them on her watch and she wouldn't know what to do.

As Ingeborg began rubbing one of her simples, as she called them, into his arms and legs, Ellie headed for her bed next door. It was time for her to move out of the surgery. She'd felt that way all afternoon. She could go back to Penny's, but she knew she wasn't strong enough to help out at the store. Besides, Rebecca was working there now and very happily. She could go visit her family in Grafton, where she would be closer to Andrew, but he'd refused to allow her or anyone to come and visit him.

"Father God, will I never see him again?" *No, don't even think that,* she ordered herself. *You've prayed for Andrew's release from jail and Toby's release from the coma, now believe that God is answering your prayers.* She climbed into bed and turned onto her side so she could look out the window. *I want to go home . . . to my house, to Andrew's and my house.*

What would the others say when she told them in the morning?

❧

"But what if you need help?" Elizabeth studied her patient, who'd become such a good friend.

"I'll run up a flag on a post. You know that I am so much better. And if I get out of breath, I shall sit down, just like I do here. Besides, I believe Toby will wake up soon and Andrew will come home. Then we'll get married, and all will be well." *If he still wants to marry me.* The thought kept nagging at her, especially after he told Olaf he didn't want to see anyone. Her mor had tried to visit him with the same results. *Did I thank you, Father, for the telegraph? What a gift that has been for us.*

Andrew, what are you thinking? What is going on in that mind of yours? Why do you cut us all out?

"I really don't think your living alone yet is a good idea."

"Well, I can't walk that far out there every day, and there are things I could be doing." Like harvesting the garden, although Astrid had assured her the beans had been picked and the corn wasn't ready yet. *But she and I can take care of that together.*

Everyone was taking care of her, but she wanted to be taking care of others, mostly Andrew. Her mind always revolved back to Andrew.

"Let me think on it." Elizabeth studied her patient. "Your breathing still concerns me."

❧

Andrew stood at attention in front of the judge on Monday morning. His stomach flip-flopped, and while he wanted to stuff his shaking hands into his pockets, he kept them at his sides.

The judge looked up from reading the sheriff's report. "Sounds like you lost your temper."

"Yes, sir."

"Has this happened before?"

"Not like this, sir."

"You better be praying that the young man pulls through. In the meantime you are remanded to jail until we know one way or another." He tapped his gavel. "Sheriff, take him back to his cell."

Andrew nodded. More waiting. *Please, Lord, let Toby live.*

Back in his cell, Andrew picked up his Bible again. *I thought . . . hoped . . .* He heaved a sigh. The judge had not changed anything. He was still in jail and would remain so. Home. He closed his eyes and sank back on his bed. Home with wide-open fields, a house of his own with wide-open windows. No bars; no stink.

Lord, I want to go home. I swear I'll never get in a fight again. Just let me go home. He waited, hoping for some kind of sign. *Toby . . .*

Don't you go blaming Toby, a small voice took up another argument. *It's your own fault you are here behind bars.*

"I know that." He thought a moment. *Do I really know that? I took the first swing. He didn't.* He sat up and forced himself to remember that day. He'd been angry at Ellie. Toby had stuck up for Ellie. *He started to say something about the barn, and I never let him finish.* What did he know? If he didn't start the fire, what did?

This is all my own fault. Lord, is that what you've been trying to tell me? He laid the Bible down on the bed and got to his feet. Back and forth across the cell he paced. *My fault. I nearly killed a man because I couldn't mind my temper. All those years Pastor Solberg tried to help me. Sure, chopping wood worked off the anger, but I missed the point.*

But, Toby . . . The other side tried to chime in.

Lord, forgive me. I sinned not only against you but against Toby. Please let him live so I can tell him I'm sorry. And Ellie and all my family. What a hothead I've been. He sat down on the bed again, then leaned against the wall, his knees bent to prop his elbows, his head too heavy to hold up. *My fault. Mea culpa.*

A verse that Pastor Solberg had assigned him to memorize floated through his mind. *"If we confess our sins, he is faithful and just to forgive us our sins, and to cleanse us from all unrighteousness."* Pastor Solberg had called that the "Christian's bar of soap."

As he continued to read the Bible and pray, Andrew grew more sure. If he got out of this with his life, he would be the man the Father meant for him to be. If only he could be with Ellie and his family again—in Blessing.

❧

Tuesday afternoon when Ellie was sitting reading the *Blessing Gazette* to Toby, she thought she heard something. But when she looked up, nothing had changed. She read an editorial by Thorliff.

"Huh."

She looked again and saw Toby's eyelids flutter. Dropping the paper onto the bed, she ran to the surgery and burst through the doorway. "I think Toby's waking up."

"I'll be right back," Elizabeth told her patient and hurried after Ellie.

Toby lay as usual, but when Elizabeth laid her hand on his foot, his eyelids fluttered again, and this time his mouth opened. "Huh."

Elizabeth took his hand. "Toby, if you can hear me, squeeze my hand." She waited. "His hand moved . . . barely, but I felt it!" She grinned at Ellie, then looked down at her patient. "Good for you, Toby. Welcome back."

A slight smile lifted one side of his mouth.

"Ellie is going to bring you some broth so you can get your strength back."

Ellie flew out of the room and made it to the kitchen before having to catch her breath. She took the broth out of the icebox and poured it into a pan to warm on the stove. While it warmed, her heart sang. *He's alive. He's awake. Thank you, Lord, Toby is alive.* She carried the cup and spoon back to the room, where Elizabeth was flexing Toby's arms for him.

"Blink if you can hear me, Toby."

He blinked, accompanied by a slight nod.

"We've been exercising your arms and legs to keep your circulation going. Here's Ellie with the broth. Drink as much as you can."

He blinked again.

Spoon by spoon he drank the broth. He sighed, and his eyes fully opened for the first time since the fight.

"Welcome back." Elizabeth set her stethoscope on his chest and listened. "Still clear, which is a miracle in action. I've wrapped your ribs because I thought there might be an injury there also. As far as we know, other than contusions, you have no other injuries. If you feel pain anywhere else, you have to tell me." She stuck her stethoscope into her pocket. "Blink once if you understand. Twice if you need something more right now."

He blinked once, and she patted his hand. "Your mother will be so glad to hear the news."

By the time Ingeborg arrived after supper, the news was all over Blessing. Toby Valders was awake again and seemed to be in his right mind. At least he could eat and respond to commands.

"Ellie," Elizabeth said the next morning, "I would really appreciate it if you would stay and help take care of Toby for me. Astrid will help too. You can read to him, get him to talk. He will be very weak for a time and still might be in severe pain due to the head wound."

Ellie felt her dream of moving to her own house slip away, but what could she say? She never stayed around when Mrs. Valders visited, though.

"Toby, I am praising our God for you every day." Pastor Solberg sat down in the chair. He took Toby's hand. "I hear the girls are giving you muscle therapy treatments. Why, you'll be going home before you know it."

Toby nodded. He cleared his throat, opened his mouth, and said, "Yes." Slowly, but it was a word, his first word.

The next day he sat up on the edge of the bed and rested his feet on the floor. "Thank you."

"You are welcome." Elizabeth sat beside him and gave him a hug. "You are my star patient, you know."

He shook his head. "Ellie."

"Yes, well, her too. All thanks to our wonderful God."

"I've come to take my boy home." Hildegunn stared at Elizabeth, her eyes and jaw both hard as a dirt clod in the winter.

"I'm sorry, but I cannot allow that."

"But I am his mother."

"I know, but I am a doctor, and Toby is under my care. I am sworn to do what is best for my patients." Elizabeth kept her voice gentle in spite of the finality of her words.

"You think you, a Bjorklund"—she made the word sound like an epithet—"can give him better care than I can?"

"Listen to me, Mrs. Valders, and listen well." Elizabeth even managed to keep a half smile in place. "The fact that my last name is now Bjorklund has nothing to do with the quality of my care as a doctor. Toby needs my skill if he is to return to his full capacity, and I deem that here in my surgery is where I can give him the most complete attention. I'm sure you want the very best for your son."

"Ja, but . . ." Hildegunn narrowed her eyes. She started to say something, then stopped.

"You are welcome to spend all the time with him that you can spare. I know he is sleeping now, and he must still sleep a great deal of the time because of the pain in his head. When he wakes, you can spoon-feed him liquids, like we have all been doing."

"Humph." Hildegunn pushed past Elizabeth and entered her son's room.

"Are you all right?" Ellie asked. "I hope you don't mind, but I was just around the corner and couldn't help hearing."

"I saw you. I was about to send you to Penny's for help," Elizabeth whispered and took Ellie by the arm. "Let's go in here so she doesn't hear us." They stepped into one of the two examining rooms, where Elizabeth leaned back against the door as soon as it was closed. "That woman!"

"You were wonderful."

"I think I have more sympathy for Ingeborg right now than I ever believed possible."

⚖

On Friday Sheriff Becker came to visit. He found Toby sitting up in the chair and answering, with a yes or no, Ellie's questions about what she was reading to him.

"Well, I can hardly believe this. I thought you for a goner for sure."

Toby nodded.

"Can you answer some questions for me?"

"I . . . can . . . try." Toby stared into Ellie's eyes.

Ellie tried to smile her encouragement but found herself chewing her bottom lip. *Do not cry, Ellie. No more crying.*

"Let An . . . drew go."

A huge tear trickled down her cheek and caught in the crease of her smile. *Thank you, Lord, thank you.*

"Yes, I will do that, but I had to make sure for myself. That young man has practically memorized his Bible while he's been in the cell. Reading it all day, every day. I never seen anything like it."

Ellie gaped at the sheriff. "But he wouldn't let any of us see him."

"Said he didn't want you to remember him sitting behind bars. Figured he was doing you all a favor."

Ellie glanced up to see a smile stretch Toby's mouth.

"Good," he said, this time with a nod.

"I'm sure Andrew will be home tomorrow." Sheriff Becker shook Toby's hand. "I'd like to hear what really happened to that barn when you are well enough to talk of it."

Toby nodded. "Yes."

"Got one question now. Did you set fire to that barn?"

Toby shook his head and winced at the pain. "N-no!"

"Guess that ties it up, then. You'll tell me all you know another day. Now just keep on getting strong again."

Toby nodded and lifted his hand to be shaken.

❧

Only Ellie and the Bjorklunds stood on the platform waiting for the train to come in the next day. Ellie wore her straw hat over a scarf made to match her sky blue dress. She kept a hand on her stomach to try to calm the butterflies threatening to fly out of her throat. What if he would have nothing to do with her? What if he was still angry? What if? What if?

The train whistled in the distance. Her heart took up leaping and twirling. As the train slowed with billows of steam and a screech of iron on iron, she searched the windows for his beloved face.

Was he not on the train?

When Andrew appeared and paused on the steps, his eyes locked on hers. He'd lost some of his tan, appearing pale in the shadows. But when he stepped down onto the platform, he strode straight toward her, only nodding at the others.

"Ellie." His word sounded like a prayer.

Her gaze never left his. "Andrew."

"I'm sorry."

She nodded. "Me too." And threw herself into his arms. "Oh, Andrew I was so afraid."

"I thought you might never want to see me again."

She thumped him on the arm. "You wouldn't let me."

"I know, but I had to . . . Well, I'm here now, and I'm free. Thank you, Lord God above, I am free." He swung her around once and then kissed her right in front of God and all who were present. Once he set her down, he looked straight into her eyes. "I have to go see Toby. Do you think he will want to see me?"

"Oh yes. He is waiting for you at Elizabeth's."

Andrew hugged his family, his father last. "Pa, I have a question. Why did you ask us to put off the wedding?"

"I finally know the answer. You weren't ready yet." Haakan stared without flinching into his son's eyes.

"Are we now?"

Haakan nodded. "I believe so."

"Thank you."

Making his way to Dr. Elizabeth's surgery, Andrew kept one arm around Ellie, keeping her safe, next to his heart.

She could hear his heart pounding when they neared the house.

Perhaps Andrew wasn't as sure of himself as he wanted her to believe. *Please, Lord, make this go right.*

"In there," Elizabeth said after hugging him close, stepping back to look at him, and hugging him again.

Andrew stopped in the doorway. "May I come in?"

Toby nodded. "Yes, please do."

Andrew took the offered hand and held it between both of his. "Toby, if you hate me forever, I'll understand, but I have to ask you." He leaned forward. "Will you forgive me?" The silence in the room quivered like an overused muscle.

The words came slowly, but they were all there. "Yes, I forgive you."

"Thank you. I cannot tell you how relieved I am." Since Toby was sitting in the chair, Andrew sat down on the bed as if all the strength had gone out of his legs. He paused, then asked the question he should have asked before flying off the handle and attacking Toby. "Do you know how the fire started?"

Toby nodded. "I think there must . . . have been a hot spot. I smelled smoke . . . came from the haymow."

"But I checked it every day." Andrew rubbed shaking fingers back and forth on his forehead. "We were sure the hay was dry enough." *It was my fault, not his. God forgive me.*

"I'm sorry. Those things just happen sometimes."

Andrew looked back at Toby. "Why were you there?"

"I was building nest boxes. Grace asked me to . . . for wedding presents."

Oh, Lord, talk about heaping coals upon my fiery head. "You're a better man than I am, Toby." Andrew sighed.

"Then this is over."

The two men stared into each other's eyes and nodded. It was indeed over.

"Right now Ellie and I are going out to see our house. I'll come by later."

Toby nodded and smiled. "Go."

Ellie let Andrew lift her into Elizabeth's buggy, and together they rode out to their house. With so much to be said, they just sat together, arms locked, and watched their house come closer.

He stopped the horse by the house. "Will you marry me, Ellie Wold?"

"Yes." She gazed into the deep blue pools of his eyes. "As soon as the threshing crew returns."

"I promise you, Ellie, that I will never lose my temper like that again. I will never strike anyone in anger."

"Oh, Andrew, can you keep that promise?"

"I can and I will . . . by the grace of God." He grinned at her. "And by chopping wood."

He kissed her then, a kiss that made up for all the loss and longing, a kiss that promised new life to be built upon the old ashes.

EPILOGUE

"Hurry, Ellie!"

"Rachel, you leave Ellie alone. This is one day she doesn't have to hurry." Goodie adjusted the sash to her daughter's wedding dress and looked over her shoulder into the tall oval mirror. "You are just the prettiest bride there ever was."

"I might be the longest waiting bride." Here it was October, Indian summer, and she had planned to be married in June. To think of all that had gone on in the last five months. She shook her head. "But I think I must be the happiest."

"I surely do hope so. You and Andrew did a heap of growing up this summer." Goodie brushed a bit of lint off the shoulder of the white lawn dress that Ellie had sewn last May. "I was afraid it would be too big for you, much weight as you lost."

"But I am fine now, Mor. If we don't hurry, we will be late."

"I told you so." Rachel clapped her hands on her hips and huffed a pretend sigh.

Olaf helped her into the buggy that waited outside the house that she and Andrew would finally move into. "You look so lovely, my dear." He kissed her cheek.

"I wish Hans could have come."

"I do too, but . . . well, you will see him at Christmas. We'll all be here for Christmas." Goodie joined Ellie in the buggy, and Rachel squeezed in on the front seat beside Olaf and Arne, who laughed all the way to the church.

The music flowed out to greet them, and the last guest disappeared inside.

"You ready?" her father asked.

"Yes."

Olaf helped her out and settled her hand through the crook of his arm. "Mother, lead the way."

When Ellie walked through the door, the congregation breathed as one in delight. She floated down the aisle, her gaze locked on Andrew's. They said their vows without a fault, accompanied by sniffs and tears at the beautiful words.

"Do you, Andrew Bjorklund, take Ellie Wold to be your lawful wedded wife . . . ?"

"I do. . . ."

Ellie's voice broke, then cleared as she finished. ". . . to love and to cherish till death do us part."

"I now pronounce you husband and wife." Pastor Solberg beamed at them both. "Andrew, you may kiss your bride."

"I love you, Ellie."

She nodded. "From this day forward. Oh, Andrew, I pray us many days, weeks, and years forward." They turned and smiled at all their loved ones gathered to celebrate this day. The day that almost never came.

Thank you, heavenly Father, she whispered in her mind. *Only you could have made all this possible. You honored your promises again.*

ACKNOWLEDGMENTS

I MEET THE GREATEST PEOPLE in all my travels, on-line, and at events. Several years ago I met Rae Lynn Schafer, who loves research, especially on-line, and she agreed to help me with mine. Thanks, my friend. Your assistance in invaluable.

It is impossible to recognize all the people who have shared their family stories with me, but I appreciate you all. Many of the details in my books come from your stories, memories, and experiences. What a treasure trove.

By the time I finish a book, I have picked friends' brains, especially Woodeene's and Kathleen's, and rejoiced in editorial help from my so very capable assistant, Cecile, and Sharon Asmus from Bethany House Publishers. I am always grateful for the entire Bethany staff, who do their jobs so well to bring a book to life and out to the readers. Heaps of thanks to you all.

God is generous and gracious to give me forty-four years of teamwork with my husband, Wayne. I could never get all this done without him, and besides we have such fun, especially with all the travel we do. Who could have ever dreamed all this?

Another book is done. To God be the glory.

Be the first *to know*

Want to be the first to know
what's new from
your favorite authors?

Want to know all about
exciting new writers?

Sign up for BethanyHouse newsletters at
www.bethanynewsletters.com
and you'll get regular updates via e-mail.
You can sign up for as many authors or
categories as you want so you get only
the information you really want.

Sign up today

Lauraine Snelling's Signature Series!

Faced with the forbidding prairies of Dakota Territory, the Bjorklund family must rely on their strength and faith to build a homestead in the untamed Red River Valley.

Laboring from dawn till dark, breaking and cutting sod, planting and harvesting what little they can, the family suffers tragedy and loss but also joy, hope, and a love that continues strong through the daunting challenges of making a home in this difficult land.

RED RIVER OF THE NORTH

1. An Untamed Land
2. A New Day Rising
3. A Land to Call Home
4. The Reapers' Song
5. Tender Mercies
6. Blessing in Disguise